INLAND

Also by K.C. Frederick
from The Permanent Press

Country of Memory (1998)

The Fourteenth Day (2000)

Accomplices (2003)

To Dan & Anne, with warmest wishes
Kat 1/28/07

INLAND

K.C. FREDERICK

THE PERMANENT PRESS
Sag Harbor, NY 11963

Library of Congress Cataloging-in-Publication Data

Frederick, K. C., 1935–
    Inland / K. C. Frederick.
        p. cm.
    ISBN 13: 978-1-57962-135-3 (alk. paper)
    ISBN 10: 1-57962-135-X (alk. paper)
    1. Graduate students—Fiction. 2. Nineteen fifties—Fiction.
3. Middle West—Fiction. 4. United States—Politics and
government—1953–1961—Fiction. I. Title.

PS3556.R3755155 2006
813'.54—dc22   2006035852

The Permanent Press
4170 Noyac Road
Sag Harbor, NY 11963

For Toni

Walking across the campus of the state university on a bright May morning in 1959, Ted Riley feels a mysterious surge of well-being. It isn't just the weather, though the end of a couple of days' rain has left the air fresh and clean, and it isn't just that he's a healthy twenty-four-year-old. God knows, he's no stranger to days when neither sunshine nor good health has been enough to banish the black dogs haunting his dreams. Whatever the reason, when he steps out of the shade of the covering elms, he can't help glancing at the sky, where a few puffy clouds sail serenely amid an ocean of blue. What would this place look like from up there? he finds himself wondering. He's only flown once and he wasn't interested in looking down during that short, turbulent trip, concentrating as he was on willing the plane to stay aloft, trying to forget he was trapped in an enclosed cylinder hurtling through the sky, dependent for his very survival on strangers in dark glasses operating machinery he didn't understand. Today, though, it seems like a pretty terrific idea to look down from up there and see things, so to speak, as God sees them. Just now he might even be able to convince himself he wouldn't mind being in the air.

Nevertheless, he's decidedly earthbound this morning, his briefcase jammed with books and notes as well as unread freshman compositions as he makes his way toward Edgar Peterson's seminar on the Victorians, which promises to be utterly unlike flying. Though, the thought occurs to him, supplying the class with bags for air sickness wouldn't be such a bad idea. There's no hint of a plane in the sky above the campus,

7

but his mind is drawn back to his earlier fancy: what would a stranger be likely to make of this place from up there? No doubt for many a flier on the long journey between the coasts, the stretches of land over which he passes amount to little more than time to be got through, blank spaces on the map. As he glances casually from his window at the sudden blistering of hills, leafy covering and open expanses, thrust of roof and the lazy curve of a river, could he guess that he's passing over a university town where on any given night people might be arguing passionately about philosophy or football while more than a few lonely and homesick souls are walking the streets pondering their futures, just as all of them have for generations? Would he have any curiosity about the lives being lived there? Ted is excited by the notion, and it pleases him to think that some stranger passing overhead, glimpsing this very spot, might actually wonder about the place whose name he doesn't know, this town called Chippewa. We're being watched, he tells himself, visualizing this imaginary traveler; only it isn't by a solicitous deity, it's by a salesman from Bakersfield, California. He wishes someone were here to tell that to, and finds himself thinking, as he often does when he feels this way, of Sally Pell.

Before he's even realized it, he's already changed his plans for the day, and his first order of business is to persuade Sally to join him. "So," he says when he finds her in her usual booth at the House of Joe, "why don't we both skip Peterson and go to the island?"

Sally looks up at him. "Am I hearing you right? The dependable Ted Riley wants to cut class?"

"Hey," he gestures toward the outdoors. "How can you refuse on a glorious day like this?"

A smile plays about the corners of Sally's mouth. It's clear she's trying to assess the seriousness of his offer. She and Ted are very good friends—amid the usual woes of grad school, they've kept each other sane on more than a few occasions. Their relationship is platonic at the moment, though for a week last winter when Sally'd been convinced she was going to leave school, they crossed the line to sex. That they'd both been able to return to their earlier status is impressive and a little perplexing to Ted, as it must be to Sally.

"Come clean," she demands now. "What brings this on? Sure, it's a nice day, but I've seen days just as nice. Let me guess: you met the love of your life at that party I couldn't go to last night and you want to tell me all about it."

"Yeah," he says, recognizing that she's right: it isn't his fantasy of the observer overhead any more than it is the weather that's buoying him today; it's something else. "Yeah, I want to tell you about that party."

"So?" she leans forward. "What is it? I'm all ears." In fact she's much more than her ears, which are hidden beneath her long blonde hair. In her genuine eagerness and curiosity, she's suddenly very beautiful, a tall, corn-fed princess of the prairies, though she grew up in a suburb of Chicago.

"You can only find out," he says, "if you come with me to the island."

She looks down at the book she's been reading, then at the clock. She closes the book emphatically and holds up her hands as if preparing to be cuffed. "O.K., Sergeant Friday, you got me."

They walk downhill from the campus area to the older part of town, where Victorian gables give way briefly to the columned stateliness of the Federal period, then to an area of amiable dinginess, what passes for a slum in Chippewa. This is the locale of Cousin Willie's, a Negro bar where some adventurous white students go to hear real blues. Just beyond the stone railroad station they cross the river on a low bridge, the gray mass of the university hospital looming like a cubist dream on a hill behind them. Not far from where an old neighborhood gives way to the green countryside, they make their way over a wooden pedestrian bridge to the island, which is slightly longer than a football field and just as flat, tapered at each end like a boat. Tall, silky grass runs between a few birches and oaks; at the water's edge the leaves of low-hanging willows dip into the slow-moving current of the river that occasionally overruns its banks and swallows up parts of the island. It's solid and dry today, though. Behind them is an old-fashioned merry-go-round that you push into motion, as well as swings and a teeter-totter, all bespeaking the turn of the century. This is one of Ted's favorite places in town, and he's grateful to the unknown genius who conceived of the little park whose modesty as well as its beauty have always appealed to him.

"So," Sally says when they'd stepped onto the island's soft grass. "Tell me what happened at the party."

"I met a guy," Ted says, and pauses for effect.

She smiles wryly. "I guess I didn't know you as well as I thought I did."

"I should have told you earlier," he says. Then, "No, really, it's just that I had a very interesting talk with this guy."

"Interesting," she points out pedagogically, "is a very evasive word."

"You're right," he admits. "Still, it was interesting." And he tells her the story, giving the bare facts, the shorthand, though nothing in the telling this morning can convey the texture of the previous night or why the encounter should have left him feeling so good today.

The party had been given by a couple of grad students in philosophy Ted didn't know, but it had a familiar enough feel. The hosts had provided some beer and chips, but it was for the most part a BYOB. He arrived fairly late in the evening, knowing from experience that the affair had probably started out quiet and tentative, the first guests exchanging nervous monosyllables between frantic puffs on cigarettes and earnest gulps of their drinks as they tried to launch themselves into a festive mood. Some faculty members had been invited and they'd have come early, producing further constraint. A record would be playing—something like *The Threepenny Opera*—but it would be barely audible, as if the hosts weren't sure whether they wanted music or not. Most of the men would be wearing suits or sports coats, the women party dresses, though there were always a few consciously bohemian types in black turtle necks. All of them would be on alert, attentive, as if waiting for someone to say the magic word.

By the time Ted arrived, though, the air was thick with smoke, lights had been turned down, ties and inhibitions loosened, a few of the women had slipped off their shoes, and people had to shout at each other to be heard over the roar that all but drowned the insistent beat of Ravel's *Bolero*. The drearier faculty members were already gone. The next phase, he knew, would be quieter, with murmurous confidences being exchanged in a kitchen where the sink was full of dirty dishes and empty beer bottles littered the table beside overflowing ashtrays and crumpled potato chip bags lying in pools of melted ice. Ted didn't mind the noise: he hadn't come here to make friends or to learn anything; he was just courting a bit of oblivion. Because Sally had work to do, he'd come alone and he'd tried to convince himself that he was having a good time simply because he wasn't correcting freshman papers. He had a few beers, talked briefly to a large number of people, some of whom he knew and others whose names he'd forgotten as soon as he heard them. Someone told him the old joke that the word "Chippewa" meant "a long way from anywhere" and he laughed politely. To this point, as far as he could tell, the gathering had been completely unremarkable: there had been no fights and no one had thrown up, at least not in his presence. All in all, fairly civilized. At a party he and Sally went to the previous month, someone as yet unidentified had thrown a firecracker into the kitchen that exploded near a woman, causing her to be taken to the hospital's emergency room, where she received several stitches in her foot. Ted was in no mood for drama tonight, though, and thankfully, there seemed little likelihood of that here.

When he became aware that things were quieter than they'd been before, he realized the party was already entering its final phase. Looking around, he saw that many of the guests had left and the ones who'd remained were engaged in what seemed to be earnest conversations, for the most part, he supposed, either late-night confessions or sexual advances, though of course the two could be combined. At least some people, he hoped, were likely to get what they'd come here for. As for himself, he'd managed to kill some time, but there seemed no good

reason to linger and he'd just about made up his mind to leave
when, turning to exit the kitchen, he literally bumped into a
short man wearing a light-colored tweed jacket. Apologies were
exchanged and introductions made, though it was soon clear
that the stranger he'd bumped into seemed to know something
about Ted. "You were in Eerdman's class, weren't you?" the man
asked, a half-smoked, unlit cigar bobbing as he spoke.

"Yeah," Ted answered guardedly. Since most of the grad students in English were likely to take Eerdman's Methods class,
there was nothing particularly uncanny in the man's making the
connection. Still, it was odd that he'd brought it up at all.

"Eerdman mentioned you," the man said, which was more
surprising: Ted hardly remembered a thing about the class and
certainly he'd done nothing remarkable there. "He said you were
a good man," the stranger continued. "Reliable."

Ted nodded vaguely, accepting the belated compliment,
which sounded like faint praise indeed, but he was slightly
uneasy and couldn't help wondering why old Eerdman would
be talking about one of his students with this guy, who'd intro-
duced himself as Sam Morelli. He worked, he said, in graduate
admissions. Morelli was dark, with neatly clipped black hair and
a thick black mustache. He was solidly built and Ted guessed he
might be pretty strong. But as he talked, what got Ted's attention
were the man's eyes. They were brown, but their color was less
memorable than a piercing quality that made them seem preter-
naturally alert, as if this man could tell you at any time exactly
how many people there were at this party.

The chance encounter and the connection to Professor
Eerdman gave way to an exchange of noncommittal comments
about the graduate program, then to the football team, which
gave every promise of doing disastrously once again, and the
best place in town to shop for cheese, a question that interested Ted not at all. It amused him, though, to think that this
talk had become part of the web of late-night conversations and
that someone looking on might well take it for a confession or
a sexual advance. His curiosity was suddenly piqued, though,

when Morelli asked, "What did they call you when you played football? 'Sure Hands Riley?'"

"Yeah," he answered, flattered by the reference to his high school exploits but puzzled too: he hadn't been that big a deal, at best a fair-sized fish in a small pond, so why would this guy know about him? Not from Professor Eerdman, he was sure: the footnote, not football, was Eerdman's passion. He looked at Morelli again, reminding himself that the man he was talking to was in grad admissions and would have access to all sorts of information about the students in the various programs. Even as he pondered this, Ted was distracted, suddenly aware of Nat Cole's "Unforgettable" playing in the background. The song brought memories of high school parties in darkened basements, slow dancing, charged silences, furtive gropings and embarrassments about unwanted erections. He remembered the time sharply, but he had no wish to go back there.

"Football teaches you a lot of things about life," Morelli declared, interrupting Ted's reverie.

"Oh, you played?" Ted asked.

The man chewed on his unlit cigar. "Like you. Just high school," he said dismissively.

"What position?" Ted was vaguely curious.

Morelli smiled challengingly. "Try to guess."

Ted looked the man over. He wasn't very tall, 5-8 or 9 at best and, though it was hard to guess at his weight, he might be around 165 or so. A kind of hunger about his face suggested that he'd been very thin as a teenager. If he was in his forties now he was likely to be twenty pounds over his playing weight, and that would have made him about 145 in high school. "I'd say halfback," Ted ventured.

Morelli laughed and shook his head. "I didn't have the speed, buddy. Actually, I played guard." Ted looked at him: a 145-pound guard? "Yeah, I know," the man said, "that's a surprise. But at St. Bernie's you couldn't be choosy and I wanted the job and the coach saw that. So I was the starting left guard my last two years."

Ted nodded. "I'm impressed," he said.

Morelli made a gesture with his cigar. "Don't be: we were lousy. We played twelve games those two years and the best we did was to tie one of them. When we lost to our arch-rivals St. Dominic, 42-13, we had afternoon classes off the Monday after the game and had a dance called the 'Two Touchdown Hop' to celebrate those thirteen points." He looked at Ted. "Not exactly like your high school experience, eh?"

Ted shook head. "We always did well in our league," he acknowledged, "so, yeah, we went to the playoffs, but we'd get creamed when we played the big city boys." The mention of those times brought back the smell in the locker room before a playoff game: sweat, liniment and anxiety. "The press loved us, though," he mused. "We were always the sentimental favorite."

Morelli narrowed his eyes appreciatively, nodding encouragement. "Like I said," he broke in, "football teaches you something, doesn't it? You don't want to be the sentimental favorite."

"I guess not." Ted answered, vaguely disoriented. What was this guy driving at? Was he making fun of Ted's achievements? And if so, why? Hold on, he reminded himself, we're talking about high school, and that was over a long time ago.

Morelli re-lit his cigar. "Our coach was a fatalist," he said. "Coach Cassidy. Honest, I think there were guys who thought Coach was his first name." He smiled to himself. "I mean, he knew we were undermanned—we finished one season with only twenty players. This was obviously before the two-platoon system." Morelli squinted as though trying to find his old mentor in the haze of this kitchen in Chippewa. "Coach Cassidy knew how bad we were, he knew we were going to get our asses whipped most of the time. He had to know he'd never hear the end of the jokes at the bar after the game—they used to call us St. Bernadette, the guys at the bar would ask him when we were going to schedule the Little Sisters of the Poor, stuff like that. He didn't have any illusions about the hand he'd been dealt." Morelli puffed on his cigar and the harsh smoke filled Ted's nostrils. "Coach Cassidy used to say, though, that even if we weren't half as good as the people we were playing, it was our job to offer resistance. Imagine, he'd tell us, that you knew you were going to play a whole season and get the shit kicked out of you and lose all your games. Imagine then that before it all started you had the chance to forfeit all those games and come out with the same record. That would be easier, he said, not only easier on us but a lot easier on the other teams. Then his face would turn purple and he'd start yelling, 'Would you want all of them, St. Dom's, Holy Cross, St. Tony's, all of them—would you want them to be able to beat you without at least feeling you were there? Christ, even if all you can be is a punching bag, you get a chance to bruise the other guy's knuckles.'"

In telling this story, Morelli had become very intense and Ted could imagine the underweight guard he'd been, rushing at a potential tackler. He was anticipating hearing more about the woes of St. Bernie's football team when Morelli asked, "You're Catholic, aren't you?"

"Yeah," he answered tentatively, though he was forced to follow with, "I'm actually not that good a Catholic." Once again, though, he was a little uneasy about the man's knowing these things.

Morelli waved it away. "That's not important," he said. "What's important is that you learned the system."

"The system?"

"The structure," Morelli pursued. "The ten commandments, the seven sacraments, the seven deadly sins, the cardinal virtues and the corporal works of mercy. It's good to know that the system was there before you were born and will still be in place long after you're gone. There's a beauty to that."

Ted laughed. "You're not a recruiter for the Vatican, are you?"

It was during the interval of a few seconds that followed, when neither man spoke and over the clink of a beer bottle and a gust of muted laughter from a corner in the kitchen, Nat Cole sang about someone's being unforgettable too, that it occurred to Ted that nothing about this meeting was accidental, and it seemed to him afterwards that he'd already known what Morelli was going to say next, though of course that was ridiculous: it had come as a complete surprise.

"He asked you to become a spy?" Sally says when he tells her the story on the island.

"Not exactly. He just said I should consider the Central Intelligence Agency, the CIA, as a career possibility." Ted can't help feeling that the punch line in his story of the momentous encounter came out disappointingly. Out here in the sunlight it just sounds like a job offer.

Sally frowns. "But he knows you're going to be writing your dissertation soon," she says.

"That didn't seem to be a problem for him. He even seemed to feel I could combine careers."

She looks at him as though he's become a stranger and the thought suddenly bothers him. "Hey," he takes her arm. "If I were really interested, I don't suppose I'd have told you, would I?"

She thinks about that. "Hmm, maybe."

"Hmm, nothing," he says, and pulls her close to him. Her blue eyes look at him steadily, her hair moves in the breeze. He can smell her skin. He remembers being in bed with her, in her apartment on Baker Street, the two of them looking at the bedroom wall, watching the stripe of green, then amber, then red from the traffic light on the corner. She had to stay in school, he pleaded with her, she couldn't drop out of the program. Things were going to get better. His arguments were muddled and not very convincing, he thought, but they were heartfelt. In the end, Sally stayed. Thank God. All at once everything that happened last night seems meaningless and unreal, an encounter with a phantom in a cave.

Seeming to sense his thoughts, Sally smiles an ambiguous smile. "Well, I'm glad," she says. "I wouldn't want you to be a spy." And then, as if she thinks that statement might seem too proprietary, she adds, "As your friend, you know."

"Yeah," he laughs. "As my friend."

She takes a step away from him. "But you were interested, weren't you?" she challenges. "Interested in what he was offering."

He shrugs.

"Sure you were. Why else would you persuade me to cut old Stringy-Thighs' class? She mimicked Peterson's voice: 'Come into the garden, Maud/ For the black bat night has flown.'"

He smiles. "You've got to work on that a little more, kiddo. But, hey, do I need a reason?" He spreads his hands. "Isn't this a great day?"

"I can't disagree," she concedes. He steps toward her and places his hands loosely on her hips. They say nothing, listening to the willows hissing in the slight breeze, aware of the soundless current of the slow-moving river, the sudden smell of lilacs. She was right, though: he had been interested. Not in the offer specifically, but more in the sense it gave him that the world was suddenly full of possibility. There have been plenty of times when the prospect ahead has seemed dreary: finishing his course work and finding a topic for a dissertation, writing it somehow while teaching freshman English to pay the rent and put food on the table. And then, after God knows how many years, trying to get a job somewhere, a decent job, he hopes, at some halfway interesting place, and not a dump in the middle of nowhere. The gloomy chair of the department, Bradford Winslow, a flinty New Englander who'd brought to the prairies where he'd been exiled a grim Calvinist view of the universe in general and the study of English in particular, seems to delight in declaring again and again that Ph.D's in English in the year of our Lord 1959 have only the bleakest of prospects before them. In the light of that, the idea that some government agency might actually be interested in hiring him suddenly pushed back the horizons of possibility to the limitless expanses the pioneers had pursued as they made their way west more than a hundred years earlier. "Think about it," Morelli said. "This isn't something you have to decide on right away." He gave him his card, which Ted put into his wallet. Like money in the bank.

"But why did he pick you of all people?" Sally asks, wrinkling her nose.

It's, in fact, something he himself has wondered about without being able to arrive at any satisfactory answer. He tries to parry Sally's question. "You mean why not you?"

"No, I mean why you in particular?"

He smiles. "First of all, it's possible Morelli does this every week to a different grad student." He doesn't really believe that, he realizes as he says it. "Hey," he challenges her, "do you mean it surprises you that someone would be interested in me in particular?"

She shakes her head. "No, not at all. I mean, you have plenty of qualifications. You're sharp, you won the Edwards Prize last year, your French is excellent."

"Don't forget," he adds, "I know some Russian. Even a little German." He smiles again. "So what's the problem?"

"I don't know," she says. "I guess I think of spies as people who live under rocks. Creepy. Not like you."

He feels a rush of warmth toward her. "Thanks for the compliment. Though actually, I think it wasn't spying he was talking about. It was more information-gathering. Sort of like research. Not all that different, I suppose, from what we do in grad school."

"Hmm," she smiles. "How's the pay? I might be interested myself."

"We never got around to that," he says. "But he did mention that the pension was great."

They fall silent. In a puff of breeze the rich sweetness of the grass blends with the fishy smell of the river. From behind them comes the creak of the old merry-go-round and a kid shouts happily. "Jesus," Ted says. "What are we doing talking about pensions on a day like today? Is it because grad school is a conspiracy to make you forget that you're young?"

Her eyes brighten. "You're right," she says. "Let's let all that go for now, let's just pretend this is all there is to the world." He looks with her toward the gentle hills that rise up from the river. In that direction is the old stone railroad station they passed minutes ago and the streets that lead up the hill toward the campus, all of them obscured at the moment by the greenness around them. "There's nothing," he says, "but this island, these trees, the grass, the hills."

"The birds," she adds, and they listen for a while to their singing.

"The fish in the water," he says.

"A couple of kids on the merry-go-round that one of their parents is pushing."

He hears a distant rumble. "A train somewhere headed in this direction."

Then they stop enumerating things and just let the world flow over them. In the silence he feels her leaning trustfully into him, feels the brush of her hair against his face. Once again he remembers their time together last year and he's acutely aware that Sally is the person he cares for most in the world. Do you remember, he wants to ask her, how the colors changed on your bedroom wall that night? The memory of those colors is bathed in a tenderness for her. How close she came to leaving, which would have been devastating for him—he couldn't imagine Chippewa without her. And yet, mysteriously, when it was finally clear Sally was going to stay in school, they stopped having sex. It was as if they'd each agreed without saying anything that it was something to be used only in emergencies. He remembers feeling very mature at the time. He wonders now, though. If they chose to stop, why couldn't they choose to start again? He's curious about what Sally thinks of their decision. Possibly she's thinking about that time too. He's looking at the flowing water, wishing that the moment would last forever, when he feels her stiffen.

"What is it?" he asks.

She steps away from him. "I just had a crazy thought. . . ." She shakes her head and gives a little sigh. He waits for more but she says nothing.

"What?" he presses her gently. "You started it; you have to finish it."

"I just thought . . ." she begins hesitantly, "I thought this is the kind of day when, at least for a few seconds, you can forget about the Bomb." She's looking at the grass at her feet. "Isn't that stupid?"

He wants to say something but can't think of a response. His tongue is dead in his mouth and he keeps hearing those two syllables: the Bomb, the Bomb.

"I'm sorry," she says, raising her eyes to him. "Maybe I shouldn't have said that. We were having a good time, weren't we?"

"No, no," he protests. "There's nothing wrong with saying what you said. It's the truth, after all." It has upset him though, he has to admit. His insides have gone light, as they had last winter when Sally first talked about leaving school.

"It's so strange," she says. "A minute ago I just felt a lifting. Then I thought about what it was that was being lifted."

"I understand," he nods. That was it: he'd felt a lifting too and now there's only a heaviness. "It's something that's always there," he says harshly.

After a silence, Sally pursues. "Do you ever wake up in the middle of the night terrified about it?"

He nods again. "Of course. Doesn't everyone?"

Though they seem to be agreeing, something hangs in the air between them, separating them. Sensing this, Sally asks, "What is it?"

"Nothing." He shakes his head. "Really, nothing." Except that he no longer feels the spaciousness of the frontier, his horizons have shrunk and everything he felt this morning is gone. Why did Sally have to bring that up? Now everything around them is changed. This peaceful island in the middle of a slow-moving river in the middle of a vast continent is suddenly vulnerable and exposed. He feels emptied of words and the silence he's fallen into lengthens until he becomes desperate to break it. "I remember when Sputnik went up," he says at last, not even sure why he's talking about this. He isn't looking at her. "That was the semester I took off from classes, when I was working full time at the library. You know I love that old building in the middle of campus, I love the stacks, shelves and shelves of books where you can get lost, those levels in the old part of the building where the floor is made of thick translucent glass blocks—it's all so mysterious, like a hidden world. I used to push that creaking wooden mail cart into every corner of the library and if I wanted to take a break and read something, I had a thousand places where I could hide. That building seemed so

safe and solid. I remember being in the mail room the day after
the Russians sent up that satellite, seeing the *Chicago Tribune*.
I remember the colored front pages that always made me think
of the hustle and bustle of Chicago—the El, the lake, the Art
Institute, people in long coats hurrying through the streets, on
their way to something interesting—and there was the picture
of Sputnik. It occurred to me that it might be sailing through
space directly over Chicago at that very moment—or over here,
for that matter—and all at once I felt that down there in the
basement working with old Ed Mieske I wasn't safe anymore."

Sally leans toward him. Once again he smells her hair. The
sound of the willow leaves shifting in the breeze, the languid
flow of the river, the shouts of children playing and the smell of
the grass all seem different now.

"I'm sorry," she says.

"You don't have anything to be sorry about," he tells her. He
doesn't want to blame her for the way he's feeling.

"Well, then I'm sorry things are the way they are," she says.
"This is such a scary time."

"Yeah," he agrees. But still, he tells himself, you have to find
some way of living in it.

After a moment she smiles at him. "It's going to be OK,"
she says.

He returns her smile. "You're right," he answers and looks
around. "Hey," he says when he sees that the children have left
the merry-go-round, "want a ride?"

"How could I refuse such an offer?" she answers, obviously
as grateful as he is for the change of subject. A minute later he's
pushing the tilting metal disc on which Sally stands, holding
on to the bar and laughing. He throws himself into his efforts,
feeling it in his calves, racing in dizzy circles as the merry-
go-round picks up speed, creaking as it whirs. As he pushes,
Sally shouts something that he can't make out until at last he
hops aboard and is propelled with her by the already dimin-
ishing force with which he set it into motion. "Come into the
garden, Maud," he hears her chant now, "For the black bat night
has flown."

Breathless, he calls to her. "Think we can persuade Peterson to hold next week's class here?" He isn't sure she's heard him, but she looks happy again.

Later that day, when he's returned to his apartment on Tecumseh Street, he fixes himself a cup of instant coffee. Impatient for the first sip, he lets the scalding, tasteless liquid burn his lips and he puts the green cup down. Things turned out OK in the end, he tells himself, thinking about the events of the morning. But if that's true, why can't he keep himself from feeling lousy when he remembers the time on the island? Nothing happened, really. What Sally said was understandable enough, legitimate enough—hell, everyone who has a brain is being driven crazy by the Bomb; it's a wonder people get out of bed at all and live their lives. But there's no way of getting around it, you have to do it, Bomb or no Bomb, future or no future. And yet he let what she said get to him like that this morning, at the island, of all places: he just started talking about Sputnik and the library and, Jesus, Ed Mieske. It's not as if there was anything crazy, or even untrue, about what he said. You can't deny there are atomic weapons all over the planet, ready to be set loose by the hundreds, the thousands even, vaporizing cities and spreading deadly clouds of radioactivity that would settle over the survivors. Who wouldn't be scared of that? Still, talking about it that way doesn't help any, does it?

He looks at the curtain moving faintly in the breeze. He can see nobody in the street. He picks up the cup. It's always disappointing to fail yourself like that. Having grown up for the most part without a father, he's used to making the most of what he has. He's worked hard, he can honestly say that he's pretty much used what abilities he has to the fullest, he's done well in school. If he and Sam Morelli had carried that conversation on football further he'd have told the guy that he hadn't had a lot of speed either, and speed was important to a pass receiver. Even more so, since he wasn't exceptionally tall. But he'd made up for it with good hands and an ability to run the routes the way they were diagrammed, something he practiced over and over. What he was proudest of was that once he had the ball, size or no size, he'd been hard to bring down. Maybe he just wanted things more than other, more talented guys did. Even while he was doing it, though, he had no illusions about his football career going beyond high school. No college coach would have been interested in him—no big-time college coach, anyway. Still, he knew how valuable he was to the Cold River Warriors. The way he played was an important reason why his team dominated their division, though it was never enough to get them a win in the playoffs, whether or not they were the darlings of the newspapers.

It was the same for three years: whatever dreams you might have early in the fall, reality always set in in November. A time always came when it slipped away. The underdog Warriors were actually leading their bigger and faster rivals from the city at half-time in Ted's sophomore year and there was jubilation in the locker room. "Just keep on doing the things you've been doing," coach Keller told them. After their first possession of the second half, their punter pinned the opponents inside their own ten-yard line. Even before the Warriors' fans had a chance to savor the situation, though, the other team, on its first offensive play, ran an option and while the defensive end tackled the quarterback, the trailing man to whom he'd pitched the ball was speeding down the sidelines on a touchdown run of almost the length of the field. A moment later the team in gold and purple was celebrating on the other side of the field and their band struck up their fight song while Ted smelled the grass and the chalk marking of the yard line, watching the smoke of countless cigarettes drift upwards in front of the light tower. That score only put the Warriors a point behind but, though nobody said anything, everyone seemed to know that play was the beginning of the end. When it was over, they'd lost by three touchdowns. And yet, up until that moment when Arnie Schultz hugged the quarterback's knees as he pulled him to the earth, not yet realizing the futility of his tackle, they'd all thought they could pull it off.

During Ted's playing days it happened three times that way, with slight variations. When it was over the outcome might seem inevitable to the smart observers but that wasn't the way it felt while he was playing: each time he thought they were going to win. All he had to counter the empty feeling at the end of the game was the hope that he and his teammates had earned the respect of the guys who beat them. "You sure are one tough sucker to bring down," a smiling six and a half foot linebacker who eventually went on to play a couple of seasons with the Packers told him in the final seconds of one of those losses. But of course in the end they did bring him down, him and the rest of the Warriors. "Be proud of yourself," the coach would tell them. "You got into the playoffs again." And then, almost under his breath, "It wasn't in the cards for us to win today." There was a question there that Ted didn't want to deal with: if it wasn't in the cards, what was the point of trying? Finally, there were things that were out of your control; all you could do was to play your part as if it made a difference.

It was true in the world beyond the football field as well: there were lots of things over which you had no control. It was a refrain Ted had recited to himself for some time. Early on, he decided that he wanted as large a life as would be permitted him; he was determined to live as if he had an unlimited future. How much of one he was allowed wasn't up to him but, whatever it was, he'd make the most of it.

He puts the coffee cup close to his face. He can feel the heat but he knows enough not to take another drink until it's cooled a bit more. That's what bothered him so much about what happened this morning on the island—he made it seem as if he didn't really believe there was a future, and how could you live that way? Given the world he's living in, it's entirely possible, he knows, that there's not much of a future ahead of him. Still, as he's told himself again and again, that's a notion that seems to have little practical value.

November in Chippewa: skeletal trees are set against a low gray sky heavy with the threat of the season's first snow. Sharp gusts send dry leaves raking the concrete walks of the campus. The wind bites, there's nothing pretty here. All of nature has turned grim: the sensible geese have already flown south, bears are sleeping in their caves. Who'd stay around for this? And yet here's Ted making his way across campus. His heart is pumping and blood courses through his veins as if there's a purpose to the cycle of the seasons, or anything else. His shoulders hunched against the cold, he's on his way somewhere, he knows, because his feet are moving along one of the familiar campus paths, but for the moment he's forgotten where he was headed. Well, it's happened before; it will be enough to follow his feet; he'll find out soon enough where he's going. November, the eleventh month. When Sally's plane went down in July, Chippewa had been hot and green and the cicadas were chanting eternal summer; now fall is already ending and only the unrelenting midwestern winter looms.

There are notices on a bulletin board: the Young Republicans are sponsoring a mixer, a pep rally for Saturday's game will be held at the field house, a fraternity is holding an auction whose proceeds will go to charity. Distinguished visitors are going to lecture on Spanish poetry, the limits of the universe and pacifism. Baha'i and Moral Rearmament compete for attention with the more conventional religious groups on campus, and some organization calling itself Dada International has put out an unauthorized flier announcing that on the last day of the 1950s the accumulated boredom of the decade will bring the world to an exhausted end. Ted takes in all these messages, though none of them gives him a clue to why he's crossing the chilly campus.

There are worse things than the numb state of forgetfulness in which he often finds himself these days. Whatever the source—God, some evolutionary instinct, or just the tidal flow of chemicals, he's grateful. The problem is, he can't control it, just as he can't predict the next assault of painful memory, with its confusion of anger and despair, sorrow and guilt. And time, which is supposed to move forward, can suddenly bend, twist and loop, yanking him back to those awful days in July, as if an endless repetition can somehow undo the events of last summer.

While he was experiencing them, Sally's last days seemed to have a happenstance quality—at any point you could believe things might turn out in a thousand different ways; after the fact, every action she took seemed directed toward that single, terrible end. Ted was working at his old job in the library for the summer and, against his mild protests, she'd decided, more or less on a whim, to go home to Evanston. "I should give it a try," she said. "I should be a good daughter. It'll just be for a week, maybe ten days—if I can stand it." It was so characteristic of Sally to keep trying to repair her relationship with her parents, and Ted admired her for it; but already after only a couple of days with her family she'd become restless. Over the phone he tempted her with the prospect of a trip to a little town north of Chippewa that the two of them had discovered where the local roadhouse, on the shore of a lake, sold cheap draft beer. "Imagine the place in midsummer, Sally: buzzing flies, nickel beer, John Deere caps and the faint intoxicating smell of cow manure."

"It sounds divine," she said, though no doubt by that point, her experiment in family reconciliation having taken a familiar turn, any place other than Evanston might have produced the same reaction. "Go ahead, keep talking," she urged him on.

"Tell them you have to get back by Friday," he pressed her. "That you've got some important research to do."

"Hmm," she answered, and the meditative syllable was filled with promise; but when she called the next day it was to tell him excitedly that she'd got a surprise invitation to visit from a favorite aunt in New York. "Isn't that great?" she said.

"What about Modena?" he asked glumly. "The Lakeside Tavern, the cheap beer?" Desperately, he added, "How can Manhattan hold a candle to that?"

"We can see Modena in the fall, can't we?" she insisted, and he wanted to tell her it wouldn't be the same. The flies would be gone, at the very least. "Hey," she said, "aren't you happy for me?"

"Yeah," he conceded, barely.

"Come on, Mister Grumpy," she pushed, "can't you do better than that?"

"OK, I'm happy for you. " He knew it hadn't sounded very convincing. Of course he was more than a little jealous of her. He'd only been to New York once but that trip of seventy-two hours fired his imagination. Now, as he delivered the mail to the various library departments, he'd have to imagine Sally doing some of the things that he treasured from his own trip: walking without any particular destination amid anonymous throngs in the shadows of midtown skyscrapers; taking the subway to the Village around midnight, where you could listen to jazz or just nurse a cup of espresso at a sidewalk cafe and watch the colorful street life go by. There were dusty used bookstores to browse and places like the Steuben Glass building where the poorest passerby could window shop; but there were so many rich surprises too: from a speeding taxi you might catch a sudden glimpse of the Brooklyn Bridge, its towering Gothic mass held together by the intricate tracery of its cables; standing on the deck of the Staten Island ferry, you could breathe in the salty Atlantic and imagine untold numbers of immigrants arriving in this harbor, carrying with them a world of histories. Afterwards, it seemed crazy for him to have thought for a second that she'd trade all that for a nickel beer in Modena—which didn't keep him from thinking anyway that he should have been able to convince her to give up her trip to New York or, more credibly, to have persuaded her not to go to Evanston in the first place.

At the same time, given the way things turned out, he couldn't help feeling remorseful about his lack of enthusiasm in their last phone conversation.

"I'll see if I can get a flight early tomorrow," she said. "That way I'll still be in Chippewa in a week." Obviously, she couldn't wait.

When Marty Reindorf called to tell him about the crash a bolt of terror went through him that was sharper and more frightening than anything he'd known since childhood. Marty kept calling, "Ted, Ted," into the phone, but Ted just held the black shape to his ear, unable to answer, and after a few moments he hung up. When he put the receiver down he realized that for some seconds he'd been shaking uncontrollably, in the grip of an immense fear: he couldn't have been more scared if he'd suddenly found himself facing the barrel of a gun, staring into the cold eyes of a stone killer. Amid the nighttime noises of his apartment, all he could do was to try to breathe deeply and to reassure himself by looking at the familiar objects around him: his Morris chair, the coffee table, the standing lamp with its shade askew, the Salvation Army sofa. He took in their shapes, their dimensions, their materiality, inhaling their familiar smells, a wordless prayer that the persistence of all this sense-data pro- vided a guarantee, however slender, that he still inhabited the same world he'd known a moment ago. Within a couple of min- utes, when Marty called back, Ted had managed to gain more control of himself, but Marty's message was of course the same: Sally was gone, irrevocably, irretrievably, forever. "I'm so sorry, Ted. I can't believe it. I can't think of her without expecting to see her again. Sally," he kept saying her name. In the silence that followed the call, Ted knew that in spite of the persistence of chair, sofa and coffee table, the beige folding door that stood half-open between rooms and the slits of windows high on the walls of his basement apartment, the world had been violently torn apart. No, he told himself, it was impossible to believe that Sally was never going to come here again, trying to resist the idea even as he understood that an enormous part of what he'd thought of as his future had just been rendered obsolete; a moment later, defeated, he said aloud: "Sally's dead," choking on the words like a man deliberately swallowing ground glass. In the end there seemed little difference in which attitude he took: this huge new fact remained beyond his comprehension.

He went a little crazy that night. Because Chippewa was virtually empty for the summer, there was nobody he could talk to. And in truth, who would he have wanted to talk to? Marty had called from Cincinnati, but even if he'd have been in town Ted wouldn't have felt like sharing his grief with him. What did Marty Reindorf know about Sally, after all? Still, the emptiness of Chippewa was ominous. The thought of staying alone in his apartment oppressed him, and he went to one of the local bars, where he ensconced himself in a booth and quickly managed to get drunk on a double shot of Canadian Club followed by an endless succession of beers. Alone in his retreat, his elbows on the black formica table, he created a little island for himself, a castaway with no desire to be found. Should he be doing something, he wondered, like calling Sally's family? The thought filled him with dread. Shouldn't he at least have stayed home, since others who knew Sally might have wanted to call him? After all, nobody would be able to get in touch with him here, nobody had a clue to his whereabouts. But that was what he wanted, wasn't it? And maybe, he slyly thought as he sipped his beer, after a couple of hours in the Old Heidelberg, he'd come home to find that none of this had happened.

A few months earlier the university town had been abuzz with the story of a Japanese engineering student who'd failed to make his expected grades and thus, in his eyes, brought dishonor to his family, whereupon he disappeared, presumably a suicide, only to have been discovered, alive, almost four years later, in the attic of a church where he'd taken refuge. "Can you imagine," Sally had said when they discussed it, "not to have anyone to talk to all that time?" Even worse, Ted had thought, would be the knowledge that the people who meant the most to you—and judging from the extremity of the man's response, they must have meant a lot—had long ago given you up for dead. The man had come down from his hiding place during the night, moving on stockinged feet, scavenging food from the church kitchen, performing calisthenics and reading such things as he could get his hands on. As his life in hiding was described, it seemed alarmingly rational, except that there was nobody to share it with. Apparently, there were even times when he sang, and his eventual discovery cleared up certain mysterious sights and sounds around the church that had baffled the people to whom they'd occurred. Ted couldn't help trying to imagine what it must have been like for the man in his refuge, feeling the vibrations of the bells each week, listening to the distant voices of the congregation among the eaves. Alone in Chippewa the night he heard about Sally's death, Ted felt a strong affinity for the recluse whose name, he was ashamed to admit, he couldn't remember.

An indistinct but familiar, seductive melody was playing in his head that night. It was a call he'd heard before, and answered. What was the point of playing by the rules, of doing the responsible thing, always doing the responsible thing? What did it get you in the end? There was a sweet glamor to letting go. He'd always been struck by the expression in the church liturgy when Catholics were asked once a year to renew their baptismal vows and to renounce not only Satan and his works and pomps, but also what was denominated the glamor of evil. The word glamor suggested that evil wasn't just something that befell you; it was something that attracted you. Just as attractive, it seemed to Ted, was the prospect of giving up, ceasing to fight, and that night he was strongly tempted to give up all fights.

In the end, he hadn't been able to find oblivion in the Old Heidelberg. Over and over he replayed his last conversation with Sally. Was there something more he could have said that might have changed the way things turned out? Somebody played Johnny Cash's "I Walk the Line," which made things worse, since it was one of Sally's favorites. Later, he remembered a cop leading him gently along the street, saying "Go home now." He seemed to have spent a good part of the night crying. At one point well after midnight he found himself passing a Catholic church and before he knew it he was pounding loudly on the thick door, incoherently asking for something, demanding something. Nobody answered, of course, and nobody showed up in the silent, empty street, telling him to be quiet. Finally, there was nothing to do but to drag himself home, where he was sick, and he had a terrible hangover the next day. It had been awful, but what followed was worse. There seemed no point to his life anymore. Everything had emptied out. When the first rush of his rage subsided, there was only a dull blank vacancy at the center of things.

And yet in the immediate aftermath of Sally's death he pulled himself together, he called her parents, he went to Evanston for the funeral where, for two awful days he had to deal with Mr. and Mrs. Pell, whose load of grief and guilt were greater than his own, and more legitimately so. To make an uncomfortable situation worse, the midsummer heat was stifling, his clothes stuck to his body, tears mixed with sweat. At the service, the candles, the vestments, the Episcopal minister's hushed words conveyed a sense of solemn elevation, as if to die at twenty-four was something to be desired. There was nothing in the cleric's solacing tone to suggest that the deceased, with thirty-seven strangers, had spent the last terrifying seconds of her life trapped inside a broken machine that tumbled awkwardly out of a stormy sky until it slammed into the earth and exploded; that the heat from its burning fuel was so great that in seconds it was melting the already twisted metal of the deformed airliner and sending thick, deadly smoke over the charred remains of the passengers before pouring out in an ominous cloud over the rain-lashed fields of upstate New York. In the cemetery, where a welcome breeze momentarily lifted the day's oppressive heat, Ted took his leave of Sally's parents, who clung to him for a few desperate, tearful seconds, then finally released him, as if they'd just realized at last that he had no power to give them back their daughter. A last glimpse of the blue dream of a lake beside which Sally had grown up brought stinging tears.

Yet it's fall now and he's teaching again. Incredibly, he's survived the worst period of his life. He's nominally taking courses, though he hasn't been doing much work there. Still, he wouldn't have believed, in July, that he'd be in the program at all. It was simple inertia that led him to sign up for a couple of classes and to resume teaching freshman English. "It's important to keep going," his mother told him over the phone, and he had no argument with which to resist her. After all, what else was he going to do? But his performance as well as his attentiveness has dipped sharply in his classes and he's headed for a couple of incompletes. Which is why it came as no surprise when he was summoned, only a week ago, to see the chairman of the department, Bradford Winslow. Old Stone Face was going to let him know, he supposed, that if things continued this way he could expect to be drummed out of the program. One of the few benefits of the zombie-like state in which he'd receive the news was that he didn't give a shit. It was even a matter of some amusement to imagine a ceremony, direct from the Saturday movies of his youth, in which old Winslow solemnly expelled Ted from the graduate program to the accompaniment of an actual group of uniformed drummers in pith helmets, with maybe a kilted bagpiper or two thrown in, playing dolefully in the background. He realized he might even be looking forward to this unambiguous shove, which was certainly more than he was likely to be able to provide for himself.

When he entered the chairman's office wearing the beat-up military jacket he'd got at the army surplus store, he felt even more like the soldier about to be cashiered for some failure that had cost the lives of his comrades. He was prepared to be stoical, possibly a little flip and philosophical; he'd already visualized the whole encounter, all the way down to his jaunty farewell salute. Winslow invited him to sit down, then leaned back in his chair and looked at him for long seconds over his steepled hands, an expression of concern on his face. A bit unnerved by the man's prolonged silence, Ted tried to make out some of the titles in the bookcase behind Winslow, but in testimony to the chairman's legendary thrift, no lights had been turned on in the office though November's early darkness had already begun to settle over the campus. In the greenish indoor twilight the older man's massive brow, gray eyes and small mouth presented a formidable facade. After a cough or two, he spoke at last. "I understand you're going through a difficult time," he said, and fell silent, as if waiting for an answer. When Ted nodded, the chairman coughed again and declared simply, "I have confidence you'll get through it." There was another long silence and Ted was still wondering whether he was supposed to get up and leave when Winslow added, "You have a lot to offer."

Ted was stunned by the simple comment, suddenly overwhelmed by conflicting emotions: on the one hand, he was childishly grateful for this commendation; on the other, he couldn't help wondering what right old Winslow had to make such judgments. What does he really know about me? Ted thought, about my growing up in Cold River, about what happened between my mother and father? What does he know about me and Sally?

The man on the other side of the desk didn't seem to be bothered by Ted's silence. "There have been excellent reports about your teaching," he said. "That's important. The teaching is the most important thing in the end." It was clear he wasn't going to say anything about the forthcoming incompletes. Wouldn't this be something to tell Sally? Ted thought, and after the sudden ache of loss, he felt a thousand different emotions connected with her. How could he communicate to anyone what he was feeling? Christ, he wanted to say to Winslow, for a time when Sally was thinking about leaving school we got so close, we were the two people in the world who knew each other best. What we had for a few days was the most wonderful thing I ever expect to know in my life. And yet, when she decided to stay, we both pulled back—I still can't say for sure which of us took the first step—and even though we were still close there was a difference. What does that say about us? What should I have done? Somehow I can't help feeling that if we'd have acted differently, it would have changed what happened later. Of course, Bradford Winslow wouldn't be able to respond, he'd have nothing to offer Ted on that subject. Still, minutes later, when he'd left the meeting, Ted couldn't help feeling a little more connected to the world, and for a moment it made him wonder whether that constituted a betrayal of Sally.

On his way across campus, Ted glimpses a solitary figure standing in front of the flagpole. A group at the university is protesting against nuclear weapons and in every kind of weather there's somebody there. They make no speeches, there are pamphlets that people can take if they want to, but the protesters just stand there silently: everyone knows why they're there. Some people yell at them, calling them commies, but they won't let themselves be provoked into a response. Ted can't help admiring them.

At last he steps out of the November chill into the warmth of the House of Joe. Coming here was a conscious choice—there's no way he can avoid going to places he associates with Sally—though when he gets his coffee and a sugar doughnut from the eponymous Joe, he avoids bringing them to the booth where he found her last spring and persuaded her to come with him to the island. Though, God knows, over time the two of them probably sat in every one of Joe's booths. Still.

Ted turns to his coffee, intent on focusing on his freshman papers. He didn't come here to socialize and he hopes he doesn't run into anyone he knows, no friend, certainly no teacher, least of all a student. After all, he came here because, as he belatedly remembered, he wanted to grade the latest batch of freshman papers from his morning class, to get that necessary task out of the way. He doesn't expect to find much inspiration in the utterances of these eighteen-year-old Midwesterners, though in truth there are four or five of them who have interesting minds. He's planned to space those papers so he can't get to one of them until he's made his way through a fair number of the likely more pedestrian efforts. The good ones are going to be his reward. He takes off his jacket and flings it into a corner of the booth. The very casualness of the gesture makes it clear that in spite of what happened a few months ago he's capable of turning his attention to this job. He brought himself out of the cold, after all, he's having a cup of coffee—and a sugar doughnut—in order to sustain himself. In every way he's acting like an animal bent on preserving life and, further, like a person who feels that the work before him is something that needs to be done. He might be on automatic pilot a lot of the time, but there's no denying that he's—how can he put it in a way that isn't melodramatic?—committed to life. He lights a cigarette, enjoys the first inhalation, and takes a sip of coffee. You were right, Mom, he says to himself.

"I don't know too much about your relationship to Sally," she said in one of her recent letters, "but I know this has hurt you terribly—that's all I need to know. I know how badly people can be hurt. But I know you and I know who you came from. You've had bad times before, I'm sure I don't have to remind you. I know you'll get past this, you'll move on." Remembering her words, he thinks of his mother fondly, the librarian back in Cold River, a trim, handsome woman in her forties, her short, prematurely gray hair always in place, almost a caricature with her cardigan sweater, the glasses on a string around her neck, yet a woman the town has talked about, a woman who married a man four years younger than she was, a handsome man without a college education who'd always been a little suspicious in their eyes and who validated their suspicions in the most satisfying way when he ran out on his wife and eleven-year-old son just after the war, not to be heard from since, at least not that anyone in town knew about. The only thing that sticks in the town's craw is that Beatrice Riley refuses to act like a spurned woman, but continues her highly public role with her head literally held high, which no doubt has won the admiration of some but just as certainly provokes others, none of whom know her madcap humor, her vivid imagination or the everyday courage with which she carries on her life. You were right, he tells himself, remembering his teary calls to Cold River this summer, the evidence suggests that I want to live.

Though, of course, that statement gives rise to the question, why? and that's not so easy to answer. Just now he's drifting, he'd have to admit to himself, he's doing what he's learned to do. He's curious about the present, he supposes—he's actually looking forward to finding out what Robert Lasher, his best student, is going to say in his essay—but—and here he waits a beat or two before allowing himself to realize what he's thinking—he can't really say he believes in a future.

Inevitably he thinks of Sally, remembering that moment on the island when she confessed her fears even as she'd recognized their momentary lifting. How much he misses her, how he wishes he could talk to her now. He remembers the smell of her bare skin and once more he remembers the colors of the traffic lights changing on the walls of her bedroom. When we were together that time did you believe in a future? he wants to ask her now. And how far ahead did you think you could see? He finds himself remembering a dream he had earlier this fall. He's thought about it so often that he can't be sure how much comes from the original dream and how much has been added in his subsequent musings about it. It's night, a black rainy night, and I'm driving somewhere, he wishes he could tell Sally. I have no idea where I am. It's dry in the car, though, and kind of comfortable, actually. I'm smoking, there's music on the radio, something mellow, the dials glow green. But the rain outside just keeps going on relentlessly as if it's never going to stop. My headlights send cones of illumination into the dark, cones that turn the rain into bright pellets of light through which I see a bit of the road before me, straight for a while, then curving. My hand moves the wheel and the car follows the road's curve. After a time the road straightens but I have no idea how long that will last, and I have to be ready for the next curve. Occasionally a pair of lights comes at me and something flies by. A rush of sound, then darkness again. Music from the radio, a different song now, dash lights glow. I can only see as far ahead as my headlights can penetrate the dark, yet somehow I know I'm on a very long trip. It's kind of scary but I feel excited—and ready for something.

Though it's crazy, he can't help feeling he's actually talked to Sally and here in the House of Joe he's warmed by her presence. Sally who fell out of the sky in a summer storm. She was brave too; she had to be: how much of a future can anyone believe in these days? And yet, though she might have awakened in the middle of the night thinking about the Bomb, she never really surrendered to despair, as far as he could know. How excited she sounded at the prospect of going to New York. At that moment, who could doubt she was looking forward to the future? He remembers the flier he saw on campus earlier today about the world ending on December 31, 1959. Yes, he tells himself, let's put this decade behind us, blow it up completely. The next one can't be worse.

I'm going to go to Modena, he tells Sally now. I've been putting it off. But I'm going to have a cheap beer for the two of us at the Lakeside. I'll look at the locals and try to imagine what you'd have to say about them.

When he takes a sip of coffee, he suddenly feels overwhelmingly alone. Maybe, after all, he wouldn't mind a bit of company just now. His eye falls on the first of the freshman papers. Well, there's always that. Even the awkward language and cliched sentiments of his students may be able to provide some solace. "I would like to say emphatically that I've always regarded myself as a positive-type person," Henry Sutter has written, "but in my opinion life at the university can bring real challenges." Ted's red pencil is already at work. And there are still twenty-three more of these.

He's working on his third paper when he hears himself being addressed by a raspy voice heavy with the accents of eastern Europe. It takes him a moment to realize that it's Andrew Kesler, the Polish guy who's been working in the Catalog Department of the library since the summer. "I hope I'm not interrupting anything," the man says, standing beside the booth with an air of expectancy, though it seems to Ted that most people seeing the batch of student papers spread out on the table before him this way would keep moving.

"No, no," he says nevertheless, and actually experiences a sense of relief as he clears a space on the table. He hadn't been planning to do the whole set of papers without a break, after all. "Sit down," he gestures, as though Kesler is his best friend when in fact his entire acquaintance with the man comes from the time when Ted delivered mail to him at the library.

"Thank you," Kesler says. He's about thirty, short, thin and nervous-looking, with a blonde crew cut and horn-rimmed glasses. One of his arms is slightly shorter than the other and the hand is correspondingly small. After a moment's formal hesitation, Kesler settles quickly into the booth across from Ted and puts down his coffee. Even seated, he has the air of someone about to make a sudden move, but for a moment he says nothing, just sits there in the tattered gray overcoat that's at least a size too large, the collar pulled up as if against Siberian blasts. He points to the papers. "At work, I see."

"Yeah," Ted answers, unsure of where this conversation can go. At best, his earlier exchanges with Kesler haven't amounted to more than a couple dozen words at a time. "Hey," he shrugs, "I've got to pay the rent."

Kesler's large eyes widen as if he's seen an apparition. He shakes his head and runs a hand through his hair before touching his glasses. "God, I can't believe you said that," he exclaims. "It's . . . it's. . . ."

"What did I say?" Ted asks.

"About paying the rent," the man smiles bleakly. "It's as if you're psychic."

"Paying the rent?" Ted is puzzled. Is the guy going to hit him up for a loan? That would be a laugh. Who knows, though? He may not have any other friends. When he worked at the library, Ted was well aware that Kesler wasn't particularly popular there. He got used to hearing complaints that the Pole could be prickly and would often get upset over what seemed like small matters. "He's a regular Miss Fuss-Budget, if you know what I mean." The man seemed perfectly sociable to Ted in their brief encounters, though it's true there was an air of distance about him, which is probably why many of his fellow workers decided that he was snobbish. The fact is, some people in the library were looking for reasons to dislike the newcomer and there was a lot of snickering about his shabby and somewhat obsolete wardrobe, as well as grumblings to the effect that he'd gotten his job illegitimately. Miss Eyre, head of Cataloging, was emphatic in declaring that she didn't need a new person in the department.

Well, Ted thinks, whatever his relations at the library, if he's looking for a loan he's certainly come to the wrong guy. "You've got problems with your rent?" he volunteers.

Kesler shakes his head. "I've got problems with my apartment." His good right hand rests on the table. Ted knows that Kesler tends to keep the smaller one hidden. "You heard about the fire on Pearl Street, didn't you?" he asks. On his face is a familiar half-smile that makes it look as if he's enjoying a secret joke. Ted shakes his head. If there's been a fire on Pearl Street recently it can't have been that bad. "It's where I've been living," Kesler declares, fixing Ted with his gaze. "The Persian on the second floor was using a hot plate, which was strictly prohibited. The fool left it unattended while he was writing a letter to his wife and, of course, it started a fire." His words are delivered in a nervous, rapid-fire way and his voice rises with excitement, his eyes growing large as he gestures with both hands. "In minutes there was smoke all over the place, there were fire engines, there were ladders and axes. God," he sighs, "it was hell." He lowers his eyes to the table. "In the end the fire caused a good deal of damage and even though the flames themselves didn't reach the third floor, I'm going to have to move out."

"You were on the third floor?" Ted says. "It sounds like you were lucky."

"I suppose so," Kesler acknowledges glumly. He's silent for a while before continuing. "But the smoke made my apartment absolutely unlivable. I have to move." He looks at his hands, which are joined on the table. "My problem is that I don't have a car." Ted feels a vague sense of apprehension even before Kesler goes on to say, "Sam Morelli said you might be able to help."

For a moment Ted is speechless. He glances toward Janet Mikkelson's paper contrasting dogs and cats as household pets as though it's part of a simpler world from which he's been exiled. Sam Morelli? Ted hasn't seen him since that party last spring when for a short time the man's oblique offer seemed to have pushed back the boundaries of the world. But what does he have to do with Andrew Kesler? He looks at the man sitting across from him, this stranger. In fact, he's not averse to helping out somebody in trouble, even someone like Kesler whom he knows so little about, but this whole thing has burst upon him before he's had a chance to get ready for it, and he has the uneasy feeling that he might be being used. "Well," he manages at last, "I do have a car. It's not much, though." He paid a hundred and twenty-five dollars for his Chevy, though there have been times like the full week last winter when the car wouldn't start when he thought he'd been cheated. There have to be plenty of people in this town who have better and bigger cars, including, he supposes, Morelli himself.

"I'd only need it for a few hours," Kesler says. "Of course I'll pay for it. I'll give you twenty-five dollars if I can use it for an afternoon this week some time when I've found a new place."

Ted is surprised by the amount of his offer. "No, no," he protests, "that's way too much." After a moment, he says, "Buy me a pitcher of beer instead." Jesus, he realizes, inside of a half minute, he's agreed to this proposition. Some resistance. In truth, though, he can spare the clunker for a few hours. Why not be big about it? He smiles and Kesler extends his good hand. "I guess we've got a deal," Ted concedes.

Kesler smiles. "Sam was right, you're a generous person." Ted would like to ask him about Morelli but something in Kesler's manner suggests that the part of the conversation dealing with business, as it were, is over for him. It's as though now at last this can be a social visit. Kesler takes a long sip of his coffee and sets his cup down on the saucer. "Troubles, troubles," he muses philosophically. "We can't avoid them, can we? I suppose it's all in the way we deal with them."

Ted nods. How else can you respond to that sentiment? But there's a dreamy look on Kesler's face and it's a few seconds before he speaks again. "Are you a lover of film?" he asks. Then, with a laugh, he corrects himself, "Are you a movie fan?"

"Yeah, sure. Who isn't?"

"I had an uncle," Kesler says. He's silent for a time, presumably in tribute to his relative. "Poor man," he continues. "Uncle Roman. He lived in what was then eastern Poland. It's not in Poland anymore." He laughs mirthlessly to himself. "Of course, Poland isn't Poland anymore either." Then he resumes in a more serious voice. "In a matter of months at the beginning of the war his village was invaded first by the Russians and then by the Germans. Later, of course, the Russians came back." What's this got to do with movies? Ted wonders. Was this uncle a Polish movie star? Those were terrible times," Kesler declares. "Uncle Roman said that for weeks on end the sky was filled with smoke, that long after the big guns stopped you couldn't get the smell of it out of your nose." It hasn't escaped Ted's notice that the man's presentation is highly theatrical, and he's suddenly curious about where Kesler himself might have been at the time. If he's about thirty, Ted calculates quickly, he'd have been about ten when the war started. "Terrible, terrible," Kesler repeats with the authority of someone who lived what he's relating. As Ted waits for more, he imagines a village somewhere on the vast plains of eastern Europe where the beleaguered inhabitants listen to the artillery of two armies, wondering when the next set of soldiers will arrive. Would those villagers have any preference between the two forces that would occupy their town? "You have to remember," Kesler says, "there was little food, nothing on the shelves. People were trading good hammers and saws for eggs that . . . who knew if they were any good?" He pauses, the familiar half-smile painted onto his face.

"But one thing they did have was an American movie." At last, Ted thinks, the movie. Kesler gives a little nervous laugh. "From the way my uncle described it," he says, "I think it must have been a Jimmy Cagney film—or maybe he didn't describe it at all and I just think that's what it was." A suspicion crosses Ted's mind: could the man be making this whole thing up? "That guy, Kesler, that Polack or whatever he is," Ted's boss Ed Mieske used to say, "I understand he tells some real whoppers. Problem is, nobody knows what to believe about him. Know what I think? I think he might be a commie. Or worse." Nevertheless, Ted can't shake the image of those villagers caught between hunger and terror, watching some American romance in which fast-talking slick-haired men blow smoke at each other and pursue glamorous women whose eyes shine like the diamonds they wear around their necks. "It seems," Kesler says, "that when supplies into the village were cut off that was the only film in town and when it was clear there wouldn't be any more for some time, the manager of the theater let the people in free. My uncle said they kept coming there and watching that movie over and over again. Isn't that something?" he asks. "The world around them is burning, they know they have only a short breathing space before one or another of those armies is going to come into town, and they already understand what that means. And they're all watching a movie!" He's silent a while. When he continues it's as if he's talking to himself. "Who knows? Given what was in the future for most of them, that was probably as sensible as any other kind of behavior."

"This uncle," Ted feels compelled to ask. "Is he alive?"

Kesler frowns. "He survived the war, but died in an automobile accident just weeks afterwards." Ted takes in the information, but he's still caught up in Kesler's story. The movie house. Crowded, filled with the harsh tang of cheap cigarettes and the stench of bodies that haven't been bathed in weeks. The darkness hides their shabby clothes, their gaunt, haunted faces, their fear. Some of them are likely to be dead soon, they know, possibly many of them. In every heart there's the secret prayer: don't let it be me. The moviegoers don't look at each other; their eyes are fixed on the screen whose images are continually being replenished by a cone of light coming from behind them. If they keep looking ahead they won't have to think about the columns of smoke on the eastern horizon, they can block out the memory of the clanking armored vehicles that have left gouges in their streets, they can ignore the rumors that are carried on the wind: there's been a reverse on the front, the retreating troops are desperate, they've been ordered to set fire to every building on their way through town; the citizens are going to be recruited into the army, the citizens are going to be killed, the occupiers are planning to take away all able-bodied men, children will be snatched from their families, local women are to be sent to the front for the pleasure of the soldiers. The Jews, there are special plans for the Jews.

Eyes ahead, the moviegoers watch the cocky protagonist in the light-colored suit. He's standing outside a night club where the orchestra is playing frenetically, his head is lowered, his feet are slightly apart, he's uncharacteristically still, his hat is in his hands. The blonde woman a short distance away has just turned him down with a disdainful laugh in favor of a suave mustached man in a tuxedo who's imperiously smoking a cigarette in the doorway. It's a crushing, desolate moment and you can see the puzzlement in the rejected man's eyes as he contemplates this thunderclap from the woman he counted on to love him. Will he be vanquished at last then, our plucky hero, this short, energetic man who's made us believe we can have what we want if we only strive for it hard enough? Our hearts are in our throats as we witness his confusion, the nervous fingering of his hat; we're afraid for him. But then, with a sudden decisive gesture that thrills us, the man puts the hat on and cocks his head, pulls out a cigarette with deft grace and, quick as quick, he lights it. He looks indulgently at the woman for a few seconds, a crooked smile on his face, then he exhales a cloud of smoke into the street and shakes his head, pushes back his hat and walks away with his familiar jaunty step. We know now that he'll be back, we know that the woman is destined to give up the shallow usurper and return to our hero. Our hearts are lifted. The jazz music that drifts into the street from the nightclub obliterates the sound of distant artillery whose rumblings we feel beneath our feet.

"So you'll do it then?" Kesler's eyes blaze. "You'll let me use your car?"

"Yeah, sure," Ted says, though for a moment he can't shake off the feeling that his car is being lent to someone who'll have to dodge the artillery shells of two desperate armies as he tries to make his way to retrieve his belongings from the devastation of the fire on Pearl Street.

"Hello, stranger." The words come slow and sultry, with the seductive lilt of a movie temptress, and the hair on the back of Ted's neck bristles because he knows at once who it is. Even as he lifts his head to confirm her identity, the rush of joy he experiences rides on a wave of sexual excitement: my God, it's Sally, here at the House of Joe, and she looks wonderful: standing beside the booth, she's smiling mysteriously, her head is tilted and her blonde hair falls in a dazzle of brightness. She's wearing a black wool skirt and a lilac blouse he's never seen before. His heart jumps at the thought that she's back, after all, in spite of the thing that happened last summer. Like the apostle Thomas seeking truth, he reaches out a hand and touches her arm, his fingers brushing the soft down there. "Hi," he says, looking up at her, and she answers, "Hi," once again in a voice that's not quite hers. Then, as if he too is someone else, he says, "You sure are a sight for sore eyes." She finds that funny and gives a little laugh, but the smile that accompanies the laugh is more than just an expression of amusement; it's clearly an invitation to sex. Sally, he's thinking, did you learn that smile in New York? even as he knows she never reached her destination. But none of this matters because somehow they're in her apartment now and it's summer again. It thrills him to find that the place looks exactly as it did the last time he saw it. The Picasso drawing is still in the corridor, he's sure, and if he were in the kitchen he'd see the picture of the two of them at last year's Winter Carnival that she'd pasted to the refrigerator. But how can he take his eyes off of Sally's naked body beside him? "Oh, Ted, I missed you so much," she

44

sighs as he runs his fingers through her hair. She takes his hand and holds it beneath hers for a moment before moving it to her breast, where he can feel the beating of her heart. Then she gently guides his hand down her rib cage, across the slight swell of her stomach, and it seems to Ted that his hand is like the pointer on the ouija board, propelled by a mysterious energy of its own. His eyes closed, he's caught up in a heightening breathless sexual excitement, his entire being concentrated in that glove of flesh that moves across her skin toward the soft, damp brush of her hair.

Awakening to a world without Sally brings a harsh letdown. Still, he has an erection, and his hand immediately goes to his cock, desperate to prolong the ecstasy of her wonderful return; but when he tries to summon her image he can't recover the seductive Sally of the dream—instead he remembers her in a familiar pose, wearing a black bulky sweater as she's curled up in a chair pondering a book, her brow creased—and he feels the sexual excitement slipping away. But he's gone too far to have this experience end in anticlimax and, surprising himself, he reaches for the image of another woman, Dori Green, the sexy Californian with the full mane of black hair and the throaty voice who's in his Faulkner seminar. The shift of images throws Ted off stride and he feels himself softening for a moment, but it doesn't take long for him to return to his previous state of arousal. He directs the fantasy figure of Dori to take his cock in her hands. "Would you like me to suck it?" she asks over and over, moving toward it without reaching it until he comes at last.

It doesn't take long in the calmer moments that follow for another feeling to rise to the surface: remorse for his betrayal of Sally, both for appropriating her in his sexual fantasy and then for abandoning her in favor of someone else; and all the remembered elation of the dream is spent, making Sally even more dead, and gone, and unattainable than she'd been up until now. The world is empty again.

It's a chilly day outside, he can see through the slit of window. The sky, he knows, has been sandblasted to a gray the color of cement; he can imagine on his skin the dry bite of the cold.

There's no place here for lilac blouses, or summer, or naked bodies, just the usual stuff of his present life. He has no classes today but he has papers to grade as well as preparations, and he should read a couple of articles on Faulkner. The real world. Yet what he felt in his dream was real too, wasn't it? He drags himself off to the bathroom, where he shaves and showers. In the steamy aftermath, he sits on the edge of the tub, flushed, drained, clean and empty. Once more he recalls the dream, he can feel his hand moving over Sally's body. He remembers his absolute conviction that his friend, who was dead, had come back: the contradiction between what he knew and what he was experiencing simply didn't matter. Jesus, he tells himself, in my dream I was a believer. But in the end it was only a dream, his belief merely the projection of his desire. When he thinks of Dori Green he feels a twinge of shame for having used her that way. At the same time it's clear to him that he finds her attractive, and interesting. But she isn't Sally and that's her problem. I've got to get out more, he tells himself, I can't keep using Sally . . . He follows the thought: I can't keep using Sally as my shield to keep the rest of the world away.

The phone rings in the middle of the morning. His first thought is that it's Marty Reindorf, trying to organize that touch football game with some of the younger faculty that he's been talking about. Ted doesn't think there's much of a chance to bring it off, though it might be interesting to see who would actually play. "We'll cream them," Marty said, "we'll really do some damage." He can't see Marty, who looks more like a chess player than an athlete, doing any physical damage to anyone, but he's obviously eager to be on a team that might deliver some bruises to the ancient enemies of grad students. Actually, just now Ted welcomes the idea of such a contest. I hope it is Marty, he thinks, I hope he does organize that game.

He's surprised when he hears his mother's voice on the other end of the line. "Mom?"

"Hi, Ted, how are you?" she asks.

"Fine, fine," he answers. "Is anything wrong?"

"No," she says. "Why do you ask?"

"Well, for one thing, you're calling long distance in the morning and that costs money."

He hears her laugh. "Cold River isn't exactly in Alaska, you know."

"True enough." Though something else occurs to him. "But why aren't you at work this morning?"

"Are you a spy for Mayor Beinecke? We do get to take days off every now and then, you know."

"OK." Ted knows enough not to press any further. "So why did you call then?"

"Just to find out how you're doing," she says. "It's still not that long a time since this summer." They both know what "this summer" means.

Ted is silent a while. "I'm doing OK, Mom," he says. "I'm doing fine."

"There's nothing wrong with recognizing that you have feelings," she says.

"I know. I appreciate your looking in on things," he says. "I really do."

They talk for a few minutes, his mother filling him in on some of the local gossip, turning it, as she always does, into an amusing series of stories about a town full of crazy people. "I love you," she says at the end of the call. The expression of the sentiment isn't unusual for her but its echo lingers in Ted's mind, and he can't quite abandon the idea that this time he heard a note of special urgency in her voice. In truth, though, he has no way of knowing how much he's embroidering a simple statement. Still, it isn't normal for her to call at this time of day and as he replays her words he can just about convince himself he detected a tinge of weariness in her voice. The dream this morning has upset him, he realizes; it's made him jittery. Maybe he should have told his mother about that, just in general terms, of course, no details. Though what if she'd have started asking? No, better to keep quiet on that score.

Ted settles into the Morris chair with his freshman papers. Amid the ramshackle collection that fills his apartment, the dark brown chair he picked up at a barn sale outside of town is the one piece of furniture he really values. Sally, who was with him, spotted it. "What a great Morris chair," she said. At the time Ted didn't know a Morris chair from an electric chair, but once Sally pointed it out, he was attentive and the more he looked, the more he liked it, especially after he'd sat in it. The pale descendant of some farmer, disenchanted with the rural life, let them have if for five dollars and it didn't take Sally's expertise to tell Ted what a steal that was. Fashioned out of solid oak in the previous century, it looks as if it can last for untold generations. Its reclinable back is adjustable to four positions by means of a bar placed into one of four pairs of metal notches behind the rear legs. With its carved arabesques in the front and the hand-turned helical spindles supporting the armrests, Ted can convince himself that there's something Venetian about it. It's ideal for reading and correcting papers, since its wide flat arms provide a sturdy backing to a book, enabling you to write in it or even have a cup of coffee; and with the beige burlap coverings Sally made for the pillows, it's damned comfortable.

He's just got into a groove with his freshman papers when the phone rings again. "Ted?" The voice on the other end makes it sound like "Tad." All it takes is that one syllable, or syllable and a half, since the speaker's intonation prolongs it, to identify Andrew Kesler.

"Oh, hi," Ted answers. It's been a couple of days since their meeting at the Joe and Ted has been expecting him to call.

"I have a new apartment," Kesler tells him enthusiastically. "On Cummings Street." Well, isn't that great, Ted wants to say, but what's that got to do with me? In fact, he knows very well what it has to do with him and his heart sinks at the prospect. "I was wondering," the voice on the other end says after a moment, "if I could use your car."

Ted waits before answering. Next time you feel inclined to make a spontaneous offer, he tells himself, think twice and bite your tongue. This is certainly something he doesn't need just now, but he can't really muster up a sense of outrage. After all, he's already agreed to it. "Sure," he answers at last. "When were you thinking of doing it?"

"This afternoon?" Kesler turns it into a question. "Say one or so?" Another question.

He should have known. Once more Ted waits before responding, though the fact is, he has no special plans for the car today. And it will be a relief to have this business over with in a few hours. "OK," he says, "I can meet you someplace with the car."

"I wouldn't think of it," Kesler says. "I'll come there."

"Suit yourself then." In some dimly-lit corridor of memory, Ted senses figures of fairy-tale characters moving through an obscure landscape: a traveler lost in a forest encounters an odd-looking stranger who shows him the way out of the dark woods on condition that some day in the future he'll fulfill an obligation. Of course, the traveler has no choice but to accept. Kesler, though, is a bad match for the stranger who makes the demand, not having led Ted out of any forest, thick or thin.

The Pole arrives precisely at one and they shake hands in what Ted supposes is the continental fashion. There's something intent, expectant about the man, as if he's come for more than the car. Here in the apartment Kesler seems particularly out of place, though the thought occurs to Ted that he'd probably look out of place in his own home town. He's wearing the over-large gray overcoat whose cut suggests it was made by one of Warsaw's finest tailors, possibly of the prewar period. Remembering Kesler's story at the House of Joe, Ted wonders if it could have belonged to his uncle Roman. "So," the visitor says at the door, "this is your lair." He makes it sound like a question, even something of a challenge.

"I suppose," Ted responds. "Not much as lairs go, though." Kesler's eyes grow large as he peers behind Ted, trying to get a look at the apartment. Though he hadn't been planning to do so, Ted invites him in and the man enters with quick, cat-like steps, his head moving from left to right as if he expects to be asked to describe the place later. It takes only a few paces to cross from the little anteroom through the kitchen and into the living room. The sliding door separating it from the bedroom is pulled closed at this hour, which is a blessing, since, in spite of a bit of minimal tidying in deference to his guest, the bedroom is in even shabbier shape than the rest of the place. "My housekeeper doesn't come in until tomorrow," Ted says. "Getting proper help is so difficult these days." Kesler acknowledges the joke with a smile but Ted realizes that he's glad his bedroom is shut off from view. The general assumption at the library is that Kesler is homosexual. What the man does with whom is his own business, as far as Ted is concerned, but he's still uneasy about letting his visitor see the bedroom. It's almost as if he thinks the other man would be able to find traces there of his dream of Sally and, more incriminating, his subsequent masturbation.

Kesler stops in the middle of the living room. Standing beside the Morris chair, he runs a finger absently along one of its arms. "Interesting,' he comments, looking at a window high in the wall, "choosing to live in a basement. I suppose it gives you a sense of security, like being in a cave." He smiles to himself. "I, on the other hand, seem to wind up in the eaves, like an owl." The man's eyebrows are so blond that he doesn't seem to have any and his face, Ted speculates, would look completely different without the horn-rimmed glasses. Kesler looks at the titles in one of the bookcases. "Do you know Milosz's *The Captive Mind*?" he asks.

Ted shakes his head. Feeling a belated obligation to hospitality, he asks, "Would you like a cup of coffee?"

"No, thanks." The look of resolve on the man's face is buttressed by the fact that he hasn't even unbuttoned his coat. "You're doing enough for me as it is. And I don't want to take up more of your time than I have to."

As they walk toward the car, Ted's curiosity gets the better of him. "How do you know Sam Morelli?" he asks.

Kesler turns toward Ted as if in response to the question. He walks a few steps before answering, "I met him at a party." In the silence that follows, Ted seems to hear him add, "The same as you."

Did Morelli try to recruit him too? Ted wonders. But Kesler shows no inclination to go any further with his disclosures. "He seems like an interesting guy," Ted offers.

The other man doesn't rise to the bait. Instead, he glances at his watch. "I should be back by 3:30," he says. "Four at the latest."

"Be it ever so humble," Ted points to the car moments later.

"It will do fine," Kesler pronounces, accepting the keys to the green Chevy. As Ted watches, he starts the engine without adjusting the rear-view mirror. "See you in a couple of hours then," he says, giving Ted a parting wave. After a brief squeal of rubber, the car darts down the street in a series of jolts. Jesus, Ted thinks, I didn't even ask him if he could drive.

Hours later, he's concerned. He's already had his dinner of twenty-nine-cent-a-pound ground beef mixed with spaghetti sauce and pasta—even with the bits of onion he sauteed with the meat and the bowl of vanilla ice cream he topped it off with, the whole meal hasn't cost him more than a dollar, for which he feels virtuous, though the virtue is accompanied by a familiar heartburn. The latter condition is aggravated by Ted's mounting concern during the past few hours about where Kesler can be. There are plenty of believable explanations for his delay and Ted has gone through them all, but why hasn't the man at least called him? Now that dinner is over and the dishes have even been washed, there are fewer diversions to keep him from thinking about Kesler and his Chevy. Finally, in resignation, he turns to Faulkner's *Absalom, Absalom*, though he knows that under the present circumstances he isn't going to be able to give the novel the concentration it requires.

After a few halting attempts, he manages to lose himself in the convoluted sentences with which Faulkner tells an even more convoluted tale. Once he's succumbed to the prose, the vividness of the language carries him along whether or not he's able to hang on to the thread of the story. The tropical heat of a lost time envelopes him as, with the inhabitants of a hamlet on the Mississippi frontier, he contemplates the arrival from the swamp of a mysterious stranger and his equally mysterious retinue of blacks.

The knock on the door abruptly brings Ted a thousand miles north and more than a century into the future, though for a second or two the afterimages of Faulkner's scene linger.

But he quickly springs to his feet and goes to the door where, gratefully, he encounters Kesler. "I'm sorry I'm late," the man says hurriedly, his breath frosting on the night air, whose chill enters the apartment. "It's nothing," Ted says, noting the evasive look in the Pole's eyes. "I . . ." Kesler begins, "I ran into a little trouble."

His tone of barely suppressed alarm sets off warning signals for Ted. "Trouble?" he asks.

"Yes," the man responds. "With the car."

Since the entrance to the basement apartment is recessed, Ted can't see the car from where he's standing. He remembers how Kesler drove off this afternoon. "Did you have an accident?" he asks.

Kesler nods. Then he clarifies, "Just a small one."

"Let me see." Ted follows the man into the street. The cold runs along his bare arms but he ignores it, intent on finding out what's happened to his car. It's been dark for some time already and the first thing he notices is that Kesler chose not to park the car under the streetlight, which would have been closer to the apartment. A sudden bolt of anger overwhelms him. What did that idiot do to the car? The anger slides immediately into self-condemnation, since he knows he was under no obligation to loan the Chevy to this man. When he glimpses it from a distance, though, he experiences a sense of relief: at least it looks intact. "It's the side," Kesler explains, and walks Ted to the passenger's side where, indeed, there's a tiny canyon that runs along the fender and across part of the door.

Given his initial fears, Ted is glad to see that the damage is minor. He looks at the car for a few seconds, trying to get used to this slight disfigurement. The dent is possibly a foot and a half long and not very deep, all in all, nothing disastrous, but by the same token, not at all necessary. "How did that happen?" he asks.

Kesler is suddenly spirited. "Some fool came out of nowhere," he gestures with his hands, "and sideswiped me."

Ted is still looking at the shallow gash along the side of his car. He resists the temptation to run his finger along the crease. "Who was the other guy?" he asks. "Did you talk to him? Exchange papers?" The damage to Ted's car doesn't warrant any insurance claims, but what about the other guy?

Kesler is ready with his answer. "He never stopped. He was gone before I knew it." Ted is dumbfounded. Somebody comes out of nowhere and hits him, then just keeps on going? It sounds fishy, especially given the configuration of the damage. His puzzlement shades toward suspicion: it's more than likely that Kesler himself was at fault. Did he hit a parked car? Is someone out there right now looking for the person who did it? Possibly the police? Ted turns his attention back to the Chevy: it's certainly drivable and the aesthetic damage is something he can live with, as long as the passenger side door opens. In truth, the car isn't worth enough to justify trying to get the dent repaired. But, Jesus, you'd think its very shabbiness would have been enough to protect it against this kind of thing. The fury that rises up in him now is directed against a cosmos that would engage in such shameful piling-on. "Don't worry, I'll pay for it," Kesler says.

And that man, Ted thinks, is the agent of the cosmic forces that determined I was having too good of a life driving around in a shitbox that cost me a hundred and a quarter. I guess I was too bold and ambitious. But that's not the only thing that disturbs him. He can't stop thinking that, in spite of what the man said, it was actually Kesler who hit another car. Maybe the other car is in a lot worse shape than Ted's. But he wouldn't have just run off like that, would he? Once again the man offers to pay him for the damage. "We can talk about that later," Ted says. Money, after all, isn't what his present feeling of impotence is all about. Suddenly he just feels tired. "What about you?" he asks. "Are you OK? Did you move in all right?"

Kesler nods, a relieved smile making its way tentatively to his face. "No problems, otherwise." He's hunched and, in his oversized coat, he looks like a refugee who was forced to flee his home, leaving all his possessions behind. He isn't, though, Ted reminds himself; he most certainly has possessions. But why did it take him so long to transfer his things from one apartment to another? There's no way that a minor accident would have delayed him that long. Ted realizes that for the moment he has no choice but to take Kesler's word for what happened to his car. It's getting cold out on Tecumseh Street and it occurs to Ted that this is just one more pain to have to endure on what hasn't been a very good day. It may have started well enough with the dream of Sally, but everything after that has been a falling-away.

"I'd like to pay you," Kesler says again. "For the damage, as well as the use of the car."

Ted doesn't like the way he's feeling: the quiet anger that's been rising in him feeds his sense of self-pity: why does all this stuff have to happen to him? The last thing he wants to do is to go back to his apartment and stew over things. He's certainly not likely to return to *Absalom, Absalom*. Kesler owes him something, that's for sure. "I said before that you could buy me a pitcher of beer," he tells him. "Do you want to do that now?"

"Oh, certainly," Kesler agrees. "That's fine with me."

"I'll drive," Ted says.

They go to the Old Heidelberg where the iconography includes elaborate beer mugs, cuckoo clocks, much Gothic script and a painting of a bearded, pot-bellied elf puffing on a pipe bigger than himself. The tobacco smoke that lazily fills the room carries a companionable sense of people bent on enjoying themselves in an unstrenuous way. Ted is still agitated, though; he has a sense of expectation, as if this interlude in the Old Heidelberg might be a chance to clear some things up, like the mystery of Kesler's accident. What the hell did he do or what was done to him? Kesler is a man whose declarations are hard to credit. Ted remembers his story about the uncle and the movie played over and over as the Russians and the Germans fought for the privilege of occupying his village. It was a tantalizing story, but really, there's no way of knowing how much, if any of it, is true. That goes for Kesler generally, he concludes.

"Kesler sounds like a German name," he says when they're seated in a booth with a pitcher of beer between them.

The other man frowns. He's taken off his overcoat and is wearing a black sweater which, like the coat, looks big on him.

His good hand is on the table near his glass; the other rests in his lap. "There are a lot of German names in Poland," he says. "In that part of the world the borders are notoriously fluid."

"But they said at the library that you came here from Germany."

Kesler looks at him a moment and takes a breath. It's hard to tell whether he resents Ted's curiosity or is simply gathering his thoughts before going on. "As the war was ending," he says, "a lot of people did everything they could to get to the west. If you were going to be liberated, or captured, everyone knew it would be better with the Americans and British than with the Russians. Much better. I was lucky: I made it to Germany." He takes a while to light a cigarette and when he's done, both of his hands are on the table. "Many people didn't make it," he says as he exhales a cloud of smoke. "I stayed in Germany and went to school there."

Ted's curiosity is aroused. "You didn't want to go back to Poland?"

Kesler shakes his head. An ironic smile plays about his lips. "Not to communist Poland, my friend, no." He takes another drag on his cigarette. "Besides, my sister was in Germany."

Ted has lit up himself. The new piece of information catches him as he's inhaling. "I didn't know you have a sister."

Kesler turns grave, he looks down. "Had," he corrects Ted. "Magda is dead."

"I'm sorry," Ted says.

Kesler continues to look at the table, where the smaller of his hands is curled into a fist. "My father was a professor," he says, "my mother was a doctor. Magda and I were the only children. She was five years older." He pauses a moment as if in tribute to his sister's memory. "At the beginning of the war I was ten and she was fifteen. My parents were political. They were taken away and we never heard from them again. Things happened, Magda and I were separated." His eyes narrow as if he's trying to see something very far away. "You may find this hard to believe, but each of us made our way separately to Bavaria, and—this is the incredible part," he says, his eyes growing large again, "—my sister actually tracked me down and found me in a refugee camp there."

"Tracked you down?" Ted says. "How long were you apart?"

"We'd exchanged some messages near the end, but I hadn't actually seen Magda in more than three years." Kesler blows a cloud of smoke and squints into the haze.

"Amazing." Ted imagines brother and sister moving through the ruined cities of eastern and central Europe in search of each other. The roads would be filled with refugees on foot dressed in rags, while tanks and jeeps rumble by, carrying victorious soldiers past bomb craters and the stumps of ancient churches. There would be smoke everywhere. It would be a landscape utterly unlike Chippewa and as he considers the flight of Andrew Kesler, it seems all the more remarkable that this should be the place where he's wound up. He waits for more, but Kesler has gone silent, and it seems as if he's come to the end of the account of his postwar travels. Ted can understand. Possibly he's thinking about his sister, who was obviously important to him. In the light of the man's past, the business of the car seems like small potatoes indeed.

Kesler puts down his cigarette and takes a long swallow of his beer, then sets his glass back on the table. For a time he's lost in thought, unpleasant thought from the look of it. "That Persian," he says suddenly. "He wanted me to believe he was writing his wife when the fire started." He laughs. "How do I know he actually has a wife?"

"What Persian?" Ted asks, and then remembers Kesler's story of how the fire started in his building.

The other man's mouth is curled into a sneer. "You can't just take things at face value," he declares. "I'd be dead if I hadn't learned that long ago." He takes a hungry drag on his cigarette, exhales, and his shoulders sag. "I don't know," he says. "I'm not saying I believe in this one hundred per cent, but I can't completely rule out the possibility that that fire was no accident." Ted is still trying to account for how Kesler got from his sister to his former fellow-tenant. "Of course," the Pole laughs bitterly, "they want me to keep moving. And after that. . . ."

Ted waits for more, but Kesler seems to have dropped into a funk. He takes another swallow of beer and puts the glass down; he says nothing for a long time, staring into his glass. Which will it be when he starts talking again? Ted wonders, the sister or the Persian?

But Kesler surprises him. When he looks at Ted again there's a completely different expression on his face, he looks younger. "When I was a boy . . ." he says, a touch of dreaminess entering his voice, "one of my schoolmates was named Antek. Antek Frytkowski. He was tall with the complexion of a gypsy and he was very handsome." Kesler laughs, becoming more animated. "He had the most beautiful eyebrows." Though Ted nods encouragingly, he feels an encroaching uneasiness. Is Kesler going to confess to some homosexual relationship? "Antek was a rarity," he goes on, "a boy who was highly intelligent and at the same time very popular. All the rest of us wanted to be with him and, like a woman of great beauty, he never had to make a move toward us. All he had to do was wait and we'd come to him." Kesler smiles wickedly. "I was no different from the others. I admired Antek, I wanted to be like him, I resented that he had so many friends." He shakes his head. "Oh, he was my friend, but he had so many others, and I was jealous."

Ted is curious about how old Kesler was when this was happening. Could the events he's narrating have happened during the war? It's hard for him to imagine that with all the killing going on around them there would be any time for personal relations of the kind that Kesler is talking about. But then, the world he's describing is completely different from the one Ted has known.

Kesler meanwhile has lit another cigarette. The noise level in the Old Heidelberg has risen and he leans forward confidentially as he continues his tale. "Oh, I was bright," he says, "and if I may say so, I was handsome enough, but," he moves his head briefly in the direction of his smaller hand lying on the table, "I wasn't . . . perfect, and children can be cruel. They called me names, of course. Not Antek, though. He was an aristocrat, he was above that. It's just that there was no reason for him to pay

special attention to me, and that's what I wanted, special attention." He expels a thick cloud of smoke. "But as I said, I was
bright, and I devised a brilliant idea to win his regard."

Kesler has become completely caught up in his story: his
eyes gleam, there's a raptness about him, and Ted doubts he's
even aware of where he is at the moment. "Antek had a toy
airplane," Kesler says, "a really pretty thing made of metal that
all of us boys admired. An uncle had given it to him. It was a
gray biplane with Polish insignia on the wings. We all wanted
to have it and, as a special treat Antek would let one or another
of us play with it for a short time, always, of course, under his
watchful gaze. It didn't take any brilliance to see how important that airplane was to him. Whether it was simply because
the toy was so well-made, or because of his love of the uncle
who'd given it to him, or possibly because he harbored secret
dreams of becoming a Polish airman, who can say? But I saw
that the way to make Antek care about me was connected to
that airplane, that if he were to lose it, he'd give anything to get
it back." The smile on Kesler's face must mirror the delight he
felt when he first came upon this scheme. His look is an invitation to complicity, as if the two of them are planning the next
move together.

Ted already knows what Kesler did next. "So you stole it?"
he asks.

The other man nods. "I devised a perfect plan; I chose my
moment well and took the plane when there was a great deal of
confusion and any number of people might have been blamed.
Then I raced off and hid it in our cellar where I knew that
nobody was going to find it."

It must have been a bold and dangerous thing for a boy like
Kesler to do, Ted thinks, not to say desperate. "Did the plan
work?" he asks.

"Yes and no," the other man answers. "The theft was accom-
plished brilliantly but, as I said, the point of the plan was to use
the theft to win Antek's regard. Yes, when he discovered that
the plane was gone, it was like a blow to the stomach, he pulled
back from all his friends, as I knew he would. He suspected all

of us. But my larger plan dictated that somehow I would be the one to find the lost toy without being blamed for having taken it. I hadn't figured out exactly how I was going to accomplish that, but I believed I could do it. I'd hurt Antek but I'd done so in order to get closer to him and for the act to have its full consequences it was necessary that it be brought to a successful conclusion." When he falls silent, the buzz of talk suddenly fills the room and Paul Anka's "Lonely Boy" is faintly audible in the background.

Ted knows this story isn't going to end well. But it's his role to ask, "Things didn't go the way you planned them?"

Kesler shakes his head, darkness clouds his face. He waits a moment before going on. "Just at that time Antek became sick with rheumatic fever. His mother said that in his fevered ravings he kept asking for the airplane. You can imagine the state I was in. I wanted desperately to return it but I didn't want, especially at this time, to expose myself as the one who'd caused him so much pain. I was determined to find a way of getting the plane back to him but I'd have to wait until he got better." Kesler's silence tells Ted all he needs to know about the outcome of Antek's sickness. "Well," the Pole sighs, "when it was over, you know, when he was dead, I was haunted by the need to get rid of the incriminating evidence and I was a madman until I was able at last to throw the thing into the river." Kesler looks drained, as if in telling the story he's re-experienced the emotions he's described. Yet he pushes on. "To this day I can remember the smell of potatoes in our basement, the feel of cool earth in the secret place where I'd hidden the plane. I can remember how I felt as I pulled the plane out of the darkness and brushed some of the dirt off its wings, then held it in my hands for a few seconds. I had the airplane but Antek was gone. You can't imagine the emptiness. I didn't believe I could go on living."

The two of them smoke in silence for a while before Ted says, "The fact that you remember the incident so vividly seems to mean it was a difficult thing for you to do. Were you at all religious as a kid?"

Kesler makes a gesture with his hand. "I was religious enough. I still believed then. But in my heart I knew I wasn't taking that plane for selfish purposes. Really, I never had any intention of playing with it by myself. In fact I believed my larger motives were very noble."

"But you said your conscience bothered you."

Kesler shrugs. "I felt terrible about betraying Antek, of course. But you have to remember that it's only because the story ended the way it did that anybody can say I betrayed him. If he'd have lived and I'd have found the plane for him, I'm confident we'd have been very good friends. I betrayed him in order to be closer to him. That betrayal, that theft, was only supposed to be one chapter of the story. But it never turned out that way."

Ted can't help thinking that, given the world in which these events were taking place, with years of death and destruction awaiting that part of Europe, there were many other, darker ways it might have turned out, even if Kesler's theft had been able to win the temporary friendship of Antek.

"We have to think the story's going to continue," Kesler declares, "But we don't have complete control of it; we don't have very much control at all."

"Amen," Ted says. He suddenly has a strong urge to tell this man he hardly knows about Sally, about his dream this morning and the way it made him feel, but the impulse is only momentary.

Kesler regards him with a mysterious smile. "I hope," he says, "that in telling you about my betrayal, I haven't made you an accomplice." It's precisely at this moment that Ted wonders whether a word of what he's just heard is true.

In one of the graduate reading rooms on the top floor of the library, Ted is having a hard time keeping his mind on the class he's preparing. The slightest thing distracts him—a cough, the scraping of a chair, even the soporific hissing of the radiators—and after a while Thoreau's declaration of why he went into the woods has become just a pattern of black marks on paper. Possibly the weather is to blame: all day long people have been talking excitedly about the impending snowstorm and here he is, inside, engaged in business as usual. Worse, he's been bothered again by thoughts of Sally. Given the way things turned out, he's used to thinking that her death robbed him of his future; but there are times when he's been visited by the worm of doubt. He and Sally were very good friends, but they'd never got to the stage of talking about getting married. Would they ever have? Or were there some things between them that would have kept them apart? These are questions, he realizes, that can never be answered.

And then, amid these musings, he feels a sudden flash of something like anger. *She abandoned me*, he thinks, *and now I'll never know how things would have turned out for us.*

"Some snow, huh?"

Ted looks up to see Gordon Wiley, who works in the reference department, standing beside him. It takes him a moment to reenter the present. "Has it started already?" he asks.

"It's been going for about an hour." Gordon, a tall, prematurely balding man in his forties, is wearing his familiar tweed jacket and knit tie. "People have started leaving early," he says, his Adam's apple bobbing with urgency. According to what Ted heard on the radio, the snow could be heavy, there might even be a blizzard. The thought brings a tingle of anticipation. From where he sits at one of the old wooden tables illuminated by green-shaded lamps, he has no way of gauging the weather outside. It could be full summer as far as he's concerned, though the heavy coats flung over chairs by the handful of people left in the room would suggest otherwise. "It's coming down fine, like dust," Gordon says, unable to contain his excitement, "but it's very heavy and it's covering everything in a hurry."

Ted looks at the clock on the wall: the place will be closing soon. "I guess I'd better get going, see if I can find my car under all that snow." The thought of his car and cold weather brings disturbing memories of last winter, when the Chevy wouldn't start for days on end, and the recollection makes him uneasy.

Gordon hovers, as if he has more to talk about than the weather. "That pal of yours," he says quietly, in deference to the others in the room, "that guy Kesler, I hear he's really giving them a run for their money in Cataloging."

Ted, who's going to leave anyway, makes a motion toward the corridor and the two men exit the room. "My *pal* Kesler?" he asks.

"Well," Gordon looks at him inquiringly, "he seems to think you've helped him when other people haven't. At least that's the story he's telling." Gordon narrows his eyes. "The guy's more than a little paranoid, you know."

Christ, Ted thinks, the last thing he wants is to have his name linked with Kesler's. And Gordon is just the kind to spread the word around. Ted has always suspected that there's a connection between the man's taste for gossip and his being a ham radio operator. "I loaned him my car for a couple of hours when he was moving," Ted explains. "That's all." He's certainly not going to tell him that the Pole put a dent in the Chevy. Oddly, whenever he's been asked about the damage, he's been content to slough it off with something vague, leaving the listener to assume that he was responsible. "I don't think that qualifies for making us pals."

Gordon shrugs. "Just as well, I guess, from some of the stuff I've heard." There's no follow-up to that but Ted can guess what he's talking about. Ted has heard the same stories. If they're true, Kesler is making no secret of his sexual preferences. "Not that that's a problem," Gordon goes on. "Not in this town, anyway." Ted recognizes the invitation to join him in decrying the presence of homosexuals on campus, but he makes no response, and after a moment Gordon continues, more cautiously. "They say his work in Cataloging is—well, erratic. Eyre says she doesn't really need him there. She makes it sound as if Kesler was kind of foisted on them by higher-ups and they don't know what to do with him." He pauses, waiting for Ted to join in. "The worst thing is," he goes on after a while, "the guy doesn't seem to care who he ticks off. I don't know," Gordon shakes his head. "I suppose he may have had some hard times back wherever the hell he came from, but I'd guess he doesn't have a great future in Chippewa." His effort to sound sympathetic is considerably less than half-hearted.

When the man leaves, Ted walks into the stacks to a window where he can look out onto the campus. Lighting in the rows of stacks is controlled by a timer and he leaves the light off, which sharpens the contrast between the darkness inside and the snow that's being driven through the night air by strong gusts, a pale, ghostly spume that comes alive when it passes into the light. Several inches have already covered the campus, erasing signs of the walkways between buildings, and the solitary figure Ted sees from his vantage point seems to be trekking through a pathless white wilderness. Around a lamppost near the library the falling snow swirls thickly like a plague of albino bees and Ted shivers at the prospect of having to make his way through the stinging cold to his car.

That pal of yours. He hasn't thought much of Kesler in the couple of weeks since he loaned him the Chevy, though sometimes, seeing the damage on the passenger's side, he's likely to be visited by a feeling that conjures up in an instant the sense of that entire evening, the anxious waiting in his apartment, the Pole's return of the car, their subsequent time in the Old

Heidelberg, where he listened to Kesler's dramatic, if dubious stories. But he hasn't given a thought to what Kesler himself has been up to since he saw him. Now Gordon Wiley's report has made him aware once again of this stranger in Chippewa, a man who doesn't seem to be going out of his way to make himself welcome, and he wonders how things will turn out for the Pole. Certainly his being homosexual shouldn't hurt him in the library. Chippewa is fairly tolerant to its community of homosexuals and there are enough of them at the library to make Gordon's attitude the exception rather than the rule. But Ted can imagine Kesler would be a hard person to get along with, regardless of sexual preference. The Kesler Gordon described sounds like someone who's daring the library to fire him and, from what Ted knows of the man, he can believe it. What's going to happen to him? Ted wonders, realizing that the Pole has become interesting to him again.

He gathers his things, puts on his jacket and leaves. The library is pretty much deserted and people who'd normally be on campus are nowhere to be seen, no doubt snugly ensconced in dorm rooms, apartments and houses all over town, which only makes him feel more lonely. He trudges through the snow. Without boots, his feet are quickly cold, and he feels the icy rills of melting snow moving down the back of his neck. Still, it's wonderful out here with the wind wailing as it drives the glistening snow, and he exhales clouds of vapor just to see his breath carried away by the sharp gusts. The snow has softened the shapes of hedge and hydrant; it's turned the campus into a vast field of white shading toward blue under the darkness. At the moment there's no sign it will stop falling soon. Possibly it will continue this way, not just for hours but days on end—he's read about storms like that—so that people will have to tunnel their way out of their homes to get provisions for survival. He welcomes the thought, remembering stories of the early settlers on these plains who had to confront such assaults of nature with far more primitive tools. He can't help feeling exhilarated at the thought that facing such a storm is a test of his mettle, far more of one—and maybe far easier in the long run—than getting a batch of freshman papers graded in time. Hearing the muted clank of chains, he glimpses the pulsing light of a snow plow laboring down the street. The sound of its blade scraping the asphalt conveys the sense of the midwestern town beginning its serious work of dealing with winter's fury, and for an instant he might be a boy again in Cold River.

The student union, outlined by a constellation of haloed lights, lies between him and his car, and its looming presence in the storm is inviting. Rather than going straight home, why not get a hot chocolate and maybe do a little reading among the few other brave souls riding out the storm in a public place? He climbs the steps and enters, feeling a sense of accomplishment as he breathes in the familiar smell of the dark-panelled lobby, the residue of generations of cigars smoked by returning alumni. He unzips his jacket, shakes the snow off of his clothes and stamps his feet, savoring the warmth while the carved life-sized Chippewa Indian looks gravely on from his station near the reception desk. Odd, he thinks, to have been visited again by that feeling about Sally, the doubt, the desperation, the feeling of abandonment. Well, Sally certainly abandoned him.

Downstairs, in the nearly empty cafeteria, Ted gets his hot chocolate and is on his way to find a place where he can indulge in a bit of solitary reverie when he hears his name called by Marty Reindorf, who's in a booth with someone else. When Ted recognizes Dori Green, he experiences a rush of delight that carries an element of guilt, and he hesitates for a moment. The guilt is mercifully short-lived and he walks over to the booth, disappointed to be losing the privacy he was contemplating only seconds ago but not entirely displeased at running into fellow refugees from the storm. "I don't want to interrupt anything," he says when he gets there, though his first impression is that he can't be butting in on anything particularly jolly: Marty, who usually looks as if he has indigestion, is even more doleful tonight. Behind his trademark horn-rimmed glasses, his thin, sharp-featured face is contracted with concern, his narrow shoulders pinched under his maroon corduroy shirt. Ted remains standing for a while. He isn't aware of any romantic relationship between Marty and this woman who's only been on campus since September, but it's possible, isn't it? that, in spite of Marty's hailing him, they really want to be alone. He hardly knows Dori, so he can't be sure.

But she joins Marty in inviting him. "Please," she appeals, "we need a little cheer in this booth." In spite of her black sweater and skirt, her dark stockings and her thick black hair, she has a sunny expression on her face, as befits her California origins.

"That's putting a lot of pressure on me, isn't it?" Ted settles beside Marty. "OK," he announces, "here I am, Mr. Cheer. What do you want: jokes, card tricks, funny sounds? I got 'em."

Dori's smile makes it clear his presence is no intrusion; Marty gives a wan shrug. When Ted has got out of his coat, Dori takes a thoughtful puff on her cigarette and exhales. "OK," she says, "we might as well get right to the point: where do you stand on the question of having kids?"

Ted isn't prepared for this. "Well," he stalls, rejecting the first flip response that comes to mind. She didn't sound as if she were joking. "I suppose eventually I'd want to have kids," he says at last. "Sure." Was that the right answer? he wonders.

Dori looks toward Marty with a look of weary triumph. "You see," she says, "another representative of the forces of life."

Marty shakes his head before taking a puff on his cigarette. A very discriminating smoker, he smokes only Marlboros in the soft pack and won't even accept a free one from the hard pack. "I didn't say I was trying to prescribe the way everyone should behave," he says a bit petulantly. "I just said that, the way the world is, I'd never want to bring kids into it." Respecting his friend's intensity, Ted nods sympathetically.

Dori's bright expression of moments ago has darkened under the weight of Marty's mood. When she bends over her cigarette, Ted notices the faint shadows under her eyes, and they make her even more attractive. "What I remember you saying," she says softly to Marty, "is that it would be a crime to bring kids into the world."

Marty nods, bringing a finger to his glasses. "Well, yeah," he sighs, "I guess I said that. What I meant is that it would seem like a crime to *me*."

Ted has already concluded that there's nothing romantic going on between these two; he's just walked in on a conversation about The Meaning of It All. Somehow this makes him feel better. "Well," he says, "that's certainly an understandable position."

But Marty has just got started. "People say things are getting better," he says, waving his cigarette for emphasis. "Khrushchev comes for a visit, he throws corn at reporters, he ogles movie stars. Fine. We all breathe easier. But meanwhile the Russians haven't stopped making bombs. And neither have we." He looks from one to the other, as if challenging them to disagree.

Dori shrugs. "That's not a news flash," she says. "We know that. Still," she adds after the briefest of pauses, "we have to live, don't we? We have to believe in a future."

Ted is surprisingly grateful for her hopefulness, and pleased to be included in her "we." He can understand Marty's position in theory but just now, his suggestion that it would be a crime to bring children into the world sounds a little crazy.

"Yeah, of course," Marty shakes his head, "we have to live. So everybody keeps on shopping and watching TV and dreaming about having next year's model that has bigger tail fins. And sure, most of the time even I can just ignore the big picture and keep on doing what I'm doing." He runs a finger along the frayed cuff of his shirt. "But eventually it comes to me that I'm living an 'as if' life, that we all are." Ted can smell his hot chocolate, but hesitates to take a drink while his friend is speaking. "We go about our business," Marty continues, "as if we had a future and at any minute the whole thing could be gone. The whole thing."

All of them are silent for a while and the few stray sounds they hear make the cafeteria seem emptier. Then Dori speaks. "OK," she says, "I'm living an 'as if' life. But maybe that's the way it's always been: the future might be taken away from me at any time; I could get hit by a car when I leave here." Marty shakes his head and she raises her hand. "I know, I know, I see your point about the present situation: with the Bomb, the future could be taken from everyone. But you know, there's just a chance that it won't. What then?"

"It isn't just me and you." Marty goes on as if he hasn't even heard her. "It isn't just us. What drives me crazy is the thought that once the bombs start falling nobody and nothing will be left, that everything we do here will go up in those mushroom clouds and be lost forever." When he pauses, nobody inter- rupts. "I mean, sure, you might say if this generation was stupid enough to let it all happen, maybe we should be wiped out— and I don't buy that for a second, by the way. But the problem is, we take everything down with us." He's looking beyond Dori. "Everything," he says. "Think of it: all human reasoning, all the counting and naming of flowers, the mapping of the earth and sky, the arguments about books and music, all that becomes obsolete when nobody's left to remember and history just ends."

Ted feels a chill. He's felt the same things himself, mostly in his solitary night-thoughts, and to hear Marty saying them aloud makes them more frightening. But he wants to think of himself as Dori's ally.

"So Khrushchev throws corn," Marty goes on, "Khrushchev has a great time in Hollywood. Let's say Khrushchev becomes a teddy bear. Still, both sides have stockpiled so many weapons that it doesn't even take somebody's conscious decision to start Armageddon. Any accident can trigger it and the law of aver- ages says there will be an accident." He shakes his head. "No, that's why I think it's a crime to bring kids into this world."

A glum silence follows. At last, Dori reaches over and pats his hand. "Marty, Marty," she says, "we all feel that way from time to time. Hell, I feel that way myself. But you can't let it get to you. You have to hope."

Marty doesn't say anything for a while. A pale man, he looks drained of blood, and tired. Then all at once he straightens and raises his coffee cup to his lips, though there doesn't seem to be any coffee in it. When he puts it down, he nods like someone trying to be convinced, but certain that he won't be. He makes the effort to pull himself together and faces Ted. "So," he says, a bright, transparently artificial smile on his face, "what can you tell me to make me more hopeful?"

Ted considers the question for a while. "Well," he says, "I think your beloved Cinci Reds are destined to rise."

"Hey," Dori says, "I thought the reds were part of the problem."

For an instant, a trace of innocent pleasure enters Marty's smile and he laughs quietly to himself, a short, flat exhalation that's close to a cough. Still, it's hard to tell what he's thinking. When he turns toward Ted, he says gravely, "I'm glad I've got friends like you two who care about me." There's an embarrassed silence, after which he says, "Look, I'm glad you dropped by, Ted. You can talk to Dori about more pleasant things. I've got to get home."

"Hey," Ted says, "I've got my car. I can take both of you home."

"No, no," he waves off Ted's offer. "I want to walk. I need to clear my head."

"Nothing like a little blizzard to put things into perspective," Dori says.

When he leaves, she brings her feet up onto the bench and grabs her elbows. Leaning back, she sighs and shakes her head. She looks tired, as if the conversation with Marty has exhausted her. "How seriously should we take him?" she asks. "I don't really know the guy. I mean, he seemed depressed in a major way."

Ted shrugs. "Marty's been saying the same things for a couple of years. He has his ups and downs. I think he'll come out of it, though." In fact, he's a little concerned. He's used to Marty's persona of gloom and world-weariness, but there was real passion behind what he said tonight; it wasn't just persona.

Dori jerks her head in the direction of the outdoors. "He's OK, walking home in this storm?"

"Oh, yeah. He only lives a couple of blocks from here. I don't think he's going to pull a Captain Oates on us."

She wrinkles her nose. "Captain Oates?"

"With Scott's expedition to the South Pole," he explains. "Oates got sick and he knew he'd slow down the others if they had to care for him, so he left their tent in a blizzard, saying something like 'I think I'll go for a walk.' Of course, they never saw him again."

She frowns. "Very heroic, very British." She takes a hungry drag on her cigarette. "As I recall, the rest of them died anyway. They might have spent some time with their friend in his last hours."

"I guess," Ted says. "But they were being hopeful, weren't they? They thought they might still make it. Weren't you arguing for hope a minute ago?" He takes a sip of his hot chocolate, which has become lukewarm. He doesn't mind, though. This is the first time he's had a chance to talk to Dori alone, and he's pleasantly surprised by how easy it is to be with her. He has a belated sense of gratitude toward Marty for providing the occasion for this meeting. In the middle of this howling storm, he feels his world expanding.

"Of course, Marty's right, in a way," Dori says glumly.

"Yeah," Ted glumly agrees. But he's eager to get the conversation away from the apocalyptic. "Wish you were back in California now?" he asks her.

She looks at him, as if acknowledging for the first time that the two of them are talking to each other now, and that Marty is no longer their concern. "You mean because of this storm?" she says after a moment. "Not at all. I love the extremity of it, I can imagine hundreds of miles of prairie being covered with snow."

"All civilized life erased," he contributes.

"Yeah, you got it." She runs a hand absently through her hair and he's aware of an energy just under the surface with Dori, a nervous quality, as if her wiry body is about to spring at any moment, and it strikes him that this is precisely the opposite of what he felt with Sally. Still, he likes it.

"Were you ever a dancer?" he asks.

She looks at him, her eyes big with amusement. "You mean like ballet, modern, that kind of stuff? Uh-uh. Though that doesn't mean that I trip over my feet on the dance floor."

"No," he says. "I don't suppose you do."

They're silent for a few seconds and Ted takes a sip from his hot chocolate. Across from him, Dori smiles mysteriously, as if she's just remembered a joke. "I just got a feeling," she says.

"A feeling?"

"Yeah, a kind of a hunch about you." Her look turns mischievous. "I'm going to guess something about you."

"OK." He readies himself for something, he doesn't know what. Whatever it is, he wants it to continue.

"I'll bet you're a fan of horror movies," she declares.

This catches him by surprise and he doesn't say anything for a moment. Then he thinks he has the answer. "Marty told you that, right?" he says.

"Uh-uh," she shakes her head. "Cross my heart." She makes the gesture, her shoulders straightening attractively. "I just guessed." She flicks her ashes into the ash tray. "Which ones?"

"Which what?"

"Which horror movies are your favorites?"

"Oh," he says, "well, the old ones, the Frankenstein movies, Dracula and the Wolf Man. Stuff I saw as a kid. And the Mummy, of course. God, the Mummy was scary. The way he dragged his foot." He can remember exactly how he felt watching the movies in the Ritz theater back home.

"And that horrible growling sound he made because they cut his tongue out. Poor Kharis," she says. "All because of his love of Princess Ananka."

"Hey," he says delightedly. "You do know this stuff."

For a time he simply basks in the memory of those movies and the fact that this girl from California seems to understand how he feels about them. But Dori isn't done. "OK, those are some classics," she says. "What about more recent flicks?"

"Science fiction counts, right?"

"Oh, absolutely."

It takes him only a second or two to line them up. "*The Thing*," he begins, "*The Thing from Another World*. That scared the hell out of me. Hey," he says, "the weather was like what we're having now." He remembers the claustrophobic military base in the Arctic, an island of humanity in a wasteland of whirling snow, the ominous silhouette under the ice, the muttered run-on dialogue of the beleaguered group of humans visited by something frightening that's beyond their understanding, their conflicts about how to respond to the creature's attacks, the unhelpful messages from Washington. "Then, of course, you have to put *Invasion of the Body Snatchers* right up there." But he's already remembering something else. "You know, though," he says, almost forgetting that there's someone with him, "maybe some of the scariest moments of all are in the opening of *Them!*"

"Oh, yeah," she nods. "You mean the sandstorm in the desert, the cops coming to that wrecked store in the middle of nowhere where something awful happened."

"Yeah," he says, "the swinging lamp and the eerie shadows it casts."

She leans forward on her elbows. "And the little girl."

"Yeah, they've already found the dazed little girl." The hair on Ted's arms bristles as her words call up the images. "And all the time the wind's wailing," he says, "again, kind of like it is tonight. So," he settles back in the booth, "you must like them too."

She smiles. "My secret vice." After a pause, she adds, "Secret until tonight, that is."

He leans toward her. "I'll never tell. But really, Marty didn't tell you that? You really guessed? How did you do it?"

She looks into her hands. "I don't know. Sometimes I think I can make that kind of guess about certain people. It's not magic or anything, just inference." She takes a drag on her cigarette, exhales and squints against the smoke. "Maybe the way you converted Marty into Captain Oates gave me a clue, though."

"So," he says after a while, "where do you come from in California?"

"L.A.," she says. "Where Khrushchev ogled starlets."

He's never been to California and hasn't really been interested in the state. But then, he hasn't known anyone from there before. "What's it like living there?" he asks. "I mean, aside from the great weather and the smog and endless driving and the lack of history."

She lifts a finger. "That's where you're wrong, my friend. L.A. is the most historic city in America." Ted waits for more, already knowing he's going to like what he hears. "Say you come out there for the first time. You're driving up Malibu Canyon and you pass a grassy spot where there are a few live oaks in a certain configuration. It looks like a hundred other places, but it gives you a weird feeling; you'd swear you've been there before." Ted nods and she goes on. "The thing is, you have. Say the next day you're in your motel watching one of those old westerns that are playing on TV all the time and you see the exact same place, that place in Malibu Canyon, and you realize you first saw it as a kid on a rainy Saturday afternoon in your hometown. Drive along some street in Santa Monica that you've never been on before and you'll have that same eerie sense of familiarity. It turns out that you saw some private eye in black and white walking that street in a movie, trying to track down a missing dame. There are dozens and dozens of places like that in L.A.—doorways, streetcorners, freeways—that you've been to before you've even set foot in the city. Every American who comes to L.A. recognizes he's been there before. That's because L.A. houses the history of our dreams."

"Jesus," Ted says, genuinely impressed. "What's a genius like you doing in a place like Chippewa?"

She smiles. "You're too kind, sir. But to answer your question, I really don't know. I'm just hanging around, I suppose, waiting for something to happen."

Waiting is precisely what he's been doing. All at once, it seems a worthy, even a noble way to spend one's time. "Waiting with hope, I gather from your conversation with Marty."

She laughs. "Always with hope."

As the storm rages outside, she tells him about her parents, Mort and Sally, old lefties, she calls them, and she talks about them with affection, though she clearly regards them as naive. Both of them wrote for the movies and were blacklisted for their political loyalties. It cost them their place on the beach, but they stayed in L.A. determinedly, managing to hang on with all sorts of marginal jobs, including her father's being a tour guide to the homes of the stars. "Poor dears," she says, "they're unrecon-structed reds, they won't give up on the party line, even after Hungary. They have to do that, I suppose. Otherwise, a huge part of their lives is a waste."

He tells her about his days in Cold River, which seem very pale compared to her story. "So," she smiles. "All that while you were knocking people around on the football field and being terrified by horror movies. I like that in a man. Anyone who enjoys getting the hell scared out of him can't be all bad."

"I can't tell you how happy I am to know there's hope for me," he says.

"Well," she says, "we can all use a little hope, can't we?"

"Amen," he nods. "Hey," he's suddenly curious, "how did you wind up here, of all places?"

She gives him a sly look. "It's a long story. Maybe I'll tell you some day."

"I'll remind you," he says.

She looks at him. "You have a very interesting look in your eyes."

"I do?"

"Yeah," she says. When she sits back and folds her arms, he senses a shift in mood. "Can I make a personal observation?" she asks.

"Shoot," he answers, eager to hear what she has to say.

"This is a guess," she says. "It's a little more of a long shot than the one about the movies." She pauses. "And maybe I shouldn't be sticking my nose in other people's business. But it seems to me you're holding on to something and you don't want to let go."

Ted feels a sudden tightening. He's felt very free up until now, but all that's changed in an instant. He feels accused, and he wonders about what she's just said. Is he holding on to some-thing? He doesn't know. Is she talking about Sally? he won-ders. She must know about her. In the end, all he can muster up as a response is, "That could be, I suppose. But then, isn't everyone?"

She looks at him without expression. "True enough," she says, but something still hangs between them and Ted is tongue-tied. "OK," Dori says at last, the playfulness back in her voice. "I've got another one for you: *Klaatu barada nikto.* Where's that from?"

He smiles back at her. "*The Day The Earth Stood Still.*" Then he adds, "Of course."

"Yeah," she says. "I gave you an easy one." He's still thinking that she's bailed him out of a potentially awkward situation when she asks, "Did you like that flick?"

Remembering the movie, he makes a face. "Ye-ah, but I'll have to confess I didn't love it. Not like the other ones."

She nods enthusiastically. "Of course, of course." Her eyes are shining. "The problem is, the spaceman's too nice, too enlightened, he's a clean-shaven Jesus." She shakes her head. "God, he's solemn. We know we're supposed to like him because he's wiser than we are and everything but the fact is, it would be a lot more interesting if he turned mean, don't you think? I mean, isn't our dirty little secret that we really like the dark forces and we want our aliens to be evil and scary?"

"Absolutely," he agrees. "Give us our giant ants or grasshoppers, give us our soulless pod-people who want to enslave us."

"It's mutants we're looking for," she joins in. "Hideous scaly creatures from the black lagoon."

"You're right," he says. "Not some noble-sounding guy dressed in Reynolds Wrap who looks like he's just had drinks with Adlai Stevenson. Though I always thought that robot Gorth might have a dark side. Hey," he says, suddenly making a connection.

"Yeah?"

"It just came to me: that Space-Jesus is precisely the answer to Marty's prayer, isn't he? The visitor who comes here to save us from ourselves."

"Yeah," Dori says, "if only. . . ." Some of the mood of Marty's pronouncements seeps into her voice. "But it just ain't going

to happen that way on this planet, my friend." It occurs to Ted
that Sally, who didn't share his love of horror movies, probably
liked *The Day The Earth Stood Still* just because it was so high-
minded. "You're right, though," Dori brightens. "About *Them!*"

"Yeah? How so?"

"The rest of the movie is good, it's fine for that kind of thing,
but nothing matches the opening. God, how could it?"

"Hey, I couldn't agree more," he says.

Dori accepts his offer of a ride home and they drive through
streets emptied by the continuing storm. The car is filled with
cigarette smoke as a radio station from a distant city plays oldies
faintly in the background and the wipers provide a steady beat
but neither driver nor passenger says much. When they talk it's
pretty much to point out things: "Look at that tree," she says,
"it's a snow tree." "The way that streetlight is swaying," he says,
"you could believe it's about to snap right off." It doesn't take
them long to get to her place, where he's moved by a sudden
impulse and insists on walking her to the door. "You have to
indulge my midwestern gallantry," he says, determined to prolong the evening. On the porch he tells her "Hey, I'm absolutely
thrilled to have discovered another horror movie fan." "So am
I," she says. As he watches the vapor from their breaths mingle,
he has the sense that each of them is waiting for the other to
make the next move. Finally, he says, "Stay warm," and turns
away.

He re-enters the car feeling happier than he has been in a
long time. When he turns the key, though, the engine won't
start. After a few more unsuccessful tries, Dori shows up beside
the car and he rolls up the window. "You got a problem, mister?"
she asks.

"Looks like," he says. "I guess I'll have to walk home."

"How far is that?"

"About a dozen blocks," he says, aware that he's making it a
little further than it is.

"Uh-uh," she shakes her head. "I can't have you going Captain Oates on me. Why not wait here at least till it's daytime

again and people can find your frozen body?" There's a gentle appeal in her voice. "You can sleep on my couch."

Briefly, he imagines the blizzard continuing for days while he stays with her, watching old movies on TV, an enticing thought. "Let me try to start this car one more time," he says. "I'll let fate decide." To his great disappointment, the engine turns over and the two of them listen to the Chevy idling.

"All right," she says at last. "Just be careful." He can't read her face and can only wonder if she's as disappointed as he is as the smell of exhaust mixes with the falling snow.

As Andrew Kesler fills his cup he's aware of how familiar, after only a few months, the sensory details of his present life have become: the thick china handle is smooth against his curled fingers, the dark liquid makes a soft splash as it's poured from the urn, the coffee smell is momentarily sharp before it's absorbed into the unmistakable atmosphere of the library staff lounge. It's the story of my life, he thinks: getting used to new things. He turns toward the tables and makes a quick survey of the room, pausing for only a second before making his way toward the corner where Bill Tuttle is sitting. "May I?" he asks the rosy-cheeked little man, and the light strikes Bill's steel-rimmed glasses as he lifts his head, dabbing quickly at his mouth with a paper napkin.

"Andrew," he smiles. "Please." He gestures magnanimously toward the place across the formica table from him. Bill, who works with Andrew in the Cataloging department, is a short, faintly plump and excessively neat man of about forty. His fussy manner raises instant suspicion that he may be homosexual, which he is, though Andrew happens to know that Bill, who lives with his mother, is extremely discreet about his sexual adventures. To some in the library he's known as "Aunt Tuttle" and even Andrew has found him to be a bit of a bore; but at the moment he prefers the man's company to that of his more sophisticated colleagues.

When Andrew takes his seat, Bill, obviously pleased to have been so visibly chosen, glances smugly toward the table across the room where Charles Cross and Ned Hanover are having coffee. He turns back toward Andrew with an expression of

stylized weariness. "I don't know about you," he sighs after a moment, "but I really need a break this morning." Andrew gives him a sympathetic nod as he lights up and exhales. Bill says nothing for a while, though his eyes have become bright with anticipation, as if he has delicious secrets to divulge. He leans slightly forward, like a penitent in the confessional, and declares, "The Iron Duke is certainly on the warpath today." Andrew catches the faint scent of orange blossoms. "If she were younger," Bill goes on, "I'd say she was having her period." He whispers the last word.

Andrew responds with a wan smile. He's aware that Bill would like nothing better than for him to join in complaining about Ellen Eyre, the head of the department, but he can't work up much enthusiasm. "It's Truscott she seems to be after today," he says at last. "We can all be thankful for that."

Bill nods agreeably, stirring his coffee, and Andrew realizes just how tired he's been feeling this morning. It isn't a physical weariness, it's more like spiritual depletion. A touch of *accidie*, Marc would have said, puffing on his Gauloise and scowling provocatively. But then, even *accidie* could be exciting with Marc. An infidel Inquisitor, Andrew called him once. He can remember the exact moment: the two of them were on that bridge on a wet spring day, the dark shape of a loaded barge sliding by beneath them, the water rippling softly around the prow, the sting of coal smoke in the air, and he'd felt everything was possible. But Andrew isn't on that bridge, he's here, in the staff lounge in Chippewa. Whether it's *accidie* or something more mundane, he isn't up to striving today. He doesn't have the stomach for bouts of forced cleverness with the likes of Cross and Hanover. The truth is, he'd just as soon crawl under a rock, and maybe Bill Tuttle is the closest he can get to that here.

"Miss Paulson is a bit touchy today too, don't you think?" Bill asks out of the blue. "I mean, she might as well announce, 'Fasten your seat belts, it's going to be a bumpy ride.'" Andrew lets it pass. Bill, he wants to tell him, you don't have to work at the gossip this morning. What Andrew would prefer just now is vintage Tuttle, his stories about growing up in Chippewa, skating on the frozen river and cooking marshmallows over a fire, the understanding teacher who encouraged his addiction to reading. Bill is fatally sentimental, for which he's scathingly satirized by others at the library. But then, his sentimentality is at least more authentic than some of the other attitudes he seems compelled to affect, such as trying to play the devil-may-care sophisticate with all sorts of shocking skeletons in his closet. What's more interesting to Andrew is the actual guilty secret his colleague doesn't dare name but can't really hide: that he loves his mother.

Rebuffed in his attempt to get Andrew to talk about Steve Paulson, Bill retreats to a more neutral topic. "Did you lose your electricity during that storm last week?" he asks, the genteel bitchiness gone from his voice.

"No," Andrew answers. "I was lucky." The storm, he could truthfully tell Bill, is the most impressive thing about Chippewa that he's seen since he got here. He'd had to fight through the blinding white cloud that buffeted him mercilessly as the thick snow grabbed at his ankles, his face stung to numbness. Out there among snow drifts that changed the very look of once-familiar streets, it was possible to believe that the town itself could be erased by the storm. Once inside his refuge on the third floor, he'd tried to read but kept getting distracted by the wind. In the end he put the book down, content to listen to the snow's ticking against the pane, a gentle, taunting invitation to come out into a world that was in the grip of furious, relentless forces. Finally, though, like so many other things, the storm only brought back troubling memories.

"Mother and I had a bit of a scare," Bill says. He takes a delicate sip of coffee and puts down his cup. "We lost power for a couple of hours. But we'd prepared: we had candles, we had heavy quilts." He laughs quietly to himself. "I'd even had the foresight to make a thermos of hot chocolate. It was actually quite wonderful sitting in the darkness and looking at all that snow swirling around, listening to the distant sound of snow plows and the power trucks."

When Bill falls silent, Andrew knows he's looking at a man who's remembering pure bliss. "Did it get cold?" he asks after a while. "Without electricity."

"Not really," Bill says. "The power wasn't off long enough." His face darkens briefly. "If it had continued, of course, that would have been another story." He takes another sip of his heavily creamed coffee. "Ah," he sighs like a man savoring the memory of a narrow escape from danger, then picks up the napkin and pats at his mouth once more.

Meanwhile, Andrew feels the tug of something unsettling, and the earlier weariness is upon him again. He can guess what it means: his present period of relative calm is coming to an end. It was signaled, as usual, by thoughts of Magda that came in the wake of his dream this morning. He's read about people who always hear a ringing in their ears so that every sound others might hear in isolation is played for them against a constant background. In his years of moving around he's come to feel that he has his own ringing that's always there, whether or not it can actually be heard. Because even when things seem quiet for a while and the world can appear friendly, so that he can entertain thoughts of ordinary comforts, like going to a movie, having a very good meal, maybe meeting someone who'll interest him for a while, that sound in the background is there, though it may be possible to ignore it. I don't have it so bad, he'll tell himself at those times, and it's true, considering some of the alternatives of which he's well aware. But as mysteriously as these periods may come, they end just as mysteriously, and that inaudible ringing in the ears suddenly becomes palpable, undeniable, making it clear that it's never stopped and that any sense of its absence he might have felt has been an illusion. Now, here in the staff lounge, Andrew can feel it returning, the sense of something lurking.

"Did they send that book over from Acquisitions yet?" Bill is asking, and it's clear that Andrew has missed something.

"The book?" He could kick himself for drifting off like that. For a moment he looks at Bill with simulated attentiveness, still hopeful he can make the connection; he takes a long slow drag on his cigarette and exhales. At last, he realizes that he isn't going to be able to fake it. "Which one is that?" he asks.

A trace of hurt crosses Bill's face. "The one I mentioned seeing in Acquisitions, the old one about legends and folktales."

"Ah, that one," Andrew responds, trying for some enthusiasm. "Yes, I remember." In fact, he doesn't.

"I thought it seemed like something in your line. Because it's got a section on the Wandering Jew."

Now Andrew recalls the conversation: "Yes, yes," he says, grateful to have his ignorance lifted at last, "the Wandering Jew. Sure, of course. Thanks, Bill. No, it hasn't come yet. It's probably still in transit. But I'll look for it."

After a few seconds of righteous silence, the other man appears somewhat mollified. "It's a wonderful old edition with woodcuts," he says. "I just love the way the paper feels and smells in those old books."

"I can't wait to see it," Andrew tells him. "Yes, I'm glad you called my attention to it. The story of the Wandering Jew has many different versions. I'm always on the lookout for ones that I don't know."

"Was that a legend you heard about growing up?" Bill asks. He seems genuinely curious.

"Yes," Andrew answers. "There was quite a lively tradition to the story in central and eastern Europe."

Bill knits his brow. "I guess I've always had a vague sense of the story," he says. "But I confess I never really knew much about it when I was growing up."

Andrew smiles. "Possibly in all his wanderings he never reached Chippewa."

There's a playful gleam in Bill's eye once more. "I wonder if I should feel offended," he says.

"No," Andrew shakes his head. "You should feel lucky. He often seemed to show up in a place just before some calamity. And so much the better if Chippewa has been spared calamities."

Bill smiles wickedly. "I don't know," he says. "What would you call the Iron Duke?"

Andrew laughs politely.

"Speaking of which," Bill goes on, "I know she blew up at you last month, but I'd have loved to have seen the look on her face when she first heard about what you did to that book by the Russian." His mouth is curled into a smile, as if he's just been offered an eclair, and it's well known that Bill can't resist an eclair.

Andrew shrugs. That gesture no longer seems as clever, or necessary, as it did when he was moved to it. The book had been assigned to him because it was in his area of specialty and he'd given it the usual technical reading, but the smug, pompous aspect of the pictured author irritated him and he spent more time with it than was strictly necessary, paying particular attention to the section dealing with fraternal relations between the Russian and the Polish peoples. When it came time to catalog the book, he classified it properly under the U.S.S.R., memoirs, politics and foreign affairs, but it was a perverse notion that led him to append a "see also" directing the reader to fairy tales.

"You must have had a vague idea that old Eagle-Eye might see it eventually," Bill says. "She's famous for not letting anything get past her."

In fact, Andrew hadn't thought about that at all. Or was it that he had a sense of invulnerability? "I could always have said I was testing the system," he suggests.

"That's true," Bill says. "After all, it might have taken years before they discovered that." He shakes his head. "Still, I think it was a brave thing to do." He looks as if he wants to go on, maybe to ask Andrew why he thinks Eyre didn't fire him. He knows the questions people ask about him. But Andrew says nothing and Bill knows enough to back off. "Well," he says, "that hysterical fit she had when she found out is just like her. But you can't run a department on tantrums. Not if you want people to do their best work over the long haul." Both nod sagely and return to their coffee.

Throughout the rest of the day Andrew is aware of that inaudible ringing in his ears. He grows irritable and impatient, snapping at the man from the mail room when he makes a wrong delivery, only to regret it minutes later. He makes it clear to his colleagues that he isn't inviting company or conversation, but he can't keep his mind on the material before him, thinking instead about the discomforts of his new apartment, the chief of which at the moment is his neighbor's loud playing of his hi-fi, made worse by its being the same piece over and over again, Ravel's *Bolero*. Andrew suspects that the man is masturbating to the music, though if that's the case, he has prodigious capacities. He's already talked to the landlady, who's done nothing. Maybe, he thinks wearily, I'm going to have to move again.

God, how many times has he done that? And it doesn't get any easier. When he put the dent in Ted Riley's car he panicked; he'd actually thought about not returning it. He even had a mad moment when he believed he might simply drive off somewhere without any destination. Lost in the New World. How ridiculous! But it took a few hours for the madness to pass, for him to convince himself to return to what he'd started out to do. Still, so close.

That evening, he makes a deliberate attempt to resist the mood that's befallen him by going to the student film society's weekly event. Tonight's offering is Bergman's *Wild Strawberries*. Andrew doesn't particularly like Bergman and he finds the film sentimental, but at least getting out of his apartment is a positive action on his part, preferable to listening to Ravel's *Bolero* through the wall. Bergman is Bergman: there's much black, much white, much existential gloom and contemplation of lost opportunities, life not lived as fully as one can dream it, some nice comic moments. The dream scenes, though, seem forced and literary—at least Andrew has never had dreams like that: clocks without hands, faceless men, confronting yourself in a coffin.

Nevertheless, the sheer visual presence of the northern European scenes works on him, provoking memories and, inevitably, he finds himself thinking of his sister. Brilliant, lively, hungry for life, she was as far from Bergman's professor Isak Borg as one can imagine, but she's never going to get the chance to reflect, in old age, on days gone by. Andrew feels a sudden rage at the professor, as if the stooped old man on the screen were responsible for what happened to Magda. She could be alive today, she could be here in America, young and free, her life full of possibilities. But Andrew's rage spends itself, leaving him with an emptiness. He knows that what happened to Magda isn't professor Borg's fault. Magda is no longer alive because of what she'd had to do for them—the liberators, the benefactors. It was all part of a deal she'd made of her own free will. Once more, he feels the ache of his own responsibility for what happened to his sister. When the war was over, Magda wouldn't believe he was dead. She tracked him down through that ruined world until she found him in the refugee camp in Bavaria, but she couldn't have done it on her own. She needed them and they in turn needed her. She made her bargain: she got their help only by promising to do things for them. That was simple enough at first but it soon became more complicated and more dangerous. Until at last it became fatal.

In his own dream this morning he was on a crowded city street—some place he'd actually been to, though he couldn't identify it. He heard her voice: "*Jędruś*, I'm here. Come to me." But though he stopped while hurrying pedestrians passed him and he looked in every direction, there was no trace of her. That moment in the street was all that he remembered of the dream, but the desolation he'd felt on awakening was immense: no, he couldn't find her there, or anywhere on this earth.

Knowing his sister's story, how can he engage in the charade of an ordinary life? What makes it worse is that he doesn't know the whole of it and in all likelihood never will, and the frustration is enough to drive him crazy. Even Morelli, the one person in Chippewa who might be able to help him, claims to know less than he does. "I don't know," he said when Andrew pressed him, "I really don't know too many of the details of what happened to your sister, what that whole deal was. Honest." The unlit cigar kept bobbing in his mouth. "They just told me to be your contact here, to help you out if I could." But how could you help if you didn't know the story?

There are times when Andrew can't help thinking that Morelli knows more than he's letting on. That's certainly not beyond belief. None of them is going to tell everything he knows, is he? On the other hand, it makes sense that the best way for them to work it is to keep individuals from knowing too much, to let each person in on only a part of the story, and the smaller the part the better. Finally, there's Morelli himself. He's smart enough, in a simple sort of way; he can probably follow a complicated set of directions without getting them confused. But he seems hardly to have the necessary depth and deviousness to hold in his mind the tangled strands of a thousand intrigues, and what Magda got caught up in had to be tangled. No, Morelli probably doesn't know.

When the lights go on, the artfully rendered world of contemporary Sweden is swept away and Andrew is returned to a beige-walled room in the basement of a university building here in Chippewa. There's much shuffling about and thoughtful muttering as people get up and put on their coats, readying themselves for the encounter with the icy midwestern night where many sober discussions of the movie will continue under the indifferent constellations. Cigarettes are lighted, attitudes assumed, radiators hiss, coughs come from all directions. As his eyes run over the departing crowd, Andrew notices a familiar face: it's Ted Riley. Given his recent thoughts, his first impulse is to be suspicious: after all, Morelli was the one who gave Andrew Ted's name. Could there be some reason why Morelli wanted him to spy on Andrew? But a moment's reflection is enough to persuade him that that's absurd. What purpose could possibly be served by noting that Kesler saw *Wild Strawberries* tonight? Besides, it's become clear to Andrew that Ted has someone with him, a dark woman who's absorbing all his interest. Very likely Ted isn't even aware that Andrew is in the room with him, in which case it's Andrew who's the spy.

He walks out into the night where the snow crunches underfoot and the stars glitter coldly above. When he inhales, the frigid air instantly freezes the hairs in his nose and he breathes out a cloud of vapor. It's actually exhilarating and for an instant a vague sensory memory from his childhood plays about the fringes of his consciousness, but it eludes him at last and once more he's reoriented himself to the present. My God, he thinks, did Magda and I endure everything that we endured, did she make so many sacrifices, even before the final one, so that I should wind up in a place like Chippewa?

But Magda could adapt anywhere. Just now, he's not so sure about himself.

Ted scatters rock salt as he makes his way up his apartment steps, climbing to street level where he can get a better look at the effects of the January storm that's blanketed Chippewa with snow. Under the bright morning sunlight, the white world is snapshot-silent, the familiar street eerily beautiful. More important, the sky is a flawless blue. According to the TV, in the wake of the storm a clear cold spell has settled over the prairie and no more disturbances are expected for a while. He's grateful for that: Dori is flying in from California today and, given the present state of their relationship, he doesn't need any meteorological complications to stoke his anxiety about her return. He pulls a draught of icy air into his lungs and holds it there for a few seconds before exhaling, hoping to empty himself of the vague uneasiness that follows him everywhere these days. The action is only partially successful: when he returns to the warmth of the apartment, he feels better momentarily about Dori, only to find himself facing another concern.

His few days back home during the break between semesters has left him worried about his mother. There was a quiet about her that bothered him, a slackening of her normal pace: she walked into a room rather than bursting into it. He thought she looked paler than he remembered; certainly she seemed more tired. Was it just that she was getting older? Guilty about leaving, he begged off from a party his last night in town to stay home with her. He made popcorn and the two of them watched Boris Karloff in *The Isle of the Dead*. "Just like the old days, eh, Mom?" he told her, and for about a half hour things were fine, mother and son sharing comments about the movie, the popcorn steadily disappearing from the big red bowl that sat between them. After a while, though, his mother's comments grew scarcer, then she began to nod off, and at last he realized she'd fallen asleep, leaving him to watch the movie alone. What made it worse was that he couldn't help thinking how much more fun it would have been to see it with Dori.

When he'd told his mother he was seeing someone in Chippewa, she smiled her approval. She'd already made it clear she felt it was important for Ted to move beyond the loss of Sally. "It may sound hard-boiled," she said, "but she's part of your past and you have to think of your future." He was used to his mother's style: love wasn't a lot of words, she always insisted; it was what you did. "You have a right to be happy," she'd told him again and again. "Remember that." He'd nod agreement, though he couldn't help wondering how happy her own life had been.

He tried to give his mother an idea of what Dori was like. "She has the, uh, look of a dancer," he told her, and he could see from the curl of her lips that she'd guessed he'd made a last-second substitution for "body." Mostly he talked about Dori's coming from California, as if that could explain something about her that he couldn't put into words. He told her some of what he'd learned about her parents, passed on a few of the more innocent stories from her childhood, all the while realizing that none of this information conveyed anything of the flavor of the relationship that's turned the needle of his compass spinning wildly. Of course he didn't tell his mother about Dori's delight in sex, her passionate, eager, even playful lovemaking that's so different from what he knew with Sally. He was necessarily selective: he told her that Dori's a fan of horror movies and Elvis Presley, but he didn't mention that she has a boyfriend back in California, the shadowy Elliott, who's come to haunt Ted's imagination. "Up until the last minute," Dori told him, "he kept trying to get me to come with him to Berkeley." Ted already knows more about this guy than he wants to know: Elliott is dark and wiry, his mood can change in a heartbeat, and it's impossible to guess what he's thinking. "He has the face of a French existentialist philosopher who's a boxer on the side. And

a pretty good boxer too," she was quick to add. The man is brilliant, if Dori is to be believed. He wears a black leather jacket,
he plays bongo drums, and he has the most amazing eyes.

"This Elliott," he asked her at last, "is he out of the picture
now?" The two of them were naked at the time. The air in the
room was heavy with the smell of sex and Dori lounged against
a pair of pillows set against the wall, the dense black bush of
her pubic hair emphasizing the pallor of her sweat-slick skin.
When he asked her the question, she tilted her head and put on
the intent look of a schoolgirl in a spelling bee who's just been
given a difficult word but who's confident that, if she takes her
time, she'll answer correctly. She looked around the room for a
few seconds, then shook her head slowly. "I don't see him," she
said with a teasing lilt. Her little joke wasn't enough to banish
Elliott's shadow, though, and it must have showed on Ted's face
because then she added, "He's not in the picture now, sweetie,
he's not here: that's what's important." He leaned toward her
and ran his hand along her bare thin arm, the feel of which had
already become so familiar, so necessary to him. She was here
beside him, yet there was a world in sunny California to which
she belonged and from which he was excluded.

Later, at the House of Joe, she brought up the subject herself. "Sure," she said, her pale face veiled by a cloud of cigarette
smoke (she smoked relentlessly—"You're simmering," he told
her—and the taste of cigarettes was always on her tongue) "sure,
you can say that Elliott's still in the picture, but he's a minor
figure in the background." She narrowed her eyes, searching for
an image. "Say there's a naughty-looking peasant boy," she said
at last, "traveling on a road at the edge of the picture, carrying a
bird in a cage. You have no idea where he's going—did he steal
the bird, is he carrying it from a lover to his beloved?—but he's
not what the picture is about." Ted appreciated the inventive-
ness of her image, but that didn't keep him from wondering
what the hell that picture *was* about. Still, the picture was an
abstraction beside the reality of this living woman across the
table from him: with her dark hair, pale skin and prominent

cheekbones, there was something vulpine about her, though when she smiled there was nothing wolfish about her perfect teeth. Looking at her, it was hard for Ted to pay attention to what she was saying. But she was deadly serious a few seconds later when she confronted him with, "I've never tried to hide that, have I? I've never said he was completely out of the picture."

"No," he shook his head, "you haven't." Asshole, he chided himself, she's here, she's with you, and you keep worrying about some jerk in California. Can't you just appreciate what you have and shut up? But he couldn't prevent himself from asking her, "Have you stopped sleeping with him?"

Her smile was gentle, considerate. She tilted her head as if trying to get a better view of him. "I'm not sleeping with him now, am I?"

OK, he told himself, that's it, that's what's important. Now shut up. And he said, "Would you sleep with him again?"

When she sighed, her thin shoulders fell gently and she didn't say anything for a breath or two. "Dear, dear Mr. T-Square," she said at last—it was one of her names for him—"how can I say for sure?" Then she leaned over and put two of her fingers on his wrist. "You have to learn to live more in the moment," she said, running her fingers slowly across his skin.

"Hi, Mr. Riley," he heard. It was a couple of coeds from his class, delighted to catch their teacher in a romantic tete-a-tete.

"Hi, Terry, hi, Jo." He pulled back his hand and straightened, while Dori barely managed to keep from laughing.

There were other things Ted didn't tell his mother: for instance, that Dori had smoked marijuana out West. "You have to try it," she said. "I'd love to see you when you're high. Really," she insisted, "it's so great: you float." Then she smiled radiantly, as if what she was remembering had suddenly got clearer. "Or maybe it's that you're still and it's time that floats."

"She isn't interested in sports at all," he told his mother, who knew that Sally had been a big fan. "I don't think she knows the difference between a field goal and a foul ball."

"Oh, dear," his mother joined in the joke, "she's practically un-American. Is that the California influence, do you think?"

Most important of all, Ted didn't tell his mother that Dori
has already decided that she isn't coming back to Chippewa
after this semester is over, a stunning piece of news she delivered a week before she left for the Coast. At first he wasn't able
to respond at all, he couldn't believe it. If she'd slammed a heavy
metal door on his fingers at least he'd have been able to yell out
in pain. Now he could only look at her. Finally, trying to sound
calm, he asked, "Why?" He couldn't just come right out and say
No, you can't, I can't believe it. What he did say when he continued was, "But that's such a surprise. I mean, you're so smart,
you love so much of this stuff. You'd be good at it."

She looked at him sadly. "Thanks," she said. "Yeah, that's
true, I suppose. But I guess I've seen enough to convince me I
don't want to be a female academic. Look around you," she told
him, "look at this department. It's like a men's club."

He couldn't deny that. Still, he searched for an argument.
"Well," he said at last, "there's Adrienne Denby."

Dori shook her head. "Poor Adrienne Denby," she said.
"Adrienne Denby," she repeated the name. "I rest my case." He
could see her point. He still couldn't see her leaving Chippewa,
though. Not after what had started between them.

But if she wasn't going to continue in grad school, then
what? he wanted to ask, though what she'd just told him made
him too depressed to pursue the question further. Was she just
going to disappear back into California, write for the movies
like her parents? He couldn't see that. Dori had a great sense of
humor and she could find the absurd everywhere, but there was
nothing trivial about her. She needed to be doing something she
thought was important; she was the kind of person who wanted
to make a difference. Without his asking, she continued, "I told
you I was hanging around, waiting for something." She sighed.
"I wanted to see what graduate school was like, I wanted to try
out the academic possibilities." She frowned. "So that isn't going
to work out and now I guess I'm waiting for something else."
She narrowed her eyes. "But whatever that something else is, it's
got to be worth waiting for." When he said nothing she leaned
toward him. She had to know what he was thinking: what about

me, what about us? "Hey," she said, and he felt her breath on his face, "I'm not leaving yet. Who knows," she added. "Who knows what's going to happen between now and June?" If she was offering him a life preserver, he was determined to cling to it fiercely.

And now as he waits for her in snowbound Chippewa, the centuries-long break between semesters coming to an end at last, he hasn't loosened his grip. Dori will be here in a few hours— that's the important thing. It seems to him that they have a lot to talk about, though whenever he's tried to push that notion further, he's come up against a blank wall: what is it in fact that can be said? Because when she made her declaration, she certainly didn't sound as if she was likely to change her mind. It's always possible, he's tried to convince himself, that being home has given her another perspective. Of course, Ted isn't eager to think about the other people in California who could influence her ultimate decision.

To make matters worse, their phone conversation last night didn't go particularly well. He wanted her to say how much she was missing him but she sounded distracted. Of course, he told himself, she's with her parents, she's been back home, she's probably feeling ambivalent, the way we all do; maybe she was even nervous about flying. "We're having a snowstorm," he told her, adding quickly that the weather would be clear for her flight. "It's really kind of spectacular," he said, hoping to tap into their common memories of the place. "The whole town's transformed." "It sounds cold," she said. I'll keep you warm, he wanted to tell her, but he held back. Of course what he wanted to know was whether she'd seen Elliott while she was on the coast, but he'd already decided that he wasn't going to ask; he didn't want to sound jealous and paranoid. Still, he was curious, very curious.

"I'll be there at the airport," he assured her, already aware that this call was costing him more than he could afford.

"You're such a sweetie," she said. "You don't have to do that. Especially if there's been a snowstorm."

"No, no, that's going to be over," he told her. "It's no problem." Absolutely nothing was going to keep him from being there when her plane landed.

Now, alone in his apartment, he picks up the copy of *Howl* Dori gave him. He wasn't crazy about the Beats, he told her, and she recited a few lines of Ginsberg's poem. "How is that not poetry?" she demanded with mock indignation. "Some of it's not bad," he conceded. "But you're probably picking the best parts." The next day she bought him the book. He looks at the inscription: "To T-Square, who's not really all that square. Go, Warriors." He'd told her about his high school exploits. He touches the place where she's signed her name under a forest of X's.

Riffling idly through the pages, he comes upon a phrase: "bodies turned to stone as heavy as the moon." Just before she left, he and Dori were talking about the pictures of the dark side of the moon that the Russians sent from Lunik III. They'd both heard laments about that technological achievement removing one more mystery from human life, but Dori's response jolted him. "Elliott says there's no point worrying about the dark side of the moon when there are plenty of dark sides here on earth," she said, and Ted's ears pricked up at the mention of that name. "Look at South Africa," she went on, "look at our own South." Ted didn't respond, though he couldn't help wondering about the context of that statement. When would they have been talking about the dark side of the moon? Was she hearing from Elliott regularly?

On the way to the airport he pushes the Chevy beyond the speed limit. Already in his mind he and Dori are at his place. She's sitting in the Morris chair, telling him all about her adventures in the Golden State, punctuating her witty renditions of events with dramatic gestures, doing clever imitations of friends and relatives. She's smoking, of course, waving her cigarette before her, and it looks as if she could talk all night; but all at once there's a moment when she goes quiet and her eyes narrow, her mouth curls into a lazy smile, her nostrils flare as she breathes in the exhalation of her own cigarette, and the two of them know that now it's time to move the conversation to the bedroom.

Ted realizes that he's smiling. The fantasy has made him all the more impatient to see Dori, and not just because he's hot for her body. Sometimes the most delicious parts of their times together have been the talk before or after sex. He's already told her things he never told Sally, like what he did after his father left. "You've got to believe me," he said. "Forget the guy you see today: I was a pretty furious eleven-year-old. I'd been betrayed, in my mind by both my parents; I'd been abandoned—somehow in the shock of his leaving, I believed that my mother was as responsible as he was. All I knew was that it just wasn't fair." He had to pause in the telling but she waited patiently for him to continue. "I wasn't always the cool customer you think I am," he said again. "I was a pretty scrappy little guy in those days. I scrambled for everything I wanted, on the baseball field, on the football field, everywhere." Thinking about the kid he'd been, it was even hard for him to believe that that boy had any connection to the person he'd become.

After a deep breath, he told her the rest of it. "My father had left his lighter behind," he said, remembering the feel of the cool metal in his hand, "and I kept it. I mean, I'm sure he just forgot it but I tried to convince myself he'd left it there for me, he wanted me to have it as a memento, like some kind of bond between us. It was the Zippo he'd had during the war. I didn't tell my mother I'd found it but I kept that lighter in my drawer as if it was some kind of talisman that could bring order back into the world, could bring him back, and I kept opening that drawer and looking at it. But it became obvious pretty soon that it wasn't going to work. One day a few weeks after he left, I was sitting at the kitchen table with a glass of milk when it was suddenly very clear that things were never going to go back to what they were—I'd felt that way before, but I'd always been able to put that kind of thought behind me. Not this time, though: this time I knew for certain he wasn't ever coming back, and the idea was devastating. Something got into me. I knocked over the glass, spilling the milk, and I didn't care: I just watched the milk flow to the edge of the table and drip to the floor.

"My mother was out, I was home alone, and I got a little crazy. I was through just waiting for things to happen; I knew I had to do something myself. As I remember it, my skin prickled when I went into my bedroom and took that lighter out of the drawer—I swear I had no idea what I was going to do until I was already doing it. I remember the click when I snapped it on, the smell of the lighter fluid as I held it for a few moments before I touched the flame to the living room curtains. The whole thing was a dream; I'm not even sure I was conscious while I was doing it, and I certainly didn't have any plans beyond what was happening right then. Maybe I thought I was just going to stand there and watch the house burn down around me. But once the flames started climbing I could see that things had gotten out of hand. The smoke stung my nostrils, I felt the heat on my face, the fire was moving on its own. I panicked and ran away, convinced, I guess, that in a little while there would be nothing left of the house. It turns out a neighbor saw the first flicker of flames and called the fire department. They got there in minutes and put the fire out, but not before it had managed to ruin a good part of the living room. And the smell of smoke, I swear, it lasted years. I remember being so scared. I told everybody it was an accident, that I'd just wanted to see if the lighter worked."

"Did they believe you?" Dori asked.

"I don't know."

"And after that," she said, "you saw how close you came and you reformed?"

He nodded. "Something like that." Why did he tell her about that when he hadn't told Sally? As his mother might put it, was he bragging or complaining? Was he telling this to Dori to make himself more interesting to her? But that act of failed arson was something he'd done; it was part of him. The kid he'd been had been hurt by the world, so he snapped on his father's lighter and carried the curling blue flame to the tip of the living room curtain, watched the fire leap from the lighter's wick to the gauzy cloth, watched the flame begin its snaky climb. All these years later, he knows that the belated recognition of what he was doing scared him, but what he's less sure about is what he was feeling in the seconds before he panicked, and sometimes he thinks he remembers that, as he watched the flames begin to dance, he felt a moment of pure joy.

Now at the airport he waits in the terminal as Dori's plane taxis down the tarmac, marveling that the unwieldy-looking silver machine has traveled all the way from the coast and found this place in the middle of the continent. Men in jumpsuits guide the plane to its spot near the terminal, where the engine coughs, the props slow, then finally stop. The ramp is wheeled to the plane's side, the door opens and people begin disembarking. Ted waits with others as meaningless strangers make their way down the stairs—coats, hats, bags and purses, frosting breath—until he sees Dori at last at the top of the ramp, looking cold in the thin black coat she's wearing. For a few seconds while others surge toward the new arrivals, he just stands there and watches her, a stranger among strangers. At last, as if aroused from sleep, he rushes to her and they embrace amid the crowd of passengers and those who've come to greet them. He feels her lean into him, shivering. Kissing her, he remembers the feel of her skin, the taste of her mouth. At the same time, there's something oddly unfamiliar about the person he's holding—has he remembered her wrong?—and he can sense that she feels the same way about him. "Christ, it's cold," she says when they pull away from each other and he leads her inside, where she lights up.

"Tired?" he asks.

She gives him a wan smile. "A little. God, it's strange being back here."

"Well, I'm glad you are." When she makes no response, he says, "I haven't seen you since the '50s," which provokes a quiet laugh.

As they walk toward his car, she takes his hand. "You know," she says, "you're going to have to get yourself to California one of these days pretty soon."

"I can't wait," he says, hoping she'll follow it up, but she doesn't, making her statement seem less like a promise than

just something to say, and he can't help feeling that the timing
between them is off. He's grateful they can occupy themselves
with the details of getting out of the terminal and finding his
car. Once they've started on the drive back to Chippewa, he
waits for her to tell him about her trip but there's a reserve about
her that affects his own responses, which are as guarded as hers
are neutral. It's as if, Ted thinks, one of us has just come out
of prison after serving a long sentence. Or maybe both of us.
Outside, the snow seems dirtier, the road is a faded gray from
salting. There's nothing picturesque about the flat landscape on
this dry, frigid day, and that only adds to the heaviness of the
atmosphere in the car. Ted knows enough to hang back, to let
her gradually readjust to her exile from the golden land. "Want
me to turn the heater up?" he offers.

She shakes her head.

"Want the radio on?" he asks a little later.

Again, a shake of the head.

"At least we have a couple of days before the semester
starts," he says.

"Mmm," she responds noncommittally.

Looking at the countryside through which they're passing,
he remembers his trip home, which reminds him of the movie
he watched with his mother. "Ever see *The Isle of the Dead*?"
he asks.

She knits her brow. "I'm not sure. What's it about?"

"It's about a bunch of people quarantined on a Greek island
around the time of the First World War. Boris Karloff is in it. It's
pretty creepy: plague, premature burial, stuff like that."

She makes a brief, snuffling laugh and he feels her relaxing
beside him. "That sounds yummy. Maybe we'll get a chance
to see that together," she says and his heart leaps. "Hey," she
squeezes his arm, "excuse the mopiness. I'll be my usual bright
self in a little while."

"Take all the time you want," he says. "Your mopiness beats
a lot of people's sweetness."

"How chivalrous," she says. "Now I know why I willingly
returned to this Siberia. Hey, after I get a chance to settle back

into my apartment, what do you say we go out tonight, sample a bit of the local night life?"

"Sure thing," he says, though he'd rather she'd suggested a quiet night at home. Still, compared to his last two weeks as a hermit, the prospect of a night out with Dori is heaven itself. In any case, the world has got a lot sweeter in the last minute or so. "You want to go to any place in particular?" he asks.

She gives him an arch look. "I was thinking something pretty square, like the Lodge."

That surprises him. "I guess you're figuring, as long as you have to come back to Chippewa, you might as well come all the way back," he says.

"Something like that, my friend, something like that."

By the time he comes to pick her up that evening, Ted is resolved about a couple of things. He's not going to bring up the question of her impending departure from Chippewa, nor is he going to ask anything about Elliott. To the extent that it's possible, he isn't even going to let himself think about those things. "Live in the moment," she's told him, and he intends to follow her suggestion.

The Lodge is a townie hangout, primarily a bar, but with a kitchen that serves a pretty good fish fry, and the two of them have the house specialty, their heavy plates covered by generous portions of breaded perch, french fries and cole slaw, accompanied by a quarter slice of a lemon. The food is good and as they eat, Ted finds it easy enough to stay off the forbidden topics. Here among the deerheads and mounted bass and pike, they talk about Marty Reindorf, who's gone into therapy and has suddenly decided to take the spring semester off. He's staying in Chippewa and Ted tells her, "He says if he went back to Cincinnati his neurosis would become a full-blown psychosis within a week." Dori shakes her head. "That's Marty, all right." When their plates have been cleared away and each of them has a beer, she asks him about his trip to Cold River. "It doesn't sound as if it was so great," she says.

He nods. "I don't know, my mother just seemed tired. She fell asleep during that Karloff movie I told you about."

"Well, champ, not everyone's a fan." She gives him a wink. "You've got to be a little crazy, as you well know."

"No," he protests, "actually, she's always liked that kind of stuff." He remembers his mother asleep on the sofa before the TV, a pale green shawl she'd knitted around her shoulders. Maybe it was the movie, but he had a sudden thought that he was seeing her dead. She'd taken her glasses off and her eyes, even closed, looked tired and sad, the lines in her face drawn downward, her mouth partially open—it was unsettling. If this was indeed a corpse beside him he'd have said that the woman hadn't led a happy life. All at once, he felt an overwhelming sadness for his mother. Uncomfortable with what he'd been thinking, he was tempted to awaken her, but thought better of it: if she was tired, he ought to let her sleep. "The thing is," he tells Dori, "I never think of her as old. But, you know, time passes and all that."

Dori looks at him. "How old is she?"

"Somewhere in her late forties. I'm not exactly sure."

"Well, then, she isn't old." She smiles. "You two actually seem to get along pretty well, don't you?" she says after a while.

"Yeah, we do." Once more he thinks of the woman asleep on the couch beside him, who looked as if she were dead. What really scared him was to see her hand trembling slightly. But dogs did that when they slept, didn't they, he told himself, dreaming of the chase? Or was this different? "I told you about what happened after my father left," he says, "when I was looking for people to blame for my problems. She was the closest so I laid a load of that blame on her. It took a while for me to get clear of that but she never let it get to her. I guess she always had her priorities and bringing me up to be OK was right on top."

Dori's smile softens. "She did a good job, I'd say."

"Thanks." Will she and his mother ever meet? he wonders.

Dori takes a drag on her cigarette and gives him a sly look. "What did you tell her about me?" she asks.

He laughs. "Enough."

"Like what?" she teases.

"Like you're a real gone chick that I dig because she's not all hung up but really knows where it's at."

She makes a face of mock disbelief. "Hey, I'm going to turn you into a full-fledged beatnik yet. You watch."

"I saw the best minds of my generation," he quotes, "destroyed by madness, starving hysterical naked."

"Go, man, go," she says, hitting the table with her fingers as if it were a bongo drum.

He reaches toward her and takes her hand. "Sweetheart, it is so God-damned good to have you back, you know."

"Hey," she says quietly, "I'm glad to be back."

"Well," he picks up his glass of beer, "there's no time like the present. Let's drink to that." And they do. He's proud of himself for not succumbing to the temptation to ask her about California, or to ask her if she's going to reconsider her decision about leaving after the semester. I'm living in the moment, he's thinking when he catches sight of someone who's just come out of the cold. It's Andrew Kesler, of all people—the Lodge is certainly an unlikely locale for him. Ted is surprised by the sudden pleasure he feels upon seeing this man he hardly knows. All at once he decides he has to introduce him to Dori and he waves at the new arrival, gesturing to him to come to their booth. The Pole, clad in his familiar overcoat, has already started for the bar but he acknowledges Ted's greeting and begins moving in their direction with the reluctant steps of a man being led to his execution. Still buoyed by a mysterious sense of bonhomie, Ted waits for him. "Dori," he says, when the newcomer is beside them, "I want you to meet Andrew Kesler." He's told her stories of the man from the library, so she knows what to expect. "Won't you join us?" he asks Kesler.

The other man stands there a while before responding, as if surprised to find himself here. "Maybe just for a minute," he says at last with a tight smile and takes a seat beside Ted, who's suddenly unsure what happens next. Did I actually invite him to join us on Dori's first night back? he thinks. What got into me? Worse, now that the Pole is there, nobody can think of anything to say. An awkward silence lengthens, Kesler coughs into his hand and signals to the waiter. Meanwhile, Dori smiles expectantly at the newcomer, but doesn't say anything. Finally Ted plunges in. "It's pretty cold out, isn't it?" he observes fatuously, quickly adding, "But you've probably seen some pretty fierce stuff back where you've come from."

Kesler seems not to have heard him. He sits there silently as though thawing out, his eyes fixed on the table. A middle-aged waiter with a dirty apron makes his way to the booth. "Just a glass of vodka," Kesler says without looking at the man. "Chilled, if you have it."

"Just vodka by itself?" the man asks.

Kesler looks at him sharply. "Of course," he barks. "What did you think I said?" After the man leaves, Kesler drums the table with the fingers of his good hand.

"I didn't know you came here," Ted volunteers.

Kesler shakes his head. "There's a waiter here who knows a little more about the world than that dunce," he says. "Unfortunately, he's not here tonight." Ted and Dori nod and Kesler continues to drum the table.

At last the waiter returns with Kesler's vodka. His face is stony as he puts the glass before Kesler and he leaves without saying a word. Kesler shakes his head. "I suppose he thinks I'm a communist just because I ordered vodka. How ignorant. But typical." He quaffs the clear liquid in a single swallow, sighs loudly, and brings the glass down to the table with force. Tears have come to his eyes and he sits there a moment breathing heavily, looking into space. Then he turns toward Ted. "I told you about my sister, didn't I?" he asks quietly.

"Yeah," Ted says. "Yeah, you did."

Kesler sighs. "Today would have been her thirty-seventh birthday."

A solemnity has fallen upon the trio. After a time Dori asks, "What was your sister's name?"

"Magda," the Pole says softly.

Dori nods. "That's a pretty name."

Kesler's smile is tinged with melancholy. "She was brilliant," he says. "Everyone who knew her recognized that. She could have been a great success at so many things." Neither Ted nor Dori says anything in response. "Magda had a sense of style," Kesler continues, his face animated, his gestures emphatic. "After the war clothes, like everything else, were in short supply, but she could take a dreary outfit and transform it with a scarf and a pin."

"Do you have any pictures of her?" Ted asks.

Kesler shakes his head. "Unfortunately."

Dori points to his glass. "I'd like to try one of those," she suggests.

Kesler smiles. "It's good for you. It clears the head."

"That's exactly what I need," she says.

"I think I'll try one too," Ted joins in. "Can I get you another one?" he asks Kesler. The man nods absently. His eyes are glazed and Ted guesses that he's thinking about his sister.

They order from the reluctant waiter. "I guess he's convinced we're all reds now," Ted says, but Kesler makes no response. When the vodkas arrive at last, Ted asks, "Can we drink to your sister?"

Kesler is roused from his reverie. "That's very kind of you."

The three of them lift their glasses and drink. "Whew!" Dori says when she's downed the vodka the way Kesler did. "This stuff will ring your bell."

The Pole is looking into his empty glass. There's a loose smile on his face that has nothing to do with amusement. Once more, he sighs. "I may have to move again soon," he announces flatly. "The new place is intolerable. It's worse than the last one."

Christ, Ted thinks, I'd hate to be a potential landlord when this guy walks up the steps. Still, as the heat of the drink makes its way through his system, he feels a flush of generosity. "Hey," he volunteers, "you're welcome to use my car again if that can be of any help."

"Many thanks," Kesler says. He lifts his empty glass as if in a salute. "You know . . ." he begins and the other two wait for what he has to say but after a few seconds of silence, he gets up abruptly, makes a bow to Dori and announces, "I have to be going now."

"A strange guy," Ted says when he's left. "He was pretty rough with that waiter, though. Hey, I'm sorry I invited him over without asking you first."

"No, no, I liked him," Dori declares. Her eyes are bright with what looks like excitement.

Ted thinks of the Pole moving through the chilly streets in his overcoat, bound for another place he doesn't like. "I suppose we should remember that he's lost, in a way," he says.

Dori nods. "He's not the only one," she says. "But you're right: you have to put yourself in his shoes."

For some reason, Ted remembers Kesler's story about the villagers who kept watching the same movie over and over while two sets of conquerors were firing at each other outside the theater. "He's had quite a life, I guess. I told you some of the stuff he told me."

Dori takes his hand. "That was sweet of you," she says, "making that offer, especially after what he did to your car last time." He feels her touch, thinking it's been a long time since they've gone to bed together. Their eyes meet and he hopes she's thinking the same thing.

She looks at him with an ambiguous expression. The Kingston Trio is singing, "Hang down your head, Tom Dooley" on the juke box and they listen to the lyrics for a while. When the song is finished, Dori lets go of his hand, settles back and lights a cigarette. The smell of the match is harsh and acrid. "I'm still planning on leaving after this semester," she says. "In case you were curious about that."

He nods and says nothing.

After a while, she asks, "What about you? You said you were waiting too, didn't you?"

He nods again and once more he says nothing. He's determined not to ask her about Elliott.

He should be feeling awful, but he isn't. Maybe it's the vodka. He and Dori are silent again and it feels all right, just the two of them sitting across from each other here in the Lodge, not saying a word. There's a comfortableness about the situation, a peace, and Ted is sure that neither of them feels the need to break the silence until one of them is ready. He's listening to a couple of guys at the bar talking loudly about mortgage payments when Dori speaks again. "You're never going to know how much I was hoping this academic thing would work out," she says. "I mean, I love books, I love the way they smell, even, and, like you, I've never found a library I didn't want to explore." She takes a drag on her cigarette. "Some things I've read made me feel—hell, they were better than sex." She smiles to herself. "Well, maybe almost." She's silent for a while, then she shakes her head slowly. "But that isn't going to be my life. I know that." Her smile becomes more distant. "Maybe I'm just a little like your Polish friend right now."

"Jesus, Dori," he says.

She looks at him a long while, and he can feel the distance between them shrinking. She reaches for his hand. "I might have a little trouble getting to sleep by myself tonight," she says. "First night back and all."

He smiles. "I was thinking something like that myself."

"Good thing you didn't loan him your car tonight," she says.

He looks at her across the table thinking, it's still a long way till June. It has to be.

Ted should be exhausted. He worked hard on his freshman papers tonight and got most of them done. Still, he's as hopped up as if he'd drunk a pot of coffee—and maybe he has—so he's giving himself a reward of a glass of Jim Beam, a cigarette and Ray Charles singing "I Surrender, Dear." Relax, he tells himself, watching the smoke curl lazily, relax. But he can't: his blood pulses in his veins, his fingers dance on the chair arm. If only Dori were here. But she isn't. She has Sam Pierce's seminar and he knows they all go drinking afterward. For a while he even thought she might call. Too late now.

His apartment is more than usually shabby tonight: a dish from dinner is still on the coffee table with some crusted sauce and a couple of dried strands of spaghetti, there are three cups in different parts of the room; his dirty jeans are flung across the orange womb chair; crumpled pieces of paper litter the floor, books are all over the place. "Hey, T., ever try smoking a pipe?" he remembers Dori asking him once. "You'd be cute." He takes another hit of bourbon. Why does that memory make him sad? He doesn't want to get into that. He suddenly straightens in the chair as if ready to spring into action, but where would he go? You'd freeze your balls off on a night like this.

He picks up the phone and listens to the dial tone for a second or two. When he puts down the phone Ray's singing fills the room. Ted likes Ray, even if George Kanaris keeps calling him a genius. Wasn't it enough to say he sings OK? Ted wanted to tell him. But maybe George is right because listening to Ray tonight, Ted gets the feeling that the man knows precisely how blue, how lowdown he feels. The words he's singing are corny:

"When stars appear and shadows fall/Then you'll hear my poor heart call. . . ." Oh, Jesus, they're corny and still, this guy's got it right.

"Dori," he says aloud and, saying it, he realizes he already has a bit of a buzz. Did he refill his glass already? Well, so what? He gets up and goes to the record player. He wants to hear that one again. Listen, Dori, he wants to say, when stars appear and shadows fall, then you'll hear my poor heart call. And she would. His poor heart is hungry for her, his hands and his mouth are hungry for her, for all the places on her, and she's just as hungry, he knows that. The first time he felt the tickle of her warm breath on his stomach, felt her mouth moving down from there, he thought he'd been taken to Paradise. He drags on the cigarette as if he wants to take the whole of it in one long, sustained inhalation, like a note on a sax that's prolonged to a point where it's almost unbearable. Yet, as wonderful as Dori's made him feel, she's made him feel awful too. Because she's going.

What am I going to do, Ray? He gets up, a little more wobbly this time, and puts the needle back to the song. They've had such great times together. "Hey," he told her last week, "your mind is as sexy as your body." But she's going to be leaving. *La belle dame sans merci*. He knows now why it made him sad when she said that about the pipe. She saw him as another professor, like Eerdman, Peterson and Pierce, the next generation. Puffing on his pipe. While she was somewhere else. Somewhere more interesting.

It happens, he tells himself, trying for the philosophical perspective, it happens all the time. Why can't he just accept the fact that his time with Dori has been wonderful but one way or another, it's going to end up with teary goodbyes at the airport, violins swooning in the background as the big silver bird carries her westward and he does a little softshoe on the tarmac, whistling ruefully, "It Was Just One of Those Things?" Because he can't, that's why; he doesn't want to. But then, what's he going to do? He's standing now, in front of the bathroom, the plywood door facing him. All at once he's hitting it, hard, his knuckles colliding with the wood once, twice, three times, and then the pain starts. He draws his fist back, staring at it as if it belongs to somebody else. Already the knuckles are turning dark, starting to swell. Christ, who was he swinging at, though? Breathing heavily, he savors the delicious ebbing of the pain, so gradual as to be almost imperceptible, and he knows his hand is already healing. He looks at the dent in the brown door, the faint smear of blood. His head is clearer now yet even as he feels himself backing away from the desperation of a few moments ago he remembers a story about his mother. As a girl she broke her leg ice-skating and her doctor father, who carried her back to the car, marveled that she didn't cry. "It's all right," he told her, "you can cry if you want to." "I didn't, though," his mother told Ted, not boastfully, just giving an accurate description.

He makes some experimental moves with his fingers: everything seems to be all right. He hopes the hand doesn't swell, though, since explanations could be embarrassing. It will be easier to make up a story about the door. He walks back to the chair where he was sitting and takes another sip of bourbon. Good. He lights up another cigarette. Things will get better, he tells himself. This is just a bad moment. It will be the weekend in a couple of days and the two of them are going for a ride in the country.

On Saturday he and Dori are in his car, making their way up a gentle hill a few miles west of town. The fields through which they're traveling lie under a covering of snow and even from inside the car you can tell that the air is cold, sharp and dry. "Just a little further," he says.

Dori looks at the wintry scene. "If my California friends could see me now," she says. "Lost on the prairies." In her fur hat, she looks Russian. "This is a landscape only a polar bear could love."

"You know the old joke," he tells her. "February in Chippewa is a Hobbesian month: it's nasty and brutish, but blessedly short."

"The first two I can believe," she says. "That last one I have to take on faith."

Once again they're playing roles that have become familiar: he's the native guide to the exotic, not-quite-to-be believed realm called the Midwest and she's the wary sophisticate from the coast. They both enjoy playing their parts, however much irony they might bring to them. "Think of this as anthropology," Ted says when he sees the sign for Half Moon Lake and they begin descending the hill. "You're getting a rare chance to observe some odd native folkways."

She shakes her head. "More than odd, T. Why in weather like this would anyone leave the comforts of home so he could spend the day staring into a hole in the ice?"

"You'd be surprised," he says. "The shanties can be pretty comfortable, even elaborate. Though I have to tell you there are guys who just sit out in the open with a rod in their hands and a pail of minnows, totally exposed, fishing through a hole they have to stir regularly just to keep it from freezing over."

Gradually the full outline of the frozen lake comes into view. Dori stares in wonderment as they approach the shanties and shakes her head. "My God, these are dangerously sick people." A couple dozen of the little buildings are clustered on the ice like a prairie settlement while a few stalwart souls are actually braving the elements without benefit of any kind of shelter. A handful of cars on the ice completes the resemblance to a town.

Ted laughs, strangely cheered by the sight. "Hey, they're just our local druggists and dentists," he says, "guys who work at hardware stores. You're looking at the heart of America."

"Then get me a cardiologist," she says, "and step on it." She continues to look at the scene. "It's so . . . so Chippewa," she says at last.

Ted pulls the car to a stop and sets the emergency brake. "OK, just keep looking carefully," he tells her. The ice is mostly clear, but low clouds of dry snow swirl in places. "Does it remind you of anything?" He waits a second or two. "Like maybe *The Thing*?"

She continues looking at the scene. "Yeah," she exclaims, "that's it, that's it, all right: the whole scene has the feel of a horror flick." She's suddenly excited. "The Land of the Ice People," she intones in the voice of a narrator of coming attractions.

"Come on," Ted says, "we're going to go out there and meet some of those Ice People." He steps out of the car into the chill, dry air, which he feels immediately in his nose. The door closes behind him flatly, the sound sharpened by the cold. Dori follows him down the snowy bank; once on to the ice, she moves like someone walking barefoot over hot coals, reluctant to stray far from the shore. When Ted points out that the ice is able to bear the weight of a few cars, she counters, "That's just what I'm afraid of: adding our weight could be the straw that breaks the camel's back."

"Trust me," he assures her, "I know the country." For no reason at all, he feels great and he steps across the ice with the enthusiasm of a boy let out of school.

"Actually," Dori says after a while, "this is pretty amazing."

The air is crisp and frigid, their breath frosts before them, and the cold comes up the nostrils like a knife-blade. "Listen to the way sound carries out here," he says. From the opposite shore comes a faint pounding that travels over the chill air, followed by a dog's sharp bark, the sound of a car starting up.

"Now," Ted says, "It's time to meet some folks." They make their way to a plump man sitting on a wooden box before a hole in the ice. He's wearing a heavy coat with the collar raised, his scarf covering his mouth. His knit cap is pulled down low on his brow, leaving very little face to be seen. When Ted asks him how he's doing, the man answers with a grunt and he points to a half dozen perch lying on the ice a few feet away. They're already frozen, their color dulled. "Nice," Ted says and the man nods. "You wouldn't happen to know if any of those shanties are unoccupied?" Ted asks, gesturing toward Dori. "I'd like to show her what it's like inside."

"Guy left that one not long ago," the man says, his words muffled by the cloth covering his mouth. "Coming back in an hour. I don't think it's locked."

"Thanks," Ted says and Dori, getting into the spirit, adds, "Much obliged." He half-expected her to add "pardner." They cross the ice to the shanty the man indicated, which is indeed unlocked, and they step inside, feeling an immediate warmth. Within its tiny confines there's a little bench with a couple of outdoor magazines and, more impressive, a small metal stove. On the wall against which a pair of rods rests, the occupant of the shanty has tacked a photo from a newspaper of a smiling man standing on ice holding a sturgeon more than a yard long. When Ted closes the door behind them, the place darkens but the water visible through the hole in the ice casts a greenish luminescent glow through the enclosed space, which is filled with the smell of wool and some kind of oil.

"I wish a fish would come by," Dori says quietly. "It looks like you'd see them the way you would on an X-ray screen. Wow, I can see how thick the ice is."

He looks at the rectangle of luminous water and the evidence of the dense crust of ice on which they're suspended over the lake's mysterious depths, seeing it all through her eyes. "Hey," he says, putting his arms around her, "did you ever do it in an ice shanty?" Many layers of clothes separate them.

She draws back her head to look at him. "I think that's one of those things that's better as a concept than in practice." She gives him a peck.

The dark, tight space reminds him of a confessional. "You know," he says, running his gloved hand along the arm of her navy peacoat, "when I was a kid the nuns taught us that to consent mentally to an impure act condemned you to Hell just as much as doing it."

"Great," she says. "Let's consent to the act and keep our clothes on." He feels her breath against his face as they stand there for a few moments holding each other, the two of them alone and for all practical purposes invisible to the world on the surface of the frozen lake. Wouldn't it be great, he thinks, if we could just stay here? Wouldn't it be great if February never ended?

When they leave the shanty they trek to the edge of the ice village where all the little buildings are behind them. "Know what else this reminds me of?" Dori says. "*Alexander Nevsky,* the great battle scene on the ice."

"Haven't seen it," he says, "though it looks like you're dressed for the part."

She shakes her head. "As I remember it, there weren't many girls in that battle." They've come to a place where someone chopped a hole that's frozen over and the leftover ice beside it has been molded into a jagged shape whose rough edges have been smoothed. "Watch this," Ted says. He kicks free a triangular piece of ice no bigger than a hockey puck and with a low side-arm motion, he sends it sliding across the surface of the frozen lake toward the opposite shore. The ice whistles shrilly as it travels with incredible ease across the frozen plain that offers no resistance, and it continues gliding until it's out of sight.

Dori claps her gloved hands. "Hey, it just keeps going as if it's never going to stop," she says. "Let me try one." He gets her a piece and she sends it sliding across the lake's frozen surface. Like his, it travels on the ice until they can't see it. She smiles. "It gives me a real feeling of power to be able to propel something like that such a long way."

On the way back to the car, Ted is desperate to prolong their excursion. "Hey," he suggests, suddenly inspired, "what do you say we pay Marty a surprise visit?"

She stops and looks at him. "What do you say we go to the dentist instead?" Then she sighs. "Actually," she says, "that's probably a good idea."

Both of them feel guilty about Marty who, in his current situation, neither taking classes nor teaching, has started to fade out of their daily lives. To make things worse, since he's working only a few hours a week at a bookstore, he has plenty of time on his hands and he's phoned each of them at inconvenient times, droning on about his miseries. It's got to the point where Ted has started consciously avoiding the bookstore where Marty works and Dori has admitted to doing the same. "Are you on, then?" he asks.

"Yeah," she nods. "We should bring him something, don't you think?"

"OK," he agrees. "Like what?"

She wrinkles her brow. "We know Marty loves Twinkies. Why not get him a box of them?"

"Sweetheart," he says, "just when I think I've seen the limits of your genius, you surprise me with more."

"Keep talking," she says. "I like what I'm hearing."

"You know," he says later when they're back on the road, "what we're doing is what Catholics call a corporal work of mercy, like clothing the naked and burying the dead."

"Oh, what category does this fall under?" she asks.

"Visiting the sick, I suppose."

"Hm," she responds. "Marty's sick, all right, but I don't think sitting around in Chippewa contemplating his navel is the right cure."

"I agree," Ted says. "If he were still in school he'd have something other than himself to think about. I mean, he's so . . . downbeat all the time."

She smiles. "Marty was never exactly Jerry Lewis. But then, you've known him longer than I have."

Ted shakes his head. "I can assure you, you haven't missed his Wacky Period."

"Poor guy," she says. "I don't imagine any of this is funny to him."

Marty's apartment is on the second floor of a large wooden house from the previous century that, with its tall first-floor windows, its columned porch and cupola, must once have been home to a single family of impressive numbers as well as their retinue of servants, though its former grandeur is a sad memory. Inside the imposing door, it's clear that large spaces have been subdivided in order to accommodate generations of students, and wallpaper that's either yellow, brown or gray has been laid over whatever once covered the walls. Amid the mustiness of the downstairs hall can be detected the faint, tired traces of countless cheap meals. As Ted and Dori climb the stairs on worn carpeting they hear the unmistakable sounds of strangers living together.

When Marty comes to the door after a couple of knocks, he stands there a moment blinking, as if he's just been roused from sleep. His attire of robe and pajamas does nothing to contradict the notion. It's obvious he hasn't shaved yet. Behind him, though, music is playing, something Slavic and melancholy. "Ted, Dori," Marty says. "This is a surprise. Hey, come on in. What's that?" he says as Dori hands him the box of Twinkies. "Oh, great," he responds spiritlessly, but Ted is hopeful, in spite of the utter mess of the apartment as well as Marty's general air of dishevelment, though it's well into the afternoon. It isn't a work day, he reminds himself.

Marty shambles off to the record player like a man unused to walking and turns down the volume.

"So, how are things going?" Ted asks when Marty has cleared them some space on the sofa. The kettle is already on for water for instant coffee.

Marty settles slowly into a chair opposite them. In answer, he shrugs. "Linsky says I'm resisting him." Linsky is Marty's therapist.

"Oh?" Ted responds noncommittally.

Marty rubs his chin, a sly smile on his face. "It's Linsky's job to get me to adjust to a mad world," he says.

Glancing around the room at the books that are flung all about, Ted catches sight of Camus's *The Rebel* facedown on an end table. In an effort to change the subject, he asks, "You reading Camus?"

"Yeah," Marty answers sourly. "When I'm reading him I can almost believe him; it's like listening to music. But when I put the book down, I can't believe in it anymore." He shakes his head. "He sees all the crap that's wrong with the world but then, out of nowhere, he gets hopeful. You have to make that jump with him."

Ted doesn't like the way this is going. "And you can't make that jump?"

"Not if I'm honest," Marty says. Both visitors nod solemnly.
"We were out at Half-Moon Lake watching the ice-fish-
ermen," Dori volunteers. "It was kind of interesting."

Marty laughs mirthlessly. "I'll bet it's really fascinating to
watch a bunch of guys who spend the whole day staring into a
hole in the ice."

"Well," she says, "that's actually part of what made it fascinating. Hey, I think the water's boiling." When Marty goes to
attend to it she and Ted exchange a look, as if to ask, what have
we got ourselves into here? and Ted regrets having suggested
this visit in the first place.

"Well," Marty says, bringing them their coffee, "do you
have any gossip about the department for me?" A good sign, Ted
thinks, though he can't come up with any immediate tidbits.

Dori takes the initiative. "This isn't exactly gossip," she
says. "Maybe it is. You know Sam Pierce?" Marty nods. Pierce
is a relatively young associate professor, recently divorced, who
makes a point of being friendly with his students, especially his
female students. "He likes to go drinking with his class after his
seminar on Thursday afternoon," Dori goes on. "The drinking
can glide into pizza and sometimes there's more drinking after
that and often enough he'll wind up making a pass at one of the
women in the class, though he's usually so drunk by then that
it's hard to take him seriously." Ted has already heard the story
and he knows that it's stirred her up.

"Trying to emulate his subject, I'd say," Marty observes. Sam
Pierce has written a book on Faulkner. In the background a
cello repeats a haunting phrase.

"I can understand his wallowing in self-pity and self-destructive behavior," Dori says. "I mean, it looks like he's got himself
a pretty shitty life, and who knows who's to blame for that?
But last Thursday he offered me a ride home—I knew what he
might try but I knew I was perfectly capable of handling it. By
that point, I appreciated the ride. Well, on the way to his car we
came across this cop and a Negro on the corner of Depot and
Huron. The black guy was very thin, about forty, I'd say, and he
was obviously drunk. The cop was about fifty pounds heavier,

beefy and blond, and he had a mean face. He'd got the Negro by the collar of his coat and when we turned the corner he was shaking him like a dog. I mean, it was outrageous, it would make your blood boil to see that. All I could think was, is this Mississippi?" She looks at both men challengingly; neither says anything.

"Well," she goes on, "when Sam and I saw him the cop just froze for a moment and looked at us as if to say, 'Keep moving, this isn't any of your business,' but I wasn't going to just walk by and let him beat up that Negro and I asked him why he was doing this, I said the guy didn't seem to be endangering anybody and why wasn't the cop going after real criminals? All the while Sam Pierce is saying, 'Sh, sh, calm down.' I wasn't going to calm down and finally I asked that cop what his name was and he let go of the Negro and started walking toward us, real slow, like John Wayne—I swear, I don't know what he had in mind, but the Negro was alert enough to slip away and by the time the cop was standing before us Sam was apologizing for me so ardently that the guy finally backed off, trying to save face by talking a little rough to Sam, making him bow and scrape a little, telling him he ought to have a little more control over his woman, stuff like that."

"Did you get the cop's name?" Marty asks, his eyes ablaze.

"No, things moved pretty fast and I understood that that was part of the deal: Sam apologizes for me and goes all humble and the cop doesn't have to give his name. As soon as that cop left, I told Sam I didn't want his ride, I was walking home." She shakes her head. "I damned near froze my ass off, but I wasn't going to take a ride from a guy who'd just been willing to watch something like that and do nothing about it." When she told Ted the story he wondered how he'd have behaved if he were there. He hoped it would have been better than Sam, but he didn't know.

Marty cackles. "Sammy, Sammy," he says, "that ain't no way to impress a lady."

Dori nods. "Oh, his ardor cooled in a hurry. He'd gotten pretty drunk but the cop sobered him up. Still, he wouldn't let me leave right away; he had to tell me something. 'I know you won't believe this,' he said, 'but I was once as passionate about justice as you are.' I expected him to give me some bullshit about heroic deeds from his youth but he didn't. He just shook his head and stood there a while, his breath frosting on the air. Then he told me what a priest said to him once: that none of us is equal to the tasks given us but we have to try to do them anyway. I guess the whole thing had been pretty humiliating for him and he wasn't offering this as an explanation or an apology. Still, he was obviously trying to tell me something."

Hearing the story again, Ted feels sorry for Sam Pierce, whose life, as Dori observed, has indeed become pretty shitty. "It's possible he was telling the truth, of course," he says. "Maybe he actually was a fiery guy in his youth, a champion of justice and all that."

"Yeah," Marty sneers, "but where did it go?"

Ted shakes his head. "Who knows? But if he was once that kind of guy, no matter what happened later, maybe he ought to get credit for that. I mean, it would have been real while it lasted, wouldn't it?"

Marty's pale face has the concentration of an axe blade. "So you're saying we should forgive Sam Pierce's cowardice just because he once was—or at least says he was—a braver guy than the weasel he's turned out to be, that we should just put up with the hypocrisy and the brutality that's going on all around?"

Ted's fists clench involuntarily; his breath is coming fast and he's angry. He's not siding with the cop, after all. And who's Marty to criticize somebody for not acting with courage and passion? He can't really see Marty jumping into battle with the cop if he were in that situation. "I'm not saying that." Ted says with deliberation, "I'm just saying that maybe Sam once was the kind of guy he says he was and he lost it. I think that's sad."

"A hell of a lot sadder for that black guy, I'd say." Marty shakes his head and holds out his hands as if he's appealing to a jury. "And this is what Linsky wants me to adjust to."

Ted is suddenly exasperated. "Well, exactly what do you gain by not adjusting?" he asks. "By sitting here and stewing in your own juices." As soon as he says it, he's sorry. "I didn't mean that," he says. "I just . . ." and he leaves it at that.

"I know," Marty says, "I know," which only makes Ted feel worse.

"Twinkies, anyone?" Dori offers, and the three of them are quiet for a while, as the Twinkies are passed around like communion wafers. Ted bites into his and the creamy filling brings back memories of his childhood. He doesn't want to be arguing with Marty, with anyone, and as he chews meditatively on the little cake, he mentally withdraws from this room, this town and university, and he's back in Cold River playing tackle football with a bunch of neighborhood guys on the sloping illuminated lawn of the library on one of those fall nights when the smell of burning leaves still hangs on the chill air long after the last fire has gone out. Chasing the flying white football, he imagines himself to be Mac Speedie about to pull down a pass from Otto Graham.

The momentary withdrawal calms him. All right, he's acted badly but it's not the end of the world, nor is it the last time he's likely to say something he regrets. Meanwhile, Dori has moved from Sam Pierce to the protesters who keep their vigil at the flagpole on campus. "You can't help admiring them," she says.

"Hell," Marty sighs wearily, "what's the use of fighting it? We all know how it's going to end."

"No," Dori insists quietly, "we don't know, and we have to fight it."

"So I send a letter to Ike? 'Dear Mr. President, abandon all your policies and work for world peace.'"

"Ike's already dreaming of all the golf courses he's going to play when he retires in a few months," she says.

"So I write to Nixon. Or Adlai Stevenson. Maybe Jack Kennedy."

Dori shakes her head. "It isn't about writing letters," she says, her eyes bright with determination. "Look what's happening down South, look at the Negro students sitting in at the dime-store lunch counters. That's where real change is starting to happen in this country."

"Yeah," Marty says. "Maybe they should sit in at a SAC bomber base."

"Jesus," Ted says when he and Dori have left. "Talk about Mr. Downbeat. It was like visiting Raskolnikov. I wouldn't have been surprised to find an axe behind the door." He waits for a reaction. "Marty's got to come out of his cave," he says. "Still, I shouldn't have jumped on him that way." Dori is smoking furiously. "Anything wrong?" he asks.

She shakes her head. "Maybe we're all in a cave here in Chippewa." He feels again the familiar encroachment of something unsettling that doesn't have a name.

"Hey," he says, leaning toward her, "I wasn't defending Sam Pierce, you know. I thought we went over all that before."

"Sam Pierce has nothing to do with any of this," she says. She looks into the snow-covered streets of the university town. "But Marty just hangs on to his fatalism. Doesn't he realize how easy it would be for the rest of us to take that attitude?" She shakes her head. "In the end you have to believe in something," she says. "You have to. Christ, I like Marty but he can be such an asshole."

"We did what we could," Ted says. "We visited him, we performed a corporal act of mercy. We brought him Twinkies."

She relaxes just a bit. "At least that's something he believes in."

"Twinkies?" he asks.

"Twinkies."

"Hey," he says. "It's a start."

Ted is in his apartment a couple of nights later when the phone rings. It's after 10 PM, so he assumes it's Dori but he's surprised to find himself talking to Andrew Kesler. From the sound of it, he's at some bar and, from the sound of it, he isn't entirely sober. "Ted," he says, and it sounds even more like "Tad," "I'm so glad you're home." A silence follows during which Ted can clearly hear Guy Mitchell singing "My Heart Cries For You." "You know," the Pole's voice continues, "I don't have any real

friends in this place." The declaration puts Ted in an odd position: he doesn't know whether the man wants him to challenge
this assertion; but before he can say anything, Kesler adds with a
touch of bravado, "I wouldn't want any of these fucking people
for my friends." Why are you calling me then? Ted wonders.

Once again the Pole is silent. Ted can see him in a phone
booth somewhere in town, head bent as he draws on a cigarette,
a wild look in his eyes. Through the receiver come sounds of
laughter, a shout, something like a ping. The heart of America,
he remembers telling Dori when they visited the ice shanties.
He has a fleeting memory of the two of them holding each other
in the privacy of the dark interior that was illuminated by the
glow of water. "You've got a lot of understanding," Kesler says
at last and Ted, jolted from his memory, can only wonder how
the hell his caller can know anything about how much understanding he has. "You know what it's like to go around carrying
a heavy burden," Kesler says.

Ted has only spoken to him a couple of times and he doesn't
recall confiding anything to him about carrying a burden, whatever that burden might be. But he has no interest in pursuing
that question; a more relevant question is why Kesler called
him. "Is anything wrong?" he asks.

The Pole laughs. "No, nothing is wrong. Everything is right
with the world. We're in America, aren't we?" His voice is suddenly harsh. "Oh, of course something's wrong, everything's
wrong."

Ted is thinking that his caller should go home and get some
sleep, which would probably take care of at least some of what's
wrong. "Andrew," he asks, "where are you?"

Again the man laughs. "I'm at the Lodge, that All-American
place where I can converse wittily with the local sophisticates
about hunting and football." Ted remembers the last encounter
he had with Kesler there. If he's been drinking glasses of vodka
all night, he's likely in bad shape. Though that's none of Ted's
business, he knows. Some ancient Catholic impulse tells him
he should offer to drive the man home but it's an impulse he's

able to resist. "How is your apartment?" he asks, remembering Kesler's problems with housing.

"I'm moving," Kesler says emphatically.

"Yes, you mentioned that."

"That place is impossible," he declares. "Simply impossible."

"Well, you know you can use my car," Ted tells him.

Again, a silence, which lengthens this time, so that the phone is filled once more with sounds from the bar. When Kesler speaks again, there's an overwhelming weariness to his voice, and he sounds like an old man. "I told you about my sister, didn't I?" he says. "I told you I killed her?" Ted goes cold, refusing to believe he's just heard what he thinks he has. There's nothing he can say in response so he simply listens. "I think I'm going crazy," Kesler says.

"Hey, Andrew," Ted says into the phone, "take it easy."

"It's been good talking to you," Kesler says before hanging up.

Did he really say what I thought he said? Ted asks himself. Here in the basement apartment on a frigid night in February he's suddenly aware of the cold, snow-covered spaces that lie between here and the Lodge; he's aware of the wider spaces beyond the confines of the little town, hundreds of miles of the interior of the country, probably covered as well by snow on this bitter night. He holds on to the phone as if the black double-headed instrument itself can somehow transmit to him the exact words of Kesler's message: *my sister . . . I killed her.* But Ted doesn't need any confirmation; he's sure that's exactly what he heard.

February is in its final days but the relentless winter shows no signs of loosening its grip on the university town. People stomping the snow off their boots in Meyer's Drugs or Sally's Sweet Shoppe wonder aloud to perfect strangers whether the cold is ever going to let up; harried mothers try to find new ways of entertaining children kept home because of a burst pipe in an elementary school; car batteries fail by the dozen and the steady clanking of tire chains in the icy streets makes the traffic sound like a column of passing tanks. Ted sees the same frigid numbers on the bank thermometer that everyone else does, but it isn't the weather that's on his mind these days. For him, everything is connected to Dori and their situation is no nearer to being resolved than it was a month ago: how is it possible that the two of them can mean so much to each other and that she's going to be leaving this place for good in the not-too-distant future? Hearing "California, Here I Come" on the radio can make his eyes go moist, though he's just as likely to plunge into bleak desolation while opening a can of tuna. So much for the rewards of living in the moment. When sleep is elusive, as it frequently is, he finds himself staring into the darkness above his bed, replaying endless imaginary scenes with Dori in which he delivers unanswerable arguments for her coming back next fall. As often as not, he awakens exhausted, which hasn't improved his disposition. Inevitably, he's thought about therapy, though that doesn't seem to have brought much peace to Marty Reindorf. Ted happened to run into him last week when the French A-bomb test in the Sahara was announced. "When is it going to stop?" a wild-eyed Marty declared in the street outside the Book Barn, his gloved hands chopping the frigid air. With his knit cap pulled down to where it touched his glasses, he seemed to be peering out at the world from under a rock. "Forget about the Lost Generation," he said; "we have a very good chance of being the Last Generation." Ordinarily Ted would have listened a while and made sympathetic noises but, given his own psychic state, he felt no qualms about cutting Marty off quickly and getting out of there.

In the midst of his present malaise, Ted can't help thinking now and then about the late-night call he got from Andrew Kesler a week ago. He hasn't heard from him since and at times it can seem as if he imagined the whole episode. Certainly, in the clear, sharp-shadowed February daylight through which the heavily-clad citizens of Chippewa make their way between mounds of crusted snow, that telephone encounter has the insubstantiality of a fevered dream. But the fact is, Ted wasn't hallucinating: Kesler did call him and he did say those things, like a man delivering a death bed confession to a priest. Remembering his words still brings a shiver; and yet, isn't there a sensible explanation for all of it? The man was drunk, clearly enough, he was out of his head, he made some wild statements, but so do other drunks; and then, he's always had a flair for the melodramatic. He said he was going crazy, but everyone feels that way sometimes. As for what he said about killing his sister, disturbing as it may have been on the face of it, Kesler wouldn't be the first person to feel guilt that he survived some ordeal when a close relative didn't. In the end, though, the strangest thing of all about the Pole's declarations might have been that he should have made them to Ted, of all people, and it's particularly sad if he actually thought Ted was the one person in town he could talk to.

This Saturday, though, Ted has tried to relegate worry and mystery to the background so that he can focus on the task before him. By the early afternoon he's worked his way diligently through most of his batch of freshman papers, taking only a short break for lunch. The apartment is a mess but he'll attend to that later. His plan is to keep going on the papers

until he gets all of them done, when his reward will be a night
with Dori. All he needs for motivation is the thought of dinner
at her place—Mexican food, wine, candles on the card table,
Sarah Vaughan on the record player and the promise of further,
sweeter delights to come—though even that delectable vision
can't hide the fact that every tick of the clock is bringing them
closer to her departure from Chippewa. How can it already be
the end of February when it seems just yesterday that he picked
her up from the airport on her return from California? Amid
the sweet, luxuriant sadness that floods him he's aware of something more prickly, the sense that Dori's decision to leave is a
kind of challenge to him, though it's a challenge that so far has
been met only by paralysis on his part. What can he do, after
all, to change her mind? He can't just drop out of the program
himself, can he? His thinking about the future never manages to
get much beyond that point. In the meantime, he's grateful for
the tasks immediately before him, like these papers.

When he hears a knock on the door, he has a momentary fantasy that it's Dori: what if she's as impatient to see him
as he is to see her? Even as he thinks it, though, he knows it
isn't likely: she'd phone first. All at once, possibly because the
memory of last week's phone call is lurking just below the surface of his consciousness, he's sure that it's Andrew Kesler at the
door, with some demand that goes far beyond the use of his car,
and for a second or two Ted just sits there among the freshman
papers, vaguely uneasy, listening to the silence that follows the
knock, as if he's prepared to wait until this mysterious visitor
goes away. When the knocking is repeated, though, he jumps
to his feet, suddenly brought back to his senses. How likely is it
that Kesler is at his door? It could be anyone, after all, like his
landlord, who did say something about draining the radiators
the last time they talked. "I'm coming," Ted shouts and crosses
the room. When he opens the door to a blast of cold air, though,
it's neither Kesler nor his landlord standing in the icy recessed
entryway, but some stranger with a deep tan that he didn't get
in Chippewa.

"Ted?" The man he's facing is nobody he's seen before, a big, middle-aged guy in a dark blue overcoat and a gray fedora who's studying him carefully, as if he's been asked to pick a suspect out of a police line-up. At the same time, the stranger's look carries an unmistakable insinuation of intimacy. Who the hell is this guy, Ted wonders, who's calling me by my first name? Is he some kind of salesman? Then the man moves his head in a way that seems oddly familiar. I know him, Ted thinks, but from where? Momentarily weightless, he reaches beyond the person standing at the door toward some place more distant, some place from his own past. He's still trying to make the connection when the visitor says, "Don't you recognize your father?"

Ted stands there, stunned, feeling the cold air on his bare arms, robbed of the capacity for speech. His father? Jack Riley? Can this really be the ghost who haunted his childhood dreams? He looks at the substantial figure before him, taking in the eyes, the mouth, the nose, mentally calculating the connections between this stranger and the remembered image of the lean young man who came back from the war to toss a ball to him for a few months before leaving forever. Though the face is wider and there are pouches under the guarded gray-blue eyes, there are the same heavy brows, the same straight nose (like his own, he recognizes), and the mouth is surely the same one that smiled as the father he once knew shouted, "Good catch!" Of course. Why didn't he see it right away?

"I guess this is a bit of a surprise," the man at the door says. His initial heartiness has given way to something more tentative, and there's even a hint of disappointment at his son's failure to recognize him right away. "It's been what, fourteen years?"

Again Ted says nothing. The confused emotions he's starting to feel are powerful but unfocused; they give him no guide about how to react to this abrupt visitation. *He left us, he left Mom and me. And now he comes back. What am I supposed to do? Roll out the red carpet?* Once more he's eleven years old.

"I probably should have phoned first," Jack Riley says. "But frankly, I wasn't sure you'd want to see me." His eyes search Ted's face as if he too is trying to account for the changes wrought by the years since they've last seen each other.

Ted clenches his fists to contain the trembling. He's on the alert, ready for something, but what? His feelings have clarified to the point where he can recognize the simmering anger at their core. What right does this man have to barge in on his life like this? Hasn't he caused enough damage by leaving? What can he hope to accomplish by coming back? Still, Ted vaguely senses that this anger is a dam thrown up against an incipient panic, a sense of the uncanny: Lazarus in his shroud would be no more astonishing a presence on Tecumseh Street than this man.

"Aren't you going to invite me in?" His father's breath frosts on the chilly February air.

Ted's instinct is to resist, to cut off this reunion before it gets started by closing the door in his father's face, just to stop everything right here, but even as he's thinking it he has the sense that none of this is really happening, that he's watching it all from someplace else; and when, after a few moments, he steps back into the apartment without saying a word, it's as if the two of them are characters in a dream, guided by the hidden will of an unseen sleeper. His father follows, closing the door behind him, and when Ted hears the sound, it's like a trap door closing. His own apartment seems strange to him now, and he sees its once-comfortable shabbiness—the cheap furniture, dishes and cups on the table, clothes on the floor, books and papers all over—through the eyes of his visitor, who seems even more alien as he crosses the worn carpet in his expensive coat and shiny shoes. He's slowed down, Ted observes—if he really is who he says he is—the quick, nervous motions of the man he remembers have been replaced by a measured, deliberate way of moving through the world that suggests either authority or wariness. He might be twenty pounds heavier than he was when Ted last saw him but he isn't fat, just solid, even in some way dangerous. When Ted gestures to the empty Morris chair, his father takes off his hat and coat, laying the coat casually over part of the sofa before settling into the chair. He's wearing a brown suit of a definitely un-Ivy League cut and a bright red tie. Ted has a sudden notion that he may be a member of the mob. As Ted drops into the womb chair, his visitor looks at the freshman papers strewn about the apartment. He seems about to make a comment but his face wrinkles into a frown and he sneezes.

"Bless you," Ted answers automatically, and immediately feels embarrassed for having said it. Running his hand across his face, he's aware that he hasn't shaved yet today.

His father pulls out a handkerchief and blows his nose. "I think I'm getting a cold," he says. "I always forget about the humidity back here." As if in response to the statement, the radiator hisses and he blows his nose again.

The interlude has dissipated some of Ted's resistance, though he's no more comfortable sitting there without speaking, a few feet from this specter from his past who's suddenly reentered his life. All he can think of at the moment is the condition of the apartment. It's not usually this bad, he wants to say, I'm usually a better housekeeper but I wanted to concentrate on getting my papers done today. His eyes dart quickly to the incriminating dent in the bathroom door. His visitor, though, seems absorbed in his cold, content to sit there quietly. Ted is anything but content; he has the feeling that if he doesn't say something, he'll lose the power of speech entirely. But what form of address is he going to use? He certainly isn't going to call this man "Dad." At last, in desperation, he asks, "How long have you been in town?"

Jack Riley looks up. "I got in about a half-hour ago," he answers. "I was at a convention in Chicago. I've got a rented car and I drove over." Ted nods as if he's actually interested; in fact, he's furious, vaguely ashamed of the way this conversation has started: the man who ran out on him and his mother shows up after fourteen years and they're talking about rental cars. What's the next question: is the car a Ford or a Chevy?

His father continues to survey the room, taking in the mess. Ted, studying him, can't help noticing the shine on his shoes. He must have had them done this morning. What kind of convention did he come from in Chicago? he wonders. "You, uh, seem to be doing OK," he ventures, doing nothing to muffle the accusatory tone of his statement.

The older man looks at him a moment before responding. "I live in Phoenix, I'm in real estate." His face brightens. "And, yeah, I'm doing OK." Ted watches him warily, still unsure how he's supposed to feel about the abrupt reappearance of this figure from the past. Why did he come here, and why now? are the immediate questions on his mind. Still, it's hard enough just accepting that this tan, well-fed realtor who looks vaguely like a mobster can actually be his father. Of the many versions of the man's post-family career that the son imagined, most were more romantic and, frankly, more doomed, than what appears to have been the case with the Jack Riley who left his wife in Cold River, and Ted acknowledges a sense of disappointment. He'd be more comfortable, he realizes, knowing that the man had turned into a skid row bum.

"Hey, let's get past all the bullshit," his father says at last, pulling out an Old Gold and offering one to Ted, which he refuses. Then the older man taps his cigarette against the pack, lights it, draws in smoke, and exhales. He's using matches, Ted notes; he doesn't have a lighter, at least not with him. "I didn't expect you to greet me with a brass band," Jack Riley says. "Hell, I don't suppose you like me at all." Ted takes out one of his own cigarettes and lights up as the other goes on. "I'll admit I've been kind of a shit." The two of them watch the space between them fill with smoke. "But I have my own story," he says. "And you know, it takes two to tango."

"It only takes one to walk off the dance floor," Ted snaps back, finally finding his voice. Out of the corner of his eye he sees his papers, the necessary work for which the evening with Dori is to be the reward, and his irritation at the man's intrusion into his life sharpens. What does this guy want? For all his Arizona tan and shiny shoes, he didn't come here just to talk about old times. Ted is sure he wants something; he just doesn't seem to be in any hurry to tell what it is.

"You're quick," his father says with an appreciative smile. "And you've got a temper. Just like always." If he's inviting Ted to a trip down memory lane, though, Ted's going to disappoint him because he isn't interested. His father shakes his head. "But all that's ancient history. I don't know that there's much to gain by going over it again." He exhales a cloud of smoke, thickening the gauzy filter between them. "You've got to remember, though, that it's a rare situation where only one party is to blame in a marriage that doesn't work."

"That doesn't mean they're equally to blame," Ted fires back, grateful that this intruder has enabled him to take the moral high ground.

The other man waits before responding, as if trying to gauge how upset his son is before continuing. His expression is bland and diplomatic, the realtor giving his potential customer room to justify to himself the formidable commitment he's about to make, and it's hard for Ted to find the gaunt, nervous face of the younger man in the fleshier countenance that confronts him. Where did the man who played catch with him go? "No," his father says wearily, "it doesn't mean that, and I'm not saying it does." Once more he pulls out his handkerchief and blows his nose. Somehow the commonplace gesture gives him the air of being at home here in his son's apartment, and that makes Ted uneasy: it bothers him that he should be talking as if it's the most natural thing in the world to this person he hasn't seen in almost a decade and a half, hasn't seen in all that time because he deserted his wife and child.

"Mom's doing fine by herself," Ted volunteers.

"That's no surprise," Jack Riley responds. "She's a strong woman. She always was." A shadow crosses his face as if he's about to say something that might shift the tone of the conversation, but he goes no further and Ted waits, thinking that certainly one difference between the man across from him and the one he thinks he remembers is his present visitor's greater restraint, his sense of things held in check. The father Ted knew so briefly was more mercurial, quick to change his mood, even dreamy, if the son remembers him accurately. One of Ted's enduring memories is of a moment when he stood unobserved at the kitchen doorway and saw his father sitting at the table, smoking and looking out the window toward the little woods at the back of the house. To the boy, who couldn't see his father's face, it seemed as if the man's whole being leaned toward those woods with the nervous expectancy of someone listening for a mysterious, seductive call. It's hard to imagine the person sitting across from him listening for any such call.

When his father speaks again, there's more of an edge to his voice. "You know why your mother wouldn't give me a divorce?"

The question catches Ted off guard. "Well, she is a Catholic," he answers after a moment.

The other nods dismissively. "Of course," he says, "but that's not the only reason. It's not even the most important reason." He takes a long drag on his cigarette and crushes it in the nearby ashtray. "The fact is, if she gave me a divorce I'd be out of her life completely."

"But you are," Ted protests. "Or were, up until a few minutes ago."

The other man makes a gesture with his hands. Ted has already noted that he wears no wedding ring. "Don't worry, I'm not trying to get back in. I came here to see you, not her."

"Yeah, well just why are you seeing me?" Ted asks. It comes out sounding like an accusation.

"Do I have to have a reason?" the other responds sharply. "You're my son, for Christ's sake."

"That didn't seem to bother you when you left," Ted throws at him.

Something flares up in the man's eyes and for a moment Jack Riley looks like someone who wouldn't necessarily play by the rules if he ever got into a fight; but once again he allows himself an interval before going on, as if he's decided to take a deep breath. "Believe me," he mutters almost inaudibly, "I did both of you a favor by leaving when I did." When he resumes after a while, his voice is measured but firm. "We were talking about divorce. Well, I may be out of your mother's life, as you say, but as long as I'm still officially the husband, the Mistake"— Ted hears the capital letter—"it's part of her martyrdom."

Ted is angry, as much with himself for allowing this stranger to make these kinds of insinuations about his mother as he is with the man who made them. "Shut up," he says, his voice rising. "Where do you get off saying things like that?"

The look Jack Riley directs at Ted carries no acknowledge-ment of a relationship between them. Something simmers there, something hard, possibly violent, and Ted has the feeling that it might not be wise to cross him. At the same time, he welcomes the challenge, he's prepared to defend himself physically if he has to; but then his father's expression softens at last and he set-tles back in his chair as if to get a better look at Ted. "Bea has got herself one spirited defender," he says. "And, OK, maybe 'mar-tyrdom' isn't quite the word I should have used. That may have been a little twist of the knife on my part." He waits a second before adding, "I'll admit I'm no saint." His eyes darken under lowered brows and it's not hard to imagine the wild young man of family legend. "But with all due respect," he says evenly, "this is a story I know better than you do."

"Don't think you're going to get any pity out of me," Ted says. He isn't comfortable talking about his mother with the man who ran out on her. Even though he's defended her, it seems like a betrayal. "And for your information," he adds, "she hasn't painted you out to be a demon, if that's what you're trying to say."

His father shakes his head. "No, I wouldn't expect that," he says more quietly. "That isn't her way."

"What are you trying to say, then?" Ted demands. His fists are clenched once more.

The other man raises a hand, a conductor quieting the bois-terous horn section of an orchestra. "Hey, calm down, buddy," he says. "It's one of the things that was attractive about her, that I could see even when she was in her twenties, that she isn't going to resort to cheap tricks."

"Yeah, well," Ted challenges him, "you just said. . . ."

"What I was trying to say," he answers, his voice calm, delib-erate, the voice of a teacher who wants to make a subtle point, "is that even now it isn't me she's battling so much as her old

man, old Dan Timilty, the late Dr. Dan." As he shakes his head,
Ted sees the formidable doctor who, if photos are to be believed,
would wear a suit to a picnic. He knows something about his
mother's conflicts with him and he recognizes that what he's
just been told him may contain some truth. "Look," his father
continues, "I may have been stupid when I got involved with
your mother. I was nineteen, a cocky shanty Irish lad who happened to be a small-town football hero and nothing more. I was
uppity enough to set my sights on a lace-curtain belle, but I
wanted something more than what was waiting for me in Cold
River. And so did she," he adds. "Yeah, so did she." He's silent
for a beat or two, as if agitated by the memory. "So we used
each other," he says philosophically. "She used me to get back
at the good doctor for sending her to that little Catholic college when she wanted to go to a real school and I used her
to . . . well, I suppose to learn something about the world."
When he finishes, he looks into his hands, apparently finished
for the moment. Ted is familiar enough with the outlines of
the story but this version of it has suddenly made him see his
mother and father as young people, as passionate and full of
life—as unfinished—as he is now, which is disorienting. "Well,"
Jack Riley says with finality, "it worked, but just for that." He
shakes his head. "They say you only get one wish and that's all
we got, a few months that summer. Then she was pregnant and
it was out of our hands."

A love child, Ted thinks bitterly, I'm a love child. What a
laugh. It wasn't anything anyone talked about, but you could
work out the numbers. He'd got used to that long ago, he
thought, but he's surprised by a belated sense of his own vulnerability, the idea that his being here today was by no means
guaranteed. "In those days," he says, "I don't suppose you had
much choice about having the baby." He feels an awkwardness
in talking about himself this way.

"No," his father snaps, "she could have got rid of you. God
knows, that was my first thought: how to get rid of this problem.
There were ways, even then, even with Catholics. But I eventually came round to her way of thinking about it." He looks off

into the distant corners of the apartment. "She kept reminding me that we had a code," he says. "The two of us had a code was the way she put it but really, it was only her code."

"Yeah," Ted asks, "and what was that code?"

The answer comes quickly, as if this is something he's gone over in his mind many times before. "That whatever we did, we accepted the consequences for." He looks down, as if he's examining his shoes. "It's something that sounds good when you're young but when you actually have to work it out in the world, it's a bit of a different story. I mean, Jesus, you get only one life. You shouldn't have to spend all of it paying for a single mistake." He shakes his head. "I tried. Maybe some people would say I didn't try hard enough. All I can say is that I made an effort and nobody but me will ever know how much of an effort it was. But in the end I felt the walls closing around me." Once again Ted remembers the young man smoking in the pale green kitchen, looking out the window, listening for the call from the woods. And that was more than ten years after the events that are being talked about now.

Hearing his father speak about a time before he was born, Ted realizes that the people being described are no longer as recognizable as they were only an hour ago, that the contours of the world have shifted, and he has a longing to go back to what he knew. Still, he can't help wondering about Beatrice Timilty and Jack Riley, the young couple who became his parents. "Did you two love each other?" he asks.

This time his father waits a few seconds before answering. Finally, he says quietly, "Oh, yeah," and smiles to himself. "Most definitely. It didn't last forever but that didn't keep it from being the most powerful thing I'd ever felt, and I think it was the same for her. But even when it was obvious that the two of us weren't much of a long-term proposition, she wouldn't back down. She'd made her choice and she wasn't going to blink."

When he falls silent, he pulls out another cigarette. Ted does the same. As the two of them light up separately, Ted is visited by an odd notion. Is it possible that this man he's been talking to all this while isn't really his father but someone pretending to that role in order to get something from him? After all, he didn't recognize him at the door. Maybe his initial instincts were correct. This guy could be some complete stranger, someone his father ran into after he left them to whom he told his story. But that's crazy; he can't let himself get caught up in that kind of thinking. Besides, he realizes that he doesn't want this man to be an impostor. Nevertheless, the idea leaves a residue of wariness towards his visitor. "Why are you here?" he asks. "And why now?"

The other man looks back at him steadily. "We're not ready for that yet," he says. "Right now I want to do some catching up about you. You never played football in college?"

Ted actually finds the shift in topic a relief. He shakes his head. "Only a bit of touch with friends."

"You didn't even try out?"

Ted shakes head. "I wasn't that good."

The older man acknowledges the answer with a nod but says, "You were pretty good in high school, though, I know that."

Ted tries to push back the rush of pride. "High school, yeah." He laughs through his nose. "But how did you know about my football career?"

His father leans forward, like a poker player studying his cards. There's a thin smile on his lips. "I still have contacts in Cold River," he says. "I tried to keep track of you, that's only natural. There was a time when I didn't do a very good job of it. But the last few years, yes. After I straightened out."

That gets Ted's attention. "Straightened out?"

The man nods. His voice is hoarse from smoking, from his cold; he looks tired. "I had a period of wandering." He laughs. "Being led by the blind. Unlike the Israelites, my wanderings led me to the desert. That's ancient history, though," he says dismissively, "for me and the Israelites. But look at you," he makes a gesture, "look at these books. So you're going to be a professor, are you?"

Ted feels as if he's been challenged to resolve his own doubts, which he isn't prepared to do just now. "Maybe," he answers defensively.

His father looks at him a moment before responding. "Sure," he says, "it's best not to close anything out at your age. What are you? Twenty-four?"

Ted nods.

"Christ, you're a hell of a lot more together than I was at your age," the other man says. "I'll give you that. I was in over my head with your mother. Jesus, she was smart for someone who was so sexy." Ted isn't used to hearing his mother called sexy, and he lets it pass. "All I knew was that I wanted something more than I was getting, I had no answers, just questions."

In spite of the resentment he feels toward him, Ted finds himself pulled into his father's story. "Did you get it?" he asks. "Something more?"

"Yeah." There's a long pause during which Ted listens to the refrigerator humming its familiar, comforting tune. He's jolted when the voice resumes. "Though something more is never all. I guess you come to realize that after a while." Jack Riley smiles. "Here's a bit of fatherly advice that you didn't ask for: don't think you can figure things out, don't think you can guess what the next chapter is going to be like. Life is always going to surprise you." He coughs lightly. "Still, the way things have turned out for me so far, I wouldn't trade my life."

Ted still finds it hard to imagine that this man he's learned to think of as guilty, romantic and doomed is a realtor who seems to have done pretty well for himself. "Your money, you mean, your success?" he asks.

His father shakes his head. "No, my journey," he says. "Even the wandering. Maybe especially the wandering."

For some reason Ted suddenly thinks of Marty Reindorf, the desperation in his eyes as he talked about the French A-bomb the other day, and the thought returns him to his own life with all its appetites and uncertainties. How much of a journey lies ahead for himself, for Dori, and for Marty? The Last Generation, Marty called them. It seems almost unfair that this man and his contemporaries should have been allowed their journeys when there's no such guarantee for their children. In the last few moments it seems to Ted that the apartment has become quieter, and this reunion between father and son might be taking place in a bomb shelter. "The world is a hell of a scary place right now," Ted says.

"Amen," the older man responds. There's no irony in his look. "Still, it was scary for me too." He pauses a moment, his eyes turned inward, before going on. "The war saved my life, believe it or not. I learned so much during those years. But Christ, it was scary. I mean, you experience stuff you think nobody could ever survive, and you do anyway. You do things you'd never imagine yourself doing and you don't think it's going to matter because who knows if you're even going to be around tomorrow? You think you're the only one but you know any GI you pass in the road might have had the same things happening to him. You. . . ." He stops abruptly. When he speaks again, it's as if he's talking to himself. "What I experienced in the war made it harder, a lot harder, to return to civilian life, at least the civilian life that was waiting for me in Cold River."

After a few moments of silence, he gets up, and Ted's first thought is that he's going to leave. His panic surprises him. Instead, the older man says, "I suppose it's OK if I get myself a glass of water?"

Ted nods. "Be my guest, so to speak." He's still seeing throngs of khaki-clad soldiers returning to the States, he feels overwhelmed by these stories of the past. They aren't his stories but they're filling his space and somehow they make his own life seem smaller. I should have stopped him at the door, he thinks. He's like an encyclopedia salesman who's got his foot in and now my life is being swallowed up by him.

But Ted still has no idea why Jack Riley is here and he means to find out. He hears the faucet hiss as his father pours himself a glass of water, then takes a swallow before returning with the glass to his chair.

"By the way," the man says when he's seated again, "I'm curious about why you never answered my letters."

Ted looks at him, suddenly alert, suspicious. "Letters? I didn't get any letters from you."

"Ah," he smiles crookedly. "I guess she didn't let them get to you then."

Once more Ted is on his guard. How can he be sure of anything this man tells him? "What did you write?" he asks skeptically.

Jack Riley looks at him, an eyebrow cocked. "I sent a couple of letters the first year. Just stuff about how I missed you, stuff like that. Corny, I guess, sentimental. I didn't want you to forget me. But you didn't get them?" He shakes his head. "I guess I can see her point if she kept the letters from you, though. She might not have wanted to complicate your life that way."

"She had a perfect right to do that," Ted fires back. "If that's what she did." He makes it sound righteous but he's not sure he believes it. Did his mother keep the letters, he wonders, or did she destroy them?

His father nods. "I'm not going to disagree with you there." He makes a weary gesture with his hand.

For all the time he's spent with her, Ted knows that he's never seen how much it hurt his mother to have this man leave her, at least he's never seen the depths of it. On those gray Saturday afternoons that first winter, he'd go off alone to ice-skate on the river. There, with an energy fueled by his rage at being abandoned, he'd push himself across acres of ice until he was far beyond the cove where others skated and at last in some deserted spot under a sky heavy with the threat of snow, he'd glide to a stop, his lungs burning as he teetered on the edge of exhaustion, hearing only the hiss of his skates, then just the wind, momentarily drained even of thought. Later, when he'd come home, his mother would make her special hot chocolate out of a paste of Hershey's cocoa and sugar mixed in Pet Milk, to which she'd add boiling water from the kettle, topping it off with more Pet Milk. What had she been thinking about as she'd paced the house while her son was on the frozen river, breathless, having driven himself to a point where for at least a few moments he could be beyond thinking? All at once Ted feels as if he's awakened from a dream. What am I doing talking to this man? he thinks; what am I doing talking about Mom this way?

After the surprise of his father's appearance, having to think of his parents as young lovers, it all seems too much, and he's overcome by an inner heaviness, as if in response to the gravitational pull of a denser planet. In his present state of passivity, he has the sense that his own life has been hijacked by this person sitting in his Morris chair who's chosen for whatever reason to re-enter that life. He has enough problems of his own; there are too many things that are still unsettled that he has to deal with. It seems hugely unfair that he should be carried back into an argument from the past that he thought was settled a generation ago.

His father takes another sip of water. "I've worn out my welcome, I can see," he says.

"What do you mean?" Ted responds evasively.

"Don't worry. So far this hasn't gone nearly as disastrously as it might have. I was actually pretty nervous." He lights up again. "And I can appreciate that you're in an awkward position."

For an instant Ted has an irrational impulse to tell him about Dori, about his own questions about his future, about his fears, but it takes only an instant for that to pass. "Well," he says, still feeling oddly depleted, "I don't suppose your position is all that comfortable either."

His father takes an especially deep drag on his cigarette, and he's silent for a while after he exhales. "OK," he says at last, "I guess it's time I got to the point. I didn't come here just to see how you're doing, though I have to say you seem to have turned out pretty well so far. At least," he says with the crooked smile that makes him seem once more like a mobster, "you haven't gone completely to hell yet. That's certainly no credit to me and plenty to your mother." Already in the way the man pronounces the last couple of words, though, Ted can hear a new note, a more somber note, and it disturbs him.

"What is it?" he asks, alert once more.

The man looks at him intently. "Your mother isn't in the best of health," he says, and Ted feels the brush of alarm, remembering his own sense back in Cold River that she seemed tired, paler, remembering the sight of her hand trembling as she slept.

"It's possible," his father continues, "that she may have multiple sclerosis."

The words drop into the space between them, ugly, frightening words, yet they convey no precise meaning. "What do you mean, multiple sclerosis?" he demands. His medical knowledge is hazy but he knows this is something serious. "Why would she have that? How do you know? I don't believe you."

The man ignores his outburst. He goes on as if Ted hasn't said anything. "The thing is, multiple sclerosis isn't that easy to diagnose or describe. It's a neurological condition and there's a lot they don't know about it just now. It sounds scary but I've talked to a few doctors and they say it can take a lot of forms, that it doesn't necessarily have to be lethal." He shakes his head. "Still, it is serious and it has to be treated."

"What kind of forms?" Ted asks almost before his father has finished speaking.

"Well," he says, "of course there's the worst case: muscular debilitation, progressive loss of control. Death, finally. But that's the worst case. There are a lot of other possibilities, milder forms."

"Wait," Ted says. It comes out as almost a shout. "How do you know this?"

"I told you I have contacts back in Cold River. One of them is Doctor Krause. He's actually pretty hopeful about your mother. I mean, there seem to be two main forms of the disease. One is progressive and the other isn't. It's his opinion that your mother has the second type."

Ted wants to feel relieved but it's hard not to be upset by what he's hearing. All this is going too quickly for him. "How much does she know?" he asks.

"A little," his father says. "She knows something's up. She's not dumb. She knows she's not OK, I'd guess."

But she hasn't told Ted anything about this, not even a little. He feels the bite of exclusion. "And you came here to tell me, then?"

"No," the man continues in the same calm vein, "that's not the main reason I came. Look, you probably know the bare facts

about your mother's financial situation: when she decided to
marry me old Doc Timilty pretty much cut her off. Oh, she got
the house, which helped, I'm sure. But your mother's a very
determined woman and she's insisted on living her life on her
own terms. Those are her words, by the way. And obviously
she's raised you, she's earned her own keep, without help from
old Dan and without help from me. I know she wants to keep it
that way."

He pauses to let this sink in. Ted, meanwhile, hearing once
more the outlines of his mother's story, feels a surge of love and
admiration for this woman who, nevertheless, hasn't trusted
him enough to tell him about her medical situation, as well as a
huge sense of sadness at the thought that she might now be in
danger. "You said that Doctor Krause is hopeful?" he asks.

His father's tone is gentler. "Yeah, look, when I found out
about this I was shook up too, but I trust Krause and I see no
reason not to believe him."

"Can she work and everything with this condition?" Ted asks.

"She may be able to function very well, from what I
understand."

It's all too much for Ted. "Jesus Christ," he says, "this is
awful."

His father shakes his head. "We've got to keep hopeful," he
says. When Ted doesn't respond he adds, more quietly, "On the
other hand, this is something you have to get used to. After a
certain age, it's going to be one thing or another."

"God damn it, she isn't that old," Ted protests.

"Hey, I agree with you," his father says. "Still. . . ."

The two of them are silent for a few moments and Ted manages to calm himself somewhat. "So what can I do?" he asks
at last.

His father pulls himself straight. "OK," he says, "I'll get to
the point. I've talked to a number of medical men in Arizona and
I know that the treatment she might need—the very best treatment—can be pretty costly, more than what she's able to pay, I'd
guess, but I've got a plan pretty much worked out that would
depend on your cooperation." He looks Ted in the eye. "I want

to help out but I know Bea would refuse that outright; it would go against everything she believes in, but I've made arrangements with Krause. If the treatment gets more expensive, he could bill her one price and get the rest from me without her knowing it if you were the middleman."

"Me?"

"You could open up a bank account and I'd put money there that you could draw on when Krause needed it."

Ted frowns. "I don't like the idea of going behind her back." He looks at the clock. How different a day he'd imagined this morning.

"Neither do I," says his father, "but doing it up front wouldn't work, believe me. And I don't want her to spend whatever savings she might have that way."

"You're sure she wouldn't take the money from you?" Ted presses.

He nods. "More than sure."

Ted feels overwhelmed. His father's plan is a large, palpable presence in the apartment, no less real for being intangible. "This is a pretty big step," he says. "I have to think about it."

"Fair enough," his father says. "But we should get in touch as soon as you decide, so we can set this thing up."

"It isn't something that's got to be done quickly, though, is it?" Ted asks. "I mean, how urgent is it? Do you know something you're not telling me?"

His father shakes his head. "No, as I understand it, the present phase could go on for a long while. It's just that I'd like to be ready." Ted nods. "By the way," his father adds, "since we might be doing business, you can call me Jack."

Ted looks at the man sitting a few feet away who's lived the last fourteen years apart from him, "wandering," to use his word, until he found himself in the desert. What the hell was that like? he wonders. Seconds pass without either of them saying anything. Ted isn't eager to return to the subject of his mother's possible illness—he's heard enough on that subject for now. Noticing again that his father isn't wearing a wedding ring, he voices a thought that occurred to him a while back. "Not being able to get the divorce, how has that affected your life?"

The other man looks at him knowingly. "You mean, does it cramp my style?" His mouth twists into a scowl. "Yeah, I can't get married, for one thing." He shrugs. "You learn to deal with stuff like that." He says no more for a while; just when it seems as if he's finished with the subject, though, he resumes. "You're probably wondering if I have any kind of compensation, aren't you? Well, I've been seeing someone for the past four years. Her name's Mollie. She's a widow with two kids of her own and we have a pretty satisfactory arrangement." Ted nods, as if giving his approval to the relationship; in fact, he's trying to visualize the situation: somewhere in the clear, desert spaces of Arizona a woman named Mollie is waiting for Jack Riley—is there a house by the side of the road, an apartment in Phoenix?—but all he can come up with is the image of a cactus. Yet how strange it is to be thinking of this man's life as going on, in progress, after having believed for so long that that story was over. "Mollie knows what I've been through," his father says. "We met in AA." Then he adds, "Maybe you'll get a chance to meet her one day," to which Ted makes no response.

"Dori," he says into the phone when his father has left. "You're not going to believe how I spent the last hour and a half."

"You've joined the priesthood," she laughs. When he makes no response, she asks, "What?"

"I . . . I'm going to have to wait to tell you till I come over tonight."

"You can tell me now if you want to," she says penitently. "I've got time."

"Not for this," he assures her. "This has to be told slowly, preferably with alcoholic accompaniment." As he says it, he can imagine himself at her place, doing exactly that. He's suddenly grateful to be talking to her, even more grateful he'll be with her later. "Jesus," he says, "thanks."

"For what?"

"Just for being there, you sweet lovely. Just for being there."

When he puts down the phone, he isn't sure how he feels. Exhausted, he thinks at first, and who wouldn't be, after an experience like that, spending part of the afternoon with Lazarus come back from the dead? But, surprisingly, he doesn't feel that way at all. As he looks at the mess of his apartment, it becomes clear to him that he's feeling just the opposite. In fact, he's restless and impatient, he has to do something. It won't be his freshman papers, he knows—at the moment, those sheets covered with typescript seem like artifacts of a lost world. Instead, he reaches down and picks up a gray sock from the floor and carries it to the hamper. In the process, he discovers a purpose: he's going to give the apartment a thorough cleaning, belated though it may be. He'll make his way through the mess of dirty dishes in the sink, he'll vacuum the floor, he'll even get after the bathroom with the X Boys, Ajax and Windex. By the time he leaves for Dori's, the place will be sparkling.

For the moment, though, he stands motionless beside the hamper, thinking about the man in the dark overcoat and gray hat who left not long ago. Right now he's somewhere between here and Chicago, from which point he'll fly back to his home in the desert. Like a crook, Ted finds himself thinking, a crook who's made a clean getaway while I've been left holding the bag. But if that's the case, what did he get away with and what's in the bag? Ted can't say. He only knows that the surprise reunion with his father has left him with unsettled feelings. Of course, the news about his mother is the most disturbing aspect of their meeting, though his father kept insisting that there was no reason to jump to the gloomiest conclusions. As for the man himself, it was a relief to find that Jack Riley wasn't a monster, but just another complicated person with adult problems, and it was fascinating for Ted to have learned things about his parents when they were around his age. Still, he feels uneasy about his own role in the encounter: it seems to him that he didn't say the right things when his father was here, didn't challenge him enough. It's true, he defended his mother, but nevertheless he feels that somehow Jack Riley got the better of him. And wasn't Ted, just by listening to the man's account of his time with her, whether willingly or not, playing the role of the voyeur?

There's something else as well. Now that he's gone, Ted is curious about why his father actually had to come to Chippewa, to this apartment? Of course, he'd say he had to see Ted in order to propose his plan but, no matter what explanations he gave, couldn't he just have contacted him by phone or by letter? And that plan itself, the bank account—why couldn't he deal with Krause directly? No, there's something not quite believable about the whole business. Ted remembers his father walking through the door, sitting in the Morris chair, going to the sink and pouring himself a glass of water—it all seems a bit like a dog's staking out his territory, an attempt to put his stamp on his son's life. Nobody's motives are simple and there were certainly more things going on in his coming to Chippewa than just his generosity toward his estranged wife. What exactly is he trying to buy with that money?

Though he tries to solace himself that he hasn't given his father a final answer yet, Ted recognizes that that's probably just a formality: given the gravity of the situation, it doesn't seem to make sense to refuse the deal. But he isn't comfortable with the idea of being tied up in a secret partnership with the man because, however benign its motivation might be, isn't it a kind of betrayal of his mother? Finally, this visit was about her. Ted can speculate endlessly about Jack Riley's motives for re-entering his life at this point but everything comes back to the news he brought about his wife's condition. Ted had already been anxious enough about his mother; now that anxiety is tinged with dread. He remembers her asleep on the sofa back in Cold River when they were watching the Boris Karloff movie on TV, the bowl of popcorn between them, remembers his momentary, chilling sense that she was dead, remembers her trembling hand. *Multiple sclerosis, multiple sclerosis.* His father said Dr. Krause is hopeful, he reminds himself. Yet even that consolation stings because once more, he's dealing with secondhand information. It's frustrating to be shut out of things this way. But what can he do? He knows he's not going to confront his mother about her health, of course; he's going to have to wait for her to tell him when she's ready—and maybe the disease won't reach a severe stage. Nevertheless, it will be impossible to think about her now without seeing her under the shadow of that affliction. All this his father has left him. Maybe that's what's in the bag he's holding.

Ted goes to the Morris chair and picks up the ashtray Jack Riley used. A smell of stale tobacco rises when he empties the contents into a wastebasket. He takes the ashtray to the sink, where he washes it and puts it into the dish rack beside the glass out of which his father drank. Now there are no visible traces of his presence here, but Ted is aware that the wastebasket contains those butts whose acrid tang invades his memory, the dead smoke carrying with it scenes from the stories he heard this afternoon: the passion of the young lovers in Cold River, the stern countenance of Dr. Daniel Timilty, GIs walking a road somewhere in Europe, a faceless woman in the desert—the lives of the previous generation. With the smell still haunting his nostrils, he takes the can of Ajax from under the sink and sprinkles some of the scouring powder onto the porcelain. As he bends over the sink with a sponge, the harsh blend of chemicals obliterates the last vestiges of his father's cigarettes and he's swept up in a sudden impatience. He wants it to be 6:30, he wants to be talking to Dori, he wants nothing to do with the past. Let me live my own life, he says to nobody in particular; let me live it while I'm still young.

Ted is in Hart Hall when Jamie Patten sees him in the corridor and comes over. "Did you hear about Marty Reindorf?" Jamie asks breathlessly. "He tried to kill himself." Ted stops in his tracks. "Jesus, is he OK?"

Jamie nods. "Yeah, from what I heard." The wispy ex-divinity student has assumed a solemn expression like a TV reporter covering a disaster and, though he hardly knows Marty, he shakes his head at the tragedy of it all. "Poor guy cut his wrists."

Ted is stunned by this turn of events; at the same time, he isn't surprised. "When did all this happen?" he asks.

"This morning," Jamie tells him.

"But you said he's all right?" Ted demands.

"I guess so. He's at the hospital. He'll be in good hands there."

Ted looks down the familiar corridor with its bowed wood floor. The Gothic red-brick building from the nineteenth century is perpetually rumored to be on the verge of being torn down but he's grown fond of it. "I've got to see Marty," he says. "Which hospital is he in?"

Jamie frowns. "I don't know but I doubt they'd let you see him right away. I'd call first."

When Ted tells Dori at the Joe a few minutes later, she says nothing for a time but "Shit, shit, shit." Then she lights up. "Yeah," she says, "we ought to go over there but Jamie's right: with a suicide attempt, they'll probably want to keep him under observation for a bit."

Ted sighs. "That's a little like locking the barn door after the horse has been stolen, isn't it?"

"That may be, but it's policy." She draws on her cigarette, exhales and crushes the half-smoked butt in the ashtray. "I just wish I'd have been a bit more understanding last time we saw him."

Ted shakes his head. "You? What about me? I practically accused him of malingering."

They're both silent a while. "Actually," Dori says, "I doubt that in the long run either of us had much to do with it."

"The problem is, he cried wolf so much. How could you tell?"

"I know." She touches his hand. "I know. But we have to go. How many friends does the poor guy have, after all?"

The next day, as the two of them make their way down the hospital corridor, Dori squeezes Ted's hand. "These places give me the creeps," she says.

"You and me both." For all his insistence on seeing Marty, he isn't looking forward to this meeting: what do you say to someone who's just tried to kill himself? Does Marty want to be cheered up or, being Marty, is he expecting commiseration for not being able to pull it off? By now Ted has heard the details of the story and it seems clear their friend was at least ambivalent about his act. For one thing, he cut his wrists in a way that was highly unlikely to cause his death. He also left the door open with music playing loudly, an invitation, it would seem, for someone to intervene, which is exactly what happened. Not really a suicide attempt, people said, more of a cry for help. Still, to have done something like that at all, to dare death to take you, is something that puts Marty on the other side of a line separating him from his friends, that makes him somehow scarier. Ted pulls Dori closer. "I'm counting on you to cheer him up with tales of California," he says.

She looks at him. "Cheer Marty up? Fat chance."

They're at the door of the room before they're ready. "Take a deep breath," he whispers.

Only one of the four beds in the room is occupied, so the solitary patient has to be Marty, but there's something unfamiliar about the way he looks. "Hey, Marty," Ted calls as they approach, trying for a casual note at the same time that he's reminding himself not to stare at his friend's bandaged wrists. But before he and Dori can get to the bed a grim, squarish woman in nurse's uniform comes up beside them and asks for their names. She meets their ingratiating smiles with a stony expression, as if she believes the two of them goaded her charge into his desperate act, and she informs them they can't stay long. Then she withdraws to a place just out of earshot where she can still watch their every move.

When he and Dori are beside the bed Ted can see what looked so different from a distance: his friend's usually unruly hair is slicked back, making him look like a little kid. Marty, who's pale as skim milk, regards his visitors blankly at first. After a moment, a glint of recognition comes into his eyes, though there isn't much hint of welcome there. He raises his head with some effort and Dori pats his pillow into place. "Well," Ted begins, but he can't think of anything to follow.

Marty's gaze is fixed on them uncertainly, as if he's still trying to make out who they are. "Ted," he says at last, "Dori," his mouth working toward a smile. "I really botched this one," he says. The words come slow and flat, like an induced confession. "Just like an amateur." He pauses before going on. "Or rather, like a complete incompetent posing as an amateur."

Ted and Dori laugh awkwardly, as they suppose he wants them to, but Marty's weak smile is already fading. He looks depleted; his drained face makes clear how much that one remark, no doubt carefully prepared, has cost him. "They say I didn't really want to do it," he tells them a few moments later with a feeble attempt at a scowl, but his voice is without inflection, like a zombie's. "They said I wasn't serious." Ted remembers enough of the old Marty to expect something clever after that, but the pale man lying there with the watchful nurse in attendance isn't the old Marty: his arms limp at his side, he looks like a discarded marionette from a children's book and he probably feels that way.

"We couldn't find any Twinkies," Dori offers, but there's no response from Marty. "We'll bring some next time," she adds.

"Is there anything else you need?" She glances in the direction of the nurse and lowers her voice. "Like a hacksaw maybe?"

"I'm not going to be here long," Marty says spiritlessly. "My brother Roger is coming up. As soon as they release me he's taking me back to Cincinnati." Roger is a lawyer and from what Marty has told him, the two of them have nothing in common but their parents. That he's coming from Cincinnati and taking his brother back with him is just about the worst news Ted can imagine, but if Marty is upset by this development he doesn't show it.

"Well," is all the response Ted can manage.

"It'll be better than this place," Dori suggests, relentlessly cheerful. "You can rest there and get healthy. Put a little meat on your bones with home cooking."

Marty responds with a half-smile. "Maybe," he says. "Maybe."

When their visit is over, Ted and Dori go to her apartment, where the first thing she does is to drop heavily into the wicker chair in her living room and sigh, "Poor Marty."

"Yeah." Ted knows how she feels. He walks to the window: trees, cars, the houses across the street are ghostly in the fog that's rising off the melting snow. You could probably stand out there in shirtsleeves today but nobody is taking the warm spell seriously: early March isn't when spring begins in Chippewa. He turns back to the room. Dori hasn't moved. Remembering Marty's pale face and his defeated expression, he muses aloud, "I don't know, it's crazy but you almost wish . . . for his sake. . . ."

"I know what you mean," Dori says. "There's no way this story comes out well."

Did I really say what I just said? Ted thinks. I didn't mean it that way. But the despair that must have driven their friend to his act was bad enough; he didn't need the humiliation of having, as he said, botched it. "And the brother's coming for him. Jesus, this is sad."

"That wasn't Marty we saw," Dori protests. The pain of remembering is etched on her face. "It wasn't even a bad imitation."

Ted comes closer. "I just have this feeling," he says, "that we're never going to see him again." The melancholy in that declaration is mixed with regret: if what he's just said turns out to be true, he wishes at least that his last memory of his friend could have been something that did Marty more justice. "You could see that even under all that medication he was going through hell: he screwed up, he was ashamed of that—and scared. You could see that."

Ted suddenly catches the dry, astringent scent of the colored eucalyptus leaves near the door—pure California, Dori calls the smell. It took a bit of getting used to but Ted likes it now. On the pale blue wall above the eucalyptus is a framed drawing of Humphrey Bogart: from under the curled brim of his hat Bogie looks out at the world mischievously, a man who's in on a private joke. Today, though, he's lost a bit of his swagger. Somehow, what's happened to Marty has followed Ted and Dori here. "Want a smoke?" he offers.

Dori shakes her head. "I'm too depressed." A fleeting look of amusement crosses her face. "Hey, wouldn't that be something? Depression as a way of quitting smoking."

"Don't count on it. Human beings are resourceful. They can manage both at once. At least I know I can."

"You convinced me," she says. "Give me a cigarette." She lights up and inhales deeply, settling back in her chair and closing her eyes as if she believes the tobacco will erase the memory of their friend in a hospital bed. With her pale, beautiful face and her dark hair, she looks like a fairy tale princess in an enchanted sleep. The smoke she expels through her nostrils seems to coil in slow motion and, momentarily, Ted is able to forget about Marty.

"You manage to make smoking very sexy," he says.

She opens her large gray eyes and looks at him skeptically. "Mister, is there ever a time when you're not horny?"

He puts on a serious face. "We're just talking about when I'm awake, right?"

She shakes her head and smiles to herself, but only for an instant. "Look," she's suddenly earnest again, "the important thing is that Marty did botch the job, thank God: he's still alive."

Ted nods agreement. He's determined to take a positive approach. "Still," he says, "it doesn't look as if that therapist he was seeing did him much good."

She leans forward tensely and drags on her cigarette. "Maybe the lawyer brother will decide to sue the guy and that will get Marty interested."

"If only. . . ." Ted can't quite push back the gloom. "That's the worst thing about it, maybe: he just doesn't seem interested any more. It reminds me of *Invasion of the Body Snatchers*."

"Exactly," she says. "But that's the drugs, maybe."

Ted has lit up too. His eyes travel across the familiar details of Dori's apartment: the cobalt blue vase from Mexico that holds a handful of paper flowers, the orange shag rug, Bogie on the wall with his hat and his mischievous smile, the *Gone With the Wind* poster, the eucalyptus—all these objects speak as unmistakably of Dori as the letters of her name. His favorite, though, is a picture in her bedroom, a reproduction of an old ad for California lemons. In colors as vivid as a child's birthday dream, a tile-roofed Spanish mission, moonlit and half in shadow, stands beside a lemon grove, a snow-capped mountain on the horizon. Above, in a blue night sky that's studded with five-pointed stars, a stubby vintage airplane trails lines of motion as it crosses in front of an unbelievably huge lemon-colored moon while on the ground a big sedan from the '30s waits mysteriously before the mission, sending rays of lemony light into the warm darkness. In spite of the machines that imply operators, there are no people visible anywhere. The whole scene is framed by a pair of lush palm trees in the foreground and at the top of the picture an arc of large yellow letters spells out "Silver Moon." Finally, modestly in the corner of this magical landscape, a glowing Sunkist lemon emerges from its paper wrapping like a piece of fruit from the Garden of Eden. Thinking of the picture, Ted wishes he and Dori could disappear into that scene. Maybe there they could be safe from—whatever it is.

"I wish I believed in prayer," Dori says, "because I think the odds are so stacked against Marty right now. I mean, he can be a pain in the neck but he's not a bad egg; he's a smart guy who shouldn't have to be dragged back to his family like a kid who's run away from home. Cincinnati," she pronounces the name in disbelief.

"I agree," Ted says. "I mean, here in Chippewa he might come across as some kind of cynic but I think he's basically a shy kid with glasses who wasn't very popular in school. He found a niche here and he'd have made a decent enough teacher." He suddenly remembers the nurse who hovered on the fringes of their meeting. "Did you get the impression that that misplaced linebacker posing as a nurse didn't like any of us, not Marty, not me or you?"

"If she's the one who combed his hair, she certainly doesn't like Marty." She shakes her head. "I'm sure she wanted to put us all under sedation. God, we have to pray that the pod people haven't got him for good."

"You're right." He flashes a bright, determined smile.

Her face falls. "I'm depressed again. You know, I have to admit there's one small part of me that believes Marty did what he did knowing it wasn't going to work and that his brother would come to take him back to Cincinnati." She sighs. "That would be the saddest thing."

Moved by her distress, he leans toward her and gently touches her shoulder. Her hair brushes his knuckles excitingly and for a breath or two neither of them says anything. When he speaks, it's in a lowered voice: "Might I suggest . . ."

She pulls back with an ironic smile. "The Male Mind, so to speak, at work."

"Hey," he laughs, "at least I'm good for a chuckle."

"Come here," she says, and pulls him back to her, fixing him with a mock-teacherly look. "'Ah, love, let us be true to one another . . .'" she declaims, then waits for him to continue.

When he realizes what she's up to, he adds, "'For the world, which seems/To lie before us like a land of dreams. . . .'" It's as far as he can go.

"'So various, so beautiful, so new,/Hath really neither joy, nor love, nor light'" she fills in helpfully, "'Nor certitude, nor peace, nor help for pain. . . .'"

At least he knows the ending, and he joins her: "'And we are here as on a darkling plain/Swept with confused alarms of struggle and flight,/Where ignorant armies clash at night.'"

"Jesus," Dori says, pulling away once more, "we're back to Marty again, aren't we?"

"That's his song, all right. We should have done that as a bedside duet. But, boy, you're good. Old Edgar Peterson's going to weep when you leave this place." As soon as he says it he realizes he's broken one of their unstated rules by alluding to Dori's impending departure. Neither of them says anything for a while, but he's managed to depress himself or, to be more accurate, to add to the depression both of them have been feeling.

Dori's eyes take on a distant look. "Remember when Marty and I were in the Union the night of that blizzard?" she says. "And you joined us?"

"What do you think? Sure, I remember. That was the first time you and I really got a chance to talk."

"And you took my side in pushing the Rosy View of Life."

"I did," he concedes. "So I did." He remembers the storm, the walk through the snow from the library, the sense of shelter in the near-deserted Union, the chance meeting and all that followed from it. Thanks, Marty, he says to himself. But that line of thought doesn't seem too promising and neither says anything until Dori pulls herself straight. "So," she says brightly, "made up your mind yet about that deal with your father?"

He moves away from her, the last lingering memories of the night of the blizzard and the pleasant feelings associated with it having fled; now they're in the realm of unfinished business and he adjusts his sights. "He said there was no hurry, so I don't need to answer yet but. . . ."

"Yeah?" she encourages him.

"Well, I know about my mother now and that's a hell of a lot more important than whether or not I let myself get involved with my father." Amazing, he thinks, that you can get used to something like that: you think of your mother as someone who's always been there, who'll always be there; and then one day out of the blue you learn that she might possibly have a serious illness from which she could die. It jolts you at first but before you know it it's part of the way you think about her. She could be dead in a matter of months, you recognize, she could be gone forever; and still you go on grading papers, preparing classes, seeing friends, doing the laundry. "I've asked around," he says, "and I guess my father was right. There are a lot of forms the disease can take and it doesn't have to turn out to be that bad. There seems to be reason to hope. And so long as nothing's changed so far. . . ."

"You don't want to get tied up with your father unless you have to?" she suggests.

"I guess. Something like that." Just talking about it has brought up some of the contradictory feelings that first surfaced when Jack Riley was here.

"You're still not sure you know how you feel about his coming back into your life?"

"Yeah," he admits, trying to put into words the discomfort he feels about the situation. "Sometimes it really pisses me off, what he did in the first place, then his showing up here after all those years. Other times I think, from his point of view, he could have just ignored her and he didn't. People aren't just saints and devils, after all." He shakes his head. "But I still can't figure out why he felt he had to come all the way to Chippewa to tell me what he did."

She gives him a sympathetic look. "It's hard to guess what somebody else is thinking, let alone to know what's driving them that they don't even know about."

"I don't know," he goes on. "Maybe part of the problem is just that I have to get used to his being out there, being a player in my life and not just part of some old story. The fact is, I am dealing with him already. I've talked to him, I know where he lives, I can't put him back in the box and lock it. And that's all so strange and different." Never again can he go back to thinking of Jack Riley as simply the Man Who Abandoned Us, the definition of the kind of person you don't want to be. Having talked to this tanned, expensively dressed realtor who'd been a high school charmer from the other side of the tracks, a James Dean before his time, for all Ted knows, a lover and a leaver, a returning GI scarred by war, a wanderer who found himself in the desert, in AA, a man who started a new life and found somebody new to love, a survivor. Ted can only wonder: how much of him is in me?

"I think I can understand that," Dori says. "I mean, it's a tough situation that, thank God, I've never had to deal with. It's got to be hard."

Grateful for her sympathy, he pulls himself back to the moment. "I'd like to think I have some choice in the matter."

She laughs. "Hey, you can't pick your parents."

Ted, suddenly aware that he's been standing the whole time they've been here, goes to the sofa and sits down. Neither of them says anything for a while and at last Dori's eyes cloud over, as if all this serious talk has exhausted her, and she yawns and stretches. Ted looks at her long thin arms, her breasts moving under the white sweater. When she brings down her arms, she takes hold of her elbows and tilts her head in a way that's unique to her. "You know," he says, "we're giving the Youth of America a bad name sitting here and moping like this."

She straightens. "You're right, amigo," she says. "Enough of all this gloom and complexity; let's celebrate the arrival of spring."

"Sure. What did you have in mind? A walk though the arboretum? Do you have an extra pair of snowshoes?"

She cocks her fist at him. "Hey, I've had just about enough of your smart mouth."

He feigns ducking a blow. "OK, OK, I surrender, dear."

"Really, though," she says, "we have to think of something to pull ourselves out of the lower depths." She goes to the brick-and-board bookcase and pulls out a record. "You know this, champ?" she asks him.

It's Samuel Barber's *Knoxville, Summer of 1915*. He shakes his head.

"I forgot what an ignorant clodhopper you are. But look, even you'll like this. It's lovely, in fact. Don't dare say otherwise."

"Hey, you know me: I'm open to everything."

She holds the record, still in its jacket, for a moment, and Ted guesses that she's remembering hearing it some other time, possibly with someone else. "This is sweet and sad . . . and heartbreaking. It'll give us a bit of summer," she adds brightly.

"Is it OK if I unbutton my shirt?" He realizes that he's suddenly, crazily happy to be here with this smart, beautiful woman. Yes, he wants to hear this piece of music that he loves already because she loves it. He loves hearing her talk about it, but at the same time he's anticipating the feel of her bare skin against his, the smell of her hair, the taste of her mouth, of other parts of her, anticipating the breathless words they'll say to each other, their ardor a music of its own. Maybe, just maybe, they can bring time to a stop.

Meanwhile, Dori puts the record on and sits a few feet from him on the sofa. From the piece's dreamy opening measures Ted listens expectantly, already caught up in the music. When the instruments are joined by a voice he senses a meaning before fully grasping the words and he picks up the record jacket, running his eyes over the text sung by the soprano, an excerpt from James Agee's *A Death in the Family*. Here the lost world of childhood is evoked in images from a summer evening long gone: people on porches rocking on their gliders, a horse and buggy passing in the street, the whine of a streetcar going by, a man putting away a garden hose after watering his lawn, the sound of locusts, murmur of talk at evening. The haunting, hypnotic music carries him back to his own boyhood in Cold River as he reads: "One is my mother, and she is good to me, one is my father and he is good to me."

He and Dori are sitting there, silently listening, lost in their own thoughts. "You're right," he says quietly, "I like this." When she doesn't answer, he looks at her. To his surprise, her eyes are filled with tears. He leans toward her and asks gently, "What's the matter?"

Dori smiles through her tears. "You're not that dumb," she says and he knows without her having to say anything that as she listens to this music that nostalgically evokes a vanished summer, Dori is already foreseeing the time when all of this—

Marty in the hospital, the two of them here on her sofa while Bogie watches and the spring fog shrouds the streets of Chippewa—will be part of an equally irretrievable past, that she's already missing this moment, this time in her life. He takes hold of her and clutches her tightly, saying nothing. Listening, the two of them are carried back by the music to a summer evening in the South almost a half-century ago that was once the present before it slipped into the past forever. His hand resting lightly on her shoulder, he feels the ache of that loss too, yet the feeling turns inside out, and from some hidden source he experiences a surge of joyful strength: my God, he thinks, what could be better than this, being here with Dori, listening to this music? True, the world outside is dark and uncertain, true, the two of them are facing a future neither of them can foresee. That future might well bring heartbreak but just now while the music twines around their present emotions—their shared sadness for Marty as well as whatever thoughts of Dori's are hidden from Ted, his own anxiety for his mother, his ambivalence about his father, and, especially, his powerful feelings for Dori—Ted is elated to be alive, he wouldn't change things for the world.

On the night of Ted and Dori's visit to Marty Reindorf, Andrew Kesler is in the basement of the student union, which is surprisingly empty, a fact that tinges his excitement with uneasiness. He's on his guard as he enters the men's room and looks around: apparently he's alone. Disappointed, he goes to the basin and runs water over his clean hands, listening for the sound of somebody else entering the room, but all he hears is the hiss of the water. After a few seconds, he dries his hands with a paper towel, taking his time, and still no one comes. At last he leaves, lingering for a while in the corridor outside before climbing the stairs that bring him back to the main floor. Here he takes up a position in the lobby like someone who's arrived early for a meeting and pointedly looks at his watch several times; then he strolls to the billboard and briefly examines the flyers for upcoming events before dropping into one of the plush chairs near a window where someone has left today's newspaper. He skims it inattentively for a few minutes, then puts it down. Enough time has passed. He goes downstairs once more, taking the paper with him.

In the corridor outside the men's room he leans against the wall, apparently reading the paper, as if he's waiting for someone. His breathing is steady though all his senses are sharpened, and under his surface calm there flows a ripple of anticipation. He studies the details of the tile floor, aware of the passing time—he can't stay too long without attracting attention. He comes alert suddenly when he hears someone on the stairs. In a moment the figure of a large broad-shouldered bald man in a gray overcoat takes shape, his tread heavy and determined as he makes his way down the corridor. Without glancing up from the paper, Andrew sizes up the new arrival and comes to an instant decision: not this one. Even though there's little chance the man is an undercover agent from the police vice squad, there's no indication he's likely to respond to Andrew either, and it's not worth the risk: he'll let the stranger pass. He's relieved when the newcomer walks by the men's room; at least he won't have to worry about being seen loitering there by the man when he leaves. Andrew listens as the echoing footsteps fade, bringing an eerie silence that bristles with the sense of something impending. Is there a reason why it's so quiet tonight? There have been whispered stories and vague warnings lately about a crackdown on homosexuals on campus and people are nervous about the situation, especially after a recent letter to the local paper in which a certain J. Mathers made vague charges about Communists and other unsavory figures being harbored by the university and going on to complain about unspecified "outrages" witnessed by citizens who've come to this rest room. Andrew is already responding to the mental clock that determines how long he can stay here without becoming noticeable when he hears someone else come down the stairs.

More promising this time, he sees at once: the newcomer is a slight man of average height who's wearing a green duffel coat, and he moves with a wary tentativeness—he's looking for somebody too, Andrew guesses. He puts down his newspaper and pulls out a cigarette as the man approaches. "Excuse me," he asks. "Do you have a light?" Though his voice is casual, his heart is racing.

There's always a sliver of a moment when time stops and you realize you're stepping into the dark, unsure of whether there will be anything under your feet. In that interval the man looks at Andrew as if he hasn't understood his question, and it's possible that Andrew has guessed wrong: the stranger might be a policeman prepared to play his role until he's trapped his prey, he may be someone who's unaware of anything more going on than a casual request for a light, he may even be a man who wants what Andrew wants but, suddenly nervous, has decided that discretion is the better part of valor. The moment is fleeting, though: a furtive smile crosses the man's face as he starts toward Andrew and he makes an unconscious gesture, brushing his sandy hair. He looks to be in his late thirties but his rosy cheeks and his clear blue eyes give him a boyish appearance. "Yes, yes, I do," he answers eagerly, fumbling in the pockets of his coat. "Ah, there," he says. "I knew I had them." His voice is soft and cultivated.

An academic, Andrew guesses. Moving more confidently now, he volunteers, "Strange weather we're having."

"Really bizarre," the other man says with a quiet laugh, his eyes making it clear they're talking about more than the weather. "The fog—it's like a movie." He's obviously pleased to have made this contact but his nervousness is evident. When he lights the match and puts it to Andrew's cigarette, his hand is unsteady and Andrew takes it gently with his own good hand. "Thanks," the man says. They look at each other without saying anything and it's clear that a basic arrangement has been agreed upon. Just to make certain there will be no surprises, Andrew brings up his other hand, but if there's any reaction to its difference, the stranger doesn't show it.

The man goes into the rest room and Andrew follows in a few seconds, discarding the paper and his cigarette outside. The stranger regards him silently from the end of a long row of washbasins, he and his reflection looking far away in the metallic fluorescent light. Andrew takes in the scene at a glance: luckily, they seem to be alone for the moment and when the man enters one of the stalls, Andrew follows him. He closes the blue door and the other is upon him at once, kissing him with a wildness that contradicts the earlier image of an innocent boy. Their coats are off now and the man's tongue is on Andrew's ear, his neck, in his mouth, and Andrew is excited by the smell of his hair. "I take it from the rear," the stranger whispers, "if that's all right with you." That's fine with Andrew, who's running his hands under the man's shirt, smelling his delicate cologne, suddenly ravenous. "I have some Vaseline," the man says, his hands on Andrew's belt. He drops to his knees and quickly undoes

Andrew's pants, finding his stiffened cock and taking it in his mouth.

Just then they hear somebody enter and the two of them freeze. Like a figure from Pompeii, Andrew thinks every time this happens, and in the space of a breath he can imagine the direst of consequences: yells, threats, banging on doors, a swarm of police. As it turns out, the newcomer walks quickly to one of the urinals and is gone in less than a minute, after which Andrew and the other man shift positions and resume in earnest. As Andrew drives his cock into the stranger's anus, his partner masturbates, pressing Andrew's smaller hand to his mouth, partially suppressing his moans. When Andrew comes with a muted cry of his own, his cock goes soft and he withdraws it slowly while the other man continues kissing the deformed hand as he brings himself off.

Purged of his need, Andrew is at peace, alive, alone, and the world around him has the clarity of steel. All the smells of this place of stealthy, hurried encounters—sweat, Vaseline, disinfectant, and other odors—rise up, the flavor of a familiar world. Once more he feels the triumph of the successful hunt, the risks run and conquered, another mysterious chance meeting of two strangers in need, disasters averted. Oddly, one part of him is already missing the sense of danger he's just skirted.

The two of them have already gotten themselves together and are washing their hands at the sink when the other man asks, "Would you like to go somewhere for a drink or for coffee? By the way, I'm Michael."

Buoyed by the temporary peace he feels, and remembering the tenderness with which the man kissed his afflicted hand, Andrew agrees, and the two of them go upstairs, where they find themselves an isolated booth. Michael, terse enough during their encounter downstairs, is almost giddy with the need to talk. He's a minister, he tells Andrew, not in Chippewa but in a town some fifteen miles distant. "My congregation is wonderful, they're good people and I hope I serve them well," he says, his eyes pleading his sincerity. He's married to a woman named Marge. They have two children and he loves his family, he insists. As Andrew listens he begins to feel that his impulsive acceptance of this invitation might have been a mistake. "Sometimes, though," Michael says, his voice going quiet, "the need gets too great and I have to do something about it." He shakes his head. "There are times I hate myself for it, I tell myself I can live without it, and then there'll come a moment when it's as if I pick up a scent in the air and all those arguments get overturned." He looks into his coffee. "We're all God's children in the end, though, aren't we?" Andrew says nothing. That phrase has always baffled him: having encountered a number of God's children who showed no hesitation about committing the most savage cruelties, he has no great eagerness to meet their parent.

"Still," Michael goes on, "there's something I get out of this that I don't get from the other parts of my life." He smiles. "I think in some ways it might even make me a better person, a better minister." The sentence ends with a rising inflection, like a question.

Andrew doesn't press him to try to articulate what it is that he gets out of what the two of them did in the men's room; he himself is satisfied with the temporary peace he's achieved. Obviously, the man has a need to talk, to confess without repenting, and Andrew knows he doesn't really expect any response, that it's enough if he listens. The fact is, he doesn't really care about this man's story because just now—and from his own experience, he knows this feeling isn't likely to last very long—he has no arguments with anyone, either on earth or in heaven, and nobody has to justify himself to him. The world is what it is, and at the moment Andrew has no problem accepting that.

"But I'm talking about myself too much," Michael says, interrupting himself. He gives Andrew a boyish smile. "You shouldn't have let me." He can imagine that smile in the pulpit, Michael in his resplendent Sunday vestments reassuring the congregation that everything is all right, that we're all God's children. "But what about you?" he asks. "Obviously," he ventures, "you weren't born here."

"No," Andrew smiles bleakly, "I was born in Poland. In Krakow." He shrugs. What can those syllables possibly mean to this Michael? There's no way Andrew can convey to the man he's just met what it was like growing up in the ancient city with its renowned fourteenth-century university where his father was a professor. He has a sudden image of himself as a schoolboy in short pants playing in the arcade of the Sukiennice, the great market hall. There, with a stick for a sword, he'd take on the roles of great historical figures, dreaming of the heroic things he was going to do one day. Moments later, in the rain-slick courtyard where the tang of coal smoke hung in the damp air, coming upon a flock of pigeons peacefully feeding on the crumbs provided by bird lovers, he might run at them full tilt, just to hear the explosion of their wings as they scattered into the gray skies, only to wonder at bedtime whether this assault on avian peace was something he ought to confess on Saturday. The boy found it comforting to know that, whether or not he was there, every hour on the hour the sound of the *Hejnal* would float above the square from the tower of the basilica of the Virgin Mary, where it was played on a golden trumpet. How could he explain that you could hear it without listening for it, that like everyone around you in the street, you were unconsciously waiting for the moment when the music would stop abruptly at the exact point when, according to the story, the Tartar bowman cut short the trumpeter's warning notes more than seven hundred years earlier? All that was lost, a fairy tale ended, when the gray-clad Germans marched in with an array of weaponry that would have leveled all the Mongol hordes of history. That Krakow, where horse-drawn wagons pulled logs felled from nearby forests, has vanished like Atlantis, though on rare occasions in different parts of the world, a sudden vagrant smell has brought it all back.

Still, as difficult as it might be to communicate that world of his childhood, it would be impossible to make believable what followed. First there was the war, six years on the calendar but lifetimes in the experience of the boy who had to live through it. Horror and evil, miracle and whim and unspeakable things—you could witness all of them before noon. It was a time when the sight of people hanging from lampposts was part of the natural order, when language was used as much

to conceal as to communicate, and the briefest of wordless
exchanges on a streetcorner could fill you with expectation
or terror. In those days you didn't need paintings on church
walls of devils and skeletons, no Christ descending on a cloud
to remind you that each day could easily be your last. And yet
to be alive at the end of it all was no honor to the survivors,
nor was it much of a prize, given what followed. People who'd
holed up in attics and trudged through sewers to stay out of the
clutches of one army were on the move now, fleeing another.
Trying to stay ahead of the advancing Muscovites meant desperately pushing westward through a ruined continent where
the grand boulevards of ancient capitals now looked like the
mouths of old people who had lost all their teeth, not naturally
but by violence, and the devastated countryside was littered
with the bloated corpses of animals and once-treasured pieces
of furniture cannibalized for firewood. On foot, in a cart or, if
you were especially lucky, in the back of a truck, you were part
of a mass of gaunt, stinking fugitives in threadbare clothes who
had lost everything except the secrets that surfaced only in their
dreams. To have made your way from one foul-smelling refugee
camp to another, surrounded by laments voiced in a dozen languages, having learned to expect nothing, and then to be found
in that hell by your sister—this is a story that can't be told to
strangers over cigarettes and coffee.

"This must be so different," Michael says sympathetically.

Andrew nods. Yes, it's different, he wants to say; you could
never know how different.

"Do you miss it?" Michael asks. "You must have memories."
There's a look of expectancy on his face.

Andrew shrugs. He doesn't dislike this man, who after all
shared something with him in that stall where they appeased
their mutual hungers—for all Andrew knows, he serves his congregation well; and he feels obliged to tell him something, if
only for the sake of politeness. "The last summer before the
war," he says, remembering those days, "my parents took us
to the lake country for our vacation." Michael nods encouragingly. "I was eleven, my sister Magda was sixteen," Andrew tells

him. Of course his parents knew, everyone knew, that war was approaching and that everything they'd known was likely to be coming to an end. It's possible they were offering this trip as a kind of carefully composed memory they wanted their children to have, to savor during the dark days ahead. "We lived in a large rustic cottage on one of the lakes and we hiked, swam and sometimes fished, or just sat in the shade outdoors reading. There were two hammocks," he adds, remembering the feel of being suspended between two trees, smelling the pine needles below, hearing the sigh of the branches above. Our little Copernicus, his mother called him, since at the time Andrew was fascinated by astronomy. He'd brought his telescope from the city and with the clear country air as a medium, he gloried in tracing the shadowy craters of the moon. "There was a town nearby and my sister and I would go there together: Magda would promenade before the gawking boys and I'd run off by myself. I'd already felt sexual stirrings and I was eager to experiment in this strange place where nobody knew me." He stops, thinking of his parents, the botany professor and the doctor who'd achieved a comfortable life with lively and talented friends like themselves, festive dinners and spontaneous entertainments when the furniture was pushed back amid laughter and clinking glasses to make way for dancing, charades, classical music and cabaret tunes on the piano. "We're going to the lakes," they told Pan Malborzynski, the mailman who trimmed his mustache so he could look like Marshal Pilszudski. He must have known as well as they did what was about to happen, though it isn't likely that any of them could have imagined the full horror of what was to follow.

"Did you get a chance to experiment?" Michael asks with a discreet smile.

"It was mostly fantasy." It's all the man needs to know. Though Andrew did meet a tall, dark boy with large eyes and long lashes named Ryszard, who lived at the resort year-round. Ryszard knew all about the flora and the fauna of the area. The two boys were shy around each other but on the last day of Andrew's stay there Ryszard suggested that the two of them go exploring in his rowboat. In his country accent, he told Andrew about a secret place he knew. A strong oarsman, he took them across the tranquil lake to the marshy shore on the other side. There, hidden among the tall reeds, they pushed through the shallow water until a flooded forest of dead gray trees came into view. As they glided quietly toward this secluded place Andrew became aware of vivid spots of white against the background of gray and green: gradually he saw that they'd come upon a haven where dozens of white herons were gathered in the marshy water and in the trees. All he could hear was the hiss of their boat gliding as it made its way through the weed-choked water. The sight of these thin-legged creatures with their long slender necks and pointed bills made Andrew breathless—for some reason they made him think of Egypt!—and when he whispered an exclamation of wonder, Ryszard took his hand. Warmed by the sun, the two of them just watched those regal birds. Then without any transition they were running their hands over each other's bodies, drawn to the places where, under their clothing, their sexual excitement was evident. Ryszard smiled and asked Andrew how he liked this secret spot of his and Andrew said he liked it very much. They did no more than that and in a short while they started back. Rowing across the peaceful lake, Andrew heard music coming from one of the cottages, a popular song of the time. "Thanks," he said, knowing he would always remember the secret place where the tall white birds stood in the water and in the trees, silent and inscrutable as the mind of God. The memory of that afternoon has come to him with almost unbearable intensity a number of times since in the unlikeliest of places, and he remembers it now. He remembers too that Ryszard and he spoke about writing each other, about seeing each other next year, though in a few weeks all such promises were obsolete. Of course it's very likely that Ryszard didn't survive the war.

Oddly, when he told Magda about seeing the birds in that secret place, he was sure she'd guessed all the rest of it.

"And how . . ." Michael begins hesitantly, "what happened to your hand?"

"I was born that way," Andrew's answer is brisk. He remembers the man's putting his fingers in his mouth, kissing the hand. He means well, no doubt, but Andrew doesn't make a practice of talking about his physical situation.

"I'm sorry," Michael says, sensing something. "I didn't mean. . . ."

"It's nothing," Andrew waves the apology away with his good hand. Never feel ashamed of that hand, Dieter told him. You're a beautiful boy, you're clever, you're superior in every way to many people who are whole. Don't ever be ashamed of it. One could only wonder what kind of future he could have been imagining for Andrew, for himself, since it had become obvious before very long that, whatever destruction the Germans had wrought on their way eastward would be matched and outdone by their enemy as it pushed westward, an aroused and bloodied enemy in no mood for mercy. Andrew has no way of knowing what happened to Dieter but, given the ferocity of the Russians and their bitter memory of what they'd suffered, the best he can hope for is that his protector didn't survive the war either.

Already Andrew can feel the distance growing between himself and the man who shared a stall with him. In a minute Michael will be saying he has to go. Back to his wife and his congregation, back to God's children. It's only to be expected, of course, though the man's passing out of Andrew's life raises once more the question of what he himself is going back to. Chippewa, Chippewa—such a long way from Krakow, an even longer way from that place along the shore of a Polish lake where he and a country boy saw those silent white birds. He has to protect himself against falling into despair. It's easy to believe that life is nothing more than a series of moves, that to live is to move, but there are times when Andrew gets tired. The last time he talked to Morelli he got the distinct impression that Chippewa was going to be the last place, that all this wandering was going to come to an end here. How strange and unbelievable; it's even amusing from some perspectives. But Andrew can accept it. After all, everything has to end somewhere.

Spring has finally come to Chippewa. For two days a soft, persistent drizzle falls from the gray skies that cover the town: water pours from rainspouts, there are puddles everywhere, and trees sag under the weight of wet young foliage. Then the clouds move off and the world is flooded with sunlight: umbrellas snap shut, glazed leaves shine; and in a few hours the pavement is dry, a familiar warmth has returned, insects are in the air, and the citizens of Chippewa are already used to this new way of being in the world. Windows are pushed open and household sounds find their way into the street, where people are in no hurry to get indoors, or to get anywhere, for that matter. Heavy coats gone, they delight in the mild air, the lacy fringe of green on the trees, the bright splashes of forsythia; they linger outdoors. On campus, dogs gambol, clusters of pale students sprawl shortsleeved on the grass, and even a trim, dark-clad quartet from the Navy ROTC loiters about wistfully, watching a pink frisbee float among the elms.

For Ted, though, the change of season is a mixed blessing. The knowledge that Dori will be leaving soon has put strains on their relationship. When they're in bed together and he feels the heave of her warm flesh beneath his hands, he doesn't believe in time and he's sure that she doesn't either. There are countless small moments—she looks up at him over a cigarette she's lighting and gives him a smile meant for him alone; he takes her hand for no reason and she squeezes his in return; the two of them suddenly stop in the middle of an ardent discussion, about politics, literature or favorite movies, and just look at each other—when he can believe that a wise and compassionate

168

deity has searched the planet to provide each of them with a soul mate. Still, there are times when for no obvious reason one or the other is likely to withdraw, shutting the other out. Ted can find himself suddenly plunged into a memory of Cold River, caught up in a dense web of connections: to his mother, with all the love and anxiety he feels toward her as well as the sense of hurt that she hasn't confided in him about the state of her health; to Jack Riley, the father who chose not to be a father and who's now returned, however fitfully; to his own vague dreams as a kid—to be a saint, to be a ballplayer, to live some kind of worthwhile life—and it seems to him that no one, not even Dori, can be part of that story. For her part, Dori too has gone silent at times, no doubt carried along similar paths as she travels through her own history, the California girlhood, the blacklisted parents, Elliott, other people and events unknown to Ted, her own deepest dreams, all of them shadowed by her imminent departure from Chippewa.

One element that has begun to complicate their relationship lately isn't so mysterious. Dori has been closely following the lunch counter sit-ins in the South and her initial excitement about these challenges to Southern racism quickly turned to anger at the increasing violence the Negro students have encountered. In the aftermath, she's felt nothing but frustration about the response to the situation in Chippewa. She persuaded Ted to come with her to a rally on campus in support of the sit-ins last week and was appalled at the low turnout and the general lack of enthusiasm among the handful of people who showed up. There were a few beards, a few women with dark stockings, a few Negroes and a clergyman or two, as well as a handful of hecklers. There were speeches, singing and a petition, and then people dispersed in small groups. "I've seen more passion at a bake sale," Dori said when it was over. When Ted suggested that the Negro students in the South were likely to continue their efforts in spite of Chippewa's tepid response, her eyes burned with indignation. "Of course they will. At least I hope they will. But this is shameful. We should be doing something." Things were tense between them for a time after that and Ted was angry, feeling she'd lumped him in with the yokels of Chippewa. "Hey," she said when her temper cooled, "I wasn't talking about you. At least you came to that rally."

Today, though, he has nothing more elevated on his agenda than a plan for a little mindless springtime pleasure: he and Dori are going to a party. A national magazine is sponsoring a literary festival on campus, a coup for the university in general and the English department in particular, however uneasy the scholars in the department might be with the unruly types who've been brought to the campus. Ted and Dori were among the standing-room-only crowd that jammed the auditorium last night for the festival's main public attraction, a symposium in which six more or less well-known fiction writers exchanged ideas. The fact that one of them, Ed Leveque, attired in his trademark dirty lumberjack shirt, was obviously drunk and got into a profanity-laced shouting match with the princely C.K. Atherton, made the event all the more sensational. Though campus cynics have suggested the whole thing had been staged, that imbroglio, it turned out, was just the prelude. Ever since the festival had been announced, some of the younger faculty had competed savagely to host parties for the writers (an all the more attractive prospect since the magazine was paying for the liquor) and Ed Hall, a rising star, was one of the lucky ones, lucky, that is, until an unruly guest (it hasn't yet been established that he was one of the writers) punctuated a literary point with an emphatic sweep of his arm that knocked over a breakfront containing the Halls's treasured Lowenstofft china, destroying a great deal of it, according to reports. All this on the first night of the festival. Though Ted and Dori weren't at that party, they've been invited to one tonight that's being given by Dan Seeley, a grad student neither of them likes much. Inevitably, it's been rumored that a writer or two from the festival may drop by.

Dan Seeley is distantly related to the fabulously wealthy meat-packing Seeleys of Chicago, and he does nothing to discourage the connection, but his own humbler branch of the

family is by no means poor. Dan, who drives an MG, is boyishly
handsome and cultivates a carefully casual but expensive style.
No intellectual powerhouse, it's known that he has his sights
set on teaching in a prep school. He's a favorite of his profes-
sors at the university, treating them with elaborate deference
and turning in all his work on time. His most annoying quality,
as far as Ted is concerned, is that this man already blessed with
money and good looks seems to travel under an especially lucky
star. He has no trouble finding attractive women, for one thing,
though it's hard to imagine any of them making a dent in his nar-
cissism. Even more irritating to his peers, Dan recently zeroed
in on his dissertation subject, Nathanael West, a writer who
doesn't excite him particularly but one who had the good grace
to die young and leave a small, tidy body of work; and he got
Tom Schmidt as his director, a man not likely to challenge him.
As if that weren't enough, everybody raves about Dan's great
apartment, which takes up the entire second floor of a classic
brick building in the heart of Chippewa's downtown. Tonight,
as Ted and Dori make their way to the party, they can hear the
noise of the crowd from the bottom of the steep stairs. "If he has
a writer there, it's going to be hard to find him," Dori says.

"Hey, Dori, hey, Ted," a beaming Dan Seeley shouts at them
though they're only a couple of feet away. He's wearing a blazer
and a pink shirt open at the neck, a casual touch that doesn't
appreciably dampen the Jay Gatsby persona he's obviously
chosen for the evening. Behind him is an avalanche of people
trying to make themselves heard. "Good to see you, good to see
you." Dan pats Ted on the back and shakes his head at Dori,
who's wearing a simple but dazzling black dress. "You're looking
more gorgeous than ever, Miss Hollywood. Hey, you guys know
the drill: drop your coats in any of the bedrooms, put your beer
in the refrigerator. It's a great night, isn't it?"

As they make their way toward the back of the apartment
they pick up snatches of music and explosions of laughter. The
crowd is mostly a mix of grad students and faculty, with more
than a few faces Ted has never seen, but there's no visible writer
yet. In the smoky living room a clutch of people is gathered near

the bay window that looks onto University Street, the faces of
some of them eerily tinged with red from the neon sign outside.
Small groups are jammed into all the room's corners; cigarettes,
bottles and glasses move in random patterns as people make
conversational points and others reach for bowls of potato chips
or plates of crackers and cheese. Passing through, Ted catches
sight of a solitary guy in horn-rimmed glasses looking thought-
fully at his beer bottle and is momentarily reminded of Marty.
"But no," he hears, "no no no." Madeleine Crecy, a red-haired
woman of a certain age who teaches French, is waving her cigarette like a baton while a trio of dark-suited young men looks on
reverently. A burst of applause erupts somewhere behind them
and Dan Seeley's voice sings out another greeting. Ted and Dori
push their way through the crowd in the dining room, where a
man with a strenuously impassive expression is pounding on
the table as if it's a bongo drum and a woman in a red dress
screams, "Harold? It can't be Harold." A pair of deadly serious
pipe-smokers is engaged in what seems like a staring match
while a fat man who resembles one of Ted's uncles looks on
with open boredom. People keep coming in and out of the spa-
cious kitchen, which is the nerve center for food and drink, and
some of the partygoers have even spilled into the bedrooms,
of which the apartment has three. For those who find it too
crowded inside, there's always Dan's back porch, where some
souls have gathered to enjoy the spring night.

"A buck to the first of us to spot the writer," Dori says.

"You're on," Ted answers just before Wally Wright emerges
from the crowd, his eyes glazed, his signature bow tie drooping.
"Quite a party, huh?" he declares. "Been here long?"

"We just got here. You been here long?"

A wan smile. "I don't really know."

A thin, ghostly man sidles up to Dori. It's Rob Selkirk,
an English grad student. Rob, who has the cheekbones of an
Indian, is a smooth homosexual from the wilds of Colorado.
"Dori Green," he purrs, "what's a disreputable trollop like you
doing in such company?" The dry laugh that follows comes in
clearly articulated segments like the muffled blows of an axe.

"This, er, event," he arches his brows, "might well be sponsored by the local Methodists. Really, dear, you must guard your reputation." He kisses her hand. "Ted," he says, "it's useless to try to reform her. She's too far gone. God," he adds in a version of sotto voce adapted to the noisy environment, "our host is practically salivating at the prospect of having a third-rate writer drop by."

"Any sightings?" Dori asks.

"Not yet. What he ought to do is hire an actor to play some minor Beat poet. Who'd know? By the way, have you seen what he's done to the bathroom?"

Dori shakes her head. "We just got here."

"I won't reveal a thing," he says, as if barely able to suppress his shock. "But prepare yourself."

And so it starts, as so many parties do, and proceeds in a familiar enough way. There are times when the clamor subsides and you can actually hear some music, and then a fresh infusion of people raises the volume. Ted and Dori are together for a time, they're apart for a time, the drinking continues, the smoke is thicker. Ted is on the back porch for a few minutes listening to someone argue about God, Dori is in a corner of the kitchen talking intensely to a Negro; then Dori is on the porch and Ted is talking to the Negro.

After a while the beer, the smoke, the cascade of sound produce a hypnotic effect and Ted is content to take it all in passively, looking on, occasionally nodding or giving monosyllabic responses, contributing little more than his most distant attention. He listens as various people near him talk about movies, nuclear war, campus gossip, the race for the Democratic nomination. "Symington," a tall long-jawed man asserts passionately. "If the Democrats have any sense we'll be calling him President Symington next year." Others deliver judgments on their host: "Isn't he great?" "Isn't he a jerk?" "What do you think he spent on this party?" They exchange comments about last night's symposium and speculate about the possibilities of a writer showing up tonight. "They say Mrs. Hall is devastated," someone reports. "They say that china was in the family for generations." Another sneers: "There wasn't an original idea expressed in that entire symposium; it was all day-old bread."

Ted remembers when he had a miserable cold during the last storm of the winter and stayed in bed all day. Dori braved the driving snow to bring him some chicken soup. The memory warms him now and when he spots her he walks over to her. "Hey, sweetie," he says, "I love you."

She's holding a bottle of beer and there's a sheen of sweat on her forehead. "I love you too," she answers, brushing up against him.

"At least we're clear about that," he says.

"We've always been clear about that, haven't we?" She looks into the crowd. "Spot any writers yet?"

"Not yet." He pulls her lazily to him, his lips brushing her hair. "Mm," he hums, "you're looking good enough to eat. And I'll remember this time to chew slowly."

She rolls her eyes. "You seem to be in a very good mood."

"Feeling no pain," he declares. "Meet anyone interesting?"

"I'll let you know the minute I do."

"Hey," he says, "I feel good. Real good. I feel strong; I can survive anything."

She punches him softly on the arm. "That's basically the Ted Riley I know."

"It's like a mystical experience," he says. "I have no quarrels with the universe tonight."

"Hey, don't go turning weird on me."

"No, child; go now and find a writer." He holds up a hand like Dave Garroway signaling peace.

"All right," she says, but as she's about to leave she turns back and plants a quick, hungry kiss on his mouth. "You . . . " she says and goes off.

Seconds later Rob Selkirk is back. "Rob, still here? I thought for sure this affair would have bored you by now."

Rob gives him a Cheshire cat grin. "Oh, but it does. Still, you never know what will turn up, do you?" he says. "Even in dreary Chippewa one must live in hope." Ted has a sudden thought of Andrew Kesler and considers asking Rob if he knows him but decides that just because they're both homosexuals doesn't necessarily mean they're acquainted with each other. Besides, it's hard to visualize that particular pair together. "Got to run," Rob says. "New people are still showing up."

Once more Ted lets himself drift into a passive attitude. He listens as partygoers discuss whether the new arrival in a black turtleneck is David Metzger, the biting satirist of New York Jewish life. That hope is punctured when somebody identifies the man as Dan Seeley's dentist.

"Did you see that commie demonstration the other day?" a man with a gray crewcut is saying to someone Ted can't see. "Civil rights, my ass; they're nothing but commie sympathizers. I'd like to turn a few ROTC boys loose on them." Ted is glad Dori isn't nearby; she might decide she's hearing the true voice of Chippewa.

He moves away. He checks his watch: it's getting late. No writer is going to show, he's sure. Next time Dori comes by he'll suggest they leave. He's managed to find himself a relatively peaceful eddy in the hallway near one of the bedrooms when he hears someone say his name. He doesn't immediately recognize the voice but when he turns he finds himself facing Sam Morelli. The man's appearance is so unexpected that it startles him and for a moment he can't say anything. There's the same tweed jacket, the sturdy build, the mustache, the unlit cigar, though somehow in this setting the man seems more weighty. Why the hell should Sam Morelli show up here? Ted wonders. "Some party, huh?" Morelli says.

"Yeah," Ted answers guardedly.

"You could lose a fully equipped army platoon in this crowd," Morelli declares with a smile that doesn't reach his eyes. He extends his hand and Ted takes it. "Keeping out of trouble?" the older man asks.

"I'm trying." Ted's earlier passivity is gone and he's suddenly clear, focussed, impatient to be through with these banal preliminaries, as if he and this man haven't met by chance but are here to settle some prearranged business.

"Hey," Morelli suggests, "why don't we step out of here, get to someplace that isn't so loud?" He gestures toward the nearby bedroom, which is empty. "Well," he says in the comparative quiet, "thought any more about that job?"

"I haven't had time," Ted answers. The bed is hidden under a pile of coats and purses—what a great opportunity for a thief, Ted thinks. "Listen," he says, recognizing what it is he wants to find out from this man, "why did you give my name to Andrew Kesler?"

Morelli frowns at the mention of the name. "He hasn't done anything crazy, has he?"

Ted shrugs. "What's crazy? But really, I'd like to know, why me?"

Morelli moves the cigar around in his mouth before responding. "Well, you got a good recommendation from Eerdman, I asked around. Not everyone would be able to put up with Andrew's act."

"His act?"

"Well, with Andrew." He shakes his head. "He's a handful, as you well know."

The mysterious Morelli, who presumably has contacts in the government, and the flamboyant Kesler seem an odd match. "What I can't figure out," Ted says, "is what you have to do with him."

Morelli frowns again, his eyes backing away. "I don't really have anything to do with Andrew." He pauses before going on. "He was kind of handed to me. We have a kind of obligation to him."

"Obligation?" Ted doesn't ask who "we" might be. He can't believe that Kesler is working for the CIA or any other government agency.

"It's a complicated thing," Morelli offers.

Ted shakes his head. An obligation seems to imply services rendered. But Kesler? "He doesn't seem very . . . stable."

"No," Morelli agrees with a frown.

"If you'll excuse my putting it this way," Ted pushes, "he's kind of a loose cannon."

Morelli nods. "You said it, not me. But, yeah, that would describe him, all right. Look," he sighs wearily, "I only know parts of his story. It's not a pretty one, that's for sure." He pauses a while as if considering whether he wants to disclose any further information. "I thought it might help him out a bit in Chippewa," he says at last, "if he had some contact with a . . . normal person."

"And I'm that normal guy?"

Morelli smiles. "Yeah, normal enough."

Ted isn't sure whether he should feel flattered or offended. "Well, anyway," he says, "I think Kesler may be cracking up. He said some things about his sister that, well. . . ."

"Ah," Morelli says, "his sister's really the one we owe." The noise of the party fills the momentary silence. "She came to us right after the war," he goes on, his tone sober, expository, "when she wanted to find Andrew. We gave her some assistance." He pauses again as Ted adds this to what he knows of Kesler's story. "She agreed to do some work for us. There was no coercion, you understand, everything was aboveboard." After a moment, he says, "But she was a casualty." Ted nods sympathetically and Morelli adds, "By all accounts she was a hell of a woman."

Ted is trying to keep the various parts of the story he knows in place. "And so you're helping Andrew because of his sister?" he ventures. "Just how are you helping him?"

Morelli's eyes are evasive. "We get him situations."

"Like Chippewa?" Ted asks. "This seems like just about the worst place in the world for him."

Morelli bristles. "Believe me, he's better off here than he'd be back there."

Ted is curious. "You mean he's a wanted man or something?"

"Look," Morelli says, "everybody back there's wanted for something. You should see some of the Kraut scientists we scooped up before the Russians could get to them. Not exactly Francis of Assisi and his pals." Ted has no response to that and Morelli continues. "Like I said, we have a kind of obligation to Andrew." Then he adds darkly, "But it isn't an unlimited obligation."

As Ted considers a response to this ominous declaration, the sounds outside the bedroom change dramatically: there's a sudden quieting, like a collective intake of breath; then there's a scream, followed by loud, urgent voices that seem to be issuing orders. Morelli's already outside the room and Ted follows. "What's going on?" he asks the first person he encounters.

"I don't know. Something in the front of the apartment. A couple of guys just told everyone to keep calm."

Out in the midst of the party, it's clear that everything has changed: the manic, nervous excitement of minutes ago has been replaced by a buzz of uncertainty, an anxious restlessness. Everybody is asking questions and it doesn't seem as if anyone has answers. Ted is part of a wave pushing toward the front of the apartment but those already there show no inclination to yield. "What is it? What's going on?" people shout, their voices rising. "I don't know," others answer. Ted is in a sudden panic. Something has happened, most likely something bad, he's sure, and he has to find out what it is. His first thought was that, for whatever reason, the cops had raided the place, but now he just wants to make sure that Dori is all right. In spite of the resistance, Morelli has managed to push his way far ahead and Ted tries vainly to follow in his wake.

"What happened?" he asks again.

"Somebody fell down the steps," a woman tells him and he goes cold with a sudden vision of Dori lying in a heap at the bottom of the steep stairway. At the front of the apartment a flustered Dan Seeley has climbed into the bay window and is addressing the crowd. "Everything's going to be all right," he assures them. "Just stay back. Everything's being taken care of." One half of Dan's glistening face is white with terror, the other is flecked with red from the sign outside. A voice is shouting authoritatively, "Let me through, let me through," and Ted sees Morelli disappear down the stairs.

"Ted." To his great relief, Dori is beside him. She's white-faced: it's clear she was as concerned as he was. "Thank God, you're OK." He puts his arm around her and buries his face in her hair. Since the partygoers have quieted, music is audible, a snatch of Vaughan Monroe's "Ghost Riders in the Sky." Lost in the fragrance of her hair, he remembers a high school football game played at night when that song came eerily from a small plane flying above. Meanwhile, Dan Seeley, down at floor level now, is trying to reassure his guests but a mood of apprehension has settled over the gathering and a couple of them have already started for the bedroom where the coats are. Ted hears Morelli's voice calling from the stairwell: "Has anyone called an ambulance?"

"Do you know what happened?" Ted asks Dori.

"Someone fell, I guess."

"They said it's one of the writers," a man near them volunteers. As Dan Seeley continues to try to salvage his party, urging people to enjoy themselves but cautioning them to keep back from the stairs, Ted can't help thinking about Morelli, who in the blink of an eye seems to have taken charge of the situation and has been out of sight since then. At last someone at the window shouts, "There's the ambulance" and everyone hears the siren, then the hurried footsteps of the ambulance crew racing up the stairs; but it turns out that Morelli and the victim are already gone and Dan Seeley has to try to explain the situation to the ambulance crew. At this point more than a few of the guests have started to leave, in spite of Dan's pleading. Ted lingers, thinking he might yet find something out from Morelli, who'd at least be expected to come back for his coat; but it doesn't take him long to conclude that the man might not return tonight. Meanwhile, the party continues in a subdued fashion, peopled mostly by those who hope to learn more about what happened on the stairs, and the few who know something eagerly repeat their sparse information to others.

With the population in the apartment thinned out, there's an air of a wake about the place and the people who are still there are gathered in small clumps talking in lowered voices. As information is pieced together it's learned that the victim was Ed Leveque, so that technically Dan can say a writer came to his party. Apparently drunk, Leveque made it almost to the top of the stairs before tumbling. According to those who got a look, there was a lot of blood, a fact confirmed for everyone who comes down those steps afterward. In some freak fashion Leveque managed to cut his arm and from the look of it, he hit an artery. Morelli recognized the gravity of the situation at once and made a tourniquet of his belt, flagging down a passing car and accompanying the writer to the hospital, from which he called Dan to tell him that the doctors got to the writer before he'd lost too much blood but that there was some breakage in the arm and wrist and that Leveque is likely to be in the hospital for a few days. Morelli showed great presence of mind, everyone agrees.

"I thought it was you," Ted tells Dori later in her bedroom. He remembers vividly the image of her twisted body at the bottom of the stairs. It made no sense but for a moment he was convinced of it. "I was in a complete panic for a while."

"And I thought it was you." Her cigarette glows and a pale spume of smoke floats on the dark air.

"Really?" he asks.

"Really."

A few seconds pass. "What a couple of alarmists we are."

"We're just children of our time," she says.

He looks at the dark space on the wall occupied by the picture of the California mission and the lemon grove. "Is that what we are?"

A steady spring rain has been falling all day. At the university the black elms sag under the weight of it, lawns are saturated, the paved walks are slick. Glistening umbrellas move about the campus like mushrooms on legs, here and there an intrepid bicyclist covered in plastic makes his hissing passage through a puddle. When Andrew occasionally peers out one of the library's windows, he sees nothing to tempt him to leave his place of work, and he returns to his desk with a sigh. The hours have moved at such a dreary pace today that he'd almost welcome some petty sniping from Miss Eyre; but the chief cataloger has been showing a delegation from the Philippines around the library and she's been too flustered to pay any attention to her department. Andrew is grateful for that— after all, he's told himself countless times that all he asks for here is a little peace. Yet peace by itself isn't enough to keep back a familiar gnawing emptiness. The available social distractions have been short-lived this afternoon. He's exchanged arch pleasantries with Charles Cross and Ned Hanover, listened to Bill Tuttle ecstasize again over *The Alexandria Quartet,* and heard a piece of gossip from Gordon Wiley that seemed to contradict something he'd said a week ago. All those encounters were distant, as if seen through the wrong end of a telescope; but where would he be looking from? When Mary Ann, one of the student interns who's taking a course in Political Science, asked Andrew what he thought would have happened if the Poles had supported the Hungarians in 1956, he told her truthfully that he didn't know; communist Poland was a foreign country to him.

It might have been that that had got him thinking, or not thinking so much as leaving himself open to images of the life, or lives, he left behind on that other continent. Though maybe it's just the relentless rain, a dangerous inducement to self-pity. In this weather it's all too easy to let yourself drift, to dwell on unanswerable questions about how different things would have been if there had been no war. After all, as the son of an honored professor and one of Krakow's most successful physicians Andrew had a right to certain expectations. But of course there was a war, the war was all but inevitable and only fools would have thought otherwise, though it's hard to overestimate people's capacity for hope in the face of all evidence. Hadn't he himself, even in the early days of the occupation, when the Germans already owned the city's streets, wanted to believe those adults who kept declaring, albeit in lowered voices, that once the French and English came to the defense of Poland its current nightmare would be over? As the motorcycles with their sidecars roared arrogantly over the ancient cobblestones, fouling the air with their exhaust, more than a few of the bystanders looked on silently, already tasting the vindication that would come when these helmeted usurpers were finally driven out. But those dreams, nourished in that bleak autumn, only lasted into the spring. After France fell, the darkness that covered Poland became thicker, more suffocating, and the boy who'd lost his parents found it harder to believe they were ever likely to return.

The muted clatter of typewriters and the murmur of voices brings Andrew back to the spot on the globe he now occupies. In this high-ceilinged room lit by fluorescent light more than a dozen people are at work: Lorraine Musso keeps nodding, a phone to her ear, eager to please anyone who might be on the other end of the line; Lloyd Puller is bent intently over a magnifying glass, looking for all the world like Sherlock Holmes on the verge of thwarting a master criminal; and Gladys Edes is at the card catalog as usual, a busy squirrel gathering nuts for the long winter. Desks are covered with papers, some of them stacked neatly in wire baskets, others scattered promiscuously about. Wheeled wooden carts standing beside those desks hold printed materials that are either to be cataloged or to be sent to some other department, ultimately to reside in the stacks on the upper floors or in one of the university's other libraries. Everything has a destination and a purpose, though before the day is over, Ned Hanover will have a tantrum about a missing document and Bill Tuttle will take offense at something Ned says to him. Jim Palazolla, the part-timer who's made it known that he's working on a novel, will shake his head and take note. Watching the process at work, carried out by people with so many quirks and peculiarities, one marvels that anything gets done at all; and yet in the end, the system is rational and orderly, even humane. For all that he's an outsider here, Andrew knows that the world he inhabits is heaven compared to either of the uncompromising systems imposed on his native land by the Germans and more recently by the Russians. So he's well aware that he should thank his lucky stars instead of complaining, just as he knows that there's no point in speculating about what might have been: what happened happened. Of course, a familiar voice reminds him, it's just as possible he'd have been miserable there, war or no war.

He finds himself thinking of Dieter—what an unlikely place this would be for him. Chippewa. What was it he said? We can't choose the time we're born in; we can only try to make the best of it. Slender, elegant and playful as he was, Dieter had a soldier's stoicism. Once again Andrew can only wish that that stoicism wasn't tested beyond its limits in those terrible final days by the avenging Muscovites.

Somehow time passes, as it always does, and the work day is over at last. Since there's been no improvement in the weather, Andrew prepares to face the rain. The sodden landscape makes the prospect of returning to his apartment even less appealing than usual and he looks forward to the brief interlude of eating out. Earlier in the day, Ned and Charles hinted at an invitation to join them but he wasn't interested. It's not that he particularly wants to be alone, but he's had enough of the library. Also, he knows himself well enough to understand that the vaguely distracted mood that's come upon him today is something he can't control; it's simply an episode that has to be gotten through, and his co-workers would hardly be able to help him with that.

He makes his way to the building's vestibule, where a dozen people are gathered before the heavy glass doors, buttoning up their raincoats, readying their umbrellas or just standing there looking into the rain, reluctant to leave the warm, dry confines of the library; and there he literally bumps into Ted Riley who, preoccupied with his umbrella, isn't looking as he steps into Andrew's path.

"Sorry," Ted apologizes before he realizes it's Andrew. "Oh, hi," he says when it dawns on him. "Hey, Andrew. Sorry." He stands there holding the umbrella, looking somehow lost.

"It's nothing," Andrew brushes away the apology. To his surprise, he's actually happy to see Ted.

"Some weather, huh?" Ted looks into the rain and shakes his head. "I don't know." There's an odd, distracted note to his voice and he seems subdued. It's unusual to see this normally cheerful and balanced young American so obviously at sea.

"I hoped it would have stopped by now," Andrew says as people, singly and in pairs, launch themselves into the wet world outside. Suddenly inspired, he ventures, "I was going to the Old Heidelberg for dinner. Would you like to join me?"

Ted glances up from his umbrella, still seemingly unsure he wants to open it, and initially he makes no response to Andrew's offer. "Well, " he concedes after a few seconds, "I happen to be free this evening. Sure." The acceptance has an unmistakable air of fatalism about it and Andrew can only guess that he's run into Ted in the midst of some emotional turmoil. Given his age, in all likelihood there's an affair of the heart at the bottom of all this. Andrew remembers his encounter at the Lodge with Ted and the dark-haired woman whose name he can't remember. Of course, as Dieter used to say with just enough irony to allow himself such a sentimental utterance, how would we know we had hearts if we didn't feel them breaking? "Yeah," Ted follows up more enthusiastically. "Yeah, thanks." Andrew is aware that he may be letting himself in for a bout of youthful *Weltschmerz*; but at least that's preferable to what he'd get from his colleagues.

The Old Heidelberg is a welcome refuge from the wet streets of Chippewa and when Ted suggests they get a pitcher of beer before ordering, Andrew agrees. The eagerness with which the American takes his first long swallow strengthens Andrew's earlier notion about the man's state of mind: like many another lost soul, he's no doubt hoping that drink will make his inner sorrows more bearable. Oddly, Andrew is sympathetic toward Ted and his problems, whatever they may be. Of course he's another privileged American, innocent of most of the rest of the world, but he's been generous to Andrew and Andrew understands that there are times when the mere physical proximity of another person is some solace against the world's indifference to our hurt. At any rate, given his own mood today, this is certainly better than being alone in his apartment.

The beer seems to have lifted Ted's spirits. "Did you hear about the writer, Ed Leveque, and what happened to him last week?" he asks, a propos of nothing.

Andrew nods. How could a story like that not be current all over Chippewa?

"I was at that party," Ted says.

"Were you?"

"I didn't see him fall or anything," Ted says. His eyes narrow. "By the way, did you know Sam Morelli was the one who got him to the hospital?"

"No, I didn't." The mention of Morelli brings a sense of alertness, as it always does. Is Ted going to say more about Morelli? he wonders. It's hard to believe that his name has come up by accident.

Ted takes another swallow of beer and seems to be considering where to go with his story. After a moment he shakes his head and puts his glass to the table. His eyes are clear, guarded. Maybe he hasn't drunk enough to push this subject.

"Sam Morelli is very resourceful," Andrew suggests neutrally.

But the waiter arrives just then and both of them order the schnitzel. After the man leaves it's apparent that if Ted was interested in talking further about Morelli, he's changed his mind. "They say the rain will stop tomorrow," he says.

"And not a day too soon, as far as I'm concerned." Andrew feels a twinge of regret: he was surprisingly eager to venture into a discussion of Sam Morelli.

But Ted has moved off in another direction. "When I was a kid," he says, "I used to love these springtime rains. I'd splash in all the puddles until my mother was afraid I'd catch my death."

"Did you grow up here?" Andrew asks. He's already conceded that there will be no return to the earlier topic.

Ted shakes his head. "No, I lived in a little town called Cold River, a hundred and fifty miles west of here."

"Cold River. That's not a very pretty name for a town."

"Oh, it's a pretty place, though. And I don't even think the river is so cold. I think some of the earlier settlers may have been oversensitive."

Andrew considers the unlikely notion. "A town of esthetes, then?"

Ted laughs. "The last one must have left a century ago. Leaving only shoe salesmen and pharmacists."

"Or is it that you're the last one?" Andrew suggests, touched by the exoticism of a small town in the American Midwest. He has a dim memory of *Huckleberry Finn*. "Tell me," he asks, "did you have a happy childhood there in Cold River?"

Ted lights a cigarette. After exhaling, he shakes his head slowly. "Yes and no," he says. "That's probably the only honest answer I can give you." His eyes burn with a sudden earnestness. "My father left us when I was eleven, and that really shook things up for a while." He takes another drag on the cigarette. "But then, you know," he shrugs, "we adjusted to it and things were pretty good."

Andrew waits a few seconds before asking, "You haven't seen your father since?"

The other man looks uncertain for a moment. "That's complicated too," he says at last with a half-smile. "But generally speaking, no, I haven't." Andrew waits for more but the expression that accompanied Ted's excursion into his past is gone and once more Andrew has the sense that a door is being closed. With a sigh, the American settles back in the booth. "What about you?" he asks. "I don't suppose you had much chance to have a happy childhood." The comment is vaguely unsettling, even accusatory, but Andrew gives him the benefit of the doubt: most likely he's just curious.

Andrew carefully lights a cigarette and takes a shallow drag. Already he feels the tightness on his skin that comes when he's pulled back into those times. The tobacco burns in his lungs; for an instant it makes him a trifle lightheaded, and he's able to look at his own youth as if it were someone else's. When he speaks it's calmly. "Until the war," he says, "I had an unusually happy childhood. My mother and father loved each other and they genuinely loved their children." He's surprised by how much emotion he feels telling this. "No," he says, "I can't claim to have been deprived in that way."

After a silence Ted says quietly, "I hope I haven't brought up something that's painful to you."

"No, no," Andrew assures him, "it's not painful remembering that you've been loved."

Ted nods solemnly, apparently moved by what Andrew has just said. There's a distant look to his eyes and Ted seems on the verge of saying something, but abruptly he takes another swallow of beer.

Andrew can see his conflict: obviously he wants to talk about whatever is troubling him—the girl, he's sure—but he's resisting at the same time, though he's barely able to contain the impulse. The fact is, the two of them hardly know each other, but possibly that gives Andrew a kind of protective distance, like a priest's. Whatever Ted may be thinking, when the waiter arrives with their orders the thread of conversation is snapped. Their food before them, the two men are silent for a while and the soft din of the restaurant rises around them: raised glasses shine dimly in the haze of tobacco smoke, the talk of a dozen conversations is refracted amid a constant low buzz broken by an occasional shout or laugh, and from time to time the growl of a Liszt prelude is audible. Andrew takes his first bite of the schnitzel and follows it with a swallow of beer. Once again he finds himself pulled back toward memories of his earlier life.

After a while, he asks, "Did you ever hear of the Wieliczka salt mine near Krakow?"

"No," Ted answers. He seems to have roused himself from a reverie.

"That's not surprising," Andrew says. "it's not well-known over here but it's an amazing place, really amazing." How long is it since he's thought about this? "They've been mining salt there for seven hundred years, which is impressive enough. But it's also been a major tourist attraction for centuries—even Goethe visited the mine. There are tunnels, strange geological formations, underwater lakes. For some reason, the atmosphere down there is supposed to be particularly healthy." Did he actually smell the difference when he walked through those tunnels, or is that a trick of memory? "But the most impressive thing about the place," he goes on, "is that over the centuries the miners have created elaborate structures out of salt, full-sized altars, statues, even a chandelier, all of extremely fine workmanship." Thinking about the passageways under the earth that connected the many chambers of the mine, he falls silent for a moment, then adds, "The Germans had an airplane parts factory there during the war because, being so far underground, it was protected from bombing."

Across from him, Ted nods, waiting for more.

"I went there once with my family," Andrew continues. "It was before the war, obviously. I was amazed to see the elaborate work of those miners who created all these marvelous things on their own time—what they built might have been done by the most skilled of artisans. Our parents wanted to make us aware of what these ordinary Poles had done." For the moment Andrew has lost the drift of his story. Amid the remembered images of the extraordinary spectacles beneath the earth, he's not sure why he brought the subject up.

"It does sound impressive," Ted comments.

"Yes, it is," Andrew says, having found his footing once more, "but something else happened when we were down there. We'd come down the long flights of stairs, we'd seen the lake beneath the ground, we'd seen the altars and the statues. It was all strange and wonderful but, you know, I was only ten and every second we were in that mine I was aware that there were tons of earth above us, and I couldn't keep from thinking how far we were from the surface. I was a little apprehensive, as you might expect, and then the lights suddenly went out—we were plunged into total darkness."

"Jesus," Ted says, "that must have been something."

"I don't know," Andrew goes on, "whether it was for three seconds or a whole minute but it seemed an eternity." His father and Magda had lingered to look at something and he was with his mother. When the lights went out she took his hand and told him gently that everything was all right. Amid all his childish terror and ignorance, he had an absolute belief in his mother and as he remembers the incident, he was calm as he held her hand in that dark place beneath the earth.

"Obviously, everything turned out OK," Ted says.

Andrew nods. Everything didn't turn out all right in the long run, of course, but it did then. He smiles. "When we got back to the surface my father suggested that the people who ran the tour might do that on purpose with every group just to give them a frisson."

"Christ, I'll bet that was a frisson and a half for a ten-year-old."

Andrew laughs. "It certainly made an impression since I remember it very vividly to this day."

Ted smiles, then looks into his beer, the smile fading into a thoughtful expression. Once more, Liszt surges and a clamor of voices fills the silence. When the American sighs, it's clear he's neither in Wieliczka or in the Old Heidelberg.

"You have troubles, my friend?" Andrew suggests.

"Well, yeah," Ted begins hesitantly. "The usual kind of stuff, I suppose." But before long he's ardently delineating his present woes: he and this woman are in love, he declares; they're a perfect match in many ways, but there's a part of her he can't get to, and she's leaving at the end of the semester.

"A part of her you can't get to?" Andrew asks.

Ted shakes his head. "She thinks grad school's too tame for her. She says she has to be able to do more." He pushes his fork through his spaetzle. "I guess in some way she's more . . . I don't know. Maybe she's braver than I am."

"Braver?" This seems like a major confession for an American male.

"She's less patient about things," Ted offers, still trying to clarify his situation. "Still, I can't help feeling that if we were just able to continue together for a while longer we could work out our conflicts—really, in some ways we're. . . ." He pulls himself up short. "Well, we don't have the time, do we?" When he speaks again his tone is more detached. "When I played football in high school we lost an important game once. We got blown out in the first half and then we made a strong comeback. When the game ended we were only down by one point and we had the ball on the other team's twenty. In the locker room afterwards the coach tried to make us feel good by saying, 'You guys didn't lose; you just ran out of time.'" He shakes his head. "I don't think anyone felt better for that." He sighs. "Hey, I don't know why I'm boring you with all this."

"No, no," Andrew insists, "what else is there but the human heart and its impulses?" He smiles. "Though I'm not sure I understood all of the football part."

Ted takes another drink. "Well, anyway, you've been a good sport about it." Having told Andrew his story, he seems like his old self once more.

"It's a fair exchange," Andrew tells him. "After all, you've listened to even more of my stories." Each of them, he's sure, has left out all the important parts.

His apartment in the eaves is even lonelier tonight for the brief bit of company he shared with Ted Riley. Listening to the steady crackle of rain on the roof, Andrew can close his eyes and momentarily persuade himself he's somewhere else; but even in his fantasy he knows that when he opens them again he'll be in Chippewa.

All through the center of Europe in the spring of 1944 there was a sense of expectation. The Russians were pushing relentlessly westward and the Poles of Krakow knew it was only a matter of time. So did their occupiers, and there was some satisfaction in watching the Germans try to keep up their facade of being masters of the earth while they were no doubt trembling inside. Here in Krakow, where the new Caesars administered the Government General of Poland from Wawel Castle, untold numbers of citizens of the Reich, civilians as well as military, had pushed the natives off the streets. They had tried to turn the former seat of Polish kings into a German provincial town: the *Krakauer Zeitung*, read by the Poles for its all-important obituary section, was everywhere; there were dozens of German cafes and even four German-language theaters. The most insular of Poles knew how to say, *Entschuldigen Sie, bitte*, stepping out of the way of one of the well-dressed conquerors. Now as the occupiers drove by in their Mercedeses and BMWs, their shiny Adlon limousines, the natives tried to catch a glimpse of their eyes, certain they could detect the apprehension under the carefully cultivated sneer of superiority.

Life for Poles in Krakow that spring was no less grim and dangerous, though by now those adjectives were just synonyms for "normal." Yet they could hear in the harsh voices of their masters more than a hint of an appeal. The Nazi occupation might have been hard, the conquerors suggested, but it was nothing to what the Russians would do. Ever since their revelations of the slaughter of Polish officers at Katyn, there had been stories in the Polish-language propaganda sheets about the Soviet intentions of enslaving Poland. What was worse was that many Poles agreed about the motives of their soon-to-be liberators and everyone knew that the free-lance partisans, "the people of the forest," the various resistance groups, mainly the London-based Home Army and the Moscow-inspired People's Army, were fighting not only the Germans but themselves; so that nobody could say for certain what lay on the other side of liberation.

For young Andrew Kesler the years had passed in a blur. He'd survived things he couldn't have believed it possible to survive, beginning with his Aunt Jadwiga's taking him and Magda from the house one night, the last time he saw his mother and father, their faces tight with willed fortitude as they stood in the dark street beside his uncle's car and bade the children a goodbye they pretended was temporary. Life apart from their parents was difficult enough for brother and sister, but it wasn't long before poor Uncle Maciej broke down under the strain, and his drinking caused him to exercise fatally bad judgment with one of the occupiers. Aunt Jadwiga, feeling she could no longer care for both of the children by herself, bundled Magda off to a cousin in Warsaw. Andrew was alone now, desperately alone, in a city of ghosts: he couldn't walk the leafy precincts of the university without thinking of his father who, along with almost two hundred colleagues, had been sent off to the Sachsenhausen labor camp in the first months of the occupation; nor could he step onto any part of Barsztowa Street without being aware that not many blocks from here was his mother's office, where she had sometimes let him play with her stethoscope. In Planty Park, where he and Magda used to play, the sight of a particular bench or tree could bring sharp memories of loss. "Always remember what your father and mother did," his aunt urged him tearfully. "You're a little man now."

And so Andrew had negotiated as best he could the time and place assigned to him in this world. "It can't last forever," his friend Roman kept saying. Roman feared it would be over before he had a chance to strike a heroic blow for Poland. All of them did small things to frustrate the enemy: they acted as couriers, not to the partisans in the forest but to resisting civilians in the city who wanted to be discreet. "How do I know I'm not just passing love letters?" cynical Staś asked occasionally. Still, they did what they could and they waited to grow up, they waited for things to change.

It wasn't all dedication and heroism. They were still boys and they wanted to enjoy themselves. He and Piotr drank some home-brewed vodka Piotr had stolen from an uncle. "Let's pre-

tend we're in a movie," Piotr slurred. "I'll be the man and you
be the woman." They groped and kissed. Nothing was said
about it afterwards. Andrew escaped the gray of occupation in
his dreams. In some of them, of course, the family was back
together. In others, he pursued his own desires, sometimes in
the plush settings of a hotel his family had visited on one of
their vacations to the Tatras. There, he was his present age, yet
he was treated like a grown man: waiters in elegant, chande-
liered dining rooms lit his cigarettes, the maitre d' called him
Pan. He and a friend walked arm in arm, looking at the mountains. The landscape was wild with promise.

His waking life provided a more muted kind of drama. His
teachers were nervous; they spoke in code. Everyone spoke in
code. A ghetto had been created for the Jews, who were rounded
up from the surrounding area and put behind its walls. The
streetcar could pass through the ghetto but no one could board
or disembark in that segregated area. Stories were whispered
of other such moves elsewhere in the country. The few letters
he got from Magda were spare; she knew what she couldn't say.
But when she wrote that she remembered the beauty of Quiet
Lake he knew she was reminding him of their vacation there
just before the war, she was reminding him of their parents, she
was urging him never to forget. When she said she was reading
a book he knew she'd already read, he remembered its story of
the brother and sister who'd been separated during one of the
Tartar raids of the Middle Ages, only to be reunited in the last
chapter, and he took it as her promise that the two of them
would be together once more. In the spring of 1944 Andrew
hadn't heard from his sister in months and of course he was
worried. These days it was only sensible to worry. Magda was
a spirited young woman and wouldn't be content with a passive role. Who knew what she might be involved with? But he
remembered her oblique promise.

"What do you think's going to happen?" people asked each
other these days. They were waiting for the first signs of the
German civilians moving westward. "There will be bargains,"
some people observed with a cunning laugh, though even they

must have wondered how long they'd have to savor those bargains before the next arduous chapter of Polish history was
imposed on them.

Andrew wasn't a hero but he was as much a patriot as any of
his fellow citizens, which is why it was so strange that he should
have fallen into a relationship with Dieter. Amid the war, the conti-
nent-wide turbulence and upheaval, a small thing like the coming
together of two such people seemed insignificant, but these things
continued to happen as they did in more tranquil times.

It was a rainy day. Andrew wasn't looking where he was
going when he bumped into a man. Seeing at once that he was
German—he was too well-dressed to be a Pole, for one thing—
Andrew apologized formulaically, *Entschuldigen Sie bitte.* The
man with the pencil mustache smiled and answered in passable
Polish, "It's no trouble, really." Already in the first seconds of
their time together Andrew was aware that the man was attracted
to him—why else would he have addressed him in Polish? He
was also aware that to follow up in any way could be exceed-
ingly dangerous. And yet there was a wild impulse to carry this
through a little further. Maybe it was just the boy's ravenous
ego, the gratification he'd feel at evoking some response from
this representative of the conquerors. Providentially, the rainy
street was empty. Andrew looked flirtatiously into the man's
eyes and said, *Es war ein Versehen*, it was an accident. As he had
already learned to do, he made his deformity evident, having no
wish to hide it.

The man wasn't deterred by Andrew's hand. His smile broad-
ened. "You're a clever little one, aren't you?" he said in German.
"Here, come under my umbrella. Would you like a cigarette?"
Dieter was slim, he moved gracefully. From a golden cigarette
case he extracted the first *Gauloise* Andrew was to smoke. He
gestured toward a Mercedes glistening in the rain and Andrew,
ignoring all caution, followed.

Dieter was from Rosenheim, near Munich. As a Bavarian,
he had little love for the tight-lipped Prussians who now repre-
sented the soul of Germany. He'd come to Krakow with the theater company, in which he was an assistant director. Slender and

elegant in his tailored suits, his black hair slicked back, he was in his thirties and he saw himself as something of a mentor to the sixteen-year-old Andrew. Because of his position, not only as a German but also as a theatrical person, Dieter was given a certain latitude so long as he was discreet, and he'd mastered the art of discretion, all the way to his having a wife back in Bavaria. His affair with Andrew was not destined to last long, he acknowledged from the beginning, and he seemed to want to cram as much as he could into their meetings. After they'd had their physical pleasure Dieter, in his silk robe, would lounge against Oriental pillows and, between puffs of his cigarette, he would tell his young companion about the world. "The *Götterdämmerung* will soon be upon us," he declared with a philosophical sigh, the swirling brandy catching the light. "Listen closely for the faint booming of the Russian artillery. That will be the prelude." His sensual mouth was turned into a smile but his eyes suggested something other than amusement at the prospect he was foretelling. "Then one set of barbarians will be replaced by a worse one." He was wickedly ironic about the Nazis. "Cloudy-headed Siegfrieds marching in their dreary gray uniforms, tight-lipped, rigid, when all they want is to be Rhinemaidens with golden tresses singing, 'Take me, I'm yours.'" The Nazis, he insisted, weren't really representative of the German people. "Still," he had to admit, "the German people adored Hitler. For that we'll all have much to pay." He hoped that Andrew would be able to see something else of German culture after the war, "though God knows if the Russians will leave one stone upon another."

It was a dangerous relationship; everything was clandestine and each of them could be thought a traitor, and yet it continued into the summer. The city was by now crazy with rumor, hope and dread. The Russians were advancing on Warsaw, there was an uprising in the capital. A flame of hope surged in every Polish breast but it wasn't long before people came to realize that the nearby Russians were not going to help the insurgents, the West was not going to help them; and yet the uprising continued bravely, hopelessly on. Hearing of all this from afar, the Poles of Krakow could only clench their fists and resolve that someone was going to pay for this. Meanwhile, as the urgency of Andrew's meetings with Dieter increased, they became more careless, it was even possible they might have been seen. It was clear they were going to have to break things off.

"Ah, Andrew," Dieter said, "remember, remember, you're a fine person, a young man of considerable gifts. Don't let anyone suggest that you're inferior in any way. Those who do are barbarians." He was drinking more these days, and his despair was more evident beneath the brittle surface. "Wagner, Wagner," he'd exclaim with a tinny laugh, "where are you when we need you? The entire Reich is going up in flames and there will be no escape for the likes of us."

When he wasn't drunk and despairing, though, he went about his business efficiently. It was too late now for morale to be lifted by frothy comedies and nostalgic evocations of *Gemmütlichkeit*. Members of the theater company had talked to him privately, expressing their anxieties, plans were being made to pull up stakes. "But where can we go?" he said to Andrew after one of those talks. "Berlin?" he laughed. "We won't be playing on *Unter Den Linden* but *Unter den Trummern*," under the rubble. "Do you know, my friend, it's the strangest thing these days. You don't need a compass anymore. Everyone I talk to seems to be turned eastward, listening."

"Go," he said at last, "get out of here. You don't have to be told about the Russians." The two had gone over this subject before and Andrew had made up his mind. The communists would show no love to the child of bourgeois reactionaries. Dieter opened his desk drawer and pulled out a small package. "Accept this," he said, "as my most important gift to you." They were papers that would get him past security checkpoints on the way west. "There may in the end have been some use to my supping with the devil. At least I have the power to help someone."

"And you?" Andrew asked, genuinely concerned.

Dieter brushed it away. "The great, the invincible Weh-rmacht will see to it that citizens of the Reich may return safely to the fatherland."

When it came their farewell was spare and unsentimental, stoic. It was then that he told Andrew, "We can't choose the times we're born in." It was after midnight and the leaves of the lime tree shone in the street light. The distant rumble might have been thunder or something else. "We simply have to make the best of them." He looked at Andrew for a few seconds and turned away.

And so this boy no longer young was set upon his journey. Krakow would be behind him; more tumult and ruin was ahead of him. A faint belief that he and his sister would see each other again was already fading. Ahead, he had no way of knowing, was a place called Chippewa.

I n early May the scent of lilacs is in the air and flyers all over
Chippewa advertise the university's annual Spring Carnival;
but many in town are talking about something that happened half a world away: the U-2 affair. After claiming for days
that the American plane shot down over the Soviet Union was
engaged in innocent weather research, the U.S. is faced with
incontrovertible evidence to the contrary and President Eisenhower has been forced to admit that the plane was, as the Soviets
claimed from the beginning, on a spy mission. For people used
to believing that only the devious Reds use subterfuge and guile
while the straightforward Americans always play by the rules,
the revelation comes as a shock and the story dominates the
news. "Jesus," Dori says over *The New York Times* that's spread
across the table of their booth in The House of Joe, "all this
time we're piously preaching peace to the rest of the world and
meanwhile we're regularly violating the air space of another
country. Maybe Ike and Dulles had their fingers crossed when
they were talking."

Ted looks at the columns of newsprint. "You wonder how
much more stuff there is we don't know about."

"This is just the tip of the iceberg, I'm sure."

"Unfortunately, I think you're right." The revelations about
the government's secret activities are shocking enough; their
impact on the state of international affairs is even more disturbing: the Cold War is suddenly much closer to getting hot
once more, and it's impossible to pretend that the world they
live in isn't a dangerous place. Khrushchev, having tricked his
adversaries, has been boastful and combative, issuing threats

and putting the upcoming summit talks in doubt. While some have urged Eisenhower to apologize for the deception, other voices on the American side have been as belligerent as Khrushchev's, and once more Ted feels the way he did in the basement of the library when he saw the stories about Sputnik on the front pages of the *Trib*: there's no place where you can hide from it.

"Ike needs some divine intervention about now," Dori says. "He's probably already on the phone to Billy Graham." She does the voice: "'Let us pray togethuh, Mistuh President.'"

"Old Ike's going to need more than Billy," Ted says. Among the sheets of newsprint spread out on the table, he catches sight of a photo of the pilot Francis Gary Powers. Ted is struck by the man's ordinariness. How did this broad-faced Southerner not that much older than Ted himself wind up being the sole occupant of the pencil-thin surveillance plane, a dark phantom with a huge wingspan that was designed to fly secretly across the entire breadth of the Soviet Union, photographically recording the tiniest details thirteen miles below, all the while passing unarmed over some of the most formidable air defenses in the world? It must have been an experience like no other to be up there, at the edge of space, alone, silent, cramped in the U-2's confining cockpit. Yet, even more intriguing than the image of Powers's solitary flight is the pilot's behavior after he was hit. "I wonder why the guy didn't commit suicide," he muses aloud. "He seemed to have plenty of opportunity before he was captured."

Beside him, Dori looks up from her paper with a quizzical expression. "Oh?" She's straightened, as if prepared for a fight, and her agitation is obvious. "Are you suggesting he should have killed himself just to save Ike's ass?" she asks.

Ted takes a sip of coffee before answering. "Did I say that?" Blindsided by her accusatory tone, he's hurt, and wary. He and Dori have to be careful with each other these days, having discovered that all too often the slightest difference can lead to a quarrel that surprises both of them. "All I meant was that it was a top secret mission. As I understand it, they had contingency plans that he must have known about when he signed up for it, so that was certainly a possibility."

Dori shakes her head. "I find it really strange," she says, an ironic smile playing about her lips, "that you should be advocating suicide as an act of patriotic duty." She waits a second before continuing. "Didn't you say you could never do something like that after Marty tried it?"

"Hey." He's stung by the injustice of her attack. "I didn't say the guy should have done it. I just wondered." In fact, the pilot's predicament fascinates him: lulled into believing that the plane's ability to fly so high made it invulnerable, how did he feel upon being abruptly found out, plucked from the sky by a Russian missile? Or had all the U-2 pilots known it was just a matter of time before the Soviet air defenses got good enough, so that sooner or later one of the planes was bound to be lost, a game of Russian roulette played at 70,000 feet? A game, moreover, where, given the secrecy of the mission, if you lost, in all likelihood only the spies on both sides would know about it. Whatever he might have felt about his chances, though, once Powers realized that the sleek, fragile machine he'd been flying was fatally struck, and with no possibility of reaching friendly territory, he must have been in a panic, reminding himself that the soldierly thing to do would be to take the poison capsule, to make sure the aircraft was destroyed, kept out of the hands of the Russians; and yet, in the midst of all his terror and uncertainty tumbling through an alien sky where, if he survived, the grim representatives of the enemy awaited him, he chose to live. As is often the case when he contemplates such a situation, Ted wonders what he'd have done in the man's place.

"Sure," Dori says, aflame with righteousness. "Swallow the pill and say 'Heil Hitler.'"

"Come on," Ted protests, "Ike isn't Hitler. That's ridiculous."

Dori doesn't back down. "Here we are pretending to be holier than thou and we're caught red-handed doing something . . ." She throws up her hands in exasperation. "Can you imagine what our reaction would be if it had been a Russian plane over the U.S., shot down over Chippewa? And you're saying the poor chump who got caught up in the middle of all this should kill himself to protect his government's dishonesty."

Though he loves this woman, Ted is surprisingly angry with her. "You're twisting my words," he says as coolly as he can manage.

"They're your words," she insists. "Not mine." She looks away and neither of them says anything for a few seconds.

They're both upset, he knows, and not just about this. Of course he's as disturbed as she is by the revelation of U.S. spying, and he shares her outrage, but his political feelings are twined around the alarm he feels about the heightened threat of atomic war. Once more he feels his impotence: what can people like himself and Dori, or even Francis Gary Powers, do when they're caught up in a vast system where the complex and elaborate machinery of destruction that each side calls "defense" seems to run of its own accord? In the midst of his agitation, he thinks about Sam Morelli, and it seems to him that Morelli would understand his interest in the subject of Powers's failure to commit suicide. But he doesn't want to be arguing with Dori. "I don't know," he says after a while, "maybe it's the kind of thing a guy's more likely to think about, since it's always possible it could be you."

Dori looks suddenly tired. She turns and leans against him. "Hey," she says, "I guess I jumped on you. I'm sorry."

"It's nothing," he counters, though he still feels a lingering hurt. His smile is forced.

"It's just . . ." she says. "We're kept in the dark. They feed us all this stuff and when it blows up in their faces they expect us to go along."

"I know," he says. "I know." In his relief, he feels emotionally depleted. This is the way it's been too often these days with Dori. In his more lucid moments, he can understand that these outbursts may be necessary to the process of separating, but his lucid moments are few because he really doesn't want to acknowledge that impending separation. He lights a cigarette and takes a deep drag, closing his eyes. The blur of sound around them could be from any day here at the Joe, and he remembers that they've had many pleasant times in this place. "You know one thing I wish?" he says, exhaling smoke.

"What's that?" Her look is eager, contrite.

"That maybe before you leave we'll have time to go to Half-Moon Lake."

"Is that where we saw the ice-shanties?"

He nods. "The very same. It would be fun to go out there in a rowboat now that the surface of the lake isn't so hard."

"Yeah," Dori nods. "That does sound nice." Neither of them is looking at the newspaper. "Think we'd see any cars on the bottom of the lake that went through the ice?"

He can imagine the two of them out on the water, the sun on their bare arms. As he pulled on the oars the only sounds they'd hear would be the creak of the oarlocks and the splash of the blades striking the water, the occasional buzz of an insect, a fish jumping. Maybe they could row all the way to the other shore, where it's marshy. Ted has never been there and he's curious about what it's like. Who knows? They might see something wonderful in that marsh, something that would make their breaths catch—the sun on the lily pads, the dark shape of a giant snapping turtle, maybe the tailfin of a pink Caddy sticking out among the lily pads, glittering dimly—some epiphany that would clarify things between them, maybe change things. "It would be nice this time of year," he says. Even as he does so, he's aware that Dori already has her ticket to California, and that he's pre-registered for the fall semester.

She takes his hand. "I'll bet it would be."

It would, at the very least, be one more memory of their time together. Just now it seems important that they have memories.

"Would we do some fishing?" she asks with a smile. He appreciates her wanting to prolong this fantasy.

"Sure," he answers. "We could. Why not?"

Dori continues smiling. "I'll bet you fished a lot as a kid."

"Hey, you're just responding to a Midwestern stereotype. But yeah, I did a fair share of fishing."

"Listen to modest Mr. Hemingway," she says.

"Actually," he says, surprising himself, "I went fishing with my father a couple of times before he left." He didn't realize he's remembered it so vividly. "We went to my Uncle Mike's place on a lake about twenty miles out of town. We'd have to get up before dawn, pack baloney sandwiches and candy bars, bottles of pop for me and beer for him, and then we'd drive out there. At first I'd be cold and sleepy, I wouldn't want to be out there at all. I knew we'd be going out in a leaky rowboat that I'd have to keep bailing. But once we were actually on the water it was great. There'd be a mist on the lake and all you could see would be a few reeds close to the boat, but you could smell the fish and you knew that the sun was going to burn off the mist before long."

He realizes as he's telling her this that he wants her to enter into his memory so that she can take it with her to California, to wherever she's going after that. He wants her to be beside the stoic little kid who grunted a few words to the older man as he listened to the squeak of the oarlocks in the mist, the two of them talking about fish and bait in a manly, minimalist language, the younger one remembering stories of Indians in bark canoes, lamenting that he'd been born into a civilized age and would have little opportunity to prove his prowess in the world of nature. He wants her to know what it felt like when his father let him have a swig of his beer later and it seemed the most natural thing in the world to expect the older man to be there forever.

"Hey," she teases, "maybe some day you'll wise up, you'll throw over this Ph.D. stuff and become a fisherman."

"You think there's no chance of that, don't you?" He likes the idea. "I could always hire out on a commercial fishing boat on the Great Lakes."

She nods. "Grow a beard, get tan as leather."

He lets himself imagine it for a moment. "Hands tough as leather too."

"A real Marlboro man."

Though she's smiling, he can see from her eyes that she's been reminded of something else and the spell is broken. When

he has no follow-up for her, the two of them lapse into silence.
From a U-2 thirteen miles above the earth, it occurs to him,
the camera could probably give you an exact count of the fish
that Marlboro man pulled up in his net. Ted is no longer up
to playing the game. He's not going to become a commercial
fisherman, he and Dori aren't going to Half Moon Lake, she's
leaving Chippewa and all over the world men and machines
stand ready to obliterate the enemy. What's the point of all these
attempts to evade reality? What is, is, and it's going to have to
be faced. It's enough to discourage anyone, but we're adults, he
tells himself, we have to act like adults.

"So," he tries to make it sound cool and matter-of-fact, "hear
from Elliott since the last time?"

Once more Dori straightens, moving away from him. Her
look is more guarded now. "No," she says. She lights a cigarette. "Not since last week." Elliott phoned her, it seems, on the
same day she received a letter from him telling of his decision
to drop out of grad school and go to Washington, D.C. "His first
priority," she told Ted then, "is going to be to make sure Nixon
isn't the next president, but the real reason he's going is because
he's interested in some groups that are being formed to help the
civil rights protesters in the South." He urged Dori to join the
effort and she told him she'd think about it. Sensing Ted's reaction, she made it clear that Elliott was talking about a political,
not a sexual relationship, but it was upsetting just the same.
Not for the first time, Ted feels morally inadequate beside the
dark-haired phantom in Berkeley who burns with an incandes-
cent zeal that's matched only by his intelligence. "Elliott is really
committed," Dori said. In the letter he sent her he included a
photo that she showed to Ted of Emmett Till in his casket in
a funeral parlor in Chicago. Ted had seen the picture before
but that didn't diminish its power. The casket was kept open
so that everyone could see what had been done to the young
man by his tormentors; and the photo shows the deceased in
a dark suit jacket and a white shirt, lying in a silk-lined coffin
like any other body prepared for viewing, except that all the
features have been scraped off of his face, leaving something

there that's far more frightening than anything Ted has seen in a horror movie. "And all he did," an ashen Dori said when she showed the picture to Ted, "was to whistle, to allegedly whistle, at a white woman. Look at that," she said. "That's the face of America."

"You think there's a chance you'll go to D.C. too?" Ted asks now, his throat dry.

She looks at him. "I don't know. It's too early to say but it certainly sounds worthwhile. And challenging."

He takes that for a yes. "Yeah," he says. "Yeah, it does." Though D.C. is closer to here than California is, he knows it will be a lot farther, since eventually Dori will want to go to the front lines, as Elliott put it. "And if you went," Ted forces himself to ask, already knowing the answer, "would you think about going south?" She shrugs. All at once California seems a safe haven— he thinks of the picture in her bedroom with its primary colors, the motor car, the airplane, the giant lemon moon—peace among the palm trees. If Dori goes to California, he can at least nourish the fantasy that he might visit her some time; if she goes south, things will be altogether different. The thought of her in that hot, violent region brings a shiver. He remembers that faceless figure in the casket. The Southern whites who did that aren't likely to welcome outsiders who come into their territory to help the local Negroes. Lord, protect her, he says to himself, recognizing once more how futile was his fantasy of the two of them rowing on Half Moon Lake. If they'd have gone to the lake there would have been no epiphany. There might have been the creak of oars, the sound of wood striking water; there might have been the sun on their arms. But there would have been no epiphany.

The possibility of Dori's going south raises the inevitable question: what about him? Would he go if he had a chance? Of course, he has his degree to finish; he can't just leave Chippewa like that. And there's his mother's situation. But if he's going to be brutally honest, he knows that these may just be excuses masking a starker truth: the thought of voluntarily putting himself in such hostile territory is something he resists on a primal level. As a kid, he'd always been interested in the gospel story of the rich young man who asked Christ what he should do to achieve the kingdom of heaven. Keep the commandments, Christ tells him. Not satisfied, the young man informs Christ that he's already done that. Then sell all you have and give it to the poor, Christ says, after which, the evangelist records, the young man walked away sadly, capable of ordinary goodness but unwilling to take on extraordinary sacrifices.

Of course, Ted reminds himself, Dori hasn't decided yet to go south. She's still thinking about it.

But for him to dwell on these things is an invitation to melancholy, which isn't going to help anyone. Live for today, Dori told him. How can you do that, though, without shutting out the rest of the world? All he can do is try is to try to manage things, one step at a time. "I've got my tux for tonight," he says. "Are you ready?"

She brightens. "You'll just have to wait and see, won't you, mister?" she says.

Dressing up for the Spring Carnival was Dori's idea. She persuaded Ted to rent a tux and told him she was going to find "a little something" appropriate in a local thrift shop. But nothing has prepared him for the vision that greets him at the door of her apartment. "My God," he says when he sees her. She's wearing a black strapless, her long hair is swept up, exposing her slender neck. Her prominent cheekbones are sharply defined by pale makeup, her dramatically outlined and blue-shaded eyes glint with some of the sparkle of the pearl drop earrings she's wearing. In high heels, she looks inches taller, all glamor and sophistication, a movie star. Ted's heart catches in his throat: no woman has ever been more beautiful.

"Hey, handsome," she says, stepping forward to kiss him, "look at you: you were born to wear a tux. Did you know that?" She walks him to the full-length mirror. "What do you say?" She makes a sweeping gesture toward the glass. "Scott and Zelda Fitzgerald? Or, let's hope, their less self-destructive brother and sister." Still awed by her transformation, Ted is speechless. "I couldn't help noticing," she prods him, "that you've brought something for us in that brown bag of yours."

Belatedly, he recovers his aplomb and, with a flourish, he extracts the bottle of champagne. "From California, of course. It's already chilled."

"So let's," she says. The cork pops, the wine fizzes, drinks are poured, and they toast each other. "To the ever-charming Scott," she lifts her glass, "the life of any party," to which she adds, after a pause, "except maybe the Communist Party."

"I raise my glass to Nefertiti, Queen of the Nile," he responds. "It just came to me that that's who you look like. And, baby, I never knew how erotic a neck could be."

"Sweetheart, it wouldn't surprise me if you told me you thought mashed potatoes were erotic."

He looks at her through the bubbles in his glass. This apartment, he thinks, I'm going to miss it. I can't believe someone else is going to be living here next fall. "This isn't bad stuff," he says, "but we don't want to drink it all here."

"Don't worry. I have another bottle."

"Brilliant," he exclaims. "Beautiful and brilliant." Soon they're on their second glass. Evening sunlight floods the apartment. Let time stop, he prays, let it stay like this always. "By the way," he says aloud, "did I happen to mention that you have the most delicious-looking shoulders?"

She waves a finger at him. "We're not going to eat till later tonight, remember?"

"I hate to drink on an empty stomach." He comes over to her and kisses one of her shoulders, tasting her perfume. "How sweet it is," he says, running his hand delicately along her neck.

She pulls back. "Whoa, boy. Let's finish this bottle. Then it'll be time for us to go. I want to see this famous Spring Carnival, remember?"

Outside, the world has taken on the tint of California champagne. Armed with the second bottle and a pair of paper cups, they make their way through the mild night air that's redolent of hot dogs and mustard, pretzels, popcorn and cotton candy.

The streets are jammed with people in all kinds of attire. A Key-
stone cop playfully waves his billy club at them and they salute
him with their paper cups. "Look at those two." Dori points to
a couple dressed like the subjects of Grant Wood's *American
Gothic.*

"You're looking at the spirit of Chippewa," Ted says.

"No," she pulls him closer. "Tonight we're the spirit of
Chippewa."

Darkness has fallen and lights of all colors blaze in the night,
attracting countless insects. Music blares from a dozen sources.
There are political signs, for Stevenson, for Symington, for Kennedy. A man wearing a bow tie who's carrying a Nixon sign is
booed good-naturedly. On a corner, they encounter Rob Selkirk
and a friend. Rob introduces them to the other man. "Really," he
declares, his voice straying alcoholically, "this seemingly whole-
some young pair is really *hope*lessly decadent. *Hope*lessly," he
laughs. "Come, come, Roger, we came here in search of more
innocent pleasures, after all." They disappear into the crowd,
where an Indian and a cowgirl stroll amiably together, followed
by a convict whose number seems to be "pi" carried to the ump-
teenth power. Near the entrance to the carnival itself they're
startled to recognize the tall, distinguished figure of Bradford
Winslow, walking solemnly through the merry throngs with
his wife. "Good evening, Miss Green," he says. "Good evening,
Mister Riley."

"I thought for sure he'd come as Cotton Mather," Dori says
when they're out of earshot.

"*Sacre bleu,*" Ted mutters, "*Tout Chippewa est ici.*"

Now the music that swirls around them comes from a hand
organ and they've come to a booth with a sign that says, "Knock
'Em Down, Win a Prize." "Hey, let's see what kind of jock you
really are," Dori teases. Behind the counter, a man with a derby
and a cigar in his mouth nods his encouragement. "You can't let
the little lady down."

"Watch this," Ted says. He throws three balls at a line of
bowling pins and wins a stuffed bear.

Dori claps her hands. "I'm going to name it Nikita," she exclaims.

"You think that's going to save you when the Russkies come?"

"If they come tonight, we're done for. We're hopelessly decadent, remember?"

He raises his cup. "Here's to hopeless decadence." He's flushed and happy. "How are you doing?" he whispers into her ear.

"I'm doing fine," she says.

They ride on the merry-go-round; they crash into each other with bumper cars and, waiting in line at the ferris wheel, they finish their champagne. Minutes later, from the swinging gondola at the top of the ride they look down on the bright patch of color and light carved out of dark prairie, from which a pair of searchlights rakes the sky, possibly searching for Russian U-2s. "Hey," Ted grabs Dori's arm lightly, "Look at what I'm offering you: miles and miles of prairie where the noble bison once roamed in numbers too great to count." He shakes his head. "And you'd throw it all away for California."

"I'm tempted," she says, "but it just isn't the same without those noble bison. Can we lift a glass to them?"

"Did you forget?" Ted says. "We drank all the champagne."

"Ah," she responds with the intonations of W.C. Fields, "so we did, so we did indeed. Pity, pity."

Back on the street, Ted is struck by a sudden inspiration. "Hey," he says, "let's call Marty." He's been carrying Marty's number in Cincinnati for weeks but he's always put off calling their friend. All at once this seems like a good time.

"You sure about that, champ?" Dori asks, but he's already leading her to a pay phone.

"Hey, Marty," he calls into the phone, his hand over his ear against the noise of the crowd. "How are you? Guess where we are?" Marty's responses are barely audible and he doesn't sound very enthusiastic. Ted is disappointed. "Here's Dori," he tells Marty.

"What did you think?" he asks when Dori replaces the receiver. "He didn't sound too interested, did he?"

"Marty's still adjusting," she says.

"That's right, he's adjusting." Thank God for the champagne, Ted thinks.

The street is thick with revelers. There's a clown and a football player, a pair of witches on roller skates, and someone who's either dressed like a soldier or is wearing his ROTC uniform. Among them are plenty of ordinary Chippewans and Ted wonders whether Andrew Kesler is here.

"Hey, look," a fat man calls out, "it's Fred and Ginger." Ted takes Dori in his arms and executes a few dance steps to the applause of the crowd.

"This stuff is beginning to get to me," Dori says a while later, when they're in a quieter place beside the brick wall near the field house. Her head sags against his chest and leaves rustle darkly above them.

"You are very beautiful, my darling," he tells her, running his hands through her hair, a strand of which has come loose, making her all the more attractive; and a sudden stab of reality breaks through the brittle elan he's tried to maintain for the occasion. "You are . . ." he begins but he can't go any further.

"Sh," she puts a finger to her lips, then brings her hands to his neck. "Everything's going to be OK."

Later, in her apartment, their sex is desperate, furtive, and rushed. When it's over, Ted feels vaguely inadequate. Everything is going too fast. The Spring Carnival will be over soon. Not that many hours ago they were in the Joe, where they had the brief argument over Gary Powers, and then they made up. Now it's already the next day. Before long Dori will be gone.

She sits hunched in a corner of the bed, smoking, sunk in her own thoughts while Ted lies nearby, his head propped on a pillow, looking toward the dark rectangle of the ad for California lemons. On a chair near the bed is the bear he won at the carnival. He smells Dori's cigarette, their sex, he smells dried champagne on his skin; and for a moment he's detached, beyond any personal feeling. How strange and wondrous it is to be alive, how wonderful this planet, revolving dependably as it moves through space with every kind of creature clinging to it. Then he's back in his own skin, dreading the future: what's going to happen to Dori, to him, to everyone? Hell, how is he even going to be able to watch a horror movie after she leaves without becoming maudlin?

"You know, T," Dori says abruptly. "Sometimes when I think about some of the stuff I might do, it scares me."

It's very quiet in the room, it's very quiet outside. "You mean like going south?" he asks. She's still thinking about it; she hasn't made up her mind yet. Please, God, he prays, let her stay in California.

"Yeah."

"It scares me too," he says, determined not to let himself examine more specifically what scares him about the prospect of Dori trying to convince Southern racists to give up their ways. "I wish I still believed in guardian angels. I'd lend you mine."

She sends a cloud of smoke into the dark room. "That's very sweet," she says. When she speaks again, her voice is barely audible. "However it turns out, it helps knowing you're thinking about me."

He wants to say something reassuring. He wants to guarantee that everything's going to be all right. Christ, he thinks, I want things to be all right for her, wherever she goes. Even if she's with that asshole Elliott, I want her to be all right. In the end, all he can say is, "Thanks."

A few days after the Spring Carnival, when Ted walks into his freshman class he senses right away that he's headed for trouble. Before he's said a word, he can feel the listlessness in the air: heads are lowered, shoulders slump, and a torpid silence prevails. It's clear that the two dozen sons and daughters of the Midwest gathered here on a spring afternoon don't want to be in this gray room reading the poetry of a New England spinster that Ted has assigned as a break from the syllabus. Of course, he has only himself to blame: poetry is always risky since students think they have to say something portentous about it and usually just freeze up in its presence. But, hell, Dickinson isn't T.S. Eliot, and she's plenty interesting in her own right. To get ready for the class, he's prepared obsessively and at the start of the period he gives a brief, manic introduction he thought was witty and insightful but which is received with stolid patience; and his opening overtures toward discussion are met with bored, stony faces and glazed eyes: nobody wants to play today. "Don't you have any questions about these poems?" he asks. No. "Were there any surprises?" Again, no. The end of the semester looms; they dream of freedom. Even the usually eager Harold Kranz is doodling spiritlessly. Ted has faced such situations before and he knows that sometimes it's just chemistry or the stars and there's nothing to do about it but to stoically plod on and get to the end of the hour.

This time, though, something about the class's massive inertia provokes him. Hey, he thinks, I worked my ass off on this stuff and the least you can do is act as though it's worth your time to be here. And Dickinson's poetry is so great. Can't you see that? Apparently not. Marcia Dane's placid smile conveys to him that in a couple of weeks she'll be back in Shaker Heights where it will be summer and she and her friends will be lying around the pool getting a tan, and they'll have lots more interesting things to do than to think about Dickinson's gnomic meditations on God and death, or, given the poet's fondness for capitalization, Death. Others in the class no doubt dream of summer in LaGrange or French Lick, Menominee or the Wisconsin Dells, Chicago or Detroit.

Facing their resistance, Ted lets the silence lengthen as he walks slowly to the window, though he isn't looking at the springtime landscape. "OK," he says abruptly, and something in his voice seems to have got their attention. The truth is, he doesn't have a clue about what he's going to do next. All he knows is that what he planned isn't working; but he isn't ready yet to give up this class for lost, so he has to come up with something. "OK," he repeats, stepping into the void. "Everybody tear out a little sheet of paper," he improvises. "Half a page is enough. Come on, come on," he urges to some grumbling. "Now I'm going to ask you to write something very fast. It's going to be anonymous, so you don't have to worry about spelling or grammar. Or saying something you think might be stupid." To one half of the class he says, "Write down an adjective or two you'd use to describe Dickinson's poetry—the first words that come into your head. Quick as you can. Not somebody else's words, something you've read, but your own words. Be honest too." To the other half, he instructs, "All right, um, give me one line or image, even a particular word from one of the poems that sticks in your mind. I don't want you to tell me why, I don't want you to interpret it. Just write it down. Just something that, for whatever reason, stuck out for you. And you've got to be quick, I'm collecting these in a minute and then I'm going to read them back to you. No thinking," he repeats. "Not even you, Harold. Just writing."

When he calls for the scraps of paper a couple of minutes later he has no idea what he's going to find but he divides them into two piles and shuffles each of them visibly to preserve their anonymity before laying one pile on the desk, keeping the list of adjectives in his hand. He can tell that the students are as curious as he is about what they've written and, for drama's sake, he hesitates a moment before reading the responses aloud. According to the anonymous writers the poems are "quirky," they're "comic," they're "morbid." One calls them "religious" as well as, intriguingly, "sly" while there are a couple of "borings," a "thick," jingling," and "weird." "OK," Ted says, "very good, very interesting. Quirky how? That's a good word, by the way. Did you know that was her nickname, Quirky Dickinson, Q for short?" This gets a laugh or two. "And how can these poems be comic and morbid at the same time? That's pretty fascinating, if I say so myself." Since all the words come from the class itself and they're not even attributed to anyone in particular, they're not burdened with the sacredness of authority and from the beginning the students join in easily trying to relate the seemingly contradictory characterizations of the poetry. *Mad* comics is morbid and funny, Sal Rizzo offers to a few titters. Ted picks it up. "OK, Emily Dickinson, writer for *Mad* comics. I can see it: Tales From the Crypt. I heard a Fly buzz—when I died—Sure." It's all right, Betty Huff suggests seriously, to make fun of grim things, it's a way of surviving, which leads to the question of whether Dickinson is "gloomy" or "cheerful." Or both. Horn-rimmed Roger Payne calls out from his slouch at the back of the room that the poet is "baroque" and that baffles them for a moment but the spontaneous energy of the discussion carries them past this distraction. It occurs to Ted that through these anonymous utterances he's got everyone to contribute, something that never happens even in the liveliest class.

Oddly, given the springtime setting, the list of images in the other pile comes mostly from Dickinson's wintry "There's a certain Slant of light." Why is the phrase "Slant of light" especially memorable? Ted asks. What difference would it have made if Dickinson had written "ray of light?" "Slant," Harold Kranz pipes in. "Can't you see? Light comes in on a slant in winter." A couple of heads nod. "But why does she capitalize 'Slant?' Marcia Dane interrupts, shaken from her dreams of Shaker Heights.

"I'm glad you asked that question," Ted responds. "I have no idea. No, really, there are a lot of theories about her odd spelling and punctuation. Obviously she's trying to give the word some emphasis." "I can see that," Harold declares, clearly a member of the Dickinson party. Another nameless critic has singled out "the Heft of Cathedral Tunes." "Good word, 'heft,' isn't it?" Ted comments. "What's the difference between that and just 'heaviness?' And listen to the echoes of 'heft' in 'Heavenly Hurt.' Now there's a concept. But an odd concept for somebody who's been called 'religious,' isn't it?" Before long, two and three people are talking at once. Caught up in the open-endedness of the process, they grope their way toward articulations and all Ted has to do is to guide the process a bit, feeding back to them their comments, shaping the rough edges in places, letting them carry the discussion with a zesty freedom. And they seem genuinely interested. There's none of the hesitation of a group waiting to learn which way the teacher wants them to go. Ted can feel the flow in all the seeming disorder, recognizing that this free-form response is addressing all the points he hoped to make about Dickinson. For their part, the students clearly surprise themselves, not the least in their growing appreciation of the poems that just baffled them earlier without interesting them. When the class is over surprisingly soon, Harold Kranz and Trisha Peters even carry the talk of Dickinson into the corridor.

Flushed with his triumph, Ted knows that when he tells this to Dori she'll be appreciative but that even she won't grasp the full dimension of the accomplishment. He feels as if he's unlocked something in himself; he's experienced a Copernican revolution in his teaching. Unscripted, the class had not only energy but purpose, even form—it went somewhere—and all because he trusted himself, and his students. As he reached for the next piece of paper like a poker player asking for more cards, he already knew he was going to be able to find something there that he could tie into the evolving shape of the communal enterprise—and the beauty of it was that it was all coming from them. Instead of sitting back passively and waiting for the teacher to tell them things, they were working together toward understanding a complex human statement, and they seemed to grasp that realization. Ted's role was to make it possible and with the confidence of a tightrope walker, he knew he could keep his balance. He's always thought he's a pretty good teacher and he's had good classes before, but this was something different.

It was like jazz, he could tell Dori, or, if you'd prefer, it was positively Kerouacian. At the same time, he knows that one of the reasons he was able to move about so freely was because he'd prepared like hell on Dickinson's poetry.

He's still thinking about the class, relishing his achievement, when he gets home and finds a letter in the mailbox. The sight of the long white envelope surprises him, since the only person who's likely to write him is his mother, and he can recognize at once that this hasn't come from her. Then he sees the Arizona postmark and once more it's midwinter and his father is knocking on the door. He feels a sudden excitement, recalling the time when Jack Riley was here, big-shouldered, wearing an overcoat and a hat, his face tanned in snowy Chippewa. Holding the envelope, Ted has a sudden sense of the western spaces where the man lives. Is his father going to offer him a job out there? Or maybe he's going to fill his son in on that journey of his that led to the desert. In the telling of that story, will he confide to him that there were many times when he was tempted to come back to his family, that he missed them? Ted resists the urge to tear open the envelope here and now—this is too important an occasion to be rushed—and he waits until he's in the apartment, where he deliberately puts down his books and papers and pauses for a moment before dropping into the Morris chair. He wishes he had a cup of coffee to accompany this renewal of contact with his father—he wants to give it his full attention, taking his time over each word and phrase—but he isn't willing to wait long enough to make one. After all, Jack Riley's visit to this apartment had been on his own terms: abrupt, unannounced, and all too brief, over before Ted had been able to think about any number of things he'd wanted to say to him. With the more deliberate medium of the written word, he can at least determine the pace at which he receives and reflects on whatever information he's presented with.

But all thought of regulating that pace is overturned as soon as he opens the envelope, unfolds the sheets of paper and sees the money. At first he can't take in the denominations, the whole thing seems so unreal. Gradually it comes to him that these are actually hundred dollar bills he's looking at—he's never seen one before—and he counts them quickly, though he has to do it twice to verify that there are five of them. Five hundred dollars! This is a lot of dough. But Ted is confused: wasn't the plan that he was supposed to open a bank account into which his father was going to deposit money? He never imagined that the transactions would involve cash. Already though, as he glances toward the two sheets of paper that were folded around the bills, he senses that this money isn't part of that plan. Something else is going on. He picks up the letter and reads.

Ted,

By the time you get this I'll be somewhere else. Even I don't know where that's likely to be but the truth is, I may be gone for a long while. In fact, it's possible we won't see each other again. I don't know, we'll just have to see how things turn out.

The fact is, things have kind of blown up in my face here and to make a long story short I've got some pretty substantial problems with the law. There's no need to go into the specifics, I'm not going to try to defend myself in a matter you don't know anything about. Let's just say that I didn't screw anyone, at least not anyone who couldn't afford it. But the truth is, I got a late start trying to make something of myself, I had to cut some corners, and a lot of people I know who cut those same corners are the pillars of society out here now. I'm not going to whine about not getting the breaks but, believe me, it's shitty the way things have turned out, especially considering how the whole business came to the attention of the authorities. Talk about Judas, talk about surprises!!! I never said anything more sincerely when I say I hope you never find yourself in this kind of spot.

The thing that galls me as much as anything else is that I won't be able to help your mother out the way I wanted to. Believe me, I wasn't just grandstanding, I had every intention of doing it. I hope you believe me, which would be some solace anyway. My financial picture from now on is going to be pretty questionable—hell, even my whereabouts are going to be questionable—but one thing I did want to do was to send you some money to be used as you see fit. A guy your age can always use a few bucks and you seem like someone with his head on his shoulders, someone whose judgment I don't have a problem trusting. A lot different from me, you might say, but then, who knows? There are always connections, right?

Hell, things could have been so different. And now, Jesus— Wish me luck. I know in a lot of ways I wasn't the father I should have been but I tried, and I think you've turned out pretty well. And my story isn't over yet.

Your father,

Jack Riley

Ted holds the letter in his hands, looking at the loops and slants of the unfamiliar handwriting. He tries to summon a picture of the man who came to this apartment but the images are elusive, though he does remember that something about him— was it his coat, the way he lit a cigarette, the way he talked?— made him think that his visitor had some connection to the mob. Could there be any truth to that guess? But what the hell did his father do to get himself into what sounds like a boatload of trouble? Ted doesn't know much about the real estate business but there must be a thousand ways to skirt the law in that line of work, especially in the wild west. He wishes the man had been a little more specific about details, though there's no mistaking the letter's central thrust, that, as Jack Riley said, things have blown up in his face. But the letter is maddeningly vague about these things and Ted can't help wondering about the scale of his father's culpability. What are we talking about here? Did he swindle rich clients out of millions or did he just nickel-and-dime a lot of ordinary folks? Was he, in spite of his protestations, robbing widows and orphans? Did he have some kind of sweetheart deal with the local politicians until somebody blew the whistle? It's possible Ted will never know. It isn't likely that an Arizona real estate scandal is going to make it to the nightly TV news, is it?

He sits there holding the letter. The money is on the arm of the Morris chair. This, he realizes, is his father's last goodbye. All the elation he felt after his successful teaching experience has drained away, and he can't help feeling that the old man has deliberately upstaged him.

But what if the whole thing is an act, after all, a cheap way of getting out of supporting his wife after his big gesture of a few months ago? Or is the five hundred bucks supposed to be a payoff to his son? Ted makes a quick computation: that would come to about $40 for each year of Jack Riley's absence. Ted's feeling a lot of things at once but he can't really bring himself to believe his father has made up the story he's just told. To tell the truth, the letter doesn't sound phony. The barely suppressed self-pity and the occasional bravado have the ring of someone who's been stung and, though at some level he may harbor a bit of satisfaction at the thought of the Arizona hotshot going down, Ted has a sudden wave of feeling for this man who, in spite of the closeness of their relation, is little more than a stranger to him. He has a vision of his father writing this letter in a bus station. He's thinner than he was when he visited, carelessly dressed, he's unshaved—he's the old Jack Riley, his son realizes, the fantasy figure he created in the wake of his father's earlier desertion. While the announcement for the bus to Albuquerque echoes through the dreary station and a sleeping Indian with wine on his breath stirs in a nearby seat, Jack Riley stealthily slips the money into the envelope and seals it. As he prepares to board a bus, is he thinking about his lady friend? And what about her? Is she going to stick by the man she met in AA now that he's apparently lost everything? Not likely, if she has a couple of kids, as Ted remembers his father saying. Could she even have been the Judas in this story? That would be a cruel blow. Whatever the story, this is one Greyhound passenger who's going to be traveling alone.

Ted feels the sting of tears before he realizes that he's crying. This is ridiculous: he knows next to nothing about the man who sent this letter, father or not, because that man has chosen to live most of his life among others. Ted can't be shedding tears over Jack Riley's troubles; and yet he's crying about something. Incredulous, he laughs through his tears. Hell, it's not everyone who can be abandoned twice by the man who sired him; it's even mildly funny. It also gives him a bit of clarity. So he's alone in the world, without a father; someday his mother will be gone too—there's nothing really new about that, is there? It's the law of nature. He gets up and walks to the bathroom, where he splashes cold water on his face, he blows his nose. He feels better; in fact he doesn't feel sad at all, as if the tears he shed were simply part of some ritual.

When he returns to the chair he picks up the five one hundred dollar bills. They're crisp and new. The multiplied face of Benjamin Franklin looks out at him, ready to instruct: "A penny saved is a penny earned." Old Ben has a crafty look and for a second Ted wonders if the money could be counterfeit but that's probably just because for him to be holding five hundred dollars in cash is unreal in itself. He returns to his image of his father in a bus station in Arizona: as he sealed the envelope, a country-and-western song would be playing, some hillbilly tenor wailing about his lost love to the accompaniment of a steel guitar. Jack Riley stops a moment to listen, he puts the letter into the mail slot and boards his bus, preparing to vanish once more in the vastness of the West. Now these pieces of paper are all Ted has of his father. He feels the weight of his absence. From the sound of it, he isn't likely ever to see him again, so that his brief appearance in the winter and this letter are very likely the extent of the adult relationship between father and son. Given the way things have turned out, it might have been better if he'd just stayed gone, out of Ted's life. Did he have to come back only to run out on him again? But oddly, Ted can't work up much anger about this second desertion. For all his faults, the Jack Riley of his imagination is a man who cuts a swath, even in defeat, an operator. Holding the fresh, clean bills to his nose, Ted breathes in an air of spaciousness that's infused with something of the outlaw. Growing up in a house where neither he nor his mother talked about the event that caused the fracture of the family, he's been used to trying to preserve some semblance of order, to keeping the peace. How much of his reaction to everything afterwards was shaped by his role there? Maybe, as Jack Riley suggested, the son isn't entirely unlike his father.

Five hundred bucks, five big ones. He has no idea of what he's likely to do with the money but his scope has certainly been widened.

For the time being this is just his, this whole experience, his father's second communication, his second abandonment, the mysterious circumstances surrounding his present situation, his grandly simple gift. Ted needs a space of time in which to hoard these things. He's even going to wait before telling Dori.

There's no denying that this letter changes some things dramatically, though. He no longer has the expectation of his father's help with his mother's medical condition. If anything develops on that front that requires more attention, he'll have to be the one to figure out what to do. Whether or not he likes it, he's on a new footing with his mother.

He calls her later that night and they talk for a moment about the weather in Cold River and Chippewa. "The windows are all open," she tells him. "There's a nice breeze." He can imagine her in the living room where they watched TV last winter and the precise smell of the house on Maple Street is conjured for him. He sees the curtains moving in the breeze. "We like our little house, don't we?" his mother told him more than once when he was growing up. It was small but it had been big enough for the two of them.

"How are you feeling?" he asks her now, thinking of the man in the bus station.

"I'm fine," she answers conventionally enough, though she may sense something in his tone because after a few moments she adds, "Why do you ask?"

He's determined to get directly to the point. "I mean your health, mom. How's your health?"

There's a silence for a few seconds before she responds. "What do you mean? Who have you been talking to?"

He's already decided he isn't going to mention anything about his contact with his father. Why complicate things? But then, why does he insist on pushing this question, especially now that his father's offer has apparently been withdrawn? The only answer he can come up with is that knowing the truth has to be better than ignorance. "Nobody, mom," he says. "But I'm worried. I could see between semesters you weren't as strong as you used to be."

She laughs defensively. "We can't turn back the clock. I'm not as young as I used to be, I guess."

Ted remains firm. "I don't mean that, mom. You seemed weak, tired." He waits a moment and when she doesn't respond, he continues. "There were other things too. Really, I'm old enough now, you know. If you have any medical condition, shouldn't I know?"

There's another long silence during which he can feel her resistance. He can imagine his mother trying to work out a response to this new challenge. Not a person given to crying over spilt milk, she has no use for mystification and illusion. When she asks again "Who have you been talking to?" he has the eerie sense that she knows about his father's visit and is waiting for him to confess this betrayal.

But he holds his ground. "I have eyes and ears, mom," he says.

"All right," she concedes at last. "I may—and I emphasize 'may'—have a touch of multiple sclerosis, but before you get upset or anything, it seems to be a mild form of it; it's something that can be controlled."

Hearing the words coming from her is upsetting—maybe up until that moment he's held out the possibility that everything his father told him on that subject was fiction. He holds his hand over the receiver while he takes a deep breath. "Dr. Krause says so?" he asks at last.

"Yes, Dr. Krause says so. And don't be so alarmed. I'm telling you the truth. He's very confident about controlling it."

"That's good," he says. "What Dr. Krause said, that's good." He remembers that first winter after his father left, when he took out his fury skating on the river while his mother, just as hurt, responded in her own way, keeping it from her son. She doesn't deserve any more suffering.

"Really," she goes on, "I probably should have told you sooner if it's something that's worried you. But if you want to, you can talk to Dr. Krause yourself."

"No, that's OK," Ted says. "Well, maybe I will." He's relieved, though. "But you will keep me posted, OK?"

"I will."

When he hangs up, he drops into a chair, lights a cigarette and takes a deep drag, exhaling the smoke into the room. At the moment, to his surprise, he feels pretty good. His girl is going to be leaving, his father, a fleeting presence at best, is gone once more, on the lam from the law out West, and his mother has just told him that she's sick. He's only a grad student teaching a couple of sections of freshman English while trying to get a degree which, if you believe Bradford Winslow, will condemn him to a pauperis life. Even the five hundred-dollar bills, magical as they might have seemed a few hours ago, are only money, and not so much of it in the grand scheme of things. Yet, for all his woes and all that he doesn't have, he feels a strength, an ability to deal with things, just like the people who created him. His mother is dealing with things, God knows his father is trying. For a moment Ted wonders if his present troubles will push Jack Riley back into drinking. It's possible. If it does, he might be able to deal with it, he might not be able to. Still, all of them are alive, trying to work out their fates. The sadness he feels is sharp and real, but he remembers his class earlier today and his decision to take things into his own hands, to walk the tightrope, even to dance on it a little. Remembering that feels good, it feels damn good.

The university has sent this year's crop of students back into the world and a great many of their teachers have followed them out of town. With only a few diehards like Ted hanging about in the interval before summer school, Chippewa has undergone its annual transformation from bustling academic center to sleepy Midwestern town whose torpid rhythms are dominated by the weather. Through the long, warm days the pavement shimmers, cicadas throb, and residents seek protection from the prairie heat in the shade of the lush oaks and maples, chestnuts and elms that line the streets. In back yards and on front lawns all over town the soporific buzz of insects is broken only by children's laughter or the clink of ice in a glass of lemonade. The steady heat lingers into the night, when Ted takes solitary walks through town, listening to the murmur of soft voices on screened porches while trees rustle with the promise of a thunderstorm. From the highest hill in the arboretum, he looks at the winking lights of the university hospital perched above the sleeping town. Alone in the Chippewa night, he has an overwhelming sense of his being here, alive, deep in the interior of the continent; and the exhilaration coursing through his veins is matched only by the ache of experiencing this by himself, without being able to share it with Dori.

Still, he's survived her departure. You can make it, he keeps telling himself, because you have to. It's like when he cracked a rib once as a teenager. He learned to breathe shallowly, through clenched teeth. Painful as it was, he got through it because he knew he was healing, and he supposes this hurt too will be over sometime. Meanwhile, his days move uneventfully. He feels the detachment of a lone survivor of some awful calamity. Since no one who wasn't there could possibly understand, there's no point in trying to communicate the experience. It's best to plod on.

He's not working at the library this summer because he got a grant that's supposed to give him time to search for a dissertation subject and it's true he's been reading, immersing himself in Faulkner, but he can't say that he's any closer to finding a thesis. Mostly he's kept to himself. On TV he's followed the stories of the collapsed summit, the upcoming trial of Gary Powers, the debate over whether or not the U.S. ought to have apologized to the Soviet Union over the U-2 affair. He's listened to the threats and accusations, the justifications traded by the two adversaries. Elsewhere lately there have been riots in Turkey and South Korea that have caused the fall of governments, Africa is in a state of turmoil. Whatever stability anyone may have felt only months ago seems to have fled, and here in the middle of the country there's an uneasy sense that things are slipping out of place. This isn't the way people had hoped the world would look as Ike left office and there's anxiety about who's going to replace him. With the Democratic convention approaching, everybody's wondering what's going to happen next.

Amid all the news from the Cold War one other item has especially seized Ted's imagination: the capture of Adolf Eichmann by Israeli commandos. Unrelated as it may be to the story of Gary Powers, Ted can't help connecting the two. Weren't both the American U-2 pilot and the ex-Nazi people who, for different reasons and a half a world apart, sought invisibility above all? The man confined to the tight spaces of the secret airplane thinking *I've done this before, only a little while longer and I'll make it again*; and Hitler's former functionary, living his false life in the depths of South America, calculating, no doubt, to get through one more day, then the next, knowing as he makes his breakfast coffee or listens to the news at night that all over the planet people are hunting for him—how solitary each of them seems. And now their being found out has set in motion the process of public exposure: soon both of them will be in courtrooms, their trials followed by millions around the world. It's one more thing Ted misses being able to talk about with Dori. "These two guys," he'd tell her, "each of them is an actor in a drama of spies and surveillance, and in the end each of their stories seems to point to a simple moral: *You can't hide; eventually you'll be found out.*" What would she say to that? he wonders.

Probably something like, "How can you compare a monster like Eichmann to someone like Powers, who seems like Joe Average, just doing his job?"

"Hey, but isn't that Eichmann's defense?" he'd say.

Then he'd see the light in her eyes as an idea takes shape. "Powers was the watcher," she'd say, "the voyeur in the sky. Only he didn't know that he was also the watched."

"And Eichmann," he'd counter, happy to find something from the movies, "was the Invisible Man who suddenly became visible."

Christ, how he wishes she were here.

The truth is, Dori may have left town but she's still very much a presence in his life. Throughout the day, he finds himself automatically subtracting hours from the time in Chippewa and wondering what she's doing on the coast. Is she on a beach, looking out toward Hawaii, is she driving up the coast with the mountains on her right, heading for Santa Barbara, a place she told him was one of her favorites, where she once imagined the two of them climbing to the top of the courthouse to look out at the blue Pacific, so beautiful it couldn't even be spoiled by the oil derricks just off shore? Or maybe she's sitting at an outdoor cafe in Santa Monica, smoking, reading. As she puts down her book, does she find herself drifting back in her mind to her time in the Midwest, a place as fabulous and distant for her now as Tibet? Still, for all the charms of California, Ted knows she isn't likely to stay on the coast for long. By the time she left, it was clear she was eager to get to Washington, to be part of what she's come to believe is the most important political movement in the country today, and she was almost as impatient with California as she was with Chippewa. Often when he's tried to think of what's so special about Dori, he'll remember a detail of her behavior, like the way she'd bend forward to light her cigarette, as if she were impatient for the first drag; or the lightness and grace with which she leapt over a puddle in the street; but more than the sum of all those details is a simple fact: whenever he was with her, the world grew larger.

Sometimes when he thinks about her now, he imagines he's seeing the country from above, the green, rolling prairie around Chippewa giving way to flatter, dustier plains as you move westward (the land rising, he knows, in spite of its seeming flatness, tilted upward, becoming more arid, the palette being drained of green and blue), until the landscape buckles precipitously somewhere west of the center, the soft earth by now having been transformed into piles of up-thrust rock capped at their heights by snow. Gradually the jagged peaks of the Rockies subside into the wrinkle of lower, browner shapes in the desert states. It's these mountains you have to pass over to reach the paradisal dream that confronted the pioneers when they finished their trek across a terrain dotted with the bleached skulls of cattle, California, a land of Spanish missions and palms and lemon trees and a friendly sun. And very soon Dori will be leaving that place, flying one of those new passenger jets back across the country's middle where she briefly lived, on her way to the Atlantic seaboard, touching down at the southern end of that densely populated urban corridor that extends all the way to Massachusetts Bay. There, set in a soft, humid landscape threaded by tidal rivers, sits the federal city of white monuments and grand ceremonial avenues, where she'll work with others, including the mythic Elliott, to overturn an unjust system that's been in place for centuries; it will be only a matter of time before she begins making her way south into the turbulent states of the old Confederacy where memories are long and fierce, where beards of Spanish moss hang from the live oaks, cottonmouths lurk in the swamps, and the violent heat seems to rise from the red earth itself.

At the airport, both he and Dori were tearful. A mother was trying to quiet her screaming twins, a businessmen trotted by clutching his briefcase, though he wasn't too absorbed in his mission to look at the trio of laughing stewardesses just in on an arriving flight. On the runway planes were landing and taking off. Jesus, Ted kept thinking, I can't believe this is really happening. Dori's nose was red, her eyes moist as they kissed and embraced. "Give 'em hell, Mr. T.," she said, running a hand through his hair, "I know you're going to be a great teacher. Teach those kids to be free, to think for themselves." "Hey," he tried unsuccessfully for an airy note, "how do you know I'm not going to just show up one day on Sunset Boulevard?" "You know my number," she said, doing her Bacall. "All you have to do is whistle." It was sweet torture that they still had time to fill. Then, when their playacting failed to slow the relentless clock, they became solemn. "I admire you," he declared, "I admire the hell out of you, Dori. You're going to change the world." "It's our generation," she said. "It's going to have to be us who are going to make the changes. Oh, Jesus, T." "Damn it, damn it, damn it," was all he could say when they called her to board the plane. Here in Chippewa, he wants to believe what she said about changing things, he wants to believe there's an alternative to just watching the news on TV and hoping that those on both sides who are in charge of the bombers and missiles will allow the rest of the world's people to live another day.

For the most part, he goes about his business, trying to act as though there's a future. Sometimes he's let himself succumb to a touch of self-pity, allowing a late-night glass of bourbon to become a few, turning on the record player and listening to Ray Charles over and over, or, more dangerously, to Barber's *Knoxville, Summer of 1915*, standing before the picture Dori gave him as a souvenir, staring at it as if there were some clue to the secret of life in that pale, red-roofed Spanish mission, the dark silent motorcar whose headlights send their thin beams into the darkness, the giant lemon moon bathing the orchards with the repose of its mysterious light. Looking at that picture can produce an immense longing, yet every time he's been tempted to call Dori, in spite of the time difference in his favor, he's resisted.

They made a pact that they won't get in touch until the fall. Breathe shallowly, he reminds himself; you're healing.

And he is, he's pretty sure. Alone, he isn't without resources. His father's five hundred dollars is in a bank account now and that gives him a sense of a horizon. He's talked to his mother, he's talked to Dr. Krause, and he's feeling better about her situation: it's entirely sensible to believe that the disease can be managed. "I feel like a Las Vegas gambler," his mother told him, more open now about her condition. "With this disease you throw the dice every day. And who knows? You can get lucky and go for years without any problems. Or it could all cave in overnight." She laughed. "But isn't that what the nuns always said?" OK, he's told himself, I'm not in control of this situation. I can live with that. In fact, I have no choice. Though he knows that nothing about his life has been solved, to his surprise, he still manages to awaken on some mornings with a sense of expectation.

He's in the graduate reading room of the library on one of those mornings when Charles Cross walks up to him with an uncharacteristically grave expression. "Did you hear about what happened last night?" he asks.

"No." Ted is surprised by the man's somber manner. Charles, who grew up in a small town in Nebraska, is a slim, fastidious man with an unlikely British accent. He usually has an eager gleam in his eye when he's about to present a tidbit of gossip. "What happened?" Ted asks.

Charles glances around to assure himself that nobody is within earshot before he goes on. "There was a police raid last night," he says quietly. "They arrested a dozen men in the rest room of the Student Union." It takes Ted only a couple of seconds to fill in the blanks: Charles is talking about a raid on homosexuals using the "tea-room." "Andrew Kesler was one of them."

"Oh, my God." Ted is thunderstruck. Kesler arrested? "What's that mean?" he asks. "What's going to happen now?"

Charles shows no particular relish in talking about the subject. The event seems genuinely to have upset him. "It will be in the local paper, of course," he says quietly. "There'll be vague phrases like 'morals charges' and so forth, but everybody will know what that means. And there will be names."

"Jesus," is all Ted can think to say at first. Can they really do this? "But what about Andrew?" he asks after a moment. "What's happened to him?"

Charles shakes his head. "He didn't come to work this morning." He lets that information sink in before going on. "Of course, they would have taken them all to jail in handcuffs—I don't know if we'll be getting any news photos of that, though. A judge would set bail and somebody would have to pay it to get him out." Charles speaks like someone familiar with these details.

Ted is trying to imagine a handcuffed Kesler being led into a police wagon. It's the last thing the tightly-strung Pole needs. "But why would the cops do that in Chippewa?" he asks. "I mean, it's supposedly a sophisticated town and weren't they all consenting adults?"

Charles sighs and lets the question pass, as if to say that's just the way of the world and that's the way it's always been.

Ted is trying to think clearly about this, though he can't shake the image of Kesler in handcuffs. "Could this hurt Andrew with his job here?" he asks.

"What do you think?" Charles responds. Ted realizes that in the last minute or so he's had to make an adjustment in his assessment of this man: he's no longer just the feline purveyor of gossip; there's an air of stoic forbearance about him, even a genuine concern for the unfortunate Kesler. "Oh, it's happened before," he says. "The police in Chippewa aren't as bad as they are in some places, but they don't have any love for homosex- uals. There's been pressure here in the town recently, people have known that. The police have been conducting surveillance since the spring." He shakes his head. "In some ways, the ones who got caught were practically asking for it."

Ted nods. He can believe it of Kesler. But what's going to happen to the poor devil now? he wonders. He remembers

Dori's account of the beefy cop manhandling the Negro. Could he have been in on the arrest of Andrew?

Charles is no longer speaking quietly. "In a way, I give them credit for their courage," he says, "but it was pretty foolhardy. This isn't a time to be bold. There's a bit of hysteria going around." He laughs soundlessly. "Wait'll you see what they did at the Student Union."

"What?" Ted asks.

"They've taken off the doors of the stalls in the men's room. Supposedly for the 'protection' of patrons. In other words, the university is caving in to a small-town police department. God," he sighs, "this is depressing."

"His name is going to be in the papers, you think?"

Charles nods. "I'm afraid so. And his number is in the phone book, so it wouldn't be surprising if he were to get a few nasty calls." He shakes his head. "It's not a pretty situation to be exposed like that in a place like Chippewa."

As soon as it's out, Ted buys the local paper. The report of the raid is on the front page. There's a photo but, thankfully, people's faces are obscured, though the story does name names. Kesler's is familiar to Ted, and he recognizes that of the dozen men identified, three seem to be connected to the university in one way or the other; the rest are presumably locals. As Charles predicted, he comes upon the phrase "morals charges" and a detective is quoted on the need to be vigilant about this "unwholesome element." Seeing Kesler's name in black and white in a story of this nature makes Ted wonder again about the Pole's future. The man is hardly popular at the library, he knows. But if he were to lose his job, where would he go?

Kesler's situation suddenly seems dire. In the brief time Ted has known him, he's had his ups and downs—mostly downs, truth be told—but this is something more than having to move out of your apartment. He feels unexpectedly anxious about him. He remembers the phone call during which Kesler declared that he'd killed his sister. He remembers thinking then that the man was mentally unstable and might do anything. Certainly something like this could push him over the edge.

Where is he now? Is he out of jail? Is he back at his apartment? All at once Ted knows he has to get in touch with him. It can't be good for the man to be alone at a time like this. He should at least hear from someone. Of course, Ted realizes, Kesler may have friends of his own and it might be presumptuous of him to think of intruding at such a delicate time, but to do nothing seems to be courting danger.

At a pay phone, he finds Kesler's number and calls him. No answer. That could mean he's still in jail. Or possibly he's out with friends who are consoling him. But it's the middle of the day, after all, and most people would be at work. And didn't Kesler himself tell him he had no friends here? Ted remembers what Charles said about Andrew's name being in the paper and his number in the phone book. The Pole may in fact be home and just be sitting there, letting the phone ring without answering it. Who knows what he might expect to hear on the other end of the line? Maybe he's already got a threatening or abusive call or two. No, Kesler's not answering his phone doesn't prove anything.

Ted has to find out more and there's only one other person he can think of who might provide help. He looks up Sam Morelli's number on campus and calls him.

"I just wanted to find out if you knew anything about Andrew Kesler," he says.

Morelli lowers his voice. "Yeah, I know about that. It's been taken care of."

"Taken care of?"

"His bail was paid, he's out of jail," the voice on the other end of the phone tells him.

"That surprises me," Ted says. "I thought you'd try to keep your distance from him. Especially under the circumstances."

"It was handled by a third party," Morelli tells him curtly.

Ted thinks about that. "What's going to happen to him now?" he asks.

"I don't know," Morelli says with some exasperation. "He's on his own as far as I'm concerned."

"But . . ." Ted starts, but he doesn't know how to continue.
He's never been sure about Morelli's exact relationship to Andrew
but he's come to think of him as Kesler's protector or sponsor.
You brought him here, is what he's thinking. Shouldn't you help
him out? "Do you have any idea where he might be?" he asks.
"He didn't show up for work today."

"That's not surprising," Morelli observes. "But, no, I don't
have any idea where he might be." He sounds impatient.

Ted has no intention of hanging up just yet. "I called his
apartment but there was no answer."

"I don't know what to tell you," Morelli says. After a silence
of a few seconds, he sighs. "Look," he goes on, his voice softer,
"I realize that Andrew's had a rough time but we've helped him.
After a certain point there's not much more you can do." He
sounds genuinely at a loss. "Believe me, I can sympathize with
him." After a while, he says, "Actually, if you did call or visit
him, that might not be a bad idea."

Once more Ted tries Kesler's number and gets no response.
He decides to go to his place and determine whether or not he's
there. At the very least he can leave him a note, though what
can he possibly say? The day is muggy, the trees hiss, and the
sky is gray with the threat of rain, giving the town a hunched,
expectant look. The Pole lives in a brown frame house that's no
different from hundreds of others in Chippewa, though in the
murky light it seems especially dismal. Things aren't any better
indoors. The downstairs hall is musty: a streaked mirror stands
over a cheap pine mail table, the plum-colored rug is stained.
The staircase creaks and the place seems to get shabbier the
higher Ted climbs. On the third floor the air is stale as he stands
before Kesler's door wondering whether the man can't afford
anything better or whether he actually prefers these kinds of
surroundings. He remembers Kesler's commenting that while
Ted seemed to gravitate toward basements, he himself seemed
to move in the opposite direction.

Still wondering what to put in his note, Ted decides to knock
on the door. There's no response. Then he calls out, "Andrew.
It's Ted Riley." To his surprise, he hears movement inside. Soon

the door opens a sliver and there's Andrew Kesler, peering out like some character from a German Expressionist film of the twenties. In this light he's even paler than usual; his large eyes blaze behind his horn-rimmed glasses, he's bent in a kind of stoop and his deformed hand plays absently with one of the buttons on his white shirt. "Andrew," Ted says, and can't think of anything to follow it up.

"Come in," the man at the door answers with a lopsided smile. The casualness of his greeting might suggest that he's been expecting Ted all along, and Ted enters a small area further foreshortened by the slope of the roof that gives the whole place an angular look. There's a trace of something like incense on the air. The apartment seems to consist of three small rooms and, judging from the one that's most visible, they're furnished in a manner that was outdated a generation ago when the furnishings were bought. The rug is worn and the walls are covered with a hideous brown wallpaper. There are a couple of cumbersome brown chairs and a coffee table. A small desk stands against the wall. Undoubtedly all this was provided by Kesler's landlady, who might be a fourth-generation Chippewan; and yet to Ted there's an Eastern European look to the place. Possibly it's the shawl hung over one of the chairs. "Welcome to my domain," Kesler says with an uneven sweep of his hand, and for the first time Ted wonders if he's been drinking. Books and clothing are scattered all over the place and Ted remembers being upset by the mess in his own apartment when Kesler came there. Actually, he may have felt quite at home.

"Sit down, please," his host points to one of the chairs. "Just put those books on the floor. Will you join me in a drink?"

Ted doesn't usually drink this early in the day but, given the situation, he judges it best to be sociable. "Sure," he says. Kesler retreats toward the kitchen and Ted notices that he's limping slightly, though his first impression as he waits for him is that he seems to be holding up pretty well, all things considered. A small fan drones feebly, doing little to freshen the air. Through the window Ted can see that the sky has darkened since he entered the house. From the looks of it, it will be raining in minutes, and that might bring some relief to the humid air outside.

Kesler returns from the kitchen carrying two short, slim glasses of a clear liquid with a faintly greenish tinge. Ted supposes it's some kind of vodka. The Pole's face shines with sweat, which isn't surprising. Ted feels his clothes sticking to his skin. After Kesler gives Ted his glass, he settles down across from him. "Na zdrowie," he toasts, and finishes off his drink in a swallow.

Ted takes a sip from his glass as if he's drinking bourbon. Whatever it is, it's strong. He assumes it's vodka but it has a sweetish flavor he can't identify. He puts his glass down. "I'm sorry to hear about your trouble," he says.

Kesler waves the sentiment away dismissively. "What can we expect from Chippewa?" He pronounces the name in such a way that the very syllables sound absurd. "My landlady has already given me her ultimatum. She was gracious enough to allow me a full week." He laughs. "She'll need another few days, of course, to fumigate this charming place before she can rent it again." He seems on the verge of explosive laughter. Then he frowns as if trying to remember something and shakes his head.

"If you want to borrow my car . . ." Ted suggests, a little less confident that his host is bearing up so well.

"Thank you, no," Kesler says. For a moment his eyes shine with what seems like real gratitude; then they darken and turn inward. "I don't think I'll be needing it," he says. His tone is subdued, his earlier acerbity gone. He looks into his empty glass and smiles weakly to himself. "I'm considering my options," he murmurs.

"Well," Ted says, wishing there were more he can say, "in case you need anything." The rain has started and he can hear it on the roof. For a few seconds both men listen and it occurs to Ted that this man must have listened to rain falling on many roofs on two continents. He looks around the room. Other than clothes and books, there isn't much. There are no photos of people. The pictures on the walls are cheap, sentimental reproductions, but the wooden crucifix on the desk is apparently Kesler's. Is the man religious?

"Do you know what you're going to do next?" Ted asks, careful not to address directly the question of whether or not Andrew expects to be able to continue at the library.

Kesler points to Ted's glass. "Drink, my friend. It isn't poison."

Ted finishes the rest of his vodka. "No," he says, his eyes watering, "not poison at all. Really, it's very good. What is this stuff, anyway?"

"It's *żubròwka*, a kind of vodka. A *żubr* is a bison and the color and flavor of that drink comes from a sprig of grass in the bottle that you might call buffalo grass."

"Wait," Ted says. "Bison, like our bison?"

"Yes. They live in the forests of eastern Poland. Herman Goering was a hunting enthusiast and amid all the devastation of the war he saw to it that those forests were preserved so that he could have his sport."

Herman Goering hunting buffaloes? Is this another of Kesler's fantastic stories? Ted tries to imagine the bearded creatures he's always associated with the American plains being pursued by Nazis somewhere in eastern Europe. Even if what Kesler says is true, it's hard to imagine those beasts who roam today on the back side of a nickel apart from the Indians who hunted them in the days when they covered the prairies.

"Will you have another?" Kesler asks.

"No, no," Ted waves it away.

"Really," the Pole presses him. "One drink is hardly being sociable."

There's an undercurrent of pleading in his voice and Ted reminds himself that he came here because of the extremity of Kesler's situation. "Sure," he yields. "Why not?" Kesler gets to his feet and goes to the kitchen, limping again. He brings the bottle with him this time and pours the drinks, then puts the bottle on the coffee table. I'm not going to do a third one of these, Ted resolves, noting the silhouette of a bison on the label of the bottle. This time, though, he quaffs his drink in one swallow the way Kesler does. "Whew!" he says. "That's potent but I like it." His host nods, his mouth curved into a smile though his eyes are more distant than they were moments ago. All at once the meagerness of Kesler's quarters gets to Ted: these dark, peaked rooms where books and clothes are scattered all over the place and the rain drives with quiet insistence on the roof—all the man's earthly possessions are here, his entire history confined to a space on the top floor of a house in Chippewa. It seems a frightening image of Kesler's vulnerability.

Meanwhile, his host has begun talking quietly, in a detached voice. "I knew it wasn't a smart thing to do," he says, as if to himself. "They've been watching those johns for weeks now. As soon as I got there I picked up something in the way things looked. You know how you come into a room and without knowing what it is, you're aware that something's wrong? I felt that and I almost passed the place by . . ." He smiles sadly to himself. "But there is, as your Poe says, an imp of the perverse, and he must have been sitting on my shoulder. I just wouldn't let myself be stopped from doing something because I was afraid." He shakes his head. "Maybe I should have had more common sense, but then. . . ." He throws up his hands airily.

"Yeah," Ted says. "I can see that." Kesler sighs and looks into his empty glass. "Were you in jail long?" Ted asks.

"Ten minutes in that dump is too long," the other man answers with sudden vehemence. Then his spirits seem to collapse as quickly as they'd been aroused. He fumbles with a pack of cigarettes he extracts from his shirt pocket, lights one and takes a deep drag. The exhaled smoke hangs heavily in the air. "It wasn't that bad for me," he says. "I've seen worse. But one or two of the men—kids, really—were upset and had to be calmed down. The cops didn't help, of course." He twists his mouth but says nothing more.

"Did the cops hurt you?" Ted asks, thinking about his limp.

"One of them tried to twist my leg off," Kesler says. "As you can see, he wasn't successful."

"The bastard." For Ted it has to be the same cop Dori saw when she was with Sam Pierce. "What the hell did he do that for?"

"I tried to kick him in the balls," Kesler says. "I didn't hit my target but I got him in the leg anyway."

"Good for you." Ted tries to imagine the improbable scene.

"What do they call this part of the country?" Kesler says after a while. "The Heartland? Well, it's a very frightened heart these days. Just now it seems as if everyone in the U.S. is looking for villains," he goes on, "and I suppose I qualify. Not only because of my sexual preferences, perhaps, or where I happen to be when I practice them. But I'm villain enough because I'm different." He runs his good hand through his hair. "I haven't always been strong and stalwart," he goes on. "I've done things I regretted. But my being labeled a villain solves nothing, and you Americans want all complicated questions settled." He sighs and when he continues there's a weariness in his voice. "One of the police called me a commie. The exact phrase was 'commie fag cocksucker.' I suppose I'll admit to the last two but the first one is laughable."

Never has Andrew been so open with Ted and he tries to be worthy of the man's confidence. He can't pretend to be sophisticated about Andrew's way of life but he has no intention of condemning him for it. As he listens to the rain on the roof, though, he has a sudden sense of dread. Maybe it's the apartment, maybe it's the weather, but he can't help feeling that bad things are lurking somewhere, even worse things than have happened already, and he's fearful for Andrew. He wants to say more, he wants to be encouraging, but what can he say? "Buck up, life can be beautiful?" He feels a vast sense of inadequacy. At least I'm here, he tells himself; he's got someone to listen to, and that might help.

"Morelli was behind getting me out," Kesler says, "but of course he didn't show up himself." He looks straight ahead, at some point beyond Ted. "Sometimes when I get angry I think about him and I try to work up some kind of animus but I can't, really. Morelli is just a cog, he's so far on the periphery of my story, and my sister's story—you have just as much to do with it as he does. Really, he's the last man in a chain that started long ago in Germany." Ted waits for more but Kesler is silent a while.

The fan drones, the rain keeps striking the roof. "Sam Morelli isn't the man who recruited Magda," Kesler continues. "He isn't the one who gave her those assignments and who felt some sort of responsibility to her after she was killed." The words come slowly, as if they have to be carried up several flights of stairs. "That man's name was Brown, or at least so he said. I've never been sure whether or not he was Magda's lover." He continues looking into the distance.

When he falls silent this time, Ted feels the need to say something, anything. "What do you think will happen at the library?" he asks after a moment. Even as he says it, he thinks: this guy is talking about death, about his sister and the man who might have been her lover and all I can think to ask him about is his job. But the past, at least the past that Kesler brings with him, is dark and tangled, a place with no bottom. How can there be any solace there? What's important, he tells himself, is the future.

"Ah," Kesler sinks back in his chair as if suddenly exhausted, "the Catalog Department. I suppose this will be enough for them. God knows there are people who have been looking for reasons to get rid of me." He shakes his head. "If I were a certain kind of paranoid, I might even suspect that somebody in the library was behind the whole thing. But there are limits, even to my paranoia. In this case it's wisest to choose the simplest explanation. Look," he says, suddenly aroused. "Have another drink with me, won't you?"

Ted puts up his hand. "I don't think so," he says. Two of these have been quite enough. He's feeling a little fuzzy. He tries to distract the man. "I couldn't help noticing that crucifix," he says. "Are you religious?"

Kesler shakes his head. "Technically I'm a Catholic but I'm not really a believer. No, that crucifix is a memento. It's something I got from someone who was important to me once." He goes over to the dresser and brings the crucifix to Ted, who runs his fingers over the smooth wood. "Do you like it?" Kesler asks. "It's very old, from the sixteenth century, as a matter of fact. The cross is made from a single piece of wood."

Ted nods. "Yes, I like it." The slender, stylized Christ nailed
to the cross seems to have moved beyond suffering and pain to
some kind of peace, his head laid gently against his shoulder
like a man enjoying a well-earned rest. Ted feels the wood under
his hands. It's amazing to think this was carved so many centuries ago. At last he lays it down very gently. Meanwhile, in
spite of his previous refusal, Kesler takes his glass and begins to
pour him a drink. As he watches the liquor rise in the glass, he
doesn't have the will to protest. What the hell, he thinks, can I
really refuse a man in such a desperate situation? "Well, OK,"
he concedes. "But this has to be the last one. I have a certain
amount of stuff I have to do today."

"Good, good," Kesler says, and he pours one for himself.
Ted lifts his glass and holds it to the light, so that the pale green
liquid glows. "Buffalo grass," he says, trying to imagine a herd
of the shaggy beasts roaming through a Polish forest, Herman
Goering in hot pursuit. Amazing. For a second or two he feels
a sense of spaciousness in this angular apartment at the top of a
house in Chippewa.

"To freedom," Kesler says, and drinks his down. Ted follows
quickly. "I'm living existentially now," the Pole declares with a
sudden reckless glee. "At the moment I'm without any kind of
ties; you might say I have an infinitude of choices."

In the silence that follows, the sounds of the rain and the
fan seem to grow louder. I may be a little drunk, Ted thinks, but
everything seems so strange here. Can I really be in this dingy
room talking to this guy whose story goes all the way back to a
place so many thousands of miles from here, where the buffalo
roam? It wouldn't surprise him if, having made his way back
down the stairs, he were to open the front door and find himself
in pre-war Krakow.

"Your father and mother," he says. "They were a professor
and a doctor?"

Kesler nods gravely.

"What were their names?"

"Fryderik and Malgorzata," Kesler answers.

"Good, good," he says, repeating the names. "You know," he finds himself saying, "I told you I grew up in a little place called Cold River and that my father left us when I was eleven. Well, this is strange, but he came by out of the blue this spring from Arizona, where it seems he was a big man in real estate. Then just a few weeks ago I got a letter from him saying he was in trouble with the law, he was on the run. I don't think I'll ever see him again." It's over almost before Ted realizes what he's said.

Kesler nods but he says nothing. His brow is wrinkled and his face sags as if he's begun to run down like an unwound clock.

"Sorry," Ted says. "I mean, you've got your own problems."

"No, no," the man says, rousing himself. "I appreciate your telling me. It must be difficult."

Ted looks around at the pinched, crowded room where he's talking to this man who, only last night, was handcuffed and led into a police van that took him to jail. "Look," he says, "this vodka is getting to me. I have to go home and maybe take a nap. But if you need anything, give me a call. You know, maybe we can go to dinner or something."

Kesler nods almost imperceptibly. He seems at peace just now, but there's something else as well. It's only when Ted has left and is standing in the soft rain that he can put his finger on it: at the end, the man's eyes seemed decades older than he was. They were the oldest eyes he's ever seen.

After Ted leaves, the apartment is quiet. Will he really go home and take a nap in the middle of this dreary afternoon? Kesler wonders. It's an appealing idea: what a luxury, to be able to exempt yourself from the day while everyone else is busy buying and selling, planning, scheming, pleading and longing, though it's such a civilized notion that it would most likely be frowned upon by most of the earnest citizens of Chippewa. Andrew thinks about the young American who was just here. What would it be like to have sprung up from the soil of the New World, to have lived your whole life in the center of this continent where the stories of the great deeds and misdeeds of that other, older world would seem less real than the random sighs of the prairie wind? What would it be like to carry on your back a history that, complex as it might feel to you, doesn't extend much beyond the brief span of your own life? Would your step be light and eager or would you hold yourself tense, afraid that in your weightlessness you'd float off the earth itself? For all the time he's spent among Americans, they remain a mystery he hasn't come close to solving.

In the present quiet it seems hardly possible that only minutes ago he and his visitor were sharing drinks like members of a fashionable club, discussing Sam Morelli, the Chippewa jail, bison and Herman Goering. Who'd have imagined that at a time like this he'd be entertaining this graduate student from a place called Cold River? And yet, for all their differences, it was considerate of Ted to come here when most people would be inclined to stay away. It can't have been an easy situation for him, that was obvious enough. All the more surprising, then,

243

that sudden rush of information about his father near the end of his visit, which even seemed to surprise him and to leave him somewhat embarrassed. No doubt the *żubròwka* was largely responsible. Still, he came here, and Andrew appreciates the gesture. For all his callow provinciality, Ted Riley is a civilized person: he's curious about the world and he seems to have a good heart. Though not that many years separate them, Kesler feels oddly paternal toward him, and he hopes Ted enjoys the sleep of the innocent this afternoon.

Andrew himself feels calm just now, as if this were an ordinary day; he savors the stillness of this place, he savors his solitude. And isn't he too enjoying a state of delinquency? He has no further obligations to others here; he's no longer part of this world of Chippewa. Standing near the door, he finds himself beset by the unlikeliest of memories from his childhood, of a dapper little man with a monocle who'd patted him on the head at some family party. Mustached, smelling of talcum powder, Professor Borowski thought it was the epitome of wit to address the young Andrew with florid language: "It is indeed a pleasure to encounter once again this august personage," his high-pitched voice directed as much toward the other guests as toward Andrew. For the boy Borowski was a comic figure, another adult one had to endure, vaguely insufferable and not to be taken seriously, which was probably the feeling of a good number of the partygoers. It was only later through Magda that he learned the full irony of the life of his father's colleague at the university. A professor of botany, Borowski was an intellectual anti-Semite, a supporter of the *Sanacja* party that advocated an ethnically pure Poland, though he deplored the thuggish methods of some of its more vulgar partisans. He himself had little against Jews personally, he always maintained, and he spoke admiringly of the intelligence of Jewish colleagues and of what he called the Hebraic people in general; but he thought Jews played too large a role in Polish culture and he consistently supported the restriction of their rights. Though his views were sharply opposed to those of Andrew's parents and their circle, they occasionally saw him socially and it was then that he young Andrew had to put up with his pretentious solicitude. But Borowski, though an anti-Semite, was also a fierce Polish nationalist and when the Germans invaded Poland, he denounced them publicly and repeatedly, regardless of the Nazis' racial ideology. Nor was he silent after the takeover. No one spoke more bravely against the invaders—"he kept at them like a rabid terrier," Magda quoted someone who'd been a witness. In the end, the pompous little man with his dreams of a Poland that never was died with many of his colleagues at Sachsenhausen.

Professor Borowski, who made an art of adjusting his monocle, who cleared his throat to signal an important pronouncement, and who always used the Latin names of flowers. A confirmed bachelor who may well have been one of history's rare asexual creatures. How, out of all the names, faces and places of Andrew's past, did this one happen to emerge just now? He marvels at this extraordinary act of retrieval. Borowski left no family and certainly had few admirers. After Andrew is gone, who's likely to remember the man's story?

He goes to the window and opens it wider so that he can feel the cool air; a few drops of rain splash against his skin as he listens to it fall with a patient, comforting steadiness. "This is the best kind of rain for the flowers," Magda would tell him when they were both children. "The flowers don't want the rain to come all at once; they want to drink it carefully and taste it." He'd nod, deferring to his sister's greater knowledge of the world, though he knew that when he liked the taste of something, like the lemonade Pani Piekarska the cook made in the summer, he was inclined to pour it down his throat as if he were trying to consume it all in a single swallow. What a little barbarian he'd been! But then he knew too that, whatever she might tell him about lilacs and roses, Magda was just as impatient as he when it came to actual lemonade. Maybe all it proved was that the two of them weren't flowers.

He turns back toward the small room. The two glasses stand beside the bottle on the coffee table. It was good *żubròwka* but it hasn't done much to fuddle him, which is just as well. He needs a clear head for what he's going to do. But first things first:

he can't just leave the bottle and glasses there. This bit of house-keeping isn't motivated by any consideration for Mrs. Wells, his landlady, who hasn't shown much interest in tidying up this or the two other buildings she owns; it's rather that his episode of socializing with Ted Riley is over and it's time to draw a distinct line between that and what's to follow. He picks up the glasses and carries them to the kitchen, where he runs water over them and puts them in the dish drainer. There are a few inches of *żubrówka* left in the bottle and for a moment he's unsure what he wants to do with it. No, he decides, he isn't going to finish it, and he leaves it there on the counter.

As he looks at the hump-backed, bearded silhouette of the bison, though, something passes through him, disturbing the calm. Feeling the weight of a great weariness, he goes back to the living room, where he drops into a chair, hoping he can keep his mind empty. Instinctively he reaches for a cigarette and lights it. At least he has a few more of them; he won't run out. He inhales deeply, trying to quiet the almost subliminal tremor of dread that's ambushed him in the last few seconds. That's all right, he assures himself, it's only natural. He'll go through stages before the time comes. In the end, all he needs is a few minutes' steely resolution, and he's sure he'll be able to manage that when it becomes necessary. The sound of the rain soothes him, as does the tobacco, and soon he's thinking again of Magda. "They tried to take everything away from us," she told him after they'd been reunited in Germany. She'd brought him to her apartment: the furniture was modern, the colorful curtains moved in the breeze, there were flowers in the window, a carton of American cigarettes on the table. "They took everything we had," she said. "Mother, Father, our home, our position in the world." Magda's eyes blazed with anger but what came through in her words was her quiet strength, and she reminded him of one of the knights in the books he used to read as a child, strong, cou-rageous, unconquerable. "They destroyed that world and they wanted us to believe there was nothing left but power," she said. "Those who've come after them are no better: they believe the same thing." The ferocity of his sister's moral force unnerved the young Andrew, who'd awakened that morning in the refugee camp: had her quest to find him changed her so much? But then she fell silent. Her eyes shining with tears, she began touching his face as if she were a blind person, she ran a hand through his hair, humming something from their childhood, and suddenly she was softer, she was the Magda of old who used to pull him close to her so that he could smell her hair, her skin, her perfume. "But we know there's more than that," she told him, her voice falling almost to a whisper. "You and I know that."

In the circles in which Andrew has traveled it's often been fashionable to adopt a pose of cynicism or nihilism but it was none other than dear fat Maurice in Brussels who said, "I know your little secret, Andrew, but I won't tell. You really are a passionate believer." He leaned into the folds of his chins that threatened to cover his bow tie, his mouth curved into the smile of a worldly Renaissance cardinal. "I can't say exactly what it is you believe in," he said, "but you're nowhere near as *soignée* as you'd like us to think you are." Maurice loved incense and English suits from the '30s, he loved to rhapsodize about Giotto and Palestrina. An acquaintance once described him as "a dozen affectations posing as a personality" but Maurice, for all his foppish ways and his melodramatic ultra-orthodoxy, wasn't at all dense about the things of the heart, and Andrew was genuinely fond of him.

"But why do you keep working for them?" Andrew kept wanting to ask his sister in the months that followed their reunion. They'd given her a cover job as a translator while she did her other business for them. The job paid well and she lived comfortably in Bavaria but he'd always felt that Magda deserved more from the world than to be a translator of other people's words. "They're not the Nazis, of course," he would have told her, "and they're not the Bolsheviks either but, for all their jazz and candy bars, are we supposed to believe they want to save the world without owning it?" He never asked the question since of course he knew part of the answer: that Magda got started working for the Americans because she was consumed by a single purpose: to find her brother, to salvage what remained of her family. Now that she'd done that and she continued to work for them, it could only be because she had other goals. "Andrew," she told him more than once, "you know history so you know we've always been used by others. We can't stop that but we can at least try to get something in return."

If Andrew is no nihilist, he knows that Magda certainly wasn't one: when she made a promise you knew she'd keep it. Honesty was important to her, honesty and honor and sacrifice. So she'd been willing to make the bargain in order to save her brother. And if she continued to work for the Americans it was because she wanted other things too. What some of those things were, he'll never know; but what he knows with certainty is that she wanted her brother to be protected, she wanted him to have an education, to have a chance to make his way in the new world that was being created out of the ashes of the war. "You've always loved books," she told him. "You were born to read and study. The Americans are the new Romans and they'll need someone to take care of all the treasures they now possess. Why shouldn't it be you?"

Magda made her sacrifice, she paid a terrible price, but Andrew has paid as well. Moving from place to place under the dubious protection of his sister's former employers, he's been a stranger everywhere. He's made his way across two continents, one of the century's tens of millions displaced by war and revolution, trying to find a foothold somewhere, never knowing whether to treasure or to discard the memories they carry with them. Along the way he's slept in five-star hotels and on park benches; he's encountered unbelieving priests, sentimental thugs, shape-shifting boasters and people of simple goodness; he's learned as much about himself as he's learned about the world; and he can honestly say that for all his disappointments, he's known what it is to love and be loved; but in the end it's tired him beyond imagining to have to continually create himself anew in a world of ghosts. It's been enough to drive him to the threshold of despair more than a few times, but through it all he's kept going because he's always felt that, like Magda, he's had a contract to fulfill. Now, though, things have come to an end point at last. He's felt it in his bones for some time and only lately has he come to understand why. In retrospect it seems likely that one of the reasons why he entered the rest room last night when all his instincts told him to avoid it was that unconsciously he felt the need for some external punctuation, though what he's going to do has nothing to do with the arrest. That will be the final irony: people are certain to think that it's shame that's brought him to this point, when the fact is that, by his calculation, he's at last paid off his part of the debt to Magda. She found him in that camp in '46 and continued working for the Americans for seven more years until her death in '53. Ever since, Andrew has been watched over by people like Brown and Morelli and, however difficult it may have been at times, he's been determined to exact from her former employers some measure of Magda's worth. Now that he's got his seven years out of them, though, he's not obligated anymore. He feels the relief of the reformed reprobate who's managed to satisfy the last of his creditors.

He looks around the room: amid all its drabness and impersonality, the crucifix Maurice gave him catches his eye, its simple elegance exposing the unremitting mediocrity of his surroundings. Strangely, the religious object gives him courage, and he feels a rising sense of expectation. He's glad there are a few more cigarettes, he's glad the sun isn't shining: this is the weather he would have chosen. He hasn't planned things meticulously, down to the second, but time is passing and the moment will soon be upon him. He certainly wants to get things over with before the other tenants return. He bought the rope a few days ago, he's already tested the place on the ceiling where an ancient light fixture once hung, he's made the knot. Everything is in order. He imagines some of his associates at the library might find the manner of his leave-taking repellent. "Poor Andrew," he can hear them saying. "It must have been hard for him to have to have done it in such an esthetically unappealing way." But they don't realize that he's no more an esthete than he is a nihilist. And the fact is, if they knew what happened to Magda, even some of those hand-wringing friends might concede an esthetic appropriateness to his action.

First, though, there has to be a note. Nothing long or elaborate, no self-pity or attempts at self-justification. There are a few things that can be given to people, there's a legitimate request. As far as he's concerned, there's at least one more thing he's owed. Of course he knows better than to address Morelli directly. The lawyer who got him out of jail will know who should get the information he'll be conveying.

Kesler sits at the desk, the paper before him, listening to the American rain.

Ted jumps awake the next morning as if shaken out of sleep by a shrieking fire alarm and before he has any time to shape the intention, he's out of bed. Bare feet planted on the cool floor, he instinctively turns toward the clock whose upraised hands tell him it's already after 10 AM and his first thought is that he's late for an important appointment. He stands beside the bed, ready, anxious, accused, though he has no idea about where he's supposed to go. There's nothing, he realizes with a wave of relief, there's no place he's supposed to be. It's summer, after all. Yet, even as he comes to this recognition, he's aware of some heavy undercurrent: not everything is tranquil, is it? Piece by piece recent events settle into sequence and he orients himself: it was yesterday when he heard about Andrew Kesler's arrest; he'd gone to Kesler's apartment where the two of them had a few drinks; then he came home for a nap. Maybe it was that nap that scrambled his sense of time: he awoke in twilight, unaware for a while whether it was morning or evening, and he didn't get back to bed until almost 2 AM. All that seems so far away now and at this distance it's hard to believe the meeting with Kesler actually took place. Did the Pole really tell him that Herman Goering hunted bison in the forests of Poland?

He goes to the kitchen and warms a cup of coffee. Still fuzzyheaded, he keeps coming back to the time he spent with Kesler yesterday. After the episode with the police and the publication of his name in the paper, the man was virtually hiding out in his apartment. Ted can understand that but, God, what a gloomy place it was. He remembers running his fingers across the smooth wood of the old crucifix. When the phone rings, his first thought is that the Pole has reconsidered his offer of his car. It's not Kesler, though, but his landlord. "Ted, this is Earl Bartlett." He can visualize the beefy man who looks like Jonathan Winters. His usually hearty manner is muted today, though, and, without being able to pinpoint his suspicions, Ted thinks, oh-oh, something's up.

"Look, there's no point in beating around the bush," his landlord says. "I reached an agreement with a guy yesterday and I'm selling that place. I'm afraid you'll have to move out at the end of the summer."

"Oh," Ted responds, as if the man has just told him he'll be coming around to fix a leaky faucet. "Sure."

"You've been a good tenant," Bartlett says, "but this other guy has different plans for the property. I realize I told you you could stay on, but things have changed."

"Sure, sure, I understand," Ted tells him. "It's no big deal." When he puts down the phone, though, he's surprised by how much the impending move from this place affects him. Why should that be? He's a student and students move all the time; it's not as if he's being forced to vacate the family estate. Still, his steps are heavy as he walks to the Morris chair. He drops into it, pulls out a cigarette and lights it, sucks down the smoke until it burns his lungs, and then exhales. There's no point in denying his disappointment. In his time here he's developed a fondness for this basement lair on Tecumseh Street where so many of the important moments of his young life have occurred, and in some way that makes no sense at all he must have assumed that he was just going to continue living here. Well, he isn't going to; time, as they say, marches on. But he can't deny the ache he feels at the thought that this phase of his life is going to be over soon, the change bringing with it the scary question: what happens next? Then it strikes him: like Kesler, he has to move now. Won't the Pole find that funny?

The cigarette has helped: already he's feeling better about the impending dislocation. After all, being in town during the summer, he'll be in a good situation to get his pick of the available apartments. He might even convince himself he's feeling good about this new development.

He showers and shaves, makes himself a late breakfast. OK, he tells himself, the main thing is to finish the God-damned Ph.D. and get on with the rest of life. As to the immediate future, he'll drive over to Kesler's later today to see how he's doing. Meanwhile, he's got a ton of reading to do and he might as well get started on it. He's a few pages into an article on *Light in August* when he gets another call, this time from Charles Cross, and that in itself is enough to put him on his guard.

"Charles?" Ted says into the phone, absolutely flabbergasted by the identity of his caller: this is the first time Charles has ever phoned him. "What is it?"

"You were his friend," Charles says, barely able to control his voice. "You still don't know?"

A sudden dread grips him. Whatever this is, it has to do with Andrew and it doesn't sound good at all. "No," he says apprehensively. "Know what?"

"It's Andrew. He hanged himself," Charles blurts out. "God, it's so awful."

Ted is stunned. For long seconds he can say nothing at all and the two men are linked in silence. Ted keeps hearing Charles's words and he resists letting them in, but that doesn't keep back the growing dread as well as a rush of feeling for the unfortunate Pole. *Andrew Kesler hanged himself.* He has a flash image of the man suspended from the ceiling of his apartment: he's wearing his tattered overcoat, his head is bent, there's an ambiguous smile on his face. In the midst of his horror Ted feels a stab of guilt: he shouldn't have been so eager to leave Andrew yesterday; he might have been able to do something to stop him.

"Ted?" Charles calls his name quietly. "Are you still there?"

"Yeah, I'm here. Jesus. Listen, Charles," he asks, gripped by a sudden need to know this detail, "where did he do it? I mean, did he hang himself in his apartment?"

"Yes," Charles answers.

I was there, in that very place, Ted thinks. He might even have done it in the room where we were drinking. "Jesus," he says again.

"I blame myself," Charles says. "I blame all of us at the library. We should have been more welcoming."

"I don't know," Ted offers. "His story goes back a long way. Even if all of us had been more welcoming it might not have made much difference in the end."

"Still," Charles says, "I can't help feeling we could have tried harder."

Ted finds himself wondering about the timing of Kesler's act. "Charles," he asks, "when did it happen?"

"I don't think there's been anything official about that yet," Charles says, "but it's presumed it happened last night. When he didn't show up for work for the second day someone at the library asked the police to check on him and they found him this morning."

Ted tries to take in all this information. He sees Kesler coming in from his kitchen with the bottle in his hand, limping slightly, he sees him walking the winter streets in his threadbare overcoat, and then he tries to imagine him swinging from the ceiling, a rope around his neck. This time he can't conjure the image.

"I didn't know if you knew about it yet or not," Charles goes on. "But I knew you were close to him in a way. I'm afraid he didn't really have any friends at the library." He sighs. "It's all too sad."

"Thanks, Charles," Ted says. "Thanks for telling me about it." Then he belatedly thinks to ask, "Was there a note? Did he explain why he was doing it?"

"I think there was a note. People I know who know people in the police department say he left something. They're not saying what it was, though."

When he hangs up Ted lights a cigarette. His hand is shaking. *I was there*, he keeps thinking, *I was in the place where he did it.* The agitation he feels shames him. This isn't about him, after all; it's about Kesler. And now the man is dead. And yet, for all Charles said, he and the Pole were no great friends, he hardly knew Andrew. He liked him, though. He appreciated his liveliness, his vivid storytelling—he had the capacity to make an

ordinary moment seem dramatic, weighted with consequence. But underneath all his hummingbird frenzy, what was he like? What stories died with him, known only to himself? "Andrew Kesler." He says the name aloud. He was a man who'd travelled a long way and maybe in the end he'd just got tired.

"May he rest in peace," he mutters reflexively. He can only hope he'd been able to be of some small assistance to the man. Still, that's small consolation in the light of the awful finality of the situation. Ted tries to suppress a shiver of terror by focusing on practical matters, like the question of who's going to take care of the final arrangements. This may be none of his business, but he can't let it go. He can't help feeling that in the end Andrew should have someone to speak for him and if it isn't Ted, who is it likely to be? The posing of the question leads in only one direction.

"Morelli here," the voice is brisk and professional. "Oh," the man says when he learns who's on the other end of the line. "I wondered when you'd get around to calling. It's about Andrew, right?"

"Yeah," Ted answers. "I just heard about it. The person I talked to said they thought he hanged himself last night. I figured you'd know as much as anybody."

"What you heard is right," Morelli confirms.

Neither man speaks for a while. In the interval Ted realizes that his earlier worries about whether or not he should have been able to pick up suicidal signals from Kesler are irrelevant now. "What's being done about Andrew?" he asks. "I mean his body and all?"

"Look," Morelli says, "things are still being worked out. But I'm glad you called. We have to meet after work. You're involved in this."

Ted is baffled. "I'm involved?"

"I'll explain later." Ever the man of mystery, this Morelli.

"OK," Ted acknowledges. "We can meet at the Old Heidelberg," he suggests.

"I think I'd prefer a more adult locale, something less student-y. What about the bar at the Hotel Chippewa? Say 5:30."

"Sure," Ted says.

"See you there."

After his talk with Morelli, Ted is restless and unstrung. There's no way he's going to get any work done today but how is he going to kill the hours until his meeting at the Hotel Chippewa? He has no trouble resisting the temptation to go to the library: he might be able to pick up more information, but the atmosphere there would be charged with melodrama. For too many people there Kesler's death is likely to be the piquant sauce that spices up a dull day, and Ted wants no part of that. This is one of the times when he really misses Dori but even though this certainly qualifies as an extraordinary situation, he intends to honor his side of their agreement not to get in touch until the fall. "If you want to jump the gun, I won't mind," he told her at the airport; but even now, maybe especially now, he's determined not to be the first to relent.

With what may simply be lack of imagination, he decides to go for a ride. "How American," he hears Kesler say, to which he could only answer, "You're right." He gets into the venerable Chevy that still bears the scratch Kesler inflicted on it—Ted will never know how that happened, he realizes. He drives through the quiet streets of Chippewa and out of town, heading west. Here the hills in which the town is nestled flatten out gradually and he has the sense that he's entered the great American prairie. All around are farm fields and silos, nothing like the vast agricultural complex Khrushchev visited a few months ago, though the farmers here seem to be doing well enough, their houses and barns clean and recently painted. If he were to continue westward, he knows, he might pass farms like this for hundreds of miles, established on land that was cleared of Indians in the last century and cleared as well of the prairie grass that was once as tall as the people making their way through it. And, of course, cleared of bison. Eventually, though, in the drier states the prairie would be a place of wind-blown sand and tumbleweed. The steppes of America, the pretentious Russell Carlyle called that part of the Midwest, trying to make a connection between the nineteenth-century Russian novel and the vast empty spaces in the center of the country. Carlyle was a visiting star from the East who'd graced the denizens of Chippewa with his presence for an academic year. "How many Raskolnikovs haunt the streets of Bismarck?" he declared in one of his lectures. "How many Karamazovs slouch behind the counters of dry goods stores in the railroad towns in Kansas?" What would Andrew have made of that? Ted wonders. Did he feel he was on the edge of the steppes in Chippewa? More likely Siberia.

When he glimpses a road sign indicating the distance to Half Moon Lake he's reminded that Dori never got a chance to see the lake unfrozen. Dori—he could just keep driving like Kerouac, couldn't he? and make it all the way to California. Of course by the time he got there she might be gone. But the idea of arriving on the coast in the early morning a couple of days from now is intoxicating. He sees himself driving past houses dripping in bougainvillea, he hears the scraping of the palm fronds, smells the mock orange on the morning air—all these sensations Dori taught him to expect—and he pulls up to her place, having driven all night, the buzz of the road still in his head. "Hi, I just happened to be in the neighborhood and thought I might as well drop in." How would she react to that? And what if the formidable Elliott were around?

The little fantasy pleases Ted: if you can think it, you're at least theoretically capable of it. He's got good bloodlines for it, hasn't he, given his wandering father. Where on those open western spaces is Jack Riley? he wonders. Hell, he might even be in California. He's landed on his feet before and it might happen again. Once again Ted can imagine Kesler's comment, "How American."

The notion of a solitary traveler moving through vast open spaces teases his memory and he realizes he's thinking about something he saw with Dori: the movie *Bad Day at Black Rock*, in which Spencer Tracy plays a one-armed World War II veteran who uncovers the dirty secrets of a bleak desert town seemingly populated only by sadistic bigots. Though they both loved it, Dori was especially taken by the film. "Everything is so stark and elemental there," she said excitedly. "There's the desert, the

railroad, and the town. There's good and there's bad. Even if
Tracy has only one arm, you know he has to wipe out those bad
guys. Anything else would be too devastating morally." She was
only talking about a movie, of course, but now he sees that conversation in a different light; he sees the passion and moral force
behind her response to the film, her sense that justice has to be
done and that the powerful and menacing forces that thwart it
can be overcome. In the light of what she's gone on to do, her
comments are almost prophetic.

Wouldn't it be something to keep going all the way to California and see her?

But the fact is, he knows he can't keep driving west forever:
he doesn't have the gas, he doesn't have the money, he doesn't
have the time. Besides, he has to see Morelli, doesn't he? The
abrupt ending of Kesler's story has left so many things about the
Pole's life shrouded in mystery. Maybe Ted can learn something
more about him, especially about his final hours. He's aware
of a dim sadness at the prospect of this meeting at the Hotel
Chippewa, since it will mark in some visible way—some sac-
ramental way, even, in the Catholic sense of things—the end
of his connection with Kesler. Possibly too the end of his connection, however tenuous it may be, to Morelli himself. For a
young guy, it seems he's having his share of endings these days.
Traveling along these rural roads bordered by fields of growing
corn, he's suddenly depressed by the realization that none of
this extravagant fertility makes death any less final. He's found
no solace here; all he's managed to do is to kill a little time; and
after a while he finds himself driving back toward Chippewa.

Later, in his apartment again, he addresses the question of
what to wear for his meeting with Morelli in what the other man
pointedly called an "adult" locale. He puts on a clean shirt, a
good pair of khakis, and his cord jacket. No tie—that would be
going a bit far—but he looks fairly presentable, almost the young
candidate getting ready for a job interview. When he remembers
Morelli's offer last year, it strikes him that this meeting will have
to be a substitute for that event.

He arrives at the Hotel Chippewa a few minutes early but to his surprise Morelli is already at the bar, well into his martini. He gestures to Ted and calls him over. "Good to see you," he greets him with the stylized enthusiasm of the salesman. "What'll you have?"

Ted was planning on a bourbon but, figuring, when in Rome . . . he asks for a martini. He hasn't had one in the longest time.

Morelli drops his cheerful persona and shakes his head. "Poor Andrew," he says. "His life was no picnic." Ted nods agreement and Morelli responds with a sigh, as if the act of conversation itself has become too much of an effort. Though he's dressed as he always has been when Ted has seen him, the man looks more rumpled somehow. And there's something else Ted can't put his fingers on, something missing. Morelli shakes his head wearily. "For starters, though, let's talk about some more pleasant topic," he says.

"What would that be?" Ted answers.

Morelli snorts a laugh that would be hearty if it were sincere. "You're right there," he says. He shakes his head. "Does it seem to you that the whole country's going nuts?" he asks with sudden animation.

Ted shrugs. "Not any more than usual." He can see that isn't the response Morelli was looking for. When his drink arrives he lifts his glass, as does the other man. Neither says anything but it's understood they're toasting Kesler's memory. The astringent sting of the cold gin and vermouth is as quick as a cobra's strike. Ted had forgotten that.

Morelli puts down his glass. His brow is knit with brooding vexation. "You know," he says quietly, "what I can't figure out is why, when we're the greatest power on the planet, we're acting like there's something shameful about being an American."

Ted says nothing. The last thing he came here expecting was a political discussion.

Morelli pushes on. "I never thought I'd live to see the day when the commies were in charge of Cuba."

"Things weren't so good for the Cubans under Batista," Ted offers.

"At least we could control Batista," Morelli says. "We knew what he was going to do." He takes a drink of his martini and Ted follows suit. "What are you?" Morelli challenges. "A Democrat, I suppose."

Ted nods and takes another sip. A martini isn't a lovable drink, it occurs to him, like bourbon, which actually looks warm. There's something steely about a martini, something Art Deco, and he wouldn't say he likes the taste exactly; but you could get used to these things pretty quickly.

"I figured," Morelli says. "It may surprise you, but I'm leaning toward Kennedy myself. For all he says about apologizing to the Reds, I think he just may have the balls to stand up to them when he gets into office. He's a cold-blooded son-of-a-bitch, which is what you have to be. I don't trust Nixon: he's devious enough but he's too much of a whiner. But whoever it is, we've got to stop just drifting and reacting."

Ted has already had another sip of his drink. At this rate, he'll be ordering them two at a time. At this rate, he'll be drunk in a hurry. Slow down, he tells himself. Then he's able to put his finger on something that's been bothering him since he first saw Morelli. "Hey," he says. "Where's your cigar?"

The other man frowns. "My doctor took it away." He pats himself on the stomach. "Says I should lose ten pounds too."

"You seem in pretty good shape to me," Ted says, still alert enough not to add, "for someone your age."

Morelli makes a dismissive gesture but his expression darkens and Ted wonders what medical situation prompted the doctor's restrictions. The man of mystery, who's signaling the barman to bring them a couple more drinks, suddenly seems vulnerable. Ted fishes out his olive, chews it and washes it down with the remainder of his martini.

A glaze has come over Morelli. He seems less substantial, a stubby mustached guy in a tweed jacket who's lost his way, not the same man who took charge so impressively at Dan Seeley's party when Ed Levecque fell down the stairs. Could Kesler's death have undone him in some way? Ted looks around. The bar is paneled in dark wood, the bottles glitter quietly before the mirror. This is an adult locale where adults, mostly male, can find shelter and protection as they engage in a bit of alcohol-assisted reflection. How many a middle-aged guy has sat here, retrieving through the haze of spirit the boy he'd once been, full of hope and energy and confidence, only to compare himself to the person he's become, a complete stranger to that boy, a little overweight maybe, being ordered around by doctors? How many responsible adults have sat here remembering that the boys they'd been had had fears as well, that they'd cried at night, wet the bed, prayed? Now these same people run the world, they're told; and still they remember those fears. Ted remembers Dori's words at the airport: it's his and her generation that's getting ready to take over now. Could that be part of what's bothering Morelli?

"Well," the man says, cheered by the arrival of their drinks, "that's better." He brings the glass to his lips, takes a sip, and puts it down. "You know, all you can do is the best you can. You work in the dark most of the time and you just hope you manage to put things in the right place."

"You lost me," Ted says.

Morelli throws up his hands. "I guess this business with Andrew just put me in a kind of philosophical mood. Andrew—and his sister—were just caught up in something a lot bigger than any of us." He sighs. "You just hope you're doing the right thing."

Ted nods.

"Look," Morelli says with some force, "I believe in what we're doing against the Russians. When all that stuff about the U-2 came out I wanted to stand up and cheer. Can you believe what a piece of work that plane is, can you believe the information it can give us? All this stuff about the commies outdoing us in technology, that's all crap, as that plane proves." He frowns. "I was disappointed in Powers, though."

Ted listens, sipping his martini. It's going down very easily now and he can't deny that the alcohol has affected him. He hears Morelli's musings with detachment. The two of them might well be a pair of souls who've come together in some obscure corner of hell, so that if Morelli's taking his time getting around to talking about Andrew there's no problem because they'll have all of eternity to discuss the subject.

"You have to know from the inside," Morelli says, "what the other guys are doing if you want to appreciate the job before us. Christ, in every two-bit country on the planet, even in some places that can only aspire to being two-bit countries, our guys are out there and their guys are out there battling over every acre of desert and jungle. It's like the old prayer to St. Michael where he's fighting Satan and all the evil spirits that wander the world seeking the ruin of souls."

"And you believe it?" Ted asks. "You believe we're fighting Satan?"

"Damn straight I believe it. Ask the Poles who they think's running their country. Ask the Hungarians. No, you don't have to ask them; you already know. They gave their answer in '56." Though the statement is delivered emphatically, Ted can't help feeling there's a kind of desperation behind it.

But he isn't interested in the Hungarians just now; he's interested in one particular Pole. "What about Andrew?" he asks.

Morelli straightens. For a few seconds he says nothing. "Andrew, Andrew," he says at last. "You saw him a few hours before he did it, you say. How did he seem?"

"I don't know," Ted answers truthfully. "He just seemed like Andrew." Morelli looks at him. "Did I detect any special signs of despair, you're asking? Nothing more than usual, I suppose. Though in retrospect. . . ." His voice trails off.

"The coroner estimates he did it around dinnertime last night," Morelli says. "When they found him in the morning it was . . . well, the less said about that the better."

"Did he leave a note?" Ted asks.

Morelli nods. "Yeah, he did. That's where you come in. He left you something."

"He left me something?" Ted can't keep the surprise out of his voice.

"Yeah," Morelli says. "A wooden crucifix. That mean any-thing to you?"

Ted nods. He remembers Kesler asking him if he liked the religious object. It was obviously something important to him. He's moved by the gesture but all he can say is, "Jesus."

"It seems like a pretty valuable piece, they tell me."

Ted isn't sure if Morelli is implying anything about his relationship to the dead man, but he isn't interested in what Morelli thinks. "What did he say in his note?" he asks.

The other man shakes his head. "Nothing much, no explanations or anything like that. Just a businesslike listing of what he wants done. Do you know a guy named Bill Tuttle?"

"He works in the library."

"Well, this Tuttle guy gets Andrew's books, you get the crucifix. That's all the distribution of property. I guess there wouldn't be much more than clothes. He had a bank account, but I guess he didn't regard that as important."

Ted has a sense that he hasn't heard everything. "But there was more in the note?" he pursues.

"Yeah," Morelli acknowledges after a while. "He wants to be buried in Germany near his sister."

Ted nods. Given what he's learned about Kesler and his sister, the request makes perfect sense. "Can that get done?" he asks.

Morelli frowns again. "I don't know. We've carried Andrew for quite a while. I'm not the one to make the decisions on that level but it's possible some people might think that would be a step too far. I mean, you'd have to fly his body back to Germany and all."

"Come on," Ted says. "We're talking military planes, aren't we? They're going there all the time, aren't they?" The idea of a coffin on a plane flying across the Atlantic brings a shiver. "Hey, if he doesn't get buried in Germany, what's the alternative?"

Morelli shakes his head slowly. "I don't really know. But listen, I intend to push for his request. I told you before, I believe in what we're doing, I believe we're on the right side and I don't know what kind of commitments were made to his sister, but I think we have to honor them."

"Yeah," Ted says, "you sure as hell better." Instead of answering, Morelli gestures to the bartender for more drinks. For a time neither man speaks and Ted listens to Sinatra singing "I Love Paris." Ted doesn't much like Sinatra but here, amid the dark paneling of this hotel bar, the two of them awash in martinis, the aging crooner's voice seems appropriate, his smooth baritone conveying infinite longing. Morelli too seems to be listening and at the moment neither man seems much aware of the other. At last, swimming to the surface of his consciousness, Ted asks, "What happened to Andrew's sister?"

Morelli shakes his head. "I don't know all of it, as I said. And if I did there are things I probably couldn't tell you. But I do know that the sister. . . ."

"Magda," Ted interjects.

"Yeah, Magda. She was apparently something. A real looker, I'm told, and smart as hell. She could speak four or five languages fluently. There was so much we didn't know in the early days; we came late to the intelligence game, so someone like her must have been quite an asset." Automatically, Morelli pats his jacket pocket as if looking for a cigar, then drops his hand. "I'm told she did very valuable work, " he says; "she took on tough assignments. She frequently went into East Germany and that's where they got her. A double agent fingered her and," he says these last words quickly, "she was hanged."

The words come like a blow. "Oh, my God," Ted says.

Morelli nods. "Yeah. That certainly throws a different light on Andrew's final decision, doesn't it?"

Ted can't say anything. Oddly, he remembers the scene from the movie *The Thing From Another World* when the American airmen move out to the edges of the shape lying under the ice and suddenly recognize what they're seeing. In knowing Andrew, Ted has glimpsed just a small part of a shape whose full dark presence remains obscure to him; but he suddenly has a better idea of just how long and complex is the story whose final chapter was played out in that cramped apartment on the top floor of a house here in Chippewa.

"They hanged her and they took her body back across the border. Left it for us to find. The bastards." He sighs. "That's what I mean about Satan and all his evil spirits wandering the world seeking the ruin of souls."

How many spies are there on both sides, Ted wonders, spying on each other, killing each other, plotting the overthrow of governments? "And we don't do that?" he challenges.

Morelli looks at him as Sinatra continues to sing the praises of the City of Light. "We do what we have to do."

"But to fight Satan we may have to get a little satanic at times."

Morelli shakes his head. "It's easy to criticize from the outside."

Maybe, Ted thinks, that's a pretty good argument for staying outside. How convenient for us that we have Satan and his evil spirits to emulate. But he's thinking again of the fact that Kesler's sister was hanged. "Of course Andrew would feel responsible for Magda," he says. "Whatever might have motivated his sister, there's no way he wouldn't blame himself." He takes a drink. "He told me once over the phone that he'd killed his sister. I figured he felt guilty about surviving when she hadn't. But this. . . ."

By now Ted is aware that the liquor has really got to him. Everything about his surroundings stands out with the vivid, suggestive clarity of a dream and the barman's smile as he wipes a glass seems sinister. Ted suddenly has the notion that this hotel bar in Chippewa is a comfortable nook on a luxury liner far out at sea. Morelli, looking mournfully into his drink, seems equally adrift. "Andrew had style," Ted declares, a propos of nothing. "He was one of a kind."

Morelli nods.

Ted suddenly remembers something. "Fryderyk and . . ." he says.

"What's that?" Morelli asks.

"Andrew's father's name was Fryderyk but I don't remember his mother's name. He told me but I forgot."

"Well, you could hardly expect to remember, could you?"

"But damn it, I asked him and he told me. I should remember. You don't know her name, do you?"

Morelli shakes his head.

"Could you find out for me?"

"Sure," Morelli says. "Yeah, I'll find out."

They're silent for a while. "Well," the older man says at last with a sigh, "I have a family to get back to; I've got to go. I'll get that crucifix to you as soon as it's available. Actually, it was good talking to you about Andrew." He looks bemused. "The guy was a pain in the neck, believe me. But you have to feel for him."

"You will try to see that he gets buried in Germany, won't you?" Ted says. "I mean, it was obviously very important to him. You owe him that much at least, don't you?"

Morelli nods. "I'll do my best. I promise," he says. He lays a twenty on the bar and waves away Ted's protest, then gets off the stool somewhat unsteadily and puts out his hand. Ted takes it and they shake. "Be on your guard against Satan and the evil spirits," the older man says, then makes a gesture of blessing.

"Et cum spiritu tuo," Ted responds as Morelli makes his way out of the bar. Ted still has some of his martini in the glass and he decides to stay awhile. In fact, he resists the impulse to drink, realizing that he wants an excuse to linger here. Possibly he doesn't want to face the loneliness of his apartment. Maybe. But he knows that he wants to think about things and just now this place seems like a good spot for that. He'll think about Andrew, of course, and his sister. He'll try to resist making out of the fragments that he knows of their separate yet connected lives some kind of story that makes sense, since he really knows so little, but it will be impossible not to try to see some meaning there.

And what about other stories going on in the world around him? He has the sense that nothing is stable anymore, all questions are open, everybody's story is unfinished. Like Morelli's. Did the undersized guard who's now a guardian, on the side of the angels, somehow lose points with his bosses for what happened to Andrew? Are they giving him heat for it? Or is this the perfect ending for them? Whatever the case, Kesler's death seems to have got to Morelli in some way. Where does he go from here, this guy who thinks the country's gone nuts? Maybe the instability of things is too much for him.

There are other stories closer to home. Ted thinks of his mother. As clear-eyed and unsentimental as she tries to be, facing this mysterious threat to her health, he knows she's a woman passionate enough to have gone against all her family's ideals in following her heart, she's capable of strong feeling. What does she feel about this impersonal, stealthy presence in her own body, so lethal, so unpredictable? She has to know that willpower alone won't be enough to thwart it. What's going to happen to her? And what about his father, wandering the country, somewhere in the West, in search of another new beginning while others— creditors, maybe, the police, for sure—are searching for him? Will he get away? Will he start over and make a new fortune or will he slide into obscurity in some western trailer park? It's one more incomplete story. Ted doesn't have the answers, nobody has all the answers, but still you have to go on.

Inevitably his thoughts turn toward Dori, who's changed the way he sees the world. What's the next chapter in her story and that of the movement to which she's committed herself? Are they going to prevail against Satan and all the other spirits who wander the world seeking the ruin of souls? They just might, you can't rule it out. Not they, he corrects himself, but us: *we* just might. It's our turn, she said. Certainly those who came before us didn't do a perfect job; we have to try to do better.

Why not be hopeful?

He reaches for the glass and takes a sip. The martini is no longer as cold as it was. He puts the glass down, knowing that his curiosity about all those other stories is really a way of asking the question: what's going to happen to me? And that question involves another: what's going to happen to all of us? Above this hotel in the American Midwest, the sky itself is full of threat and menace: unseen satellites orbit the world collecting information, spy planes soar at high altitudes taking pictures; all over the globe the bombers and missiles are ready. People walking the streets on both sides of the Iron Curtain are not who they say they are; a thousand plots are in various stages of development. Life is fragile, nothing is guaranteed. Maybe in some sense it's always been like that and only the technology is different. The important thing is that, like everyone else who's lived on this planet, Ted is going to be alive for only a while but, Jesus, being alive is the important thing: as long as you're alive there's a chance you can make some things come out right. He looks at his watch and follows the jittery progress of the second hand. One more second, one more second. As long as that hand keeps moving, there's still a chance.

About the Author

K. C. FREDERICK is the author of *Country of Memory* (1998), *The Fourteenth Day* (2000) and *Accomplices* (2003) as well as many short stories, a number of which have been anthologized. Born and raised in Detroit, he now lives in the Boston area.

MORE FROM K.C. FREDERICK

COUNTRY OF MEMORY

ISBN 1-57962-013-2 cloth

"Part Kafka and Millhauser and Calvino, Frederick's first novel evokes a world that is full of mystery and longing— where every lie, dream, and desire takes you farther from yourself, to a place that is strangely familiar. *Country of Memory* is odd and beautiful and deep. Go there. It will enlarge your heart."
— PAUL CODY, author of
Stolen Child and *So Far Gone*

"Frederick mines a vein of literary styles from Kafka to Kundera. . . . Old world gloom described with irresistible New World bounce."
— *The New York Times Book Review*

THE 14th DAY

ISBN 1-57962-065-5 cloth

"Meditating on love, death and national loyalty, Frederick pieces together a delicate, thoughtful allegory of war and displacement. Painted in shades of black and blue, this landscape of exile is by turns a thriller, psychological novel, meditation and romance, difficult to penetrate but well worth the effort."
— *Publishers Weekly*

"Focused sharply on those for whom personal and national identity have become traumatically entwined. Frederick's tale is as inexorable and engrossing as a recurring nightmare."
— *Kirkus*

ACCOMPLICES

ISBN 1-57962-091-4 cloth

"Two residents of a central Eastern European country come together amid the turmoil and panic of a nation whose social structure has been unpended. It's curious mix of Kafka-like meditation and postmodern thriller proves quite fascinating."
— *Booklist*

"Succeeds because of Frederick's insights into the ways that ordinary people try to live their lives as they navigate the murkey politics of a dour, repressed country."
— *Publishers Weekly*

Visit www.thepermanentpress.com

Available wherever books are sold, or call 631/725-1101